True Indigo

A TIPSY COLLINS NOVEL

STEPHANIE ALEXANDER

This is a work of fiction. Names, characters, organizations, places, events and incidents are either the products of the author's imagination or are used fictitiously. Any resemblance to actual persons, living or dead, or actual events is purely coincidental.

Cover art by Caroline Staley
Design and distribution by Bublish

ISBN: 978-1-647047-70-2 (paperback)
ISBN: 978-1-647047-69-6 (eBook)

It's a rough journey…we've braved its ghosts often together, and dared each other to stand among the graves and ask them to come… if I dare you now, will you venture? If you do, I'll keep you…they may bury me twelve feet deep…but I won't rest till you are with me. I never will!

—*Emily Bronte, Wuthering Heights*

If you want a happy ending, that depends, of course, on where you stop your story.

—*Orson Welles*

Although rice was king in antebellum Charleston, indigo claimed its own dukedom. Caribbean planters brought indigo to the Lowcountry, and by the late eighteenth century, it was the second most important crop in the region. South Carolina's beloved state flag, with its distinctive palmetto and moon design, is set against a deep purplish-blue background in homage to the indigo trade. Indigo cultivation disappeared with the horrors of the plantation system, and the genus of the plant that produced the celebrated dye, Indigofera tinctoria, *known as true indigo, is not common in South Carolina. Many southern gardeners, however, sing the praises of true indigo's rival,* Baptisia australis, *known as wild or false indigo. Both plants produce lovely clusters of blossoms, with true indigo flowers usually being pinkish. In an example of natural irony, it is the false indigo plant that typically produces blooms of the deep purplish-blue hue associated with the color commonly known as indigo.*

After Tipsy Collins exorcised the restless spirits of the Doctor Rene Bonneau House, she experienced a two-year ghostbusting dry spell. As had been the case throughout her thirty-eight years of life, she saw random phantoms as she zipped around Charleston, chauffeuring children and delivering artwork to clients. Any such sighting induced curiosity in her, and no small amount of guilt. Since her divorce, life had doled out many lessons, including supernatural ones. Tipsy knew how to free ghosts from their hauntings, but life was hectic enough. She had no time to seek out spirits in limbo or ruminate on mysterious, gruesome deaths.

That's what she told herself, anyway. Each night, before she swan-dived into a pool of dream-soaked sleep, anonymous pale faces flitted through her mind.

Morose, befuddled, hysterical, catatonic.

Each one a distinct being, with a unique reaction to a confoundingly permanent existence.

Each troubled mind hiding personal narratives—*auto-necro-graphies*, if you will—that could set them free.

Stories that Tipsy could release.

In those brief moments, Tipsy wondered if she was letting her abilities go to waste, but she couldn't perseverate herself into an existential crisis, because she'd never been busier. She was producing and selling her celebrated artwork at a record pace. Her three kids—Ayers, now twelve years old, and twins Mary Pratt and Olivia Grace, easing into double digits at ten—were evolving into productive members of society with their own onerous schedules. Her relationship with Dr. Scott Brandt,

MD, had evolved from unexpected meet-cute in the psych ward, to whirlwind romance (briefly interrupted by Tipsy's early relationship jitters and resulting meltdown) to the best thing that had ever happened to them. A month ago, Scott got down on one knee at the end of Mount Pleasant's Pitt Street Bridge and popped the question. Now Tipsy was running around town with a pretty emerald ring on her finger while they planned a small wedding and gradually combined households with their collective five kiddos. Even her relationship with her irascible ex-husband, the Big Ayers to her son's Little A, was humming along like an old Toyota. Clunks and whistles now and then, but it got their family from point A to point B.

Everything was joyfully complicated, but supernaturally speaking, things had been kind of dead, haha. As Miss Austen might say, however, it is a truth universally acknowledged that a clairvoyant with a spectral roommate cannot avoid unearthly challenges forever. And so, on a Monday morning in early April, Tipsy unexpectedly hopped back on the supernatural roller coaster.

She dropped her kids at school, drove home to her house on Bennett Street in the Old Village of Mount Pleasant, and came upon the familiar ghost of Henry Mott on her front porch. He sat at the glass-topped table, his enigmatically handsome face and bright red, tousled hair half-hidden behind a mason jar full of sunflowers.

The sight of him surprised her. Of late, the perpetually brooding Henry had been increasingly reclusive.

"Hey, Mott," she said, as she walked up the porch stairs. "Haven't seen you much lately. How's it going?"

Henry stared into Tipsy's old laptop. It was glitchy and slow, but he needed only a single Word document. She didn't understand exactly how Henry was typing his magnum opus, the novel he referred to as THE GREAT STORY. She assumed he manipulated the keys with his telekinetic power.

When he didn't reply, she crossed the porch and pulled out the chair beside him. She'd lived with Henry for four years, and knew he sometimes needed to be drawn—ahem, *yanked*—out of his shell. Before she could sit, he minimized his Word document. She glimpsed her own reflection in the darkened screen before Henry snapped the computer shut. Wavy chocolate brown hair. Big gray eyes. Her professional artist's attire (Scott's old Tennessee Vols sweatshirt and cheap paint-splattered leggings).

"I hate to disturb a fellow creative at work," she said, "but I haven't had an update on THE GREAT STORY—"

"I'm *mid-sentence*, Tipsy." He hunkered over the closed computer like a hangry badger guarding a dead mouse.

"You want to catch up when you reach a good stopping point?"

"Not especially."

"Jeez, Henry. Are you pissed at me for some reason?"

"No. I'm *very busy*. I'm—damnit. The electricity is almost depleted in this thing." He looked around. "Where's the plugger?"

Tipsy picked up the charger and plugged it into the wall. She started to insert the charging end into the computer's port, but unseen forces ripped the cord from her hands.

"I can *do it*," said Henry, as the wire floated toward the charging port. It poked and prodded, but his telekinesis couldn't find the right path.

"Let me help—"

"I *said* no!" The supernatural force of his annoyance wobbled the mason jar. The sunflowers jiggled, as if trembling in fear of Henry's famous temper.

"Watch those flowers. You don't want your computer getting wet—"

"You've told me that a thousand times!"

Tipsy scowled at him. "What is your *problem?*"

"You—you're trying to look at my work!"

"I promised I'd never look at your work without your permission."

"You may have secret, voyeuristic ways of looking! With your powers, or through the Interwebs!"

"It's the Inter*net*, and I can't use my powers to look into a computer. Computers are the *opposite* of supernatural."

"I've seen what computers can do. I watched *The Matrix* with you and Scott!"

"That's just a movie—"

"Stop *yelling* at me!"

"What the heck? If anyone is yelling, it's you—"

"Argh!" Henry grabbed two handfuls of his crimson hair and pulled. His edges blurred, until his white button-down shirt and tan pants blended into a smear of beige. The mason jar and the computer shot across the table, stopped, and spun in place. The laptop opened and started beeping and chirping like a robotic squirrel. It rotated itself over the table's edge and *thwacked* against the wooden floorboards. As Tipsy stooped to pick it up, the whirling mason jar succumbed to gravity. Tepid water doused Tipsy's right arm and splashed her face. She flinched and spun to protect the computer.

With her chin on her chest, and the computer still open, she couldn't help but see the screen. One large black character in the middle of an empty expanse of glowing white.

A single question mark, in fifty-something point font.

The computer wrenched itself from her hands and floated toward Henry. He grimaced as it gently landed on the table. "Is it broken?" he asked.

"No. They can usually tolerate that kind of fall, but you're lucky it's dry."

She wiped her eyes on her sweatshirt sleeve, but the question mark lingered in a yellow outline behind her eyelids. Henry claimed to be mid-sentence, but the sentence hadn't made it to the screen.

There were no sentences at all. No flowery run-ons. No clumsy phrases, or heated subject-verb disagreements. No dangling modifiers, comma splices, or improperly conclusionary prepositions. Not even a lonely fragment, waiting to discover its own ending.

Henry spent *hours* in front of that computer. What had he been doing all this time?

Despite her curiosity, she refused to subject herself to his hissy fit. "Let me know when you're in a better mood," she said, with her hand on the doorknob.

"Tipsy, I'm *sorry*."

She looked back at him. His grumpy, irritable frown had morphed into a sad, pensive one.

"I'm not angry with you," he continued. "I've been difficult lately—"

"You're *always* difficult. This is not your run-of-the-mill disagreeableness."

He rested his elbows on the table and glared into the Microsoft abyss. She took in his furrowed brow, trembling hands, and the weary set of his shoulders. Dark circles always lined his eyes, as if a nearsighted makeup artist had applied his smokey shadow in the wrong place. Today's blue-gray smudges were worse than usual. He looked like he'd had a run in with a UFC fighter.

If he wasn't already dead, I'd say he looks near it, said Tipsy's Granna, straight from her own head. Granna was long dead, but Tipsy had inherited her psychic powers. In life, they'd been able to communicate without speaking. Miraculously, Granna's death hadn't severed their connection.

I hear you, Granna, said Tipsy. *He acted like a jackass, but I feel bad for him.*

Tipsy returned to the table. "What's *really* bothering you, Henry?"

He looked up at her. "Something is not right. I have no bodily fibers, of course, but if I did, I'd say something is amiss in every fiber of my being."

"I don't understand."

"Nor do I. But something is *very, very wrong*."

Tipsy collected the strewn sunflowers, walked into the kitchen, and refilled the mason jar with water. She left the jar on the window ledge above the sink, where it would be safe from Henry's volatility. She changed into a dry sweatshirt—this one, emblazoned with a scowling rooster, represented her own alma mater—and returned to the porch.

She sat across from Henry. "You going to spill it?"

"I already did. I assume that's why you left it inside."

"I mean what's happening with you. Or *not* happening, given what I saw on that computer. *Accidentally* saw. You know I'd never—"

"It's fine. Have your look."

The open computer spun around. The question mark floated on stark white, like the official flag of the State of Confusion. Tipsy lowered the screen's brightness. "Maybe your brain isn't used to typing."

Henry's brow wrinkled and the keyboard keys clicked and clacked. Words appeared below the question mark.

TYPING IS EASY. I ENJOY IT.

The cursor moved around the screen. The words bolded themselves, changed from black to red to neon green, and then switched fonts from Comic Sans to Helvetica. Tipsy shrugged. "Okay. Typing isn't the problem."

"You know I've written many short stories," said Henry. "Some decent poetry. And yet, after over a century of trying, and umpteen promising ideas, I've never finished a novel. I have no trouble *starting*. The challenge is in the *finishing*. I get about seventy pages in and I fall into a plot hole. Like stepping into an abandoned cliché mine, or through an open manhole into a sewer of improbable situations and superfluous characters with no legitimate motivation."

"I'm not a writer, but isn't that what second drafts are for?"

"Perhaps for some wordsmiths, but I've never managed to climb out of those chasms, or find a rescue ladder in the form of a workable plot outline. It never fails—I start off with a bang, and run out of gunpowder. Lately, though, I haven't written so much as an opening line."

"I see you working regularly, so you're putting in effort. You must have written *something* since I gave you this computer."

"Over the past two years, I've started over at least five times, given up, and erased the whole lot."

"You don't have to delete everything! You can save those drafts and return to them."

"No, my friend. I know when my own work is, pardon my language, a pile of steaming cow offal. I conducted my last grand obliteration over a month ago. That's when things got truly…bleak. Nothing but silence in my head, as if my internal narrator smoked too many cigars and lost his voice."

"Hence the question mark."

"Yes. When I close my eyes, I see nothing but that damnable, glowing white void. I had to fill it up with something."

"I felt the same way when I had painter's block. Blank canvases all in my head. I wish you'd talked to me about it, instead of hiding out or giving me an attitude. I would have tried to help you, or at least *commiserated*."

"I'm truly sorry. In life, I attempted to shelter my loved ones from my turbulent emotions. When I recognized them, anyway. Oftentimes, my melancholia consumed me. You saw that side of me when you moved into this house after Miss Callie passed on, and found me and my sweet Jane."

Tipsy nodded. During her first summer in the house, she'd witnessed Henry's cold, neglectful, sometimes outright cruel treatment of his wife, Jane Robinette Mott. She'd observed them in person (ghostly person, of course) and she'd also used her paranormal talents to peruse Jane and Henry's memories. Solving Jane and Henry's murder had taught Tipsy how to set ghosts free. Unlike Henry, Jane had long since moved on to the next phase of her afterlife.

"From what I've seen, you were a real piece of work in life, *and* in death, but you've changed over the past few years," she said. "If you hadn't, you wouldn't be one of my best friends. These days, you're like, a *paragon* of wisdom and loyalty. You're my sounding board for everything."

"I don't know what a sounding board is, but I sense you're trying to flatter me out of this foul mood."

"I'm serious. I tell you everything that's going on in my life. I thought you reciprocated about your death, but instead you've been shutting me out. All over a creative brain block, which is something I *totally* understand. It doesn't make a lot of sense to me."

"It's not *just* about the writer's block. I also meant to avoid your… questions."

"About THE GREAT STORY?"

"Yes, but also about the *message*."

"Jane's message? From the next…plane?" Tipsy always struggled to understand the destination of ghosts who *moved on*, but two years ago, Henry had unexpectedly received a supernatural voicemail from that unknowable place. Before she moved on herself, Catherine Porcher, the teenage schizophrenic psychic (say that three times fast) who had haunted the Bonneau House, had delivered a message from Jane. Only Henry had heard the message, and at first, Tipsy had questioned him about its content on a daily basis. After months of his deflection, she'd given up, under the assumption that he found it too painful to share.

"Come on, Henry," she said. "I'd like to hear something from Jane, too, but if you truly don't want to discuss it, I would have let it go."

"You shouldn't have to let it go. Jane is my wife, but she's your friend."

"Then why have you been so tightlipped about it?"

"It drove me zonkers—"

"*Bonkers*."

"—that I couldn't understand it. The woman I love found a way to reach me through space and time, and I can't decipher what she's telling me."

"I got the impression your rewriting of THE GREAT STORY had something to do with Jane's message."

"I thought so, too. I tried to incorporate what I *thought* she *may* have meant into new versions of THE GREAT STORY, but I got nowhere." He looked past the porch rails, into the awakening garden. The budding tea roses that always found their way through the porch steps. Creeping wisteria vines, so old they had knobby wooden trunks, like true trees. Two cracked cement bird baths and patchy flower beds. Bedraggled boxy hedges.

His dark blue eyes stopped on the towering magnolia tree at the edge of the property. The magnolia had its species' trademark broad, shiny leaves, but its horizontal profile and cumbersome, low slung limbs were reminiscent of a live oak. A glorious arboreal hybrid, and the centerpiece of the yard. Jane had planted it a century ago.

"Perhaps it's all interwoven, like the limbs of Janie's tree," said Henry. "I can't write. I can't understand her message. And lately, I can't breathe."

"But you *don't* breathe."

"I don't, but it still feels like I'm suffocating. Something is crushing me. Weighing me down. It's becoming more difficult to leave the house."

Unlike most spirits, who were tied to their haunting place, Henry's lifetime clairvoyance allowed him to leave Miss Callie's house for short periods of time. After thirty minutes or so, however, the house's paranormal magnetism pulled him back.

"Harder to leave in the first place?" asked Tipsy. "Or more painful when the house calls you back?"

"Both. Leaving itself takes more effort, as if I'm jumping rope while wearing a suit of armor. Once I escape, I feel the house's walls closing in on me after a quarter of an hour, even if I'm standing on the wide open beach on Sullivan's Island at low tide."

Sounds like a recipe for serious cabin fever, said Granna.

As if validating Granna's observation, Henry said, "Traveling helps me regain my mental clarity. Now I'm experiencing all these contrarian emotions, and I can't even get the relief of a stroll along the Battery."

Tipsy felt like Scott sizing up a new patient during a psychiatric consult. She held up her hand and started counting on her fingers. "Sadness, irritability, writer's block, frustration over Jane's message, lack of mobility…any other symptoms?"

"My thoughts are like soap bubbles," he said. "I can balance them on my fingers for a moment, but then they burst. I'm afraid I'm losing the parts of my mind that I recovered over the past four years."

"I don't understand why this would be happening *now*." Tipsy stood and paced the porch. "You've been haunting this house for a century. There are only so many variables, and Jane's message is the most obvious one." She stopped and planted both hands on her hips. "It's time to *fess up* about the message, even if you don't understand it."

"I won't argue with you. I'm getting nowhere on my own." Henry twirled one finger and the computer spun in his direction. The keys resumed clicking and clacking, and then the computer magically faced

Tipsy again. Henry had deleted the giant question mark, reduced the font, and typed up a few sentences. Tipsy squinted to read the words, as he'd changed them into a swirly script. The kind of writing one might find on the back of an old black and white photo.

> *Henry, my love, more than anything I want peace for you, but you must understand our whole story. There's more to it than either of us know. We can only truly be at peace if you understand everything.*

"Is this *exactly* what Jane said?" asked Tipsy, as she looked up at him.

"Catherine said that she memorized it, word for word. She seemed very sure of herself."

Tipsy traced her finger along the words. "Jane wants you to be at peace. You've always sensed that, right?"

"Yes. That's why I believe she wanted me to finish my book before I move on. She knows how I've suffered over my literary failures. Do you think the message is about my novel?"

"Honestly…no. It doesn't sound like she's referencing fiction. She said *our* story—so, *y'all's* story. But don't y'all *already* understand your story? Haven't you felt at peace since you learned the truth about your deaths?" Tipsy shrugged. "Your gloomy, moody version of peace."

"I've never felt as peaceful as I did those first few years after you helped us discover the truth. Not in my life, nor in my death." He shrugged. "Apparently, my peace was fleeting."

"But how can there be more to your deaths? Being murdered is pretty definitive, and we know what happened. Your death, and the events that led up to it. You remembered your *lost week*." Like all ghosts, when Tipsy met him, Henry had no recollection of the last week or so of his life.

"I don't remember *everything* that happened during the week before my death. It's like…if I ask you what happened on an important birthday, or a specific holiday celebration. Do you remember *all* the details? Perhaps you wouldn't recall a conversation from that day until someone reminded you of it."

"Henry, this is really complicated. So many supernatural what-ifs." Tipsy folded her arms over her chest. "You know I love you. I'll miss the hell out of you, and I want you to be at peace as much as Jane does. But the time has come for you to *move on.*"

"Definitely not."

"Huh? Why? You've always said that you'd move on in time. Now you have reasons to go. *Imminent loss of sanity* being the most pressing one."

"Are you sure you're not pushing me to evacuate the house before Dr. Brandt and his children move in?"

"You know Scott and I already discussed your lingering presence. He's good with it, or we wouldn't be buying the house."

In a stroke of incredible fortune, as Tipsy and Scott were getting hot-housing-market anxiety, Miss Callie's house had become an option. Tipsy's landlord and former brother-in-law, Jimmy Lathrop, had finally settled the lawsuit over his late mother's estate. His siblings agreed to fire-sale the place, *as is*. That meant a 1960's kitchen, tiny bathrooms, no closets, leaky roof, flood-prone backyard, cracked driveway, wood floors in need of refinishing, the aforementioned overgrown landscaping, and a questionably stable foundation. Tipsy and Scott were willing to live through years of renovations to get the size and location, and with a sale pending on Scott's house and the stroke of a few pens, they had Miss Callie's house under contract. They'd scheduled the Big Move in phases, starting after their Memorial Day weekend wedding.

"I told Scott you'd move on eventually," said Tipsy. "He's accepted the idea that you come with the house. Like the hideous linoleum and the drafty windows."

"I like Dr. Brandt, but I find it hard to believe he's thrilled by the idea of sharing his home and his new family with another man that he can't see."

"I mean…yeah, but…" Tipsy knew that Scott also liked Henry, as much as realistically possible, since the two men could never actually meet. It had crossed her mind that Scott found the whole *haunted house* thing weird, but he had assured her that he was onboard. She repeated his sentiments. "It's all good. He's onboard."

"Hmm." Henry's noncommittal response hinted at doubt, but other matters were more pressing. "Jane said *we* need to understand our whole story, so that means *she* needs to understand, too. What if she's in distress on the other side, and the only way to help her is to discover…whatever she wants me to discover?" He shook his head. "No. I'm not going anywhere."

"I can't answer those questions, but *you* can't sit in this house and do nothing."

"Exactly." He stood and walked straight through the computer and the table. The computer beeped and shut down, as if he'd tweaked an invisible electrical field. "With every mystery we've solved," he said, "we've spoken with others to get information. The living, and the dead. There's one person left in this world with a connection to me and Jane."

"Proctor James," said Tipsy. The man who had killed Jane and Henry. Who—as far as Tipsy knew—still haunted the graveyard at St. Philip's Church.

"If he knows Jane is in need, perhaps he'll help me."

"It's possible. There's no doubt that Proctor loved Jane to the point of obsession—uh, you okay?"

Henry's face reddened like a strawberry in the sun, and his jaw worked like he was chewing a hunk of tough beef jerky. He tugged at his collar. Tipsy thought he might rip his shirt off. A freaky idea, as she'd never considered whether ghosts could be naked.

I hope not. That would be so awkward—

Tipsy! Focus! said Granna. *Talk the man down before he moves on to his pants.*

"Henry…it's okay. Shhhh…shhhh…shhhh…" She instinctively shushed him like a newborn infant. If possible, she would have picked him up and bounced him on her hip.

The shush-and-bounce routine had always worked wonders on her babies, and even sans bouncing, it worked on Henry, too. "I'm…fine," he said. "I'm…alright." His face gradually blanched to his normal pallor, the shade Tipsy thought of as *undead white*. He let go of his collar. "But it's difficult to hear you speak of her and him."

"Are you sure you can handle *seeing* him?"

He nodded. Given the skinny line of his pressed-together lips, she wasn't convinced, but she couldn't think of any other way to kick off this mystery. "Okay. If you're set on it. It *does* seem likely that Proctor will remember something from that last week of y'all's lives. He may even know more than you do—"

The computer rattled against the table again, and the ancient ceiling fan squeaked into motion above their heads. The whole fixture wobbled in its gaping socket. Tipsy added *porch fans* to the list of household items to be replaced. She moved out from under it. "You're in a bad place," she said. "How about if I go first, and talk to him?"

"*Noooooo.*" Through some herculean effort, Henry got control of himself, and the fan's menacing whirring stopped. "I *must* visit him myself. But I'd appreciate your company, and your discerning opinion. Can we go tomorrow? I need to rest, if I'm to make the trip downtown."

"I can meet you at St. Philip's after I drop Little A at school."

"Thank you," he said. "I'll go now, and try to prepare myself. Will you put my computer away after it's properly charged?" Henry had mastered some IT terminology—*computer, laptop, cursor, wi-fi, mouse*—but it was still strange to hear her friend use such modern lingo.

She nodded, and Henry Mott disappeared into his supernatural repose like an email sent into cyberspace.

Over the past two years, Tipsy's dear friends Shelby Patterson Callahan, Pamella Brewton, and Jillian Porcher Yates had overseen her artistic renaissance. Each woman had her own powerhouse personality and lofty social connections, and thanks to their collective efforts, prestigious galleries in Charleston, New York, Atlanta, San Francisco, Miami, and Seattle had shown Tipsy's work. Accolades rolled in, demand grew, and her prices ticked up. In addition to supplying multiple galleries, she managed a constant stream of commission work. She had no complaints about her success, but she'd gone from tossing a few balls in the air to professional juggler. The learning curve was steep, like the hill Granna bemoaned climbing on her childhood walk to school. In other words, one hell of a country mile.

In the early days of Tipsy's career, she'd spent most of her waking hours drawing or painting. Her painter's block had coincided with the most physically grueling years of motherhood. As a result, she'd never carried such a heavy artistic load while also managing a family.

She'd developed a frenetic routine: drop off kids at school, squeeze in some exercise, spend four or five hours painting, pick up the kids, run said kids to after school activities, make dinner while monitoring homework, bedtime routine, paint again if she still had any functioning brain cells, shower and pass out. Nothing slowed down when she wasn't actively painting or wrangling kids. She still had to coordinate and monitor every aspect of the children's schedules (academics, extracurriculars, healthcare, and social lives), including keeping Big Ayers informed about what was happening and what role he needed to play. She ran errands, scheduled appointments, made phone calls, answered texts and emails. She managed the business side of her artwork, which included billing, taxes, cashflow in and out of her business account, coordinating with clients and galleries, and at least attempting to regularly post artwork and monitor comments on social media.

Tipsy's form of painting was not manual labor. She did not stand on a twenty-foot ladder in a hundred degree heat and slather Sherwin-Williams on planked wood siding. Still, her body was showing strain. Being on her feet all day literally got on her nerves. The ache of carpal tunnel syndrome had settled into her right wrist, and the sciatic nerve pain that had plagued her throughout her pregnancies returned with a vengeance. It ran from the middle of her back, down through her right hip, and into her right calf.

The idea of slowing down never crossed her mind. She'd always dreamed of being an in-demand artist, and even with their very comfortable combined income and the house's *as-is* state, Tipsy and Scott had stretched to purchase Miss Callie's house. Her substantial contributions to their family coffers eased her mind, even as they wreaked havoc on her back.

Stretching eased the discomfort temporarily, so she'd perfected some amateur contortionist moves. She promised herself, Scott, and Pamella that she'd join a yoga studio, but a daily hour of *namaste* seemed an indulgence. Instead, she continued to run and lift weights, which provided the most bang for her workout buck. On the morning Henry confessed his inexplicable problems, she took thirty minutes she didn't have and hit the pavement.

Clipped thoughts kept time with the rhythm of her own footfalls. *Jane's message. Writer's block. Slipping sanity. Anxiety, depression, can-tank-er-ous-ness. Blended family. Blended family. Blended family.* Since the day she found Henry Mott existing in her house, his problems had been her problems. By extension, his problems would soon be Scott's.

Ugh, Granna. It's going to be stressful enough moving three more people into the house. Now we're also dealing with Henry's mysterious malaise and the destruction that may accompany it.

Wait till Dr. Brandt comes home to his neatly folded underwear strewn across the bedroom, or his beloved Swiffer splintered into pieces like a used toothpick.

That will go over like an overweight pelican with one wing. Tipsy scowled as a bead of sweat dripped off her nose. *Hell, Henry himself might not enjoy another alpha male in his house, plus the added chaos of two more kids.*

Reality is, Henry should move on sooner than later. For everyone's sake.

I will really miss that undead fool, but given the big picture, you're right.

Her heart hurt at the thought of never seeing Henry again, but even her big ol' house could feel crowded with seven living people and one dead one residing inside it. She was fixing to create one jacked up version of the Brady Bunch, especially if the resident ghost started destroying the furnishings. Henry Mott was no Alice Nelson.

With visions of airborne boxer briefs dancing in her head, Tipsy sprinted toward the corner of Venning and Bennett Streets. She slowed for her cooldown walk, then paused on her driveway to stretch her perfidious nerves. She grabbed her right knee in her left hand and pulled it across her midsection. She clung to her picket fence with her right hand and sunk into a squat until her eyes watered.

"You okay over there? That looks darn uncomfortable."

Tipsy looked up. A woman stood beside a red Cadillac parked in front of her next door neighbor's house.

"I'm fine, thanks," said Tipsy. "Just working out some kinks—"

At the sight of the woman's face, déjà vu washed over Tipsy. She was a wiry African American lady who appeared to be about seventy years old. Her long salt and pepper braids framed her round face, and pink glasses outlined her dark eyes. She wore a short-sleeved white button down shirt, a long skirt with a blue floral pattern, and flat sandals.

The Walking Lady! Tipsy thought.

The woman flinched, as if Tipsy had shouted at her, then her polite smile widened to a warm grin. A voice spoke up in Tipsy's mind. She's heard it once before, on Rifle Range Road. *Look who it is! Is that what you call me?*

Tipsy unfurled her contorted limbs. "Yes. Since I see you walking on Rifle Range Road all the time."

"I remember you. There was traffic, and you were thinking hard, and—"

"You spoke to me. Told me I wasn't alone with…*you know*."

"The *ghosts*," said the woman, matter-of-factly.

"Right. I'm getting used to talking about them, but it's still weird."

"I've had a few more decades to get comfortable with it. What's your name, honey?"

"Tipsy Collins. I live right here." She pointed up at her house.

"I'm Helen Stokes. Nice to meet you. I'm dropping off dry cleaning for Mr. Quattlebaum."

"Mr. Q. had another bad fall, didn't he?"

"Yes. His family finally convinced him to give up driving. He can't pick up his shirts. He's been a customer of ours forever. My family owns Stokes Cleaning and Alterations on Coleman Boulevard."

"Ah! I don't have a lot of dry cleaning in my line of work, but I've had dresses cleaned there. Everyone is always super friendly."

"Nice to hear. My son runs the business. I go in a few days a week to help out—"

"That's where you're always walking!"

Helen nodded. "I help with bookkeeping and things. But I'm a busybody. Always have been. I told Mr. Q.'s daughter I'd drop off his clean shirts and pick up the dirty ones."

"That's nice of you. It's sweet how he dresses up every day. I used to see him puttering around the neighborhood in a suit and fedora, but not so much anymore."

"That's the old generation. Sharp dressed men."

"I know all about men like that. There's a ghost in my house. Henry Mott, circa 1923."

"Tall, red-headed fellow?"

"Yes!"

"I saw him on your porch when I picked up Mr. Q.'s shirts last week. He struck me as a bit gloomy."

"Oh, he is. He's even more gloomy than usual lately and..." A loose light bulb sputtered in Tipsy's head. She screwed it in tighter, and spoke. "Hey—random thought. Henry is having some issues that I don't quite understand. Maybe we could have a cup coffee and discuss? Since, as you said, you've been at this for longer than me."

"Sure," said Helen. "I'd be happy to—"

A buzzing roar cut Helen off. Only a chainsaw or a biblical plague of locusts could produce such a sound. Tipsy looked over her shoulder, where a construction crew was framing an addition to the house across the street.

"Mercy," said Helen. "Mr. Q. is lucky he's hard of hearing."

"No kidding. Their ruckus is louder than my kids, and that's saying something. They've been at it for weeks."

"That's an...*interesting* house," said Helen, as she looked the place over.

"I suppose so," said Tipsy. "It's different, anyway." The house was a big three-story brown brick colonial with a single round turret. There were few brick homes in the Old Village, and even fewer turrets. It looked like a puritanical minister had started out building a church, lost his faith, and settled on a rather ugly house. It appeared to be at least as old as Miss Callie's house. In another Old Village aberration, it had no front porch. Just a set of crumbly cement steps.

That house had always struck Tipsy as forlorn and misplaced. It belonged up north somewhere, in a cold city where people avoided eye contact with their neighbors. A place with no need for front porches.

After the last owner passed away, it sat on the market, uninhabited, until a retired lawyer from Columbia bought it and started renovations. He turned up every few weeks to check on the progress, but otherwise, it remained empty. The boarded up windows resembled closed eyes, as if the house slumbered under general anesthesia.

"What are they doing to it?" asked Helen.

"Rearranging every wall and adding a couple thousand square feet, apparently. I'm ready for them to finish. The sawing and hammering are worse than the landscapers' gas-powered leaf blowers. Anyway, let me get your phone num—"

"What's that?" asked Helen, as she pointed in the direction of the chainsaw's intermittent screeching. "Or—*who* is that?"

Tipsy followed her line of sight, and to her surprise, she caught flickering purplish-blue light smack in the middle of the addition. The workers bustled past an unmoving, gossamer human shape. "Is it a ghost?" asked Tipsy.

"It sure looks like it."

Tipsy squinted. Given his closely-cropped haircut, she guessed the small, thin ghost was male. A short man, or a tall child?

As if sensing their eyes on him, the ghost turned in their direction, but she couldn't make out his features. His unusually bright cerulean glow threw off sparks, like Bunsen burner flames in a high school science lab.

"I've never seen him before!" As the words left Tipsy's mouth, the ghost disappeared. "Then again, I haven't been inside that house."

"I've known spirits who spent decades haunting a single room," said Helen. "Even one who refused to come out of a broom closet. The noise and chaos might've driven that fellow outside."

"Maybe, but…jeez. Now I want to know more."

"So you can help him *move on*?"

"You know about all that?"

Helen laughed. "I've been helping ghosts *move on* for most of my own life. I was about ten years old the first time I looked into a ghost's memory, witnessed a nasty death, and sent her on her way. My first one was a *her*. A young woman, poor thing. Gored to death by a pack of feral hogs."

"You saw *that* when you were ten?"

"I did. Threw up as soon as I woke up from the memory. But I watched her find peace and move on, and I was hooked like a tight belt buckle. I've released…*oh*…fifty-odd ghosts?"

"*Fifty?* Good lord! How did you know how to do it?"

"My mother and my auntie taught me everything they knew, and *they* learned it all from my granny. Helping spirits is considered a calling in my family."

"Wow. You *definitely* know more than I do, since I've only been doing this for a few years. My list is only…." She counted ghosts on her fingers. *Jane-Henry-Louisa Bishop-John Huger-Ivy Brewton-Camden Brewton-Catherine Porcher-Thomas Bonneau.* "My list is only eight spirits long. And Henry won't go, so I don't know if he counts."

"If he chooses to stick around, that's not your fault. You did your part."

"When can we get together and talk? About Henry, and now…" She pointed at the house. "About this mystery guy, too."

"Text me and we'll find a time for me to come by. I'd like to meet your gloomy, dapper ghost."

"Hmmm. You mind if we meet somewhere else? Henry is in a poor frame of mind. I don't know how he'll react to me discussing his issues with a stranger. He was a clairvoyant in life, you see, so he can—"

"Move things around with his mind? Accidentally cause a lot of damage?"

Tipsy grinned. "It's so nice to *not* have to explain everything! Here's my number."

They exchanged digits and wishes for a good day, and Tipsy headed into her house to start the day's painting session. She texted Scott as soon as she stepped into the foyer. HEY BABY. I'M HOME, ABOUT TO START PAINTING. EVERYTHING GOOD AT WORK?

He replied as she removed her running shoes. HEY BABY. EVERYTHING'S FINE, JUST VERY BUSY, ER BLOWING ME UP AS USUAL. BTW, MY KIDS AREN'T COMING OVER TILL TOMORROW, SO I CAN COME TO YOU FOR DINNER.

TIPSY: YAY! I'D LOVE TO TALK TO YOU ABOUT HENRY ONCE MY POSSE IS ASLEEP. HE FINALLY OPENED UP ABOUT WHAT'S BEEN BUGGING HIM.

SCOTT: SURE. I'LL TRY TO HELP. AS LONG AS HIS PROBLEMS ARE NOT DIRECTLY RELATED TO BEING DEAD.

TIPSY: EVERYTHING SOMEHOW RELATES TO HIM BEING DEAD, BUT HE'S DEFINITELY STRUGGLING WITH HIS MENTAL HEALTH.

SCOTT: THEN THAT'S RIGHT UP MY ALLEY.

TIPSY: ALSO, MR. Q NEXT DOOR IS GETTING HIS DRY CLEANING DELIVERED, BY A WOMAN WHO HAPPENS TO BE A FELLOW GHOSTBUSTER!

SCOTT: WOW! SOUNDS LIKE WE HAVE A LOT TO DISCUSS, BUT I GOTTA RUN. LOVE YOU!

TIPSY: LOVE YOU TOO!

Tipsy plugged in her phone, chugged some water, and got to work. She removed the sheet covering her latest gallery piece and sized up her progress. The painting depicted a cherry red parrot with a blue head. The bird's curved beak, scaly feet, and piercing eyes were bright yellow. She wasn't sure what kind of parrot it was—a macaw, maybe—because she'd never seen such a bird. It could have originated in the Amazon jungle, or it may have come straight from her brain. Her imagination's idea of how a parrot should look.

Tipsy usually painted from real life. Her mental camera would click on a scene, and she'd store it away in the file cabinets of her mind. Lately, however, she'd found herself...dare she admit it...*bored*...

with reality. She'd painted every Charleston scene imaginable, and her commission clients usually requested Lowcountry lore. Lovely, but she was tired of painting marsh-scapes, and nautical scenes, and dreamy ladies languishing on piazzas. And the *birds*.

So. *Many*. Birds.

Herons. Egrets. Pelicans. Sandpipers. Seagulls. Ospreys. She despaired of finding originality in anything avian.

Tipsy had always had vivid dreams, so when she woke up with this new, unknown, wonderfully *exotic* bird clearly in her mind, she seized on it. Silky crimson and blue feathers, sunny yellow points, and the fiercely intelligent look in his eyes. This bird knew what was up, and he wouldn't hesitate to tell you. She imagined he enjoyed every brush stroke as she preened over him. Such a haughty creature would revel in the attention.

In her dream, the bird perched on a silvery crown, which in turn rested on a bed of purple and green fabric. Parrot, crown, cloth—none of it matched, but somehow it all did. She'd started the painting immediately, and several weeks later, it was almost complete.

Ol' Fussy Feathers is looking damn good, said Granna. *What does Shelby think about this new direction you're taking?*

Shelby, as Tipsy's oldest friend and the owner of the Good Queen Bess Gallery on Queen Street, always got first dibs on Tipsy's gallery pieces.

She's being supportive, but I can tell she's a little skeptical. If she poo-poos my parrot, I won't send him to the GQB. I'll send him to The Flamingo Gallery in Miami.

They have to accept exotic birds in that joint. What's next in your fairytale repertoire?

Almost finished the storm landscape. Then there's that castle that came to me as I was running along the Battery last month. The one on the cliffside. Not sure where that came from either, but I like it.

She sensed Granna squinting at the painting. *So what* is *the source of all this imaginary stuff?*

I'm just bored with my usual repertoire, said Tipsy. *And O-Liv has been reading tons of fantasy books. I'm surrounded by once-upon-a-time. Probably sneaking into my subconscious.*

That explanation didn't feel exactly right, but she didn't have a better one, and Granna accepted it.

That makes a whole dollar's worth of sense. You're feeling good about this painting. How are you feeling about Henry?

Better. She squeezed blue and red paint onto her pallet and mixed shades of purple. *As Helen said to me a few years ago on Rifle Range Road, I'm not alone.* She backtracked. *I'm never truly alone. I have you. But Helen—*

She's like the GM of the Martinville Piggly Wiggly, while I never made it past second assistant manager of the bakery. Tipsy started to protest, but Granna shushed her. *It's okay, sugar. I've taught you everything I know. It's high time someone expanded on my lessons.*

Tipsy dabbed purple paint on the rolls of lush fabric. Velvet, or something like it. Soft and warm and wintery. *I agree, Granna. Helen turning up is an unexpected gift, like my recent doldrum-busting imaginary artistic visions. I know I'll learn a lot from her. I mean, the woman has freed fifty freakin' ghosts!*

Tipsy might not have a complete understanding of her latest creative inspiration, but she had no doubt that Helen Stokes was a woman with answers.

Last fall, Little Ayers had started sixth grade at Pinegrounds School, Charleston's most storied private educational institution. Big Ayers and his sister Mimi Collins Lathrop were Pinegrounds alums, and Mimi's kids had been at PG since first grade. After visiting the local public middle school at the end of their son's fifth grade year, Big Ayers had asked Tipsy to consider sending Little A to his alma mater.

"I can afford it, Tipsy," he'd said, when they met for coffee to discuss their options. "The academics are top notch, but so are the extracurricular activities. Their art programs are amazing. If Little A has a good experience, we'll enroll Mary Pratt and Olivia Grace when they start middle school, too."

Tipsy had agreed to a tour. Once she met some teachers and walked the school's grounds—the towering oaks, the rolling green grass, the view of the Ashley River from the playground—she hadn't been able to say no. Shockingly, Ayers didn't ask her to contribute financially, and she admitted to herself that her trepidation stemmed from her own insecurities. She wasn't sure she'd fit in with the Pinegrounds moms, but at least she had Mimi.

Little A was nervous about the transition, but he put on a brave face. Lots of kids switched schools in sixth grade, so he wasn't the only new guy. By Halloween, he was loving his new friends and teachers. He didn't even complain about his uniform, but he did grouse about the increased homework.

After dinner on the day Tipsy met Helen Stokes, Little Ayers was desperate for mathematical reinforcements.

"Uhhhhhhh." He rested his forehead on the kitchen table. He smushed his freckle-covered nose against his forearm and his floppy dark blonde hair pooled on his placemat, as if the strain of his after-dinner math assignment had melted his head. "Scott? Help."

"Hang tight, dude," said Scott, as he straightened the dish towels. Even at Tipsy's house, Scott always insisted on cleaning up after meals. His OCD couldn't tolerate anyone else's version of tidying, organizing leftovers, or loading the dishwasher. Tipsy had long since given up trying to contribute.

"I'd help if I could, buddy," said Tipsy, "but I'll add to your confusion." Tipsy's artist's brain rebelled against the utilitarianism of mathematics. Thankfully, Scott was a borderline math genius, so once he wiped down the counters, he came to Little A's rescue.

Mary Pratt and Olivia Grace had already finished their comparably simple fourth grade homework. They bopped around the kitchen on their long, gangly legs. Their curly brown ponytails bounced as they practiced the viral dance moves they picked up from TikTok. Mary Pratt still wore her volleyball practice clothes, but Olivia Grace had changed into a sundress the minute she walked in the door. She'd slathered sparkly pink lip gloss over her mouth.

"Can we watch *Tangled*, Mamacita?" asked Olivia Grace.

"Oooooh, yes," said Mary Pratt. She broke into one of the movie's signature songs, the one where Vikings, pirates, and other animated scallywags professed their hidden creative and romantic desires. In an off-key singing voice she inherited from her mother, she yodeled about piano concertos, interior design, and ceramic *un-i-cooooorns*.

"M.P., *come on*!" said Little Ayers. "I'm trying to concentrate."

"Go to your room if you need to use your brain." She narrowed her big brown eyes at him and stuck out her tongue.

"You're such an opp," said Little A.

Lately, her kids' constantly evolving Gen-Z slang made Tipsy feel as clueless as Henry talking about pluggers driving him zonkers. She kept a *KID WORDS* list in the Notes application on her phone. From her understanding, *opp* was shorthand for an opponent, or an enemy. A low blow from Little Ayers.

"Ayers, your homework is your nemesis, not your sister. How about this plan," said Tipsy, as she looked up from jotting notes in her day planner. "Girls, y'all take all the laundry upstairs, and put yours away, and when Ayers is done, we can watch *Tangled*."

"As long as y'all—" M.P. pointed at Tipsy and Scott. "—don't get all *mushy* during the boat scene."

O-Liv giggled. "Like Scott is Flynn Rider."

Scott looked up from Little A's worksheet. "Wait for it…y'all ready for…" He flipped his dark hair out of his eyes, raised one eyebrow, and pursed his lips. Scott made a pretty good Flynn Rider, if Flynn was a forty-one-year-old psychiatrist with blue eyes and a beard. "The *smolder*."

Tipsy pretended to swoon at his passable F.R. impression, which made the girls shriek and gag over the grossness of their mother and soon-to-be-stepfather. Their laughter echoed down the hallway as they raced for the laundry room. Tipsy felt her heart might burst with happiness at their appropriate mock disgust about her healthy, affectionate relationship.

"Two more problems." Scott squeezed Little A's shoulder. "You hanging in there?"

"Barely. But I'll be glad when I'm done. Thanks for your help."

"You got it."

Early on, Little Ayers had struggled with his father's negative (and tactlessly expressed) opinions about Scott, but Scott's patience and goofy sense of humor had won him over. The friendship between her fiancé and her son heartened Tipsy. She relished the idea of Ayers growing up under the influence of such a kind, gentle man.

Damnit, Granna. I'm so lucky.

You are, but so is Scott. So are all five of y'all's kids.

I know, said Tipsy, but an increasingly familiar anxiety vibrated in her stomach. Like the thrum of cicadas, she only noticed it when another noise brought it to her attention.

Why has the universe dumped such good fortune on me, while so many people suffer? Such questions plagued her, unanswerable and tinged with inexplicable guilt. *Do I deserve this happiness?*

She smothered those thoughts before Granna offered sensible insight about the multitudes of good people who suffer, and the bad people who prosper, and how *deserving happiness* had absolutely nothing to do with achieving it. Granna was right, but with much happiness comes an intense desire to protect it.

She tried to ride out the worry-bugs' intolerable buzzing, and like their real insect compatriots, they shut up when the sun went down. Once ensconced on the sectional sofa in the den, sandwiched between Scott and O-Liv with Little Ayers and M.P. sprawled on beanbags on the floor, she felt better. They watched the first hour of *Tangled* before Tipsy sent the kids upstairs to get ready for bed. Scott answered his never-ending emails while she kept bedtime on the straight and narrow. By the time she tucked everyone in, Scott was on the front porch talking to his own kids.

Tristan and Chloe were naturally more reserved than Tipsy's children, and Tipsy knew their mother—Kate Brandt-Collins, who *also* happened to be Big Ayers's wife—regularly undermined Scott, Tipsy, and their relationship. She had always gone out of her way to be nice to Kate, but despite Kate's frisky friendliness, Tipsy had no illusions that Kate had any genuine positive feelings toward her. Tipsy had *left* Kate's current husband, therefore supposedly breaking his heart. Tipsy was also marrying the former husband who left *her*. Their unique family dynamic, with crisscrossing parents and stepparents, had many advantages, but Kate's double whammy passive aggressive dislike of Tipsy was not one of them.

Given his kids' personalities, Kate's interference, and Scott's limited parenting time, Tipsy hadn't bonded with his kids like he had with her brood. She had made headway with Chloe, his eleven-year-old daughter, but thirteen-year-old Tristan remained an enigma.

Still, Tipsy kept trying. She poked her head into the FaceTime frame and waved. "Hey, y'all!" she said, over Scott' shoulder.

"Hey, Tipsy," replied Chloe, a pretty girl with her dad's features, blue eyes, and long, straight dark hair that she always wore in a high ponytail. "I like your earrings."

Tipsy fingered her silver hoops. "Thanks, honey. You can borrow them."

"Tris," said Scott. "You still there?"

Tristan leaned into the frame. Like Chloe, he had Scott's dark hair and blue eyes, but he favored his mom in the face. "Yeah. Hey."

"Hi, Tris," said Tipsy.

He muttered something unintelligible, so Tipsy simply smiled reassurance. Scott asked about their homework and got sports updates, and they said goodnight.

Tree frogs had taken over for sleeping cicadas. The frogs' chirping sounded happier than the cicadas' collective drone. Like laughter compared to snoring, or fiddle music juxtaposed with an out-of-tune bassoon. Tipsy sat beside Scott on the loveseat and rested her head on his shoulder. He slid his arm around her and squeezed.

"I wish I had the kind of relationship with your kids that you have with mine," she said.

"You will someday." He kissed her forehead. "Your kids made it easy for me."

"Because they never stop talking to anyone who will listen?"

He chuckled. "Pretty much. I know mine are tougher nuts to crack. They're like whole walnuts—"

"And mine are mushy boiled peanuts."

"An apt comparison. What's up with Mr. Mott?"

"This might sound weird—"

"We're talking about *a ghost*."

"Right. So…I found him on the porch this morning…" She summarized everything Henry had told her, from his worry about Jane to his mysterious symptoms. "… and he's more irritable and anxious than usual, which is saying something, because he's usually irritable and anxious. He's having trouble leaving the house, and let's not forget that he may be losing his mind again. He thinks its connected to Jane's message, and she's trying to tell him there's more to their murder than we realized."

"Depression can manifest in anger, or physical symptoms. Maybe he's struggling with his wife's absence, and this is a natural paranormal presentation."

"That's possible, but Henry has been missing Jane for years. This feels different to me. More…acute."

"And he wants to talk to this guy Proctor, who had an affair with his wife, and was responsible for their violent deaths?"

"Yes. They haven't spoken since the day of the murder. Henry found out that Proctor was Jane's paramour, and about ten minutes later, Jane and Henry were both dead."

"Yikes. Sounds like an intense reunion."

"Everything with Henry is intense. I offered to visit Proctor first. To prepare him for Henry's appearance, you know? But Henry insists on going. Tomorrow, in fact."

Scott frowned. "What if one of them loses it, and…I don't know… squashes you with a gravestone? There are some big memorials in the St. Philip's graveyard, and they're old and dilapidated."

"Crushed by an overturned sarcophagus. Not the way I plan to go." She shrugged. "Proctor wasn't a clairvoyant. He can't hurt me. As for Henry, projectile floral arrangements are more his speed."

"Baby, I don't love this plan. Have you thought about—"

"I *do not* appreciate the two of you talking about me behind my back."

Henry appeared on the rocking chair across from them. The butterfly bushes on the other side of the porch railing vibrated. A few of Tipsy's laughing froggies hopped out of the shrubs and onto the porch.

"Oh, he's here. Hey, Henry," said Tipsy.

"Uh…hi." Scott always took a moment to acclimate to Henry's invisible presence.

"Please tell Dr. Brandt that I appreciate his opinion," said Henry, "as diseases of the mind are his area of expertise, but this is not some function of my typical misery. This is *nouveau* miserableness."

Tipsy delivered Henry's message to Scott.

"I wish I could help," said Scott, "but this kind of thing wasn't covered in my residency training."

"Tipsy, I know you mean well," said Henry, "but please refrain from plotting new strategies without my approval."

"We're not *plotting*. We were talking about the best way to—"

"Tomorrow morning I shall speak to Proctor! Perhaps we'll even reconcile. That murdering, deceitful, conniving—"

"That doesn't sound like a reconciliation in the making."

"—and he'll apologize to me for seducing my wife and killing us and—" Henry vigorously shook his head. His red hair flopped across his forehead and covered his eyes.

Alarm must have showed on Tipsy's face, because Scott asked, "What's happening?"

Before she could reply, Henry stood. "I'll be at the graveyard in St. Philip's at half past eight. Come or don't come, I don't give a damn."

The bulbs in the porchlights exploded. The center plank on Miss Callie's old joggling board flexed and creaked as if ten-thousand chirping tree frogs were jumping on it. Henry stomped right through the porch railings, missed the staircase, and fell into the bushes. "Damnation!" he yelled. "*Infernal* shrubbery!" His cursing voice lingered for a moment after he disappeared.

"Tipsy, what's—"

"He's gone," she said to Scott.

"Shit. We have to clean that up." He pointed at the broken glass. "Should we expect more of this kind of thing?"

"I...maybe. *Probably.*"

"He *could* hurt someone."

Tipsy couldn't lie to him. "It's possible. I worried about that when I first moved in, before we found out how he and Jane died and he went into remission, or whatever you want to call it. But he'd never hurt anyone intentionally."

"I see."

"Please don't worry about it. I'll get him under control." She scooted closer to him. "You okay?"

He smiled. "Of course. I'm just worried in general. But you know that's how I roll. OCD and all."

She *did* know. He perseverated on everything. Hospital infrastructure. Stubborn mildew. Supreme Court decisions. The fluctuating price of eggs. The rates on their new mortgage. Tennessee football. Now, he'd worry about ghosts, too. She ran a finger over his scratchy cheek. He usually felt better once he talked, so she asked, "What's front and center on your worry scoreboard at this moment?"

"The move, I guess. We've already talked about how it's going to be an adjustment for all the kids. Mine might seem stoic, but they won't do well with a malignant invisible presence in the house. Chloe is prone to nightmares. Afraid of the dark."

Tipsy's intestines were suddenly made of Jell-o. She had to reassure him. "I'll take care of it. I promise. Chloe *will* feel safe in this house."

"I know you will." He laced his fingers through hers. "And it's not only that. I'm worried about your stress level, and now you're dealing with ghost problems, too. You're working so hard, and planning the wedding and the move. I'm not helping enough—"

"Eh. I'm lining up caterers and movers. A few floral arrangements and matching dresses for the girls. You have *way* more stress than I do. Work. Kate."

"You work, and you have Big Ayers."

"Yours is worse. I worry about your blood pressure."

"I worry about your pinched nerves." He chuckled. "You want to fight about who is more stressed and more worried about the other person?"

"Sure," she said.

"I win." He poked her side, and she squirmed.

"Even if I am stressed," she said, "it's nothing like the stress I used to feel in the dark ages before…us."

"I know what you mean. Knowing you have my back makes everything else manageable. Team Scipsy, right?"

She smiled. "Always. Scott and Tipsy, rahrahrah!"

"But seriously, with minimal stress in our relationship, the rest is more evenly distributed."

"You always know how to say what I'm thinking."

They sat in comfortable silence for a few minutes. Tipsy's gelatin guts went still, but it wouldn't take much to start them jiggling again. She had to solve Henry's conundrum, for Henry *and* all his living bystanders. Her kids and Scott's kids (even if they didn't know it) and Scott himself. She hated the thought that a paranormal challenge would strain their family blending or exacerbate Scott's anxiety. Given the problem's supernatural nature, the responsibility for solving it fell on her. She vowed to do so, stat, and leave Scott out of it.

Tipsy, I don't know about that approach, said Granna. *You've always said you and Scott are a team. Hell, y'all both just acknowledged that with your Team Scipsy cheerleader routine.*

I know. And we are. But—

He's as worried about you as you are about him.

As if to reiterate Granna's point, Scott broke the silence. "I *am* concerned about your safety tomorrow."

"I've dealt with worse. Thomas Bonneau was a serial killer, remember? Henry is a moody dude with a tragic backstory and a good heart."

"I believe you, but I reserve the right to worry. Maybe your new clairvoyant friend can help. Tell me more about her."

"Her name is Helen Stokes. We had a little…telepathic…meeting of the minds a few years ago on Rifle Range Road. What I mean is—"

"Don't explain. It will just confuse me more."

"Anyway, today I saw her on the sidewalk, and we recognized each other. She's, like, a paranormal expert. She's been freeing ghosts for years, and she's got the eagle eye for it. She noticed a ghost across the street, in the construction site. I've lived here for *four years* and I've never seen him."

"Another one, huh?"

"A male person of indeterminate age. Helen suggested that the construction chaos drove him out of the house. He could have been hiding inside for a hundred years. She's known ghosts who haunted *single rooms*. I didn't know *that* was a thing." She squeezed Scott's hand. "We're going to get together soon. Who knows what else she'll teach me? So exciting!"

"I wish she'd give you some lessons before you try to referee two dead romantic rivals in a graveyard. Promise me you'll be careful."

"As careful as I can be. Always."

His phone buzzed. A text from Little Ayers. Scott opened it.

LITTLE AYERS: THANKS FOR HELPING ME WITH MY MATH

He followed his grammatically unembellished message with a gif—a flummoxed-looking meme guy surrounded by floating algebraic equations. Scott smiled, and started typing. Tipsy rested her head on his shoulder and closed her eyes. She knew Scott would find the perfect response. Supportive and funny, without making a big deal of Little A's friendly overture.

She felt another surge of protective gratitude. Aside from her kids, Scott was the greatest blessing in her life. A thoughtful, compassionate, loyal man who always seemed to know what to say, not only to his own kids, but to hers.

As those thoughts flickered behind her eyes, her mind regurgitated a scene from her own childhood. One of those strangely vivid recollections she thought of as her *movie memories*. In this one, the only male figure in her childhood did and said just about everything a father shouldn't.

Tipsy is ten and going into the fifth grade. School starts in two days, and she's standing on a slippery foot-measuring thingy. It's her yearly visit to Clodhopper's Shoes, the kids' shoe store in Greenville, an hour drive away from Martinville. Granna doesn't have much money, but she always makes sure Tipsy has a nice pair of shoes before school starts. Clodhopper's is the best place to get Nikes and Reeboks and Keds for a hundred miles.

The young saleswoman—her nametag says Marnie—is measuring Tipsy's feet. It tickles when she runs her finger over Tipsy's socked toes. "This might be your last year getting shoes here," says Marnie. "You're tall, little lady, and your feet are catching up with the rest of you."

Tipsy squirms and curls her toes. She hates being so tall, and now she has big feet, too. Her own personal clodhoppers.

"If this is her last visit to Clodhoppers, it's a good thing I'm the one who brought her," says Tipsy's daddy, Randy Denning, from behind her.

Tipsy looks over her shoulder at her father. He's very tall, and slender, with straight light brown hair that's long in the back and short in the front. He's got hazel eyes and dark eyelashes, a square jaw, and the kind of twisty mouth that looks like he's always about to smile. He wears jeans and tan work boots and a tee-shirt from Trusty Trout Taproom, a restaurant on Lake Keowee. Daddy worked there as a bartender for a few months earlier in the year. Lake Keowee is thirty miles from Martinville, and Mama hated him driving all that way, especially at night. She also hated how much he drank when he was there. Good thing for her that job didn't last long. Daddy got fired for sucking down too much of the bar's product himself.

Daddy smiles at Marnie, who is a cute blonde with shiny blue doll baby eyes. She smiles back, but she's looking at the floor all embarrassed-like, and Tipsy remembers overhearing Mama and Granna talking last summer. "I bet Randy is flashing that toothy-ass grin at every pretty face in that bar," Mama had said, "and they're all melting into puddles of Budweiser and lemon drop shooters. Same damn thing he did to me."

Tipsy supposes *Daddy is handsome, just like she* supposes *Mama is pretty. Sometimes it's hard to tell whether your own parents are nice looking or not.*

"Glad I'm here to help y'all," says Marnie.

"Me, too."

Tipsy normally likes this outing every year. She usually goes with Granna, but Mama has taken her, too. Today, Granna is working at the Piggly Wiggly and Mama has a bad cold. Since Daddy isn't working anywhere at any time, Daddy brought Tipsy to Clodhopper's. Tipsy was a little nervous when Granna told her, because she rarely spends time alone with her father. Turns out it was alright being in the car with him and listening to him talk about his favorite music. Like Guns-N-Roses and Metallica, and other bands she likes better that aren't quite so loud. Boston and REO Speedwagon. She didn't feel weird till they got to the store, and Daddy started chatting with Marnie instead of the old man who is the owner. For some reason, the conversation between Daddy and Marnie makes her more uncomfortable with each word.

"What kind of shoes do you want, honey?" asks Marnie.

Tipsy shrugs. "Dunno. Tennis shoes, I guess."

"You play tennis?"

Randy laughs. "Hell no. We ain't tennis sort of people. She means sneakers. Something she can run around in. Kickball. Jump rope. That kind of thing."

"Okay," says Marnie. "All our sneakers are over—"

"Why don't you go take a look, Tipsy? See what you want."

Tipsy wanders over to the shoes, but her mutinous ears keep listening to their conversation.

"You in college?" Randy asks Marnie. "You look like one of those pretty little college girls."

"I graduated from high school last spring, so I'm taking classes at Upstate Tech. I'd like to transfer to Clemson next year, if I keep my grades up."

"I bet you will, as long as you don't let the boys distract you. I bet you get a lot of attention from boys."

She flips her hair. "I'm not much interested in the boys I know. They're so…immature."

"Ah, right. You're all grown up. I can tell by looking at you."

"My mama always says I'm mature for my age." She clears her throat. "How old are you?"

"Twenty-nine."

"Oh," says Marnie, clearly awed by Daddy's adultness. "That's proper grown."

"It is, although I sometimes long for those carefree days when I was your age."

"Isn't that your daughter? Your carefree days must have stopped when she came along."

"Yeah, I got started early. Too early. But don't tell my wife that."

"I wouldn't say a word. I'm no gossip."

"Hmm. You don't strike me as one to run off at the mouth."

Tipsy bristles, even though she isn't quite sure why. Whatever Daddy was saying to this lady—who is the same age as Tammi Reedy, Tipsy's babysitter—is just not right. *"I want these, Daddy," she says. She points at a pair of light blue low top Reeboks. She likes the high tops better, but the low tops are cheaper. "The blue ones."*

"Good choice," says Marnie, with a grin, but Tipsy scowls at her. She sits on the chair in a huff as Marnie goes to the backroom to get the shoes. When she returns, she tries to help Tipsy put them on, but Tipsy takes them herself and stuffs her foot inside. She meticulously tightens the laces and ties them. Marnie presses on her toe. It hurts, and Tipsy jerks her foot away.

"She's got room to grow. They'll last her at least through the winter. Walk around in them, honey," says Marnie. She tries her charming smile again, but Tipsy is having none of it. She stalks around the store. The shoes feel good, but everything else feels wrong.

"How do they feel?" asks her father.

"Fine," she says.

"Just fine? Those are some nice brand new sneakers."

"They feel good. I like them." She squirms. "Can we go now?"

"Yeah, sure. Hold your horses."

Tipsy puts on her old shoes as Marnie places her new ones back in the box. They walk to the cashier. Tipsy tugs on her father's arm. "Let's go, Daddy."

"Calm down, girl," he says. "I gotta get my money and pay."

"Granna's money," says Tipsy.

"What's that?"

"It's Granna's money for my shoes. Not yours."

Marnie pauses with her fingers on the cash register. Daddy says, "Wait in the truck, Tipsy."

He hands her the keys, and Tipsy strides out the door into the early September sun. The heat feels much better than the air conditioning in Clodhopper's. Cleaner. Less tainted. She unlocks the driver's side of daddy's old pickup truck, climbs across to the passenger side, and unrolls both windows to let the breeze blow through. She watches her father through the window as he keeps chatting with Marnie. It seems like she writes something on the receipt when she gives it to him.

Even at age ten, Tipsy has an idea what it is. She bets it's Marnie's phone number.

Randy comes out of the store and gets into the truck. "You like your new shoes?" he asks, but Tipsy stares out the window.

He steps on the clutch and puts the car in reverse. "How about a Happy Meal?"

She doesn't respond, even though she's hungry and a Happy Meal sounds like bliss.

"What's the problem, Tipsy?"

She glares out the window as the wind whips her hair. She isn't sure how to say what she wants to say. "You. Talking to that girl. It was…weird."

"I'm just being friendly."

"You were like…it was like you were…" She's heard the word she needs, but she's never had a reason to say it out loud in her young life. "You were flirting with her."

"Naaaah. Nothing like that. I thought if I was nice, maybe she'd give us a discount."

"Mama would have been mad."

"Huh. You think so?"

"I know so."

"Then I guess you shouldn't tell her. No need to upset her. Especially since it was nothing. Wouldn't want her to get mad at you for making up stories. It ain't right to lie, is it?"

Tipsy looks over at him. She wishes he would disappear, like the ghosts she sees around town. She knows they are ghosts these days. Not fuzzy people *like she called them when she was younger. They're dead people, stuck in this world.*

It's dumb to wish he'd disappear, *she thinks.* Then the car would crash and I'd end up a ghost, too. *She shoves the thought aside. She isn't afraid of ghosts, but she is afraid of becoming one. Besides, it isn't Christian to think about her father being a ghost. Even if—as Granna says—he can be a real turd.*

"Do you love Mama?" she asks, without thinking. "Are y'all going to get divorced?"

"I…don't think so. Not anytime soon."

She notices he didn't answer the first question. It's disturbing to think about why, so she says, "I'm hungry. Can we get a Happy Meal?"

"Sure thing, Tipper," he says.

He used to call her Tipper when she was little. He rarely does it anymore. Hearing him say it makes her sad and happy at the same time. It's too much confusing thinking, so instead, she thinks about her Happy Meal. What kind of toy she'll get. If they'll give her enough ketchup packets. Burger or McNuggets?

She's only ten, after all.

Chapter 2

St. Philips's cemetery seemed as permanent as the names carved into its granite headstones. As Tipsy waited for Henry, she peered through iron bars into a time capsule of grief and remembrance. A peaceful place of bittersweet beauty, where the bereaved of five centuries had mourned their dead. Half-sunken sarcophaguses reminded her of the tipped over refrigerators and washing machines in the Martinville junkyard. Overhead, thick oak limbs split into smaller branches, like tributaries diverging into ever-narrowing rivers and skinny creeks. Waving star-spangled banners and Palmetto flags beckoned guests to stop and visit with the deceased occupants. Tipsy imagined twittery voices behind the snapping and fluttering. *Don't forget us! Please, don't forget!*

The analogous newer monuments were like private school students; they wore the required uniform, but tried to stand out with personalized details. At Pinegrounds, kids showed their individuality through quirky jewelry and trendy shoes. On the rectangular gravestones, uniqueness came in the form of carved borders and inspirational quotations. The massive marble tomb of the Great Nullifier, John C. Calhoun, watched over them like an unpopular vice principal. Tipsy pictured the man she'd read about in high school history classes. His thin-lipped scowl and wild hair. Those piercing eyes lit by the flames of fanaticism. Given his abhorrent beliefs, he deserved to be trapped in a haunting, but she hoped she never ran into him.

Local professionals and C of C students rambled up and down Church Street, but this hour, no tourists and amateur genealogists perused the cemetery. She'd purposely arrived twenty minutes early, as she still hoped to speak with Proctor before Henry arrived.

"Where are you, Proctor?" she whispered. She didn't see the minister's hazy form, and Henry might appear at any moment. A tense situation, made more stressful by three rapid fire texts from Big Ayers.

She wanted to ignore him, but she was too much a mother. It could be a child-related emergency that somehow got to Dad before Mom. She swiped over his messages.

AYERS: HEY, STUFF IS GOING DOWN OVER HERE

AYERS: CAN WE TALK @ LITTLE A'S GAME TONIGHT?

AYERS: IF NOT LET ME KNOW WHEN U HAVE TIME

Tipsy reread the texts, twice. With Big Ayers, such messages could mean anything, from everyday banalities to life-changing trauma. He might want to tweak his parenting schedule to accommodate a fishing tournament, or he may have been diagnosed with terminal cancer.

TIPSY: YES. WE CAN TALK TONIGHT. IS EVERYTHING OK?

She rehashed the past two years as she awaited his reply. When Tipsy and Scott first started seeing each other, Ayers and Kate were scraping through the first of many rough patches, but their mutual enmity toward Scipsy's blossoming love affair created a brief alliance. Common rage distracted them from their own issues, and served as a defibrillator during their marriage's initial cardiac arrest. Unfortunately, it was a temporary fix for a systematic problem. Miscommunication, jealousy, simmering resentment, and hot-headed contrarianism increasingly clogged their relationship's arteries.

Last summer, after months of arguments and complaining, Big Ayers moved out for two weeks. He stayed with his parents, May Penny and Trip Collins, at their waterfront oasis on Sullivan's Island. He threatened to divorce Kate, but he'd ultimately returned home, like a wandering housecat who realized that a regular bowl of Friskees is better than mouse hunting.

Then around the holidays, weeks of building tension resulted in a seemingly trivial explosion—a ferocious argument over white lights versus colored lights. Predictably, Kate wanted sedate, solid white, while Ayers insisted on a seizure-inducing, twinkling rainbow. Kate snuck into the attic and used Ayers's own wire cutters to annihilate every string of colored lights.

That ballsy move had shocked even Scott, a hardened veteran of Kate's décor-wars. Ayers retreated like Camo Napoleon fleeing the Duke of Lululem-ington. They agreed to reunify at Christmas for the kids' sakes, and by New Year's Eve, Ayers had returned to his icicle bedecked abode.

When he needed a couple days of space, he planned his escapes for Tipsy's parenting time, but during the longer stints, the kids joined him at his parents' house. May Penny and Tripp enjoyed extra time with their darling son and precious grandkids, but they fretted over Ayers's marital status. Like political fact checkers stalking a wishy washy congressman, May Penny, Mimi, and Tipsy conferred regularly about Ayers's constantly shifting positions.

As for Kate, she maintained her superficial perkiness, but when things got bad, she closed the wagons around her own kids. She limited Scott's time with them and refused to communicate, while simultaneously griping about his lack of involvement. When Tipsy commented on her weird paradoxical complaints, Scott had simply shrugged and replied, "She's weird."

Big Ayers was equally weird, but in a behavioral development of particularly bizarre proportions, he increasingly relied on *Tipsy* for emotional support. He griped in her ear about Kate at drop offs, pickups, kids' sporting events, field trips, and back-to-school nights. He vented via phone calls and texts. She sensed he felt a warped kinship with Scott, who had survived life with Kate for over ten years.

Tipsy hardly put all the blame on Kate, for she knew the challenges of living with Ayers. Ayers and Kate had run smack into a concrete karma wall by marrying each other. Still, Ayers was the father of her kids. If confiding in Tipsy stabilized him, and kept her and Scott informed about the goings on in their house, so be it.

She sent him another text. IS EVERYTHING OKAY, AYERS? PLEASE LET ME KNOW.

"You're here early." Henry stood inside the gate. He scanned the graveyard. "This is where that coward has been hiding all these years."

"He doesn't have much of a choice." Tipsy pointed toward the rear of the cemetery, in the direction of the Circular Congregationalist Church. "He used to hang out around y'all's grave. That way."

"So he's still lurking in our affairs."

"There's a bench under that big oak. I'll meet you—"

Henry disappeared, then reappeared beside the stone bench. He crossed his arms over his chest and tapped one foot while Tipsy navigated the path through the cemetery. As she looked for Proctor, she reminded herself that the minister might be gone. He had the capability to *move on*, but his fears of holy retribution had kept him moribund for decades. Maybe he came to peace with his actions and he—

Seems like not, said Granna. *Look there.*

A tall gravestone topped by a weeping stone angel seemed to shimmer, as if vibrated by the angel's violent sobbing. Proctor James's trim form swam into focus in front of it. White beard, thinning white hair, white shirt, suspenders, dark trousers, and misty legs that hid his stocking feet.

Henry shoved his hands in his pockets, as if his fists were fighting roosters that had to be restrained. Tipsy stepped into the space between the two ghosts and faced Henry. His mouth had contorted into a crooked lightning bolt of rage. Despite the lack of wind, the heavy branches above his head swayed.

"Henry," she said. "Remember, you're here to *talk* to him."

"Murdering bastard—No. I won't…" Henry hopped in place and cleared his throat. "Just a chat among old..." His mouth twisted again. "He seduced her and then he…he…"

Tipsy clapped her hands in front of Henry's face. "Get it together, Mott. This is about *Jane*, remember?"

Henry's features smeared and sharpened and smeared again, until he settled on a reasonably neutral expression. The tree limbs went still. Tipsy turned to beckon to Proctor, but he had vanished. "Great, Henry. You scared him off."

"I don't scare that easily, Miss Seer. It's nice to see you again."

There he was, right in front of them. The man whose obsession with Jane had annihilated the remains of Henry's life, but only after Henry himself pretty much destroyed it.

"Thank you for visiting me, Tipsy." Proctor looked Henry up and down. "And *you* haven't changed at all, sir."

"I never had the chance to age."

"Facing eternity with a youthful face doesn't sound so bad."

"I would have traded a few wrinkles for several more decades of life. Silver would have been lovely in Jane's dark hair."

"It would have, indeed." Proctor smiled wistfully, and Henry's lip curled again.

Tipsy cut in. "That's why we're here. Right, Henry? To discuss Jane with Proctor."

"I'm happy to discuss Jane! She's just about my favorite topic of discussion—"

"You still *dare* to speak of her with so much familiarity!" said Henry.

"—but first, what about *you*, Henry? Are you well? As well as we can be?"

"No need to make polite conversation with *me*."

"It may seem like small talk, but I'm curious. I thought you would have moved on by now, given the repaired relations between you and Jane."

"You know *nothing* of our relations."

"I know Tipsy revealed the truth of your deaths, and Jane forgave me, *and* she forgave you. Why would you linger?"

"I had tasks to accomplish before I moved. Janie knew that. She… uh…" Henry's voice sloughed into a gruff mumble. "Ah. You. *Proctor*. Hateful bastard…Jane was…she knows…" He ran his hands over his face. "Argh…it's *calling* me, Tipsy."

Tipsy looked at her phone. It had only been about ten minutes since Henry appeared by the gate, but he already felt the pull of Miss Callie's house.

"Can you speak up?" asked Proctor. "What were you saying about Jane?"

Henry's voice sharpened with each word. "Don't. You. *Say. Her*—"

"Y'all," said Tipsy. "Maybe try to resolve the issues between *you two* first. Proctor, start by apologizing for sleeping with his wife, and then killing both of them."

"That's certainly a good place to start." Proctor smiled beatifically, as if explaining the divine meaning behind a boring sermon. "Henry, I have nothing but the deepest regret over the unfortunate results of my love for Jane. While my time with her was the most precious—"

Hysteria tinged Henry's laughter. "Is that your apology? Is it?"

"Proctor told me the same thing," said Tipsy. "How he repented every day of his life, and every day of his death—"

"Yet he can't resist reminding me of what passed between them! My *batty old mother* redeemed herself with more finesse! *She* managed a genuine apology!"

"What I'm trying to say is, although I loved Jane—"

"Don't you dare say her name! Not one more time!"

"We have to talk about her, Henry," said Tipsy.

Henry paced before the bench. Oak leaves rained down on Tipsy's head and floated through both ghosts. Tufts of tender spring grass ripped out of the mushy earth, and a blob of cold mud splatted against Tipsy's bare calf. She turned to the minister and spoke in a hissing whisper. "For a man tasked with providing emotional support to an entire church congregation, you can be pretty obtuse. Henry doesn't want to hear about how much you *loved Jane*, or God forbid…" She further lowered her voice. "…how she may have felt about you!"

"Ah, yes. I'm as dense as a stale biscuit." Proctor peered over Tipsy's shoulder. "Henry, son. Forgive me if I'm blundering this apology. I haven't spoken to anyone but Tipsy since 1949—"

"Don't you *dare* call me son!"

As Henry stormed toward Proctor, Scott's fears nearly came true. The nearest gravestone cracked down the center and tipped over. The next two followed like granite dominoes. They weren't big enough to squash Tipsy, but she jumped anyway to save her feet.

"You called yourself my friend in life!" screamed Henry. "*My friend!* I'll never forgive you. You vile *hypocritical murderer!"* Another tombstone shattered and peppered Henry with gravel buckshot. When the granite dust settled, he was gone. Vaporized, like a cloud burnt away by the solar flare of his own anger.

~

"Damnit," said Tipsy. "What a disaster."

"I'm sorry. I did my best. As I said, I'm unaccustomed to conversation," said Proctor. "Henry's exit can't come as a surprise to you. Jane was the actress, but Henry had his own flair for the dramatic. You must know that by now."

"Damn skippy." Tipsy sat on the bench. "You questioned Henry about lingering, but *you're* still here."

Proctor sat beside her. "Why wouldn't I be?"

"Jane forgave you for murdering her and Henry. After contemplating that mercy, I thought you'd get up the gumption to move on."

"I'm grateful for Jane's compassion, but that doesn't mean *God* has forgiven me." He stroked his beard. "If Henry can't stand hearing me speak about Jane, why did he come here to discuss her?"

"He's worried about her."

"Why on earth—or in heaven, pardon the pun—would he be worried about Jane? She's in eternal bliss with all her loved ones."

"All her loved ones except Henry."

"If Jane is missing Henry from the other side, the blame is on him for keeping her waiting."

"He's been trying to finish his novel."

Proctor raised one bushy eyebrow white eyebrow. "A ghost, writing a novel?" He smiled for the first time. "A ghostwriter, pard—

"Pardon the pun, right," said Tipsy. "He learned to type, and…it's not *just* about his novel. He also promised Jane that he'd look after me. But things changed when he received a message from her—"

"A message? How?"

"That's a long story." Tipsy gave Proctor a summary of Jane's message from the beyond. How Jane spoke with Catherine Porcher through the doorway to the next realm, and Henry sat on Jane's message for nearly two years, refusing to discuss it with Tipsy, because he couldn't fully decipher it. "He clung to the idea that the message pertained to his book. Then his literary plumbing got…blocked up. Like the toilet when my son uses too much T.P."

"T.P.?"

"I mean he couldn't write, and everything else went shootin' downhill from there. It's like a ghost's version of the flu, coupled with depression. He started *obsessing* over the message. Mostly the part about how Jane said *we* can't be at peace, and there's more to *our* story. He's afraid she's having some…problems…on the other side. Problems related to their deaths."

Proctor took a moment. "I suppose no one knows more about their deaths than me."

"Do you have anything to share from the last week of their lives?"

"I don't think so. Before that fateful last morning, I hadn't seen Jane in over a month. Spoke to her on the telephone several times, but those were brief, stilted conversations."

"Damnit."

"I'm truly sorry I can't help. It pains me to think that Jane is suffering in some way."

"We don't *know* that she's suffering. Maybe Catherine Porcher got the message wrong. Like a game of telephone from Jane, to Catherine, to Henry, across different dimensions instead of wires. Henry's own thinking isn't very sharp right now. I'm sure his worry for her is only exacerbating his own issues. He loves her so much. You probably disagree with me on that last point."

"No, I don't. Their last years together were terrible, but I knew them their entire lives. Henry loved Jane from the time they were children, and Jane always had a protective streak. She watched over younger children, small animals, and Henry. He was like a cornered kitten in those days. Terrified, yet prone to hissing and spitting when anyone got too close.

When he returned from Europe, Romeo himself couldn't have been more ardent."

"I wish I'd known them then."

"You would have thoroughly enjoyed them both. I did."

"You mean you enjoyed Jane."

"Henry, too. I felt a kinship with little Henry Mott in the old days. I understood him, as I'd lived through other children teasing me, so I looked out for him. Even as he grew up and over me, in both height and intellect, we remained close. We were indeed friends for years, but obviously, in the end, we were friends no longer." He shivered, and the mistiness spread from his feet and calves up toward his midsection. "Now I must leave you. I haven't spoken since your last visit. It's tiring."

Tipsy took in Proctor's swollen nose, the heavy bags under his hazel eyes, and the deep wrinkles around his mouth. The ravages of his lifetime of sadness and hard drinking.

"Okay. Get some rest," she said. "I'm sorry that I haven't been back to visit you."

"I wouldn't visit the man who murdered my dear friends, either."

He disappeared, and Tipsy walked a couple blocks back to her Tahoe. She unlocked the truck, got in, and retrieved her keys from her purse. Suddenly, a booming voice filled the truck, as if she'd forgotten to turn down the radio when she shut off the ignition.

"What did he *say* about me?"

She jumped in her seat. Henry sat beside her like a distraught passenger in a crowded Uber. She reflexively blasted him with the little bottle of mace on her keychain, but the cloud of chemicals harmlessly dissipated into his semi-translucent form.

"Good lord, you scared me. You're lucky you're a ghost, or you'd be temporarily blind." She cranked the engine and rolled down the windows. The residual mace floated out of the truck. "I thought you went home," she said.

"I did, but I came back as soon as I could," he said, as he solidified. "I want to know what Proctor told you. He surely mentioned my legendarily terrible temper and tiresome gloominess. He must have elucidated on how he despised and disdained me."

"He didn't say *anything* like that. He acknowledged that y'all had an…uh…falling out." Proctor shot Henry in the head, so *falling out* didn't do it justice, but Tipsy couldn't think of a more diplomatic phrase. "But otherwise, he was nice."

"Nice. Ha. What a bunch of C.S."

"C.S.?"

"You *know*. Chicken…manure."

"You mean B.S. As in *bull manure*, not chicken. *Chicken manure* refers to…someone cowardly. Like, so-and-so is a total chicken…poo."

"That applies, too, because Proctor is the biggest chicken poo in Charleston, living or dead."

"Would you like to know what he *really* said?"

Henry tapped his long fingers on his knee until his curiosity got the better of him. "If you want to tell me."

Tipsy rehashed her conversation with Proctor. "…so he doesn't think he can help you, but he acknowledged that you truly loved Jane, going back to childhood. He said the two of you—I mean you and Proctor—were close before things went bad. It made me realize you've never talked much about *your* relationship with Proctor."

"How could I talk about it? The fact that he was my friend—one of my only friends—made it all so much worse."

"He told me he felt a kinship with you, since he suffered through his own childhood outcast phase. He said he and Jane were protective of you—"

Henry pressed his fists into his eyes and his shoulders shook. The Tahoe shook right along with him. The horn tooted and the wipers slid across the windshield with the squeal of rubber on dry glass. Tipsy gripped the doorframe.

"I'll stop talking about him if this is too much for you—"

"No. No. You see—you're reminding me of—" He held up his hand to her, palm forward. Others might think he was waving her off, but Tipsy recognized the gesture as a summons. A request to dip her fingers into the river of Henry's past. She was safely in her car, and could brace herself against those rushing currents, so she accepted.

She raised her own hand, and touched his.

Tipsy opens her eyes to a cobblestone version of Broad Street she's seen in old black and white postcards. In the distance, she recognizes the Old Exchange and Provost Dungeon, on East Bay Street at the end of Broad, but the People's Building, Charleston's first sky scraper, does not yet exist. In Tipsy's day, the trees are bigger, more wires crisscross overhead, and cars, trucks, and busses cram the street. In this time, everything seems more open—the road, the space between the buildings, the sky.

Most of the vehicles are operated by old school horse or mule power. The few automobiles, with their cushioned bench seats and spoked wheels, really do look like horseless carriages. The women wear flouncy blouses and long, bustled skirts; their waistlines cinched to impossible dimensions. The men's clothing is more familiar. Except for stiffly-starched, asphyxiatingly tight collars, a man's suit in this era is similar to a modern one. Everyone over the age of twelve, male and female, black and white, wears a hat. Bonnets, newsboy caps, bowlers, boater hats.

Tipsy focuses on the hats directly in front of her—a brown bowler with a red silk band, and a saucer-shaped white bonnet topped with black feathers. Red hair peeks from under the tall man's bowler, and the stocky woman beside him is blonde. At first, she thinks the man is Henry, but when he moves his head, his profile is different. He looks over his shoulder, and his eyes are light brown. He must be Henry's father, Frederick Mott.

The woman also turns, and Tipsy recognizes Henry's mother. Patience Lewiston Mott, known in her girlhood as Patty. She's around forty years old. Her youthful voluptuousness has given way to thickness around the middle, but she's still pretty in her uninteresting way.

Frederick Mott says, "Henry, get your nose out of the clouds and keep up."

A boy in dark short pants, tall black socks and black leather boots, and a crisp white shirt trots past Tipsy. She looks down at the top of his head, capped with bright red, wavy hair. She picks up her own pace to catch up with the child, who is now a few feet ahead of his parents. She walks beside him and inspects his serious, pinched, freckly face. Long chestnut eyelashes frame his dark blue eyes. He's muttering to himself.

With the exception of the psychopath Thomas Bonneau, the hosts of these ghostly recollections have always unknowingly revealed their emotions to Tipsy, and not only through their words and gestures and body language. She experiences the memory along with the memory holder. Joys, desires, fears, anxieties, and conundrums. She knows exactly what's going on in Henry's intense young mind.

Henry is thinking about ghosts—the softly glowing, pale people only he can see—and how the dead are sometimes better company than the living. Dead or alive, people talk too much, and sometimes ghosts are puuuuure *crazy, but at least the dead only speak of olden times. Their stories are carved in the past tense, like in the novels he loves. Like the narrators of his stories, ghosts only want to be heard, so he simply listens. The living talk in unpredictable, contradictory circles, and expect him to speak, too. Henry flounders for the correct responses, and the living listener finds whatever he comes up with to be wanting. Even his own parents scowl at him, as if questioning his intelligence, or his sanity.* As if my crazy is just as pure, *he thinks. An analogy pops into his head, as they often do, and he whispers out loud, "Spring water crazy."*

"Quit talking to yourself, Henry," says Frederick. "I thought you were past all that."

"I'm…singing a tune. A hymn, from church." Henry might think on ghosts, but he never speaks of the them. When he was little, he told his mother, and you would have thought he'd admitted to regularly conversing with Satan. Patience had promptly boxed his ears.

It's taken a decade of living, but now he knows that no one else sees the ghosts. He doesn't speak about them to anyone. He no longer talks to them when living people like Mother and Papa are around. Henry Mott is eleven. He understands how the world works.

Like he knows his father will re-box his poor unfortunate ears if he does not appear spring water sane at Mrs. Marie-Laure Lamboll's seventy-fifth birthday picnic. Patience is in a tizzy about the party, as she always is about such affairs, like a pot of stew brought to a fast boil but dangerously close to burning. Unlike his wife, Frederick is unimpressed by Ms. Lamboll's palatial home on Tradd Street, near the corner of Tradd and Legare.

"If she's so high and mighty, why doesn't she live on her own family's street?" he asks, as the Motts approach the conglomeration of wood and stone that will one day be the Catholic Cathedral of Saint John the Baptist. Frederick Mott glances in the direction of the half-finished church and subtly makes a sign of the cross across his forehead and chest.

"Don't be ridiculous, Freddie," says Patience. "And stop that papist hand-waving. God forbid someone sees you."

There's irony in that last sentence, but Henry can't articulate it, and it's too pretty a day for ear-boxing.

Patience straightens her bonnet. "Miss Marie-Laure is only a Lamboll by marriage. She's a Gibbes, and the Gibbes have their own street. The Lambolls don't own anything on Lamboll Street anymore. Langdon Miller and his wife bought the Isiah Lamboll House two years ago—"

"I am aware of that, since you wanted me *to buy it."*

"— and Tradd Street is so much grander. I wonder…Mrs. Lamboll is getting on in years. Which of her children will inherit the house? Perhaps Chester. She's partial to his wife…"

Henry tunes out her chatter and focuses on the seasonal beauty around him. They turn right on Legare Street, and walk south toward the harbor and the Doctor Rene Bonneau House. How odd, thinks Tipsy, that the lunatic Thomas Bonneau is haunting a house on the edge of Henry's memory. She squints, but the pink bulk of the Bonneau House is several blocks closer to the harbor, hidden behind tall brick walls and a canopy of tree branches.

*She makes out the words that jostle around in Henry's mind, elbowing one another for space to describe the scenery around him. Nouns (*oak trees, jasmine, azaleas, mansions*), adjectives (*fragrant, bulky, pastel, elegant*), and verbs (*chirping, growing, sashaying, looming*). He pushes them all into ordered sentences.*

As Henry and his parents sashayed toward Mrs. Lamboll's house, he smelled the fragrant jasmine, and listened to the robins chirping away.

His brain shifts into storytelling mode. A settled story, where everything turns out to his liking. His own personal novel, with himself as narrator.

The Mott family walked into the party, and everyone said hello and the other children invited Henry to play ball with them. Henry caught every ball the fellows tossed his way. They cheered for him and his father patted him on the back. He ate delicious fried chicken and a slice of pecan pie. The Motts had to leave early, because Henry's brother Edward stayed home with a cold. When they said goodbye, old Mrs. Lamboll told Mr. and Mrs. Mott that their boy Henry was a joy to have in Sunday school, and on the walk home, Mr. Mott gave Henry a dime for making him proud. The End.

Of course, that's not how the party turns out at all. The Motts arrive at Mrs. Lamboll's yellow clapboard estate, walk under a wisteria-covered trellis and down a cracked flagstone path, and the whole afternoon flashes past Tipsy in a matter of moments. Sad, lonely, nervous moments; a montage of preteen misery.

Henry stands on the sidelines while the other children run about in the garden. His father encourages him to join them, but Henry is as frozen as one of Mrs. Lamboll's garden gnomes. There is no fried chicken; only chicken salad. Henry detests chicken salad. Patience forces him to take a plate and shove a few mouthfuls into his mouth. His eyes water at its sliminess. He asks Frederick when they can leave, and tries to remind him that Edward is home under the weather, but Fred is smoking cigars with Pierre Robinette and his friends. Henry hovers near his mother, but she shoves him toward the other children and their games. Tipsy wishes she could offer him some comfort. Instead, she has to follow him like an unseen foreshadowing of his far-flung future.

Henry walks in the general direction of the other children, but then turns down a gravel pathway, and continues toward the stone wall almost an acre away. Tipsy creeps along behind him like a fox stalking a bunny. He passes the old slave quarters, sturdy brick buildings that appear to be storage spaces in this age.

He traipses silently through the garden, aimlessly taking rights and lefts. She senses him thinking about the people who had lived in the slaves' quarters.

All the stories they told, and lived. He stops abruptly when the path ends, as if he might walk off the edge of a cliff instead of onto Ms. Lamboll's lush green grass. A man sits on the ancient iron bench under a magnolia tree.

The man is black, and he wears a cream colored cotton shirt, dark trousers, and scuffed leather shoes. He looks to be about Tipsy's age, with broad shoulders and a finely arched nose that hints at Indian blood. His reddish brown skin has a gray cast to it, as if he's peering at Henry through an ivory veil.

The man blinks when Henry's eyes meet his, and his mouth falls open in shock. He probably hasn't made eye contact with anyone, free or slave, black or white, in at least forty years. Henry gives him a tentative smile. No one else is around, and perhaps the man can tell him stories to pass the time until his mother calls for him.

"Hello there," he says, softly. Like Tipsy, Henry knows ghosts must be handled with kid gloves. Spring water crazy, remember? If they're agitated, they either become frightened and disappear, or they start yapping away worse than living people. Henry has learned to talk to them softly, and that's when they share their interesting memories with him. "Lovely day, isn't it?"

"Hey there, Mott! Henry Mott!"

Henry turns, and his blooming smile wilts. "Johnny," he says.

With one glance, Tipsy knows this new child can only be one person. She knows him as John Huger. To Henry, he's just Johnny. In Henry's opinion, Johnny is a stupid, beefy boy who lives only to prove where Henry himself is lacking.

Johnny's arms are crossed over his chest. He's not much taller than Henry, but that's where the similarities end. John has straight white blonde hair and light blue eyes. His shoulders are already broad; his legs straight and strong below his short pants. It isn't fair that a boy his age should have such a square chin and such a steady, level stare. It's as if he knows his painted portrait will someday hang above a fireplace in his family's Meeting Street mansion, where his condescending gaze will intimidate his descendants for the next few centuries.

In stark contrast, Henry has that crimson, slightly poufy, highly unmanageable hair. His dark blue eyes tend to have darker circles under *them, and let's not forget those copious freckles. His skinny, knock-kneed legs and clunky feet dangle under his equally skinny torso like two croquet mallets.*

Johnny stands in front of several other boys. Their names march through Henry's brain, and hence, through Tipsy's. Tradd Smith, Reed Hamilton, Andrew Bishop. *The smaller boy is* Camden Brewton, *John's younger cousin. Tipsy peers into his face, but the child is so boringly adorable that it's hard to pick out hints of the comely man he will one day become. The man who will someday marry John's one true love, Ivy More, after John himself perishes under suspect circumstances. The man who will become one of the ghosts Tipsy helps to move on.*

Tradd, Reed, and Andrew are like imitation statues done by a less talented sculptor; not quite as blonde, robust, or good-looking as John, but still better than average. Tipsy senses Henry's horror as he notices the two girls at the back of the pack. Jane and Constance Robinette, *Pierre's daughters. Tipsy immediately recognizes the younger versions of Jane and her sister. Unlike John's minions, the Robinette girls have unique good looks: delicate elven features, shiny dark hair, creamy skin, and bright blue eyes. Constance, who is younger than Jane but still taller, watches her dainty white shoes, as if embarrassed to be caught running with a pack of boys. Jane—petite Jane with her black braids, long black lashes, and inquisitive expression—stares at Henry as if she's trying to look inside his head.*

"You see me?" The ghost's voice jerks Henry's attention back to the bench. "Young sir! Help me. Please. My name…my name is Joseph. You see Joe?"

Henry swallows and his eyes flick between the dead man and his living peers. The ghost stands and shambles toward him. Tipsy knows that Henry isn't particularly afraid of him. No ghost has ever done him harm, so he doesn't see why people are so fussed about them. He's warier of Johnny and company. When they were all little children, these boys poked fun of Henry's habit of talking to unseen people. He doesn't want to give Johnny a reason to bring up his old peculiar behavior, especially in front of Jane and Connie.

"Want to play kickball with us, Hen-ro?" asks Johnny. It's the kind of request Henry's daydream narrative had imagined. Tipsy thinks he might jump at the chance, but she remembers that in Henry's daydream, he

controlled all the outcomes. John follows up his question with, "We got an odd number."

"He's an odd number all right," says Tradd, and Reed laughs. Little Camden's giggle is particularly shrill.

"Stop it, Tradd," says Jane, and Tradd hushes.

Henry's mother says that Jane Robinette is unladylike, with her running around and yelling and her bossiness, but Henry wishes everyone would listen to him like that.

"What do you say? Come on, before they call us for cake." John turns, as if he expects Henry to automatically follow.

"Young sir. Where's my Claudia?"

The grumbly voice startles Tipsy, and Henry gasps and jumps in place. While Tipsy and Henry focused on John, Joseph crept up on Henry. He's a big man, and he looms over the boy. Cold air wafts off him like winter wind off the harbor. Henry steps back, and his heel hits the brick garden border. He stumbles, and sits down, hard. Unfortunately, he plops onto a rose bush. He yelps as thorns dig into his rear end through his thin cotton pants.

The other boys burst into noisy laughter, and Johnny turns around. "Have mercy, Mott. Get on up out of that bush before Mrs. Lamboll sees you crushing her roses."

"Young sir, please. It's my gal, Claudia. Master can't sell her. He can't—but he did." The black man grabs his head and squeezes. "Did he? Didn't he? Claudia? Claudia!"

Now the ghost is screaming, and the boys are cackling, and the thorns cling to Henry's pants as if the bush wants to further embarrass him by holding him down in the dirt. Henry tries to address two problems at once. "Quiet down," he says, loud enough that the ghost and the other children hear him. "Be calm. Everything is fine. Just fine."

The ghost is beyond soothing. He screams for his missing Claudia as if she might hear him over half a century of time.

"We're all calm, son," says John, as if they aren't the same age. "You're the one floppin' around in the bush."

"Master!" screams Joe, the ghost. "Damn you! Taking my gal. You an evil, hateful man. God will punish you!"

Henry stands. Blood runs in shiny rivulets down his legs and stains his gray socks purple.

"Henry," says Jane. "You're bleeding—you should—"

"I know I'm bleeding," he snaps. Jane frowns, and Tipsy knows that Henry regrets his snarky response. Once again, he's said the wrong thing. The ghost's screaming is monotonous yet overpowering, like being too close to a tolling church bell. One of the boys, maybe it's Reed, makes a joke about Henry losing a fight with a shrub. Jane steps back from the group, and puts a hand on Johnny's sleeve. She tugs him backward, but John watches Henry with curious, discerning eyes.

Henry feels the sting of tears. Panic builds in the back of his throat. The pain of their teasing cannot compare to the mortification of letting them see him cry. As is often the case, his anger wins out over caution or prudence. He turns on the frantic ghost beside him.

"Shut up, you! Just shut up, boy!"

"Who are you calling boy?" asks Johnny.

Henry rounds on John. "You shut up, too! Shut your damn hoity-toity mouth!"

Joseph's eyes cloud over, as if he's forgotten that Henry can see him. "Claud. Claud. Where ya be, gal?" He turns in a slow circle, and lapses into Geechee, Charleston's nuanced version of Gullah. As always, Tipsy finds the dialect difficult to understand. She can only catch a familiar word here or there. Joseph's nineteenth century version of Geechee is a fully foreign language to her modern, Upstate ears. As she listens, however, she feels Henry's mind translating for her. Henry is used to listening to Geechee talk when the negro servants and tradespeople speak to each other.

"They took you, my sweet love," says Joseph. "The Lord only knows what they did to you…I want to kill them all but they must already be dead… dead, dead, dead. We're alllll dead!" He laughs right along with Reed and Tradd and Andrew. So much laughter, yet so little is funny.

As Joseph's hysteria increases, Henry can't make out what the man is saying anymore, and hence, neither can Tipsy. It's lyrical, nightmarish gibberish that stings Henry's psyche like alcohol poured over the fresh wounds on his legs.

Henry's interest in and compassion for the ghost is gone along with his learned caution about speaking to spirits. "Shut up and disappear. I don't see you. No one does," he mutters.

The ghost turns to him, and suddenly his voice rings clear, to Henry and Tipsy. He speaks standard English in a slow, direct manner. It's patronizing, as if Henry is a monolingual idiot who can't make out the Geechee tongue he hears every day in his own home. "You, white boy. I should have known you'd be no help to the likes of me. None of your kind have every done right by any of mine. You bring us nothing but suffering. That's all you're good for. Even though I'm dead, y'all can't bring me nothing but pain."

Henry stares into the man's dark eyes. Tipsy senses his chagrin. He starts to apologize, but then he remembers his living company. He tries to convey his regret by squinting and biting his lip, but the ghost shakes his head and disappears.

"Damn, Mott," says Johnny. "I came over here to be friendly-like and ask you to play with us. You're the one yelling' like a fool and fallin' in the bushes. Stay there, for all I care, with thorns in your ass. Come on, y'all. Let's leave Henry alone to talk to his imaginary friends."

The other boys, and Connie, turn and walk back toward the main house, but Jane remains. Still, she stares at him. For a second, Henry is angry with her. He wants to tell her to go away. But when he looks closer, he sees compassion on her lovely face. He wants to cry again, which makes him angrier. He bites his lower lip again to keep from saying something stupid that he'll regret.

"You should get your mama to clean those scratches," says Jane.

Henry nods. His eyes burn.

"Well…" Jane looks over her shoulder at her sister and her friends. "I'm sorry about all that."

"Wasn't your fault." Now that the ghost is gone and things are quiet, Henry has a little more control over the conversation. Not as much as he will have when he reimagines it in his bed that night. In that reimagining, he will know exactly what to say to make Jane Robinette laugh. He asks her to sit on the bench with him, and no ghostly negro appears to distract him and reminds him that he's a useless white man in the making, and he shows

her that he's much cleverer and more fun than John Huger. Instead, all he manages to say is, "Thanks."

"You're welcome," Jane says. She pauses a moment, as if waiting for him to say something else, but Henry doesn't dare risk it. So she turns and walks toward the house in her dark blue springtime sailor dress. Henry is sure he's never seen anything so beautiful.

"Good afternoon, Miss Janie," says a grown up voice. It's too deep and strong to be the voices of the other children, but too calm and melodic to be a ghostly enslaved man.

Henry tears his eyes off Jane, and looks up at one of the few people who does not instill anxiety in him.

Jane stops. "Hello, Mr. Proctor," she says.

Henry repeats after her. "Hello, Mr. Proctor."

"Y'all," says the slim young man in his late teens. He has dark hair and hazel eyes. Tipsy saw this version of him once—he was not quite so young, but young enough that she recognizes him. He's a precursor of the man who will someday kill these two children. In that moment, Proctor James smiles fondly at both of them. "You make me feel old when you call me Mister. I'm not so much older than you two."

"You're learning to be a minister, at minister school," says Jane. "You're much further along in life than me…or Henry." She looks at Henry and blushes. "Or Connie. Or Johnny—"

"You're right, Janie. I am a little further down the path. But just wait, y'all will catch up before you know it." Proctor leans down and whispers to Jane. Henry can only catch a few words. "Good of you to stand up for him…good Christian…"

"Yes, sir…thank you, ah…Reverend. I try…er…Mr. Proctor." She can't quite figure out how to address him, so she runs off.

"You alright, Henry?" asks Proctor.

"Yes, sir…Proctor."

"That's right. No need for formalities. Eight years ago, it might have been me sitting where you are. Maybe you, in little Camden Brewton's place."

"I couldn't be in his place. He's Johnny Huger's cousin. They're like brothers. No one will laugh at him."

"You have a big brother, too."

"He's sick today. But he wouldn't speak for me. He'd laugh along with them."

"I know what it's like to be laughed at."

Henry can't imagine it. Proctor seems so wise and calm. Everyone professes the deepest admiration for him. Still, come to think of it, Proctor spends his time with the real grown people. The parents and grandparents. Henry doesn't see him laughing and carousing with Reed Hamilton's teenaged brother, Crawford, and his friends.

The idea brings Henry comfort. Perhaps there are other ways to win respect besides throwing a ball and running fast and speaking louder than everyone else.

Proctor puts a hand on his shoulder. "Hold fast, Henry. You'll grow up and over those boys."

"Not Johnny."

"Ah, well. I'll admit, young Mr. Huger has a certain something about him. But that doesn't mean—"

"All the girls like him."

"Seems like Jane Robinette had more interest in you than him. He walked off, and she stayed."

"She felt sorry for me."

Proctor smiles. "Whether she felt sorry for you or not, she didn't follow Johnny. She's a sweet girl, and she doesn't much care what the crowd thinks." He gently claps Henry's back. "Now, let's walk back to the house for cake."

Henry nods, and follows Proctor. He relaxes some, because no one will dare tease him when he's walking alongside the man who will be the next minister of St. Philip's. He can speak to Proctor without worrying about every word that comes out of his own mouth. Proctor really does seem to understand. It feels good to think he might have a friend, and an important one at that.

Tipsy stood on the running track beside Pinegrounds School's athletic field and watched Little Ayers goof around on the sidelines. Little A and his buddies wore black lacrosse helmets and red jerseys over their clunky shoulder pads, so the top of their bodies clashed with their skinny legs. Sticks waved about their heads like plastic war lances. The sound of their laughter floated across the manicured grass.

Only a few hours had passed since she visited Mrs. Marie-Laure Lamboll's seventy-fifth birthday party via Henry's memory. Lingering physical discomfort usually accompanied her supernatural voyeurism, but her symptoms were manageable. A slight headache, fatigue, and false-feverish achiness in her shoulders; like supernatural PMS. Observing a lacrosse game was the perfect post-time hop activity, as she had only to clap now and then.

She finally understood the rules of this Yankee import sport, and she was glad Little Ayers liked it. If he played lacrosse, she could put the kibosh on football. She wouldn't tolerate his sweet, sensitive brain being knocked around more than necessary. Not that he'd showed any serious interest in the ol' pigskin. Little Ayers enjoyed sports, but he lacked the killer instinct required to rise in the athletic ranks at a school like Pinegrounds. He'd squeaked onto the lacrosse team through hard work and a positive attitude.

"Go, go, go!" he yelled from the sidelines, as his teammates sprinted down the field after the kid in the number twelve jersey. "Whoooo!"

Number twelve—Trey was his name—did *not* lack killer instinct. Every game, he scored multiple goals and plowed over his opponents like a steamroller in cleats. When he removed his helmet, his fierce expression dared anyone to come between him and that little white ball. With his dark shaggy hair, he was an earthbound Harry Potter going after a rubber Snitch.

Tipsy turned to Big Ayers, who stood beside her. He watched the field with his big brown spaniel's eyes, his arms crossed over his Pinegrounds lax tee-shirt. He wore a COCKS baseball hat to hide his thinning brown hair. He shifted his weight—left, right, left—as if he were standing on a land mine.

"That Trey kid is something else," said Tipsy.

"Uh, huh." Big Ayers shoved sunglasses on his face and chomped on his omnipresent blob of gum. She assumed Little A's athletic mediocrity annoyed him, as Big Ayers had been an all-state baseball player. To his credit, he didn't push his son. He faithfully espoused the theory that sports should be fun.

Given his own ego, I figured he'd be cracking the whip at Little A's heels, said Granna. *Screaming at the coach and getting into fisticuffs with the referee.*

You know what I've always said about Ayers. Predictably unpredictable.

The electronic scoreboard ticked down the final minutes of the first half. As the sun sunk behind the two-story bleachers, no-seeums emerged from the marsh grasses like a forcefield of crackling electricity. She waved her hands to fend off the tiny insects, but they still found their way behind her ears and into her hair and under her sunglasses. She'd sprayed herself and the kids with bug spray, but this time of year, even poison couldn't deter the no-seeums from a meal. Mary Pratt and Olivia Grace were working on homework at the top of the stands, out of reach of the bugs' spring bloodlust. Soon they would wander to the playground to mess around with the other younger siblings. Tipsy silently thanked them for their patience. They didn't have volleyball practice, so they could be at home, relaxing.

Speaking of patience, she was still waiting for Big Ayers to address the topic that required an in-person conversation. He rarely beat around the bush, but tonight, he silently sulked beside it.

"Soooo…what did you want to talk about?" She couldn't read his expression through his mirrored, wraparound black sunglasses. *Basic dad glasses,* as the twins called them. Big Ayers had a largish noggin, so his shades dug into the sides of his head and left white tan lines on his face.

He did not respond to her friendly inquiry. He chew-chew-chewed on his gum. Between chomps, he blasted his bubblegum breath into the cloud of gnats circling his head. His attempts to blow them off course failed miserably. They were tiny Boeing 747's plowing through mild turbulence.

Tipsy removed her own sunglasses, as if to encourage eye contact, and tried again. "Something about the kids? Your parents? Work?"

Nothing. She felt like a therapist cajoling a stubborn patient.

At least if you were his therapist, you'd be getting paid, said Granna.

Tipsy watched her own warped reflection in his orange lenses. *Instead, I'm trying to see into the crystal ball of his Oakleys.*

In the past, his tense silence would have incited panic, but she refused to succumb to Ayers-xiety. "Look, *you* asked to discuss something tonight—"

"I'm getting a divorce." He waved at the bugs and moved over a few feet, but they gleefully followed him.

"Oh." She'd heard this line before. "Y'all are having problems again?"

"There's no *again*. It's ongoing. Never-GD-ending."

"But you've said that in the past, and—"

"I'm moving into my parents' house."

Tipsy smacked the no-seeums congregating on the back of her thigh. "You've done *that* before, too."

He removed his shades and hung them on the collar of his tee-shirt like a plastic necktie. "Tipsy," he said, in an oddly calm voice. "I've stayed with my parents a few times when I needed space. But this time, we've *discussed it*. Me and Kate."

"But you talked about separating around Christmas, and—"

"Last night's talk was different. We had a serious conversation about logistics. Lawyers. Money. The house."

"She wants to get divorced, too?"

"No. She wants to stay married, even though she complains about me so much, you'd think she'd be hightailing it like a spooked doe. She realizes I'm serious this time, so she's promising she'll change. She wants to go to couple's therapy."

"Shouldn't you at least hear her out?"

"I'm *done* hearing her. I've been listening to her crazy shit for years." He scuffed one sneakered foot against the track. The sound of grinding gravel grated on Tipsy's nerves. "You know *I've* tried to make things better," he said. "You and me have talked about it a thousand times. But she *never* tries."

"Maybe this is a wakeup call for her—"

"Nope. I'm *done*." He wiped his mouth and spit. "Damn these bugs!"

Tipsy wished the no-seeums would take a hint for once. They were fingernails on the chalkboard during a nerve-wracking lesson. "What does this mean for the kids?" she asked.

"I'll talk with them this weekend. I wanted to tell you what's going on first, because we'll be staying at my parents' house—"

"Maybe they should stay with me."

"Negative. It's my time with them. I'll discuss everything—"

"Don't talk to them yet. You can't be sure what's going to happen—"

"I'm trying to be up front with you so you can help me do what's best for them. But I'm telling you, I'm *not* losing time with the kids, so they need to understand the situation. Little Ayers is twelve and a half, and he's more observant than a convent full of nuns. The girls are ten and they're just as perceptive. They *know* shit ain't right in that house. Pretending things are fine and dandy isn't helping."

She understood his logic, but it still felt wrong, given her experience with Big Ayers's changeability. For the moment, he seemed determined to go down this road, so she yanked the conversational steering wheel and switched lanes. "But it's so much change for them. Y'all get divorced, and we get married—"

"My life isn't stopping because you and Scott are getting...married." He glared at her. Red lines squiggled around his chocolate brown irises like the swirling bands of a hurricane. He clearly hadn't been sleeping well. "I've been cool about...*y'all*...all this time. Cool with you. Even cool with Scott."

"I know. I appreciate how we've been getting along. I mean...ah..." After veering into the fast lane, she had nowhere else to go, so she drifted off the road into a drainage ditch. "Ayers. *Ayers.* Ayers," she repeated, before dissolving into frantic babbling. "You can't underestimate the magnitude of this. It will have a ripple effect on everyone. Our children, and the Brandt kids. Y'all get divorced, and Kate will be so angry. Not only at you, but at me and Scott—"

He snorted a harsh laugh and smacked a gnat on his arm. "Ah! So it's about keeping things *peaceful* for you and Scott."

"No, but if Kate is on the warpath against us, that affects our kids *and* theirs. They're already facing an adjustment period. This is a terrible time to pile on more stress!" She didn't mention that the kids' stress pile would include existing alongside a mentally unstable telekinetic spirit.

"Yeah, but—" He looked down at his phone. Four texts and two missed calls from Kate. "She *knows* I'm at Little A's game. Damnit." His scowl migrated from the phone to Tipsy's face. "Thanks for making my divorce about *you*, Tipsy."

"That's not fair at all. I've been *trying* to support you. Help you. I know this is hard, but *please* don't give up yet. If she truly wants to work at it, y'all should try—"

"I know you're itching to remind me that you warned me against marrying Kate without getting to know her. Pure idiocy on my part, right?"

"That's ancient history. Ouch!" *Bzzzz. Whack!* To her disgust, her quick reflexes left a dead gnat and a splotch of blood on her thigh. She wiped her leg until the blood disappeared back into her skin.

"You said it. So did Mimi. My own sainted mother warned me. Now y'all can get together for a validation celebration. Have mimosas to celebrate my stupidity."

"Come *on*. We won't revel in your misery."

"Right. Sure. I'm—"

"Hey! Are y'all Ayers's parents?"

Tipsy turned to face a tall, smiling, dark-haired woman. Her smooth ponytail, polished makeup, and neatly tailored, dark green dress spoke of boardrooms or courtrooms. She wore tasteful diamond studs and a simple gold cuff bracelet. Only her footwear—pink flip-flops—clashed with her elegant, professional ensemble.

Tipsy returned her smile. "Hey. Yes. We are."

"I'm Trey's mom. He wants to invite Ayers over to our house, so I thought I'd say hello."

"That's so nice. I'm Tipsy, and this is—" She pointed at Big Ayers. "—the original Ayers."

Despite his tense posture, Ayers also smiled at the woman. A natural masculine reaction to such a pretty face.

"I'm actually the *fourth* Ayers, so not much originality coming from me," he said.

"My son is the third in his line. Hence, Trey." She waved her hands around her head. "These bugs, right?"

"Little vampires," said Ayers. "My dad is Tripp. We love our family lineages around here. Your boy is damn good." Ayers looked at his vibrating phone. Kate's name screamed up at him from the screen.

Tipsy leaned toward him. "Why don't you take it? You're putting off the inevitable."

His nostrils flared, but he nodded. "Nice to meet you," he said to the woman. He waved at the gnats and whispered furiously into his phone as he walked toward the bleachers.

Tipsy turned back to Trey's mom. "I didn't catch your name?"

"LeeLee Moretz," she said.

Tipsy immediately recognized the name. "Oh, right! You're Mimi's friend. The lawyer!" Mimi had given LeeLee's card to Tipsy a couple years ago. When she started dating Scott, and Big Ayers went nuclear.

"That's me. Hence my weird outfit." She pointed at her flip flops. "I was in court all day. My nanny picked up my other kids and I came here straight from work. Couldn't take two more hours in pumps."

"I'm glad my professional attire doesn't require heels."

"You're an artist, right?"

"Yup." Tipsy flinched as a no-seeum tangled itself in her eyelashes. Her eyes watered and she wiped them.

"That's so cool." LeeLee reached into her purse and handed Tipsy a tissue. "A lot more interesting than what I do."

"I don't know about that. If you're a divorce lawyer, you must hear some interesting stories. Then you stand up in court and you *tell* your client's story." Tipsy crouched to rub paint off her bare calf. She thought of Henry, years ago, commenting that Tipsy's paintings told their own tales. "I guess we're *all* storytellers."

"Excuse me?"

Tipsy straightened. "A writer friend once reminded me that I'm a storyteller, too. So are you."

LeeLee stared at Tipsy for a long moment. She didn't blink against the swarming no-seeums. Her bright greenish hazel eyes stood out against her dark hair and olive skin. In a city of Charleston Dress Code Blondes and Instagram vampires, she had a fresh, natural appearance that Tipsy admired. She strove for a version of that look herself.

LeeLee finally opened her mouth to reply, but Big Ayers cut her off from fifteen feet away. "Tipsy, come here, will you?"

"Excuse me for a sec," said Tipsy. "I gotta see what he wants."

"No worries. In my line of work, it's nice to see divorced parents communicate peacefully."

"We have our moments, believe me. Thanks for introducing yourself. I'm sure Little Ayers would love to come over. We're happy to have Trey at our house, too. I'll get your number from the school directory and text you."

"Perfect," said LeeLee.

Tipsy trotted toward Big Ayers. He paced in a circle with his baseball cap clenched in his hands. "I cannot take it. Not for one more night—"

"What happened—"

"Same shit as always! She reamed me out!"

"Okay, I—"

"Don't say anything. Just *don't.* I'm getting a divorce. I'm going straight to my parents' house. I'm calling my lawyer tomorrow—" He looked like he was about to have a heart attack and a seizure while simultaneously passing out. "I have to get out of here. I can't breathe."

"Are you sure you're okay to drive?"

"Yes. I'll get the kids after school on Thursday—"

"Please think about waiting to tell them—"

He leaned in until she smelled bubblegum and bug spray. He didn't scream—there were too many people around—but his voice shook. No-seeums swirled around his head like an expulsion of rage. "I will tell them *exactly* what I think is appropriate, when I'm *damn well* ready to tell it."

He stalked off in the direction of the parking lot. Tipsy drifted back to the sidelines. It wasn't purposeful, but she found herself beside LeeLee Moretz again.

"Maybe y'all *aren't* blissfully coparenting," said LeeLee.

"Like I said, we have our moments, and that was one of them. You must be pretty good at reading such situations."

"I have indeed heard *a lot* of stories."

"Big Ayers is my everlasting story. He's a long, confusing poem that always seems to have one more stanza." She grimaced. "Sorry. Too much information for someone I met fifteen minutes ago."

"No problem. TMI also comes along with my line of work." Her gaze followed her son as he ran onto the field.

"I promise we're not usually like that—"

LeeLee turned her intense green-gold-gray stare on Tipsy. "I understand, Madam Sosostris."

"I'm sorry, who?"

LeeLee's pretty dark lashes drooped until her eyes were half closed. Tipsy noticed that her fingers were clenched around her phone. Her voice dropped to a stilted whisper. "He who...was living...is now..."

"What was that? Hey...you okay—"

"Mama-mia!" Out of nowhere, Olivia Grace careened into Tipsy. "Can we get a Coke at the snack stand?"

Mary Pratt was right behind her. "I want a Snickers, not a Coke. Or M&M's, or—"

LeeLee's phone rang and she seemed to wake up. She looked at the phone, and said, "Work call. I'm gonna take it in my car. Text me about the boys getting together." She backed up.

"I will. So nice to—" But LeeLee had already turned away with her phone beside her ear. Tipsy looked down at the girls. "Y'all. *Relax.* You can get a snack."

"Does a Coke count as a snack?" asked O-Liv. She rubbed her nose. "*Omigosh,* these bugs!"

"Coke *is* a snack. It's got sugar in it." M.P. looked at the adults around them. "Where's Dad?

"But you *drink* a Coke, you don't *eat* it—"

"Whoa! Dad had to get going. You can each have a drink and a snack for being so patient—"

"Mom!" Little Ayers appeared behind the girls. He hopped from one foot to the other. "I drank all my water. Can you fill it up for me?"

"Yes, but are you sure you want more water? I'm all about hydration, but you're doing the pee-pee jog."

His face reddened behind his mask. "Ugh. Mom, don't say that."

"So *cringe,"* agreed M.P.

"No one is around, y'all—"

A shout went up from the crowd as Trey Moretz scored another goal. In the hubbub of getting her girls fed, making sure Little A didn't pee his pants, cheering on the team, and being eaten alive by no-seeums, Tipsy didn't have time to think much about LeeLee Moretz's odd statement. It wasn't until she hustled the girls into her Tahoe and slid into the driver's seat that it popped back into her head.

Madam…what was it? She rolled down the window. "Ayers! Come on, buddy!"

M.P. leaned over Tipsy's shoulder and yelled her own admonishments. "Ayyyyyy-errs! Hurry up!"

"Mary Pratt, my eardrums, please," said Tipsy. He daughter's shrill pre-teen screech roused her sleeping headache. *Madame…Sosoro?*

Something like that. Sounded Greek to me, said Granna. *Literally. As Greek as Aristotle and company.*

Something about it was familiar…

Little Ayers was still gabbing with Trey and a couple other kids, so Tipsy pulled out her phone. She googled *Madame S-O-S* and the search engine finished the rest for her. *Madam Sosostris The Wasteland T.S. Eliot.*

She clicked on the link and read the line. *Madame Sosostris, famous* clairvoyante, *had a bad cold, nevertheless, is known to be the wisest woman in Europe, with a wicked packet of cards.*

"Holy shit," she said.

"He's coming, Mom," said O-Liv. "Don't freak out."

Tipsy looked up at Little Ayers trudging across the parking lot. "All good, honey," she said to O-Liv. "Talking to myself about something else."

Granna spoke up. *Madame Sosostris, famous*... clairvoyante?

I knew I'd heard that somewhere before, Granna. Apparently, in AP English Literature.

Maybe LeeLee Moretz loves T.S. Eliot, and it was a co-in-ki-dink.

I doubt it, said Tipsy. *If she figured out that I'm a clairvoyant, she's got something supernatural up her own sleeve.*

Chapter 3

Aside from Granna, Tipsy had met only one other living clairvoyant—or, *clairvoyante*, to borrow Mr. Eliot's poetic French spelling. The teenaged Sophie Yates, resident of the Bonneau House, niece of the deceased Catherine Porcher and one-time love interest of the equally deceased serial killer, Thomas Bonneau. Love interest in her own mind, anyway. Given that Thomas Bonneau was a psychopath, relationships with him were one-sided, in life and death. Throughout her mentorship of Sophie, Tipsy was the one in the know. The interpreter of the supernatural birds and bees. As she'd told both Scott and Granna, she couldn't wait to rub elbows with Helen Stokes, paranormal grand dame. Finally, someone to answer *her* questions.

She'd wasted no time scheduling their rendezvous, and the morning after Little A's lax game, she felt like no-seeums were buzzing around in her stomach. Once she picked up her paintbrush, Tipsy rarely made mistakes, but anticipation of some ghostly canoodling interfered with her focus. She was down to the minute details of her parrot—tiny brush strokes on his scaly yellow legs—and twice, the skinny paintbrush *almost* strayed outside the lines of his feet. *Almost* a mistake was a *big* mistake in Tipsy's perfectionist world.

She imagined the parrot jerking his foot away from her clumsy hand. He'd stare down at her with his sharp yellow eyes and speak up in a voice like a squawky English butler. *Darling, do take care, you know I'm ticklish.*

"Sorry, Sir Parrot," she muttered to herself. "Maybe not the best time for precision work."

She gave up and answered emails until it was time to meet Helen. It was a balmy day, so they planned to meet at the foot of the Ravenel

Bridge and join the legions of people strolling, running, and biking across the Cooper River. As Tipsy sat on the staircase in her foyer lacing up her running shoes, Granna spoke up. *You and Ms. Helen give a whole new meaning to the phrase* power walk, *sugar. I hope she can share the kind of know-how I never got from my own relations. I've told you Grandma Meyers stayed tight-lipped about it all.*

Granna had inherited her own supernatural abilities from her paternal grandmother, Mavis Meyers. In Tipsy's family, such things tended to skip a generation.

I assume she had to be, said Tipsy. *Our little upstate community isn't very open-minded.*

You damn tootin'. In Grandma Meyers's girlhood, her own father asked the preacher to dunk her in the Chattooga River in January to cast out her demons. They made her sit in that icy water until she broke down and said she was making it all up.

Tipsy shivered. *I'm grateful they didn't burn her at the stake, or neither of us would have existed.*

You double damn tootin', said Granna. *Still, I wish Grandma Meyers had seen fit to confide more of her own knowledge in me. That's why I told you* everything *I knew, sparse as it may have been. Now, you got a chance to learn more from a single person than we both learned in years of trial and error. You make the most of it.*

Tipsy saluted her invisible grandmother as she got to her feet. *Yes, ma'am.*

By half past noon, Tipsy and Helen were ascending the Ravenel Bridge. The concrete pedestrian path's first few hundred yards crossed a swath of marsh. The bridge steepened as the mouth of the Cooper River widened below it. To Tipsy's left, the conglomeration of condos, hotels, parks, and marinas known as Patriots Point sidled up against a floating museum of nautical warfare, the permanently moored U.S.S. Yorktown. Tipsy maneuvered toward the inside of the pedestrian path. Cars blasted past, on their way from downtown to Mount Pleasant. Scary, but not as unnerving as the slowly increasing elevation. Helen Stokes was braver than Tipsy. She walked the bridge several times a week, and didn't seem the least bit bothered by the height. She pointed out the steeple of Mother Emmanuel A.M.E., where her father's family had worshiped for generations. She didn't mention the unspeakable mass shooting that had occurred inside the church, but she did say, with bittersweet knowledge and pride, "There are no ghosts in Mother Emmanuel. I can *attest* to it. All those good spirits found peace, praise God."

Tipsy was not particularly religious, but she nodded and agreed. "Praise God."

Below them, small boats navigated the whitecaps dotting the harbor. Tipsy pitied those seafarers. She'd been in that precarious position. Soaking wet and clutching her baseball cap and her sunglasses; her teeth rattling as the hull slammed against the gray water. The whitecaps didn't faze the larger vessels, like the ferry chugging past the collapsing brick fortification of Castle Pinkney toward the more historically significant Fort Sumter. Three huge docked cargo ships snoozed at the industrial port on the downtown side of the river, like giant pack mules waiting to load up and hit the trail once more. Rows of multicolored cargo containers reminded her of neatly stacked hard candy. *Jolly ranchers, haha,* she thought. *Giant Pez dispensers.*

They seemed impossibly top heavy. Her rational mind understood that physics kept them afloat, but she couldn't comprehend how those ships made it around the world without tipping over and spilling their strange confections into the ocean. How many jolly rancher containers were moldering away at the bottom of the ocean? The creepy image added to her vertigo. She tuned out the wind and the traffic noise, imagined her feet on solid ground, and focused on her fascinating company.

"So your mother *encouraged* you to engage with ghosts?" she asked Helen.

"She did," said Helen, who wore a red scarf over her braids, red sweatpants, and red tennis shoes. "Carefully, as Mama knew ignorant folks might accuse me of dealing with the devil."

"Sounds familiar. My grandmother worried they'd assume me crazy, or worse, possessed. Especially our Christian church brethren."

"If they did, they wouldn't be *very good* Christians, right? I believe the *Christian* thing to do is help these spirits on their way. My mother, and *her* mother, thought of this ability as a calling to do good. That's how I see it, too."

"I've started to think of it that way in the past few years, but so far, I haven't managed to put it to good use unless I have a dog in the fight. A personal reason to spend hours tracking down memories and getting sick. My life is so busy." She cringed. "That sounds like such a lame excuse."

"I understand. You're a young woman with a family to care for and support."

"It's also intimidating. There's still so much I don't know. That's why I'm *so glad* we met. I need a mentor."

"I'll do what I can, honey. I enjoy chatting about it all, and I'm happy to answer questions, but so much of this ability of ours can only be learned by experiencing it."

Tipsy thought about everything she'd learned over the past few years. How to manage her physical symptoms, and intervene in ghostly temper tantrums, and even shove Thomas Bonneau into the afterlife. No one could have explained how to do any of that to her. She had to figure it out. "I understand what you mean."

"My mama made me sink or swim when I got started, and she was as much an expert as one can be. She lived past ninety, and she kept freeing spirits until her last days."

"Wow. She must have been a strong lady. It takes something out of me, and I'm not even forty."

"She was. I remember that last ghost Mama sent on. We took her to a family reunion at my cousin's house on Yonges Island. Must have been fifty relatives there. All of us modern people, wearing jeans and tee-shirts that read *Parker Family Reunion*. She peered through all that cookout smoke with her eagle eyes, and picked out a man in gray homespun pants and a straw hat hunkered beside my cousin's shed."

"She set him free, right there in front of your entire extended family?"

"No," said Helen, with a laugh. "We aren't *that* loosy-goosy about mingling with ghosts. Mama didn't get up from the picnic table, tell the young people to turn down the damn rap music, and announce her plan to free a haint. We stayed overnight, and I brought her outside after everyone else went to bed. I offered to look into his memories myself to save her the effort, but she wanted the satisfaction of helping a lost spirit find his way, one last time."

"Did you ever run into ghosts you *couldn't* help?"

"Several. Some were too crazy to talk to me, or something about their deaths prevented them from remembering."

"I knew a ghost with that problem," said Tipsy, thinking of John Huger, who never saw who killed him, and hence couldn't remember the incident. "I had to see the memory via the man who killed him. Fortunately, he was also a ghost."

"If there's missing information and no one to help, then nothing can be done. It gets harder the longer they're dead. I tried for years with a little girl who haunted a patch of woods near my school. Never figured out what happened to that poor child, so I treated her kindly. My teachers would yell at me to get away from the woods."

"Sounds like y'all weren't super secretive, but you aren't out *proclaiming* your abilities, either."

"Some in our community knew my family as…*touched*. But it's like being the town drunk, or having a wart on your nose. People pretend not to know, or notice."

"That's still amazing. I was always so grateful I had my Granna. It really does seem to run in families, except for my friend Henry. My ghostly roommate. He never knew anyone like us until he met me, ninety years after he died."

"That must have been difficult. He surely questioned his own sanity."

"Yup, and he's questioning it again." Tipsy told Helen as much as she could about Henry. His background and character, his relationship with Jane, his tragic death, her own close friendship with him, and Jane's strange message from the beyond. "Lately, it's like he's having a long, gradual nervous breakdown. We think its connected to Jane's message."

"Never heard of anything like that," said Helen. "I can ask my auntie. My mother's younger sister, Aunt Talia. She's well over ninety herself.

Still lives on James Island on our family land. She's a seer, too. Tell me about this message he received from his wife."

Tipsy told her the story—which required significant background about Catherine Porcher, Thomas Bonneau, and the Dr. Rene Bonneau House. By the time she wrapped up, they reached the precipice of the bridge, where clusters of chattering people were taking selfies. Helen stopped and placed her hands on the railings between herself and the gusty, wide-open nothingness. She squeezed her face between the bars and inhaled deeply. Tipsy stopped beside her, but her fear of heights made her keep her hands and her face to herself. She talked to Helen's narrow shoulders as she finished the Tale of the Mysterious Message from the Beyond. "…so the message hinted that there's something *more* Jane and Henry have to understand about their deaths."

Helen stepped away from the railing. "Sounds like the next step is a clean sweep of Henry's mind. If you have some idea of what you're looking for, you can push his memories in the right direction."

"Yes, I've done that in the past."

"Do you think he'll cooperate?"

"With Henry, you never know, and this is one of the most confusing supernatural problems I've come across. It's not like anything has changed about his *death*."

"Nothing to be done but poke around in his memories—"

"*Tipsy!* Help me! *Please!*"

Tipsy and Helen jumped, but none of the amateur photographers heard that frantic yelping. Tipsy turned toward the sound, and to her horror, she saw Henry standing in the roadway. Cars flew past at sixty miles an hour. Some drove straight through her friend, who shimmered and sputtered with each non-impact.

"Henry! Get out of there!"

A nearby couple looked around with alarmed expressions, as if expecting to see a jumper trying to clamber up the slick vertical railings. Helen placed a hand on her arm. "In your mind, Tipsy," she said, in a low voice.

Tipsy tried again. *Henry, please get out of the road!*

"What? *What?*" The expression on his face was pure flabbergast-ery, as if he had no idea how he'd gotten here, and no idea where *here* was. A screeching motorcycle drove through him, followed by a beat up minivan spewing rank exhaust, but he didn't flinch. He flickered like a dying lightning bug, and his hair blew back from his face, but otherwise, he stayed as firmly planted as a statue.

"Those cars can't hurt him," said Helen.

"I know, but it can't be *good* for anyone to be repeatedly run over, especially in his mental sta—eeek!" She winced as a UPS truck ran through him. "I can't watch this!" *Henry! Get over here!*

He vanished, and the sound of his pleading voice jerked her line of vision back toward the harbor. His new location was worse than the roadway. He floated on the other side of the bridge railing. "Tipsy, please. I don't know what's wrong with me—"

Go back to Bennett Street, Henry. Right now. I'll be there as soon as I can.

Help me—

I'll try, but you must return to the house!

As had happened in the past in stressful situations, Tipsy felt her own power rising inside her. She'd sometimes thought of the sensation as the building tension before a thunderclap of a sneeze. Something that must be expelled with great force. Simultaneously uncomfortable and welcome.

She pictured Miss Callie's house, in all its beloved messy detail. The faded black mailbox. The cracked flagstone path through the yard. The lopsided shutters she wished she could straighten with the touch of one hand, the way she adjusted crooked paintings on gallery walls. Those two creaky boards on the front porch. If her steps were timed just right, it sounded like she was stepping on a tiny donkey. *Eee-errrr.*

The foyer, with its cluttered console table covered with random items that must be offloaded the second one walks into a house. Mail and Amazon packages. Keys. Water bottles. Lip balms. Lacrosse mouth guards. School forms. The shoes and books and baseball caps and piles of laundry that Tipsy placed on the stairs in that eternally hopeful way of mothers. Someday the children would take that stuff to their rooms with no reminders, instead of walking past with selective blindness.

She envisioned Henry descending from the second floor to the first, as he often did when she arrived home and dumped her purse on the much-abused console table. His gliding ghostly locomotion made the staircase seem like an escalator. His big hand slid down a banister he couldn't truly touch. He graciously welcomed her home to his prison.

In her mind, she took Henry by the shoulders and spun him around, so he faced the general direction of the house. *Go home, Henry Mott.*

She pushed.

Henry stumbled in thin air, and then glanced down like Wile E. Coyote. He'd chased the Roadrunner off a cliff, only to realize nothing held him up. He gasped, cried out, and plunged toward the water. Tipsy held in her own scream as he disappeared.

As had happened in the past, when confronted with supernatural necessity, she'd somehow known how to handle him. Unexplainable, yet doable. Like Helen said, some things had to be experienced to be learned.

Something shattered inside the house as Tipsy jammed the key into the lock. A *thwack* and a *boom* followed, rounded out by a good ol' fashioned *crash*. She flung open the door, and ran through the foyer and down the hall. She stepped into her destroyed kitchen.

The refrigerator door hung open; the plastic shelves, detached and piled in a pyramid in the middle of the room. A disgusting stew of spilled condiments and broken glass covered the linoleum floor. One corner of the kitchen table was buried in the drywall beside the stove. Tupperware and dishtowels floated amidst the spilled ketchup and salad dressing and maple syrup. Steak knives impaled the apples, pears, and pomegranates in the cracked bowl on the counter. The microwave languished in the sink.

"Holy shit," she muttered.

The fridge door slammed, revealing Henry crouched on the floor. He sprang to his feet. "Who the hell are *you*?" he demanded.

"Henry—"

"How do you know my name? What are you doing in my house?" He advanced on her, and Tipsy retreated toward the doorway. She was a wary ringmaster; Henry, a circus tiger that had been prodded too many times. His lips curled back in a snarl, and he roared, "*Get out!*"

"*Henry*!" Tipsy yelled back at him. "Henry Mott! You know me." She clapped—*slap, slap,* like she had clapped in this face in the cemetery—but this time, the sharp sound had no effect on him. He vanished, and reappeared only two feet away from her. The pressure of his presence was like walking around a corner into a strong wind. "You tracked me down on the Ravenel Bridge," she said. "You asked me to help—"

"*Get out of my house!*"

Shockingly, he cocked his arm. He'd strike her, if only he had solid bones to make a fist. Tipsy instinctively raised both hands to deflect him. Supernatural energy surged through her again. In an act of instinctive self-preservation, she grabbed him as she had on the Ravenel Bridge. This time, instead of reaching for him through that frightening void between the bridge and the roiling harbor, her power only had to traverse a few feet of old linoleum. She had a surer grip. More precise control.

Like a conductor leading a crescendo, she chopped the air between herself and the unhinged ghost. "Sit *down*, Henry!"

He stumbled backward, as if he'd slipped on spilled salad dressing. She pointed at the floor. "*Sit…down…*"

Henry sunk to his knees.

She imagined herself standing over him, pushing on his broad shoulders. "Sit. *Stay…put.*"

He plopped onto his rear end, and she leaned toward him. "Henry Mott," she whispered. "It's me. Tipsy Collins."

"Tipsy?" Recognition dawned on his face. "Oh, dear. *Tipsy.*" He took in the carnage around him. As his focus sharpened, a squashed banana covered in barbeque sauce levitated up from the floor and hovered in front of him. "What…what happened?"

She somehow knew how to release some of the supernatural pressure that held him in place. As she eased off him, she asked, "We good?"

"No...*no*...not good." The banana landed on the floor with a splat.

"I mean can I let you go? You know who I am?"

"You're...holding me down?"

"You were *attacking* me."

"Why would I...and what...oh, hell's bells. What did I do?"

"I don't *know*, Henry. What *did* you do?"

"I don't remember. But I must have...how did I not know you? It was as if I'd never seen your face before. I forgot I was dead." He pointed at her black leggings. "You were a strange woman in my house, wearing obscenely tight pants. Only a crazy person would wear such pants and...I thought...Jane is sick...this lunatic will hurt her and I'm afraid and I..."

"It's *okay*. Can you get up?"

"I'm *so sorry*. I'm mortified. This mess—I'll tidy up. I promise."

"That would be helpful. I don't have time to clean up before I pick up the kids, and I don't want them to come home to this."

"Right away." He stood, and waved weakly at the table. It shifted ponderously, then clunked back into place.

"Give yourself a minute," she said, and he melted onto the floor again. She found a clean spot outside the ketchup's range, and squatted beside him. "Whatever happened in here, it must have used a lot of your energy."

"I *knew it*. I'm losing my mind, and here is proof. What if I hurt your children...or Scott's. What if I hurt one of your beautiful drawings..."

Everything he said was already running through her head, but she tried to soothe him, anyway. "We'll talk about that later—"

"We *must* understand what's happening with me. But how?"

"We only have one strategy at this point."

"Look into my memories. Can we look right now?"

"Not now. You're not in the right emotional state."

"Alright. Whatever you say."

"Think of some memories that might help us. Anything."

"I will. Right now, I'll clean up." Henry stood on shaky, wispy legs. He raised his hands and a thousand shards of glass rose in the air. At his direction, they floated toward the trash can like a school of sparkling minnows. "I know where you keep the washrags and clean-spray. When you get home, this place will be as good as new." He pointed at the hole in the drywall. "But…I'm not sure how to use my powers to—"

"Scott will fix it," she said. "That man loves to repair drywall. Just get everything tidied up if you can, and then rest."

"Yes. I promise this won't happen again."

There was nothing to be done but believe him. Afterall, she and Scott were under contract to buy the house, and it didn't seem like Henry Mott was going anywhere.

That night, Tipsy had plans to meet Shelby and her other bestie, Lindsey Starkey, to celebrate Lindsey's birthday. She called Henry out of his ghostly repose, and his demeanor struck her as sane. He remained appropriately contrite over demolishing the kitchen, and he'd cleaned up his mess. Aside from the dinged up drywall, the kitchen was spotless. With a benevolent smile, Henry assured her that rest had done him a world of good. He planned to retreat for the evening and continue sleeping off whatever had set him off.

The kids were old enough for Tipsy to sneak out for a few hours, but she wasn't comfortable leaving them alone with Henry. In addition, she'd walked up the Ravenel Bridge and sprinted back down it, and twice used her supernatural power to ghost-handle Henry. She felt like she'd run a marathon and topped it off with a few Crossfit classes. She considered cancelling, but she'd had plans with Lindsey and Shelby for weeks. For Lindsey's birthday, she had to suck it up.

Scott didn't have his kids that night, so he offered to hang with hers for a couple hours and keep an eye on things around the house. She set the girls up with a movie, Little Ayers with his PlayStation, and Scott with his never-ending stream of work emails.

"Thanks, baby," she said to Scott as she kissed him. "Text me if anything *weird* starts happening."

"Sure thing," he said, as if he monitored poltergeist activity on a regular basis.

"You sure you're okay with…all this?" She shifted her head from side to side, but it didn't relieve the stiffness in her neck.

"Yeah. You said Henry was a little off today—"

"Off, right." Tipsy hadn't given Scott the details of Henry's meltdown. He didn't know that the ghost had failed to recognize her, and then threatened her. He certainly didn't know about the condiment swamp, the misplaced microwave, or the impaled fruit.

That splattered pomegranate juice added to the murder scene mood, said Granna.

Scott would have a panic attack if he stumbled into that mess. I can't tell him—

"…but you said he's feeling better, and you're only a few blocks away. I know you'll come rushing to our rescue."

"Okay, but…you have all this work to do—"

"When do I not have work to do? I'd be doing it at my house if I wasn't doing it here. At least here, I get pizza." He took her hand. "You sure *you're* okay?"

"Yeah. Just tired. These things make me—" She stopped herself. If she dumped on him about her physical symptoms, he'd start worrying. She smiled instead. "All good! As long as you're okay, I'll have fun."

"That's the goal. Relax, baby."

"I will. I promise."

She ordered the requested pizza, grabbed a birthday gift bag of Ulta skincare treats, and left the house before she talked herself into staying. She drove to Vickery's Bar and Grill on Shem Creek, home of Muddy's Deck Bar. Vickery's sat on the northern side of the creek, between the Shem Creek Inn and the Shem Creek Park. It overlooked the bustling, skinny waterway and a meandering boardwalk over the marsh. She walked around the marsh-side of the two-story building, past clusters of brightly colored Adirondack chairs. The short grass below her feet transitioned to a man-made beach leading to a rustic bar. White *and* multi-colored Christmas lights dangled above the bar (a major yuletide *faux pas* according to Kate and Big Ayers) and the bartenders had stapled confiscated fake IDs to the wall above the cash register. To make sure no passing boaters missed the party, a huge sign made from oyster shells spelled out *MUDDY'S*.

Kids played in the sand and swung on dangling hammock chairs while their parents sipped margaritas. People milled around with open beer cans and admired the big fishing trawlers tied up at the dock. On the other side of the creek, a DJ spun tunes at Saltwater Cowboys, the rowdiest restaurant in Mount Pleasant. It was a Wednesday evening, but the carefree patrons of Saltwater Cowboys didn't care. Booming bass carried across the water. Tipsy vaguely recognized a popular tune by a famous Latino artist. She couldn't put a name on the song or the singer, but her kids would know. The thought made her feel ancient.

"Tips! Hey!"

Tipsy turned to find her friends waiting for her in civilized, thirty-something mom fashion. Shelby and Lindsey had dragged bar stools away from the cocktail tables and set them up beside the bar. Both wore their blonde hair twisted up in claw clips. After calling out to Tipsy, Shelby recommenced a dramatic story—mouth open, eyes bugging, fingers pointing. "My brother's kids are *hellions*. Benji got suspended *again*. If my family hadn't kept Pinegrounds in business for the past three generations, they would have drop kicked his ass out months ago—"

"What did he do this time?" asked Lindsey, her brown eyes wide. Lindsey lived and breathed gossip, and Shelby was her oxygen tank.

"Happy birthday, sister!" said Tipsy as she dropped the gift bag in Lindsey's lap and slipped onto the barstool beside her. She inhaled the ubiquitous Shem Creek smells of fried food, boat fuel, and pluff mud. She glanced at her phone. Nothing from Scott, so all must be well at home. For the moment, she could indeed relax.

"Thanks, honey," said Lindsey. "Let the festivities begin!"

Tipsy reached around Lindsey's back to squeeze Shelby's shoulder. "Good evening, darling," she said to Shelby.

"And to you, my darling-est," replied Shelby. Whatever Benji Patterson had done to almost get his ass drop kicked out of Pinegrounds School would remain a mystery, as Shelby had already moved on. "You look gorgeous!"

They exchanged outfit compliments all around: Shelby's white bellbottom jeans and bright pink, low cut top. Lindsey's new logo-covered Louis-Chanel bag (Tipsy still couldn't keep those things straight). Tipsy's long gingham sundress and sparkly tennis shoes. "I am officially in my prairie schoolmarm era," she said. "Ever since Mimi and Pamella turned me on to this sodbuster chic, I can't ever go back. I feel like I'm wearing a trendy, cozy nightgown."

"Your butt has been draped in boho for ten years," said Shelby.

"You're the least preppy mom in Mt. P.," said Lindsey. "It's that *artist thing*. You can't be a creative genius in Lily Pulitzer."

Tipsy pulled out her own claw clip and twisted her hair up off her neck. "Y'all have baby-minders lined up for Saturday night's big birthday candle blow out?"

Tipsy and Scott, Shelby and her husband Brian, and Lindsey and her husband P.D. had Saturday night reservations at Hall's Steakhouse on King Street. For years, Halls had been a prime place to see and be seen. Exactly what Lindsey wanted on her birthday. "I've had my sitter and my outfit lined up for weeks!" said Lindsey. "I've got *so much* fun birthday stuff planned, y'all." She listed the week's celebrations, as if her birthday was Charleston's version of Mardi Gras. "Tonight, happy hour with you ladies. Tomorrow, drinks with some fellow interior designers. Big family dinner on Friday at my parents' house. Hall's is the *culmination* of the festivities."

"Damn," said Shelby. "You've got more energy than me. And more babysitters."

"Emma is watching Paulie for me tonight and tomorrow night," said Lindsey, in reference to her fourteen-year-old daughter and two-year old son, respectively. "But Em has a sleepover Saturday night, so my mom is taking over."

Shelby scowled. "I understand Grammy taking over Saturday night. You don't want to infringe on Emma's middle school social life. But why isn't P.D. watching Paulie *tonight*, and *tomorrow night* while you're schmoozing with your design comrades?"

"He's working late." Lindsey shifted uncomfortably in her seat, as her butt had broken out in a sweat.

"Text Clarice and remind him it's your birthday week," said Shelby.

"Ha. I'm on good terms with Clarice, but he's still P.D.'s rich, mysterious, oddly sexy boss. He's not on my speed dial."

Tipsy cringed at the mention of Clarice Andrews. She wondered if she'd ever be able to hear his name without being reminded of her mortification during the infamous Windjammer Incident three years ago, wherein the alpha she-wolf of Clarice's pack attempted to bite Tipsy's head off. She'd fled with her tail between her legs, and avoided Clarice ever since.

"Clarice should be more understanding of P.D.'s responsibilities." Shelby had no qualms discussing Clarice, the owner of BROCo, Inc., a vast fishing and sporting equipment empire. As vice president of sales, P.D. was Clarice's right hand man, and that honor came with long hours and lots of travel. Shelby sniffed her derision over Clarice's not-family-friendly work environment. "I'm so glad Brian's boss doesn't expect him to work until nine every night."

"It wouldn't matter if he did. Brian would take the baby night shift," said Lindsey. "He *wants* to play daddy. He's *so good* with y'all's kids."

"He *is* a natural." Shelby sounded as if she'd created Brian herself, like the breeder of prized hunting dogs. "Some things can't be taught."

Shelby had every right to brag, as she and Brian were a dynamo parenting team. Their second child, Brandon, was about six months old, and their daughter Lottie had recently turned two. Tipsy had rarely seen a man take to fatherhood like Brian, and for all her personal dramatics, Shelby calmly and lovingly managed her tiny humans like she'd been born to wipe butts and wield a baby spoon.

"What can I get y'all?" asked the bartender, a bearded, twenty-something hottie with a man bun. "I gotta see that ID first, birthday girl."

Lindsey's eyes twinkled when she smiled at him. She'd always had a thing for younger guys, especially flattering ones. "Give us a second, *handsome*," she said.

"Sure," he said. "I'm Jason, and that's Chris over there. Give one of us a holler."

"Oh, boo. Don't I get *personalized service* on my birthday?"

"If you put it that way, I will be *personally* at your service. All night, if you need it."

"That's *exactly* what I need." Lindsey leaned under the bar, found the bag hook, and fished around inside her Louis-Chanel. She ran sparkly pink gloss over her lips.

Shelby rolled her eyes as she sipped her water, and Tipsy responded with raised eyebrows. They hadn't seen Lindsey flirt like that in a long time. There was something ominous about it. A price beyond the huge tip the bartender clearly expected.

Maybe he's expecting another form of payout, said Granna.

Hardly an unrealistic expectation after that borderline proposition, replied Tipsy.

"Linds, should we get a pitcher of margaritas?" asked Shelby.

"It's water for me," said Lindsey.

Tipsy looked up from the menu. "Water? That means—"

"Yup," said Lindsey. "Another little man on the way."

Tipsy and Shelby hugged Lindsey from both sides. Shelby's hair got stuck in Lindsey's lip gloss. Lindsey wiped the resulting sticky line on her cheek with a cocktail napkin.

"This is so exciting!" said Shelby. "Your little guys and my Bran will be such good buddies…" She chattered on about the fun her son would have with Lindsey's two boys, but Lindsey simply nodded and smiled wanly. Even after she reapplied her lip gloss, she seemed to have lost her usual sparkle.

"…so P.D. better man up," continued Shelby. "That second kid is *no joke*. During my pregnancy with Bran, I figured, *I already know how to do this*. Maybe I understood the nuts and bolts of keeping one baby alive, but not *multiple* babies."

"I already have two—"

"But not two *in a row*. You've never had two in *diapers*. Someone always needs something," said Shelby, as she adjusted her top around her famously ample cleavage, "so it will be even *more important* for P.D. to be on his game. He's got to cut back on his hours. And his traveling! He can't be gone for days on end…"

Lindsey stared at her left hand through Shelby's diatribe. Her huge diamond engagement ring, diamond wedding band, and the diamond eternity band P.D. had bought her as a *push present* after Paulie's birth. She clearly didn't want to talk about P.D., so Tipsy subtly changed the subject. "Speaking of men who aren't natural baby whisperers, Ayers is back on his bullshit, y'all."

Lindsey looked up from her diamond encrusted fingers. "What's the latest?"

"He claims he's getting divorced."

"Whatever," said Shelby. "How many times has he said that?"

"Many. But this time, he says he's going to discuss it with the kids."

"Ayers is no Brian when it comes to the dad skills," said Lindsey, "but he loves y'all's kids. I don't think he'd put them in that position if he wasn't serious."

Tipsy nodded. "He usually acts without thinking. Even his marriage to Kate was off the cuff. If he's planning, that's significant."

"If he's miserable, maybe they *should* get divorced," said Shelby.

"Ayers is always unhappy about something," said Tipsy. "It's not like he'll magically find contentment by divorcing Kate. He'll end up with *someone else*, and then decide he's not happy with her, and then find *someone else*, and—"

"Kate is a known entity," said Lindsey, "and even though I gave you hell about Scott when y'all started dating, this two-family system y'all have works pretty well. I imagine Kate won't take too kindly to y'all skipping off into matrimonial bliss while she and Ayers limp into the family court."

"She will *not*," said Tipsy.

"What are you going to do? Will you talk to the kids yourself?" asked Shelby.

"No way. Not my place. But I have to leave communication open so I know what's going on. I have to be nice to him so he'll keep coming to me, and I can help him work through this."

"Unbelievable," said Shelby. "You handle that man like a skittish horse."

"I know," said Tipsy. "But me playing therapist is the best thing for my kids, and Scott and his kids."

"I could never be Barker's therapist," said Lindsey, in reference to her first husband. "But Barker doesn't have any genuine emotions, so he doesn't need one."

"Barker-type men are the most in need of therapy," said Tipsy.

"Barker is sixty-three years old. He's cold and distant and uninvolved. Thinks he's father of the year because he pays the bills. It's his generation." Lindsey snorted. "For some men of *our generation*, that mindset is lingering."

Tipsy frowned. Everything out of Lindsey's mouth bespoke discontentment. P.D. was a bit of a bubba, and no intellectual. He was not the perfect father Lindsey had hoped he'd be. Still, Tipsy would never describe the man as *cold and distant*. In the past, she'd envied Lindsey's relationship with P.D. He seemed to adore his wife, and he was always amiable and jolly. They had been an affectionate, dedicated couple, and P.D. often spoke of how much he wanted kids. They obviously both wanted another one, since Lindsey was preggo again. It didn't seem fair for Lindsey to lump him in with Barker, a notorious asshole and womanizer.

Shelby turned to the bartender. "Hey, Jason," she said. "Our birthday girl is doing sweet tea tonight, but I'll have a margarita."

"A Bud Light for me," said Tipsy.

"You sure you don't want anything else, birthday girl?" asked Jason.

Lindsey gave him a pert smile. "Can you whip up a mocktail?"

"That's more up Chris's alley. Congrats, by the way. Only one reason the birthday girl would be sitting at my bar asking for a mocktail."

"Thanks, you're a doll."

"No problem," said Jason, with a distinctly un-flirtatious tone in his voice. Flirting with a married woman was one thing, but apparently, he drew the line at flirting with a married *pregnant* woman. Lindsey watched him move on to a group of younger women standing under a rusty, dust-covered fan.

"So what else is going on?" asked Tipsy, before Lindsey tried to recapture his attention. Shelby started in about her kitchen renovation, then she moved on to the latest Mount Pleasant gossip.

"I heard that Glen finally divorced his wife," said Shelby, "but now that he's *officially* single, he ditched Whitney."

"Good lord," said Tipsy, as she pictured Scott's disastrous post-divorce girlfriend, Whitney Morrison. She of the inky black dyed hair, many tattoos, and air of not-very-quiet desperation. "Whitney has been waiting around for Glen's sorry ass for like two years, and now Glen is finally truly single…" Hard to believe, since Glen the Skeevy Charter Fishing Captain had been waffling between his wife and other women for years. "…and he ditches her?"

Lindsey nodded. "I heard she moved back to Tennessee."

"Bless her heart," said Tipsy. She and Scott had been dodging Whitney all over town for years, but Tipsy still felt sorry for her.

They blabbed on for a while. Tipsy touched base with Scott twice, and he assured her that all was quiet on the home front. As the sun went down, Shelby checked her phone. "I'm gonna go, y'all. Bri got the babies down and he's waiting for me on the sofa. Got to get home and catch up with him before he passes out."

She paid her tab, gave out kisses, and left. "You ready to head out?" asked Tipsy.

"I guess." Lindsey didn't look ready for much of anything. Her makeup didn't hide the dark circles of exhaustion under her eyes.

She's so tiny, Granna. It must be hard for such a small body to grow an entire human.

Granna clucked her sympathetic agreement. Lindsey's petite feet in their sparkly flip-flops dangled under her barstool. She resembled an overtired little girl avoiding bedtime.

"You must be *exhausted*," said Tipsy. "The first trimester—"

"Yeah. Tired. Right." Lindsey wiped at her eyes.

"Linds, honey—"

"I'm okay. *Really*. Sorry. Just hormones."

"Right, but it sounds like things are strained at home right now."

"I complain about P.D., but it's not *that* bad. I have two beautiful children, and another on the way. My husband loves me and the kids. And he wants this baby."

"Of course he does."

"I have the life I always wanted."

"That doesn't mean it's always easy."

"This is my happily-ever-after," she said. "I'm good with it."

That didn't sound like a fairytale ending to Tipsy, but she smiled. If Lindsey described her life as happily-ever-after, it seemed like poor form to disagree.

The house was still quiet when Tipsy got home. She released Scott, who was on call and had to be at the hospital early for a staff meeting. "Go home to total peace and quiet while you still can," she said, as they hugged on the front porch.

He kissed her. "I'll be home with you every night soon enough. Wherever you are, that's my peaceful place."

"Hmm. Love you, you sweet man." Henry's nuclear meltdown had proven that Miss Callie's house would have no peace until Tipsy solved his conundrum. Her neck seemed to re-stiffen at the thought.

She watched Scott's black Yukon back down the driveway, went back inside and upstairs, and peeked into Little A's room. "How's the homework coming, buddy?" she asked him.

When he looked up at her from his desk, and she saw hints of the teenager he would become. His shoulders were widening out, as if they were preparing to hold up the rest of his expanding frame.

"I'm almost done," he said. "Scott helped me. Math will be a lot easier when he lives with us. Can I game with Aidan and Trey? I already showered."

"Yes. But when I come in and say *lights out*..." She flipped the overhead light switch off, and then back on. "And don't forget to brush your teeth."

"I won't," he said, but he probably would.

"What have the girls been up to?"

"Facetiming about top secret fourth grade drama."

She blew him a kiss and followed the sound of giggling down the hall. She'd recently given the girls their own rooms, since the house had plenty of them. She poked her head into M.P.'s room, but the twins had no time for their mama. They both sat on M.P.'s bed with their noses in O-Liv's phone screen. They promised that they'd eaten pizza and fruit salad, finished their homework, and showered, then shooed Tipsy away from the door.

"Mom," said M.P., in a whisper-yell. "We're...*you know!*" She pointed at her sister. O-Liv was doing an impression of a boy from their class. Their friend in the Facetime frame shrieked and fell over backwards.

"He's so...*gross!*" said O-Liv. "Do you think he likes me?"

Tipsy chuckled and left them to their silliness. She retreated into her own bedroom and closed the door. The girls reminded her of herself and Shelby. And Lindsey, too, during happier days. She changed into her trusty College of Charleston *COUGAR MOM* tee-shirt and favorite taco print pajama pants, then slipped into her cramped bathroom to brush her teeth. Toothpaste splatter blurred her reflection, courtesy of her bathroom vagabond children. Three other bathrooms in this place, and they always ended up in hers.

She retrieved Windex and paper towels from under the sink and spritzed and wiped the mirror. She ran water into the basin, but said water went nowhere. M.P. and O-Liv often fixed their hair in here. They stole Tipsy's claw clips and hair ties and experimented with her hairspray. Between Tipsy and both girls, the drains constantly clogged up. Soon, Chloe would add another head of constantly shedding long hair.

Tipsy fondly imagined Scott stocking up on industrial-sized bottles of drain cleaner. He would not be defeated by the drain clog villains. He was Captain Liquid Plumr, the Clog Destroyer. Mr. Clean, but with good hair.

Tipsy poured Drain-o into the sink and picked up her phone to touch base with him. Texting made her achy wrist hurt, so she dictated a message into her phone. "Thank you for helping tonight. Love you so much! *Smiley face.*"

"Is smiley face a term of endearment?"

A minty scent wafted into the bathroom and overrode the chemical odor of the *glurp-glurp-glurping* Drain-o. Tipsy knew that smell. Henry's personal cologne, *Eu de Brooding Manly Spirit.* She poked her head around the bathroom door frame. The ghost sat on the edge of her bed. He hunched, as if he had a belly ache.

"My phone knows to add a smiley to the end of my text," she said. "Like, a little technological kiss."

"How charming," said Henry, who did not look the least bit charmed. "I'm sorry to burst in on you when you're doing…" He pointed into the bathroom at her moisturizers and makeup wipes. "Lady things."

"No worries. Doing more cleaning than cleansing at the moment." Truth be told, it *was* a rather abrupt entrance. Henry usually gave a spectral knock on the bedroom door before entering. "Are you feeling better after more rest?"

"I feel *nothing*. Nothing good. Nothing bad. Once again…I feel… *nothing.*"

"You feel—" Comprehension dawned on her. "Wait, what? You mean, you can't…*feel*…your hands? Or warmth, or… tingling?"

His voice cracked. "No. It's *all gone.*"

"Shit, Henry. You have to go," she said. "Right now. *Move on*. Please."

"I cannot."

"You mean you *will not.*"

"No. I *cannot.* I've lost the ability to feel…and I've lost the ability to move on."

"That's impossible!"

"You're a clairvoyant. You know that the impossible can become possible. That only leads to the supposition that the possible can also revert to impossible." He flopped backward onto the bed and stared at the ceiling. A sparkly tear snuck out of one eye and traced a glittering trail down his white cheek. "I'm such a fool. I'll be trapped here, for all eternity. I can't help her and now I'll never see her again. We *always* found our way back to one another, Tipsy. Over mountains and across the oceans. Through wars. Now, I've finally lost her."

"I don't believe you're trapped here. I don't!"

"It's true, and it's *my fault*." He sat bolt upright like invisible hands had reached up through the mattress and tickled him. He punched himself in the face, and his fist disturbingly passed right through his own cheek. Two of Tipsy's bed pillows levitated behind him like gathering clouds. They split, and cotton floated around the room, as if a giant had had sneezed into a field of dandelion puffs.

"I'm so stupid. Faithless! Selfish! Naïve—"

Tipsy had to stop him before the windows shattered. Rationalize with him. Distract him. Anything.

"That's not true," she said. "You're the epitome of faithful. You just said you found way back to Jane over oceans and through wars. The First World War, right? When you were in Europe?"

He nodded. "I never forgot her. I thought of her every day. I told people about her. Sir Nigel, my mentor. The members of Sir Nigel's philosophy club. Young men I met at the cafes in Oxford and hooligans in the pubs. Her name was famous. I spoke to Anne about her."

Tipsy remembered something he'd told her several years ago. "Anne! Anne Boleyn?"

"Yes. The Lady Anne."

Several perfume bottles on Tipsy's dresser started spritzing of their own accord. The bottle of Windex blasted blueish mist around the room, and the sink ominously regurgitated Drain-o. *Glurp-glurp-bla-blurp!* Floral and chemical aromas mixed with Henry's minty scent. Tipsy coughed and her eyes watered.

"*She is my death*," said Henry. "*And I am hers*. Anne said that, about Mary Tudor."

"I've always been fascinated by Anne Boleyn. Can you show me how you spoke to her?" If Henry relaxed into a memory coma, he couldn't ransack Tipsy's bedroom or poison her with chemical fumes. "Maybe thinking about those days in London will ease your mind. Remind you of how much you loved Jane."

Tipsy waited. She inhaled in shallow breaths as the perfume and Windex fog dissipated. Henry finally held up one hand. "*She is my death, and I am hers*."

~

Tipsy had visited London with Ayers and his parents, and places like the Tower of London don't change much over a mere century. She immediately recognizes the Tower's West Gate, but at first, she doesn't see Henry. It's hard to tell one male person from the others. They're all wearing dark clothes and hats.

An unusually tall someone brushes past her. He's wearing a flat-brimmed gray hat Tipsy associates with old Irish farmers. The man is slender, with pale hands and a familiar ambling walk. "Henry," she whispers.

He's disappearing under the stone archway. She's afraid she'll lose him, and she doesn't want to waste time maneuvering around people who can't see her. She locks her limbs against her sides, and walks into the crowd clustered on the stone passageway leading onto the Tower's grounds. Those people don't realize an invisible voyeur from the future is stepping through their arms and legs and torsos. No one feels Tipsy's brain momentarily melding with his or her own.

For someone accustomed to being on the living side of such encounters, it's terribly unsettling. If Tipsy had real skin, it would be crawling. She picks up the pace until she's running. Once she clears the crowd, she pauses with her hand over her thumping heart. She scans the crowd for Henry.

She identifies him by the hint of red hair visible between his hat and his tan scarf. He has a package tucked under his arm. As she catches up to him, she hears him muttering under his breath. "Shouldn't be this damn cold in October, but at least it's dry."

He looks up at the fat grayish clouds that hover over the White Tower like natural zeppelins. Tipsy senses Henry's desire for home as he huddles deeper in his woolen overcoat. He longs for the baking heat of a Charleston autumn day and the brilliant blue of the Lowcountry sky. He shivers. No matter how much London's drippy melancholia agrees with his overall persona, he'll always be thin-blooded.

Tipsy garners a sense of urgency as he makes his way toward the Tower Green. She understands that he visits several times a month, for the Tower of London is heavy with drama and tragedy and plot twists. When he feels a drought of creativity, he absorbs the Tower's stories like shea butter into dry skin. This may well be his last visit, and he wants to soak up all available inspiration.

His ruminations flutter beside Tipsy's own thoughts like different species of butterflies attracted to the same flower. His mother has demanded that he return to Charleston by the end of the month. There is a war on, and if he doesn't get out soon, he risks being trapped in England with German bloodlust building on the other side of the English Channel. Mother is right for once. Best to get back to America now, during the relative calm following the Battle of the Marne. Across the ocean, he's reasonably assured of avoiding violence. Henry has no tolerance for blood, his own or anyone else's.

Over the years, he's lost much of his tolerance for afterlife macabre as well, and not only in the pursuit of appearing normal. Charleston ghosts, with their quirky, annoying chatter, had nothing on the ranting and raving of old world spirits. Many had lingered for centuries. The longer the haunting, the more unhinged they became. During his time in London, he'd religiously avoided making eye contact with spirits, lest they harass him endlessly.

Henry had come to London at the recommendation of his boarding school headmaster, an Englishman who had recognized brilliance in moody, sullen Master Mott. After Henry was expelled from the University of South Carolina, the headmaster sent a letter of recommendation to his old Oxford chum, Sir Nigel Pence-Priestly, noting that the lad was rather temperamental, but he might also be a genius.

So here he was, nearly two years into his tenure as Sir Nigel's personal assistant. Sir Nigel's London townhouse was mercifully spirit-free. If Henry had to live with a six-hundred-year old plague victim screaming nonsense at all hours, in indecipherable Middle English no less, he would have been forced to immediately return to Charleston and its humdrum, mildly disturbed dead population.

As Tipsy follows Henry across the Green, she observes multiple doddering, mumbling ghosts. No surprise, given the long and gruesome history of the Tower. Their attire represents various centuries and stations in life. They stumble and fidget amid the living visitors. Sometimes they scream, but Henry does not jump and attract their attention. He avoids their darting, crazed eyes as he sits on his favorite bench, in front of the Waterloo Barracks and across from the White Tower.

He removes a brown envelope from his package, and a letter from the envelope. Tipsy reads over his shoulder as he scans it. Patience Mott's letter professes her agony over his absence, and delivers thinly veiled threats to rescind his allowance if he does not return home immediately. "She's been sending such lamentations since the July Crisis," whispers Henry. "Does her hand never tire?"

He refolds the letter and turns to a small pile of newspaper clippings from the Charleston News & Courier.

Tipsy understands that Patience's letters always include updates about his former peers' accomplishments: graduations from university, employment news, civic awards, and marriages. Henry cares little for her transatlantic gossip, unless it involves the Robinette daughters. Last fall, Patience sent the announcement of Connie's engagement to Andrew Bishop. This time, she includes a photograph of a wedding party standing beside the altar at St. Philip's.

Tipsy smiles down at the smudgy photo of Constance and her husband, their respective parents, Jane, John Huger, the Reverend Proctor James, and a few other family members. She reads the caption under the photo. Saint Philip's Church, Charleston. The wedding of Constance Mary Robinette to Walter Andrew Bishop. *The announcement lists the bride's parents and the groom's parents, followed by,* Maid-of-Honor, Jane Alice Robinette and Best Man, R. John Huger, Junior....

The list goes on, but Henry cares only for Jane. Even in the black and white photo, he admires the lightness of her eyes.

He removes a worn envelope from his pocket and starts flipping through Patience's earlier clippings. Tipsy squints down at a photo of Jane in her white debutante gown, walking up the marble stairs of the Hibernian Hall to the famed St. Cecilia Society Ball. According to Henry's thoughts, his mother thumbs her nose at the St. Cecilia Society as the height of snobbery, but only because the Motts do not have the social standing to be invited to join.

As for the Robinettes, they make frequent appearances in the News & Courier *due to their position in the highest societal echelon, so Patience has unwittingly encouraged her son's overseas infatuation. Tipsy picks out Jane's dark hair in several panoramas of church gatherings. Henry pauses on a solitary photo of a sixteen-year-old beauty portraying the lead in the Dock Street Theater production of* Romeo and Juliet. *It's yellowed from much handling. Tipsy has seen the original of the same photo. Jane's niece, Billy Childress, gave it to her several years ago. She stored it safely in her desk in her bedroom, along with Jane and Henry's wedding portrait.*

Henry turns the two-dimensional picture this way and that, as if he might somehow find another angle. There's something about her hair...the way it cascades over her shoulders. Henry feels he will never find the words to describe it. Sometimes he uses this photo as a writing prompt. When he finds himself knee deep in a short story plot hole, or his novel's outline refuses to cooperate.

The wedding photo turns up at the top of the stack again. As Henry stares at Jane, he tries ignore the figure of John Huger standing beside her like a black and white Thor. With every letter from his mother, he fears he'll unfold Jane's wedding announcement, to Huger or one of his minions. He's relieved to see that at age nineteen, she appears to still be single.

Henry isn't sure why he cares. He knows he's changed over the years, and while he doesn't have the classic conquering hero look of John Huger, he has no lack of female companionship. He's learned to clench his jaw, turn up the corners of his mouth, and straighten himself to his full height of well over six feet. What was social awkwardness in a scrawny boy is brooding charisma in a handsome man. Even the London society ladies blush and fan themselves when he turns his melancholy charm on them. More than a few had allowed him intimate liberties, so to say, so he long ago solved that pleasant mystery. Still, it all rings rather hollow for him, for he's a romantic a heart. He knows nothing will come of any of his London dalliances—he's a moderately wealthy American from a backward Southern town, no matter how oddly compelling. Jane Robinette is equally out of his reach, given their respective places in a Charleston society that is nearly as rigid as London's.

His mercurial mind continues to weave circles through Tipsy's consciousness. She feels herself relaxing into his thoughts. If they were her own, they would have exhausted her with their intensity, but second hand, they were like pleasingly solemn, lonely poetry. Perhaps Henry's loneliness serves him well, as writing demands one be accustomed to solitude. What is a writer without desperation and longing, anyway? The memory of Jane inspires in him the kind of longing he always imagined he'd write about someday. Perhaps it's simply because she had sometimes been kind to the anxious boy he was back then. When he's being realistic, he acknowledges that he doesn't even know her. Still, he finds himself pining for the person he imagines she is. No one else he's met can compete with that pretty girl in the sailor dress who silenced those boys with a few words.

He slides the photos back in the envelope and breathes in the acrid London air. Chattering visitors cluster around a placard that notes the spot of Anne Boleyn's execution, but if Henry's research has served him well, he suspects the true site of the scaffold where the disgraced queen lost her head is closer to the Waterloo Barracks. He closes his eyes, and the weak sunlight sets yellow orbs dancing in the blackness. Of all the doomed characters of the Tower, Mistress Boleyn most fascinates him. What a woman she must have been, for Henry VIII to upend his kingdom and risk damnation of his soul out of love for her. Such passion made for a great story.

How could he love her so, and then so easily cast her aside? *he wonders.* Your majesty, good lady, how did everything go so wrong between you? How did your fairytale end up with such a sordid ending?

"How indeed," says a soft voice beside him.

Henry opens his eyes. A pale, slim woman sits beside him. She wears a white cap over her dark hair, and a white petticoat peeks from below her long gray gown. Some have claimed to see her decapitated ghost roaming the Tower, but her head is firmly attached to her neck. Not a scar or a drop of blood. She has a thin, aristocratic nose, and a small mouth. Her brows are plucked clean in the style of her day. As Tipsy has read, her eyes are dark and piercing.

"Anne Boleyn?" asks Henry. "Er…I say, your majesty?"

"You can see me, sir. In all these long years, only a handful have."

"Uh. Yes. You…" His caution about speaking to the dead falls by the wayside in the face of one so historically significant, but ironically, he can think of little to say to her. His eyes fall on her primly folded, delicate white hands. "You have ten fingers," he blurts out.

"Should I have more, or less?" she asks.

"The legends say you had eleven."

"Such would have been an evil sign. Would the king have married a woman so obviously touched?"

"He didn't seem to care much about what others thought about his marriages."

"He did not. But let us speak of you, seer. How did you call to me?"

"I didn't know I did."

"Yet I heard you, and here we are."

"You speak modern English well."

"I spoke French as well as I spoke English in life. I understood Latin, and a little Greek. It has not been a great hardship to learn your new manners. When I take my walks, I listen to the common folk speak, for I long ago gave up caring about the great problems of the world. I saw my enemy, Thomas Cromwell, lose his own head. I saw my cousin, Katharine Howard, put to death here, silly child that she was. I cried every day and night of my daughter's imprisonment, but once she became queen in accordance with her birthright, I ceased to care what happened with important people and their torrid problems. So many great questions filled my life. I'd rather listen to mothers chiding their children, and friends gossiping, and the ravens chattering."

"I've been here many times, and I've never seen you. I believe I saw the Countess of Shrewsbury, but never you."

"Nasty thing, her death. The axman chased her around the scaffold, hacking away at her."

"Was your own death frightening?"

"I don't remember. Last I recall, I fell asleep in the queen's chambers, on the night before my trial. I woke over there—" She points across the Green. "— stiff and dead, but with my head attached. I imagine that the king believed mine enemies, and found me guilty of their lies, and had me killed. But I have no memory of it, or the trial. Only the terrible shame of their accusations."

Tipsy feels for her. She doesn't believe the salacious and borderline absurd accusations against Anne. She would have known that she risked both her own life and her daughter's if she betrayed the king.

Henry shares her compassion. From what he's read, the lady comported herself with the utmost dignity at all times. He doesn't want to pain her, this pretty woman whose dark hair reminds him of Jane. So instead, he casts about for a question to ask her. "Did you love King Henry?"

"We all loved him. It would be treason not to."

She seems surprisingly sane and rational for one so long dead, but then again, he's speaking to a woman legendary for her own intelligence, and who had given birth to arguably the most brilliantly successful female ruler of all time. "But did you truly love him?" he asks.

"He was a great man. I pray for him still."

"No need to be coy, your majesty. You've already lost your life, what else is there to lose?"

She regards him with those fascinating black eyes, made even darker by her pallor. "He was a man of intelligence and high spirits and passion. These things I loved about him, true. And I loved how he loved me, for all the same reasons. I am sure of it."

"How could he have done what he did to you?"

"Because the things a man worships in his lover when they are parted are rarely the things a man loves in his wife when they live side by side each day."

"If that's true, it seems that no love could ever survive marriage."

"Only truly great loves survive the doldrums of married life. The people who find as much joy in the small things as they do in the majestic ones. Henry was a king. He only lived for the majestic things."

"I love someone," Henry says, and blushes. "Or, I think I do."

"Why do you love her?"

"I haven't seen her in many years, but back then, I loved her because she was smart and kind and honest about her thoughts. She had a wonderful laugh. Her smile drew people in like a whirlpool. Everyone admired her."

"I once knew a girl like that." Anne Boleyn gives him a rueful smile. "What is your name, young man?"

"Henry Mott, your majesty."

The ghost reaches for his hair, but stops short of touching him. "Tall, comely, ginger-haired Henry. Who loves a girl of high spirits. How appropriate."

"I loved her when we were children. Perhaps she's changed."

"If that is her true nature, it will not change. You must remember that, Henry Mott. The heart of her will be ever as it is, whether she is a dream to you or a reality."

"It doesn't matter. I stand no chance with her. I'm below her station."

"I was below the king's station, and look how high I rose."

"And how far you fell."

"It is true. But do not chase your high-spirited girl, and expect her to be something different if you finally catch her. Love her for what she is."

"I will. Always," says Henry, as Anne Boleyn stands. "I'm sorry you must stay here. I wish we'd spoken sooner. I'm returning to America soon."

"Where is that?"

"Uh…the New World. Across the ocean."

"Ah, I heard of such. Barbarians and gold."

"The few remaining barbarians are subdued now, poor fellows. And most of the gold has been dug up."

"That many years have passed?" She shakes her head. "It is hard for me to understand the passage of time. But I'll remember this conversation. Will you?"

"Every day of my life, gracious lady. How could any man forget you?"

She flashes him a flirtatious smile. "I'm glad you spoke loud enough for me to hear you. Maybe the Lord placed us in one another's paths today."

"Do you still believe in God?" asks Henry.

She nods. "For it is not God's fault I'm still here, but the fault of the men who bore false witness against me. And, since, as you say, I have nothing to lose, my fate is the fault of the king, who turned his heart from her whom he promised to love forever, and who had promised to love him. No man would help me, or listen to me. My own father abandoned me."

"Cowards, all of them," says Henry.

"Most men are cowards, and no woman had the power to be brave for me. Not a one, until my daughter." She smiles. "And so…here I am. Perhaps his majesty lingers in his own sadness somewhere."

"I wish y'all could speak once more. Maybe find peace."

"Peace has always eluded me. In life, and in death. I have lingered in this state for so long, but I still do not understand it." She rubs her eyes. "Forgive me, sir. I have not spoken to anyone in…perhaps centuries. I find it exhausting. I'll leave you now. If you ever return to this spot, call to me. I'll hear you."

"I will," says Henry. "God bless you, your majesty."

She curtsies, and walks toward the crowd around the placard. As she approaches, they shiver and turn away, as if a cold wind proceeds her. She fades as she strolls, until only her white cap and a bit of lace remain. The Lady Anne, late Queen of England and mother of Elizabeth, disappears.

Chapter 4

Henry's memory of Anne Boleyn presented Tipsy with several novelties. First, she'd never traveled to a foreign country in a memory. She'd only gone as far as Jane's family plantation on the Wando River. Second, Anne Boleyn was by far the oldest spirit she'd ever observed, and the first of historical significance. Finally, and most mind-boggling, Tipsy was probably the only living person who knew what Anne Boleyn looked like, since her loving husband had destroyed all contemporary depictions of her. She owed it to humanity to paint the late queen. It was a moral imperative.

Such a significant memory—for Henry, for Tipsy, and for the historical record—required serious contemplation. The next morning, after she dropped off the kids at school, she returned home, dumped her purse and keys in the foyer, spun around, and marched right back out the front door for a long, mind-clearing run.

Waving palmetto fronds *scritch-scratched-squeaked* against one another as she stepped onto the pollen-covered sidewalk in front of her house. Her legs felt stiff and heavy, and she watched enviously as a blue heron flew over Mr. Quattlebaum's roof on delicate wings. She squinted up at it, and it honked encouragement, so she picked up the pace. She thought of the Lady Anne, trapped forever under drippy London skies. She knew nothing of the palmetto trees' chatter, or a heron's wraithlike yellow eyes. The Lowcountry's landscape would be alien to her. Tipsy would feel the same way if someone plunked her down on the African savannah. As she jogged down Bennett Street, she considered different angles from which to paint Anne, but her mental camera didn't click. She could depict the infamous queen exactly as she'd seen her—in her simple death-day gown, waif thin from worry and despair, most of her black hair covered by the chaste white cap, her concave cheeks and the dark circles under her eyes—but Anne deserved better. A salute to her brainpower, and legendary grace and charisma.

She pondered as she turned on Venning Street, then onto Pitt Street. She ran through the Old Village's little business district. Her thoughts bounced around in her head as she hopped over cracks and crevices in the uneven sidewalk. Painting inspiration aside, how amazing, that Henry actually *met* Anne Boleyn! Tipsy wondered if she remained trapped at the Tower. Unless some knowing clairvoyant had come by and peeked into her memories, she must be there. Tipsy and Scott had discussed visiting Europe when they had the time and spare cash for a real honeymoon. She imagined herself giving him their Tower of London itinerary.

Visit the famous ravens, see the crown jewels and Henry VIII's armor, right a terrible historical wrong by setting Anne Boleyn free from her haunting.

H8 wouldn't approve of that agenda, said Granna.

Maybe he would, if he's trapped in his own haunting in Whitehall Palace. Lord knows that man had plenty of unresolved issues. The release of the beloved wife that he unjustly killed might bring him some closure.

Tipsy turned to her own problematic Henry. Both of his recent shared memories—the visit with Anne and his early trauma in Mrs. Lamboll's garden—were heavy with meaning. His childhood infatuation with Jane, his lingering love for her as a young man, and Anne Boleyn's canny wisdom about the ways we romanticize one another, yet cannot live with the reality of our notions. Henry had done exactly what Anne warned him not to do. He came to resent Jane for all the reasons he adored her in the first place. He was more comfortable with a dream girl than a real person. Henry's young hero worship of Proctor heightened the tragedy. The man who brought him rare comfort would be the instrument of his greatest heartbreak, deepest regrets, untimely death, and century of limbo.

Now, after finding the means to evade that limbo, purgatory had reclaimed him. He was like a stubborn fox who had escaped a snare, only to be re-trapped by his own voracious appetite for chickens. The events of the past few days left no doubt about his deteriorating mental state. His appearance on the bridge. The destroyed kitchen, his failure to recognize Tipsy, and his aggressive defense of his territory. She'd narrowly averted him unleashing destruction on her bedroom.

She now felt certain that his predicament would negatively affect the imminent Collins-Brandt family blending. It would be hard enough for Tristan and Chloe to move into Tipsy's house, which they'd naturally think of as the Collins's kids' territory. If unexplainable, scary things started happening, the welcome wagon would grind to halt. Even Tipsy's kids wouldn't understand random explosions or stuff going missing or falling apart. It had the makings of a bad horror movie, and Tipsy and Scott would be unable to offer truthful answers. She had to get Henry stabilized, even if he couldn't move on. So far, she had only two sources of information. His own memories, and Helen Stokes.

After a three-mile loop of the Old Village, she turned onto Bennett Street and slowed to a walk. She pulled out her phone and texted Helen. HI! MY GHOSTLY ROOMIE HENRY IS SLIP-SLIDING INTO INSANITY AND TAKING MY FURNISHINGS WITH HIM. I HAVE GOT TO SORT HIM OUT! ON THAT NOTE, ANY NEWS FROM YOUR WISE AUNTIE?

Helen's reply came through as she answered Shelby's question about pricing for the parrot painting.

HELEN: I'M WORKING ON IT! AUNTIE IS ONE BUSY LADY! AND SHE DOESN'T HAVE AN ANSWERING MACHINE!

TIPSY: OKAY NO PROBLEM! ☺ I HOPE I'M BUSY WHEN I'M HER AGE!

She tucked the phone back into the pocket on her leggings and shook out her wrists to prepare them for the next few hours of heavy painting action. Construction trucks were parked on her side of Bennett Street so she crossed the road to circumvent them. As she approached, the stripped down brick house seemed to cringe away from her, as if embarrassed by its unfinished state. The dingy tarp separating the main structure from the addition was a ratty shower curtain that only half-covered its nakedness. As she passed the overgrown front walkway, she noted purplish-blue lights reflecting off the semi-translucent tarp.

Only ghosts or disco balls produced such colors. She walked down the sidewalk to get a better look, and there he was. The scrawny spirit Helen had identified on the day Tipsy met her. Just waiting for a sweaty clairvoyant to wrap up her morning run in front of his haunting.

Tipsy had been feeling guilty about wasting her talents, but as she'd lamented during her walk with Helen, gratuitous ghost-busting could be damn inconvenient. This ghost was *right there*. On her doorstep, ripe for the send-off.

And like Helen said, action is the best way to understand our talent. Hopefully an easy fix, but if he's complicated, maybe I'll learn something new.

Hmmm. I recommend saving your energy for Henry, sugar, said Granna. *There's a whole slew of messing around in his head in your immediate future. You don't need any more headaches. Literally.*

I'm offended, Granna. I can handle it. I have extra time today. It's Thursday and Ayers is picking up the kids.

Don't you have to paint? And call the wedding caterers? And make Little Ayers's next orthodontic appointment? And—

Tipsy started whistling over Granna's recital of her to-do list. Granna retreated, miffed, into the back of her mind.

Tipsy approached the brick house with still hands and soft footballs, as if the ghost was a cracked bulb on a string of holiday lights. As she got closer, she sized up the ghost as neither boy nor a man, but something in between. A couple years older than Little Ayers. He wore a lumpy, too-big sweater and had short, straight, slicked down brown hair. His severe side part and short pants tentatively placed him in the mid-twentieth century. He was skinny, but not malnourished. Sand covered his large bare feet and his slender calves.

She looked over her shoulder at the construction crew's white pickup trucks. The workers were probably on a Home Depot field trip, or went to Chick-fil-A to score some biscuits before breakfast ended. She turned back to the ghost. He had a pleasant profile, with a strong chin and a straight nose. He watched the fluttering tarp. When he shifted, she noticed a tear up the back of his sweater, like the seams of the pillows Henry had destroyed in her bedroom. She saw his pale, sharp shoulder blades.

"Hey." Her hushed voice sounded breathy in her own ears.

The boy didn't move.

"Hey, there. Hello? I can see you. You want to talk?" She tiptoed closer. "I'm happy to listen."

The boy turned and looked at her with wide brown eyes. A reddish splotch covered much of his right cheek.

Tipsy gasped and recoiled, as it appeared someone had beaten on him. When she realized the red spot was a birthmark, she tried to cover her insensitive reaction with a smile, but the boy turned away in a cloud of crackling blue energy. "Hey," she said. "Hey, wait—"

He lowered his chin, stormed toward the tarp, and vanished before she said anything else.

Damnit. How tactless of me! Now he won't want to talk to me.

That's not the end of the world, said Granna. *Before you got all sassy with your whistling, I was about to preach the gospel truth. You got more than enough ghostly whoo-ha right now. You're not leaving Miss Callie's house. You can help that boy when things are more settled with Henry. And with you and Scott and the kids—*

There's the key word, Granna. That ghost is a kid. I can't leave him there. What if he's only coming out because of the construction? Once they're done, he might go back to hiding in a closet. Or the attic. Or the damn chimney. I appreciate what you're saying, but my mind is made up like a hotel bed. I'll poke around over here when I get a chance.

You and your bleeding heart, sugar.

And where, pray tell, did I inherit that perpetually hemorrhaging organ?

This time Granna chuckled her acquiescence, so Tipsy cast one more curious glance at the construction site, then went into her own house to get to work. She painted for the rest of the day, much to the chagrin of her tender nerves. When she could take no more, she sprawled on the parlor floor and contorted herself into makeshift yoga poses. She texted Scott from the rug.

TIPSY: I'M TRYING TO RELAX AND RELEASE NERVE TENSION, BUT THIS OLD CARPET SMELLS LIKE MISS CALLIE'S CAT PEED ON IT IN 1980.

SCOTT: IT STRESSES ME OUT JUST READING THAT. WE WILL NEVER HAVE A CAT.

TIPSY: I LIKE CATS, BUT REMEMBER, THE KIDS WANT A DOG.

SCOTT: AS LONG AS IT'S NOT A DOODLE, I'M DOWN FOR A FAMILY POOCH ONCE WE GET SETTLED IN. BUT BACK TO YOUR NEED FOR RELAXATION...A BEAUTIFUL SUNSET ALWAYS DOES THE TRICK. NO KIDS TONIGHT. HAPPY HOUR BOAT RIDE?

Tipsy and Scott had joined a boat club the previous summer. They were tired of hitching rides with their friends, but they didn't want the expense of boat ownership, and neither of them had grown up boating in the Lowcountry. Scott insisted on getting his sea legs under him before he'd even consider owning his own vessel. The boat club was a damn good deal, but they usually had to reserve a boat in advance.

TIPSY: CAN WE GET A LAST MINUTE BOAT?

SCOTT: I GOT THE DOCKHANDS ON SPEED DIAL THIS YEAR. MADE IT WORTH THEIR WHILE. THEY TEXTED ME ABOUT A CANCELLATION.

TIPSY: I'LL TAKE THE SMELL OF PLUFF MUD OVER CAT PEE ANY DAY! YES PLEASE!

The boat club tied up its fleet at the Daniel Island waterfront on the Wando River, at the end of a long avenue of oak trees that would look at home on South Battery. Scott parked his Yukon in front of one of Daniel Island's retro antebellum office buildings. Tipsy got out of the truck and shook out her long skirt. She brought a sweater in case it got chilly, and Scott grabbed their little sunset cooler. They walked past the bandstand, spray fountain, and playground. Attractive young families spread out picnics, kicked soccer balls, and wrangled their rambunctious doodle dogs. Well-dressed couples walked into the crowded Kingstide Restaurant, another building constructed in an ode to Tara or Twelve Oaks. Tipsy and Scott crossed a short pedestrian bridge and then walked down the long main dock toward the boat club's little office on the covered pierhead. The dock hands jumped when they recognized Scott.

"Good tips pay off," Scott whispered to Tipsy, as one of the young men grabbed the cooler from him. The dock hand led them down to the floating dock, where they climbed aboard a slightly worn but highly functional dual-console Seafox. They boarded and the dock hand connected their Bluetooth. Scott cranked the motor. The dockhand untied the lines and gave the boat a push. Tipsy brought in the lines and bumpers, got them each a beer and a koozie, and took her seat beside Scott. He turned up the stereo. Eric Church sang about Springsteen, first love, and that old Jeep he had when he was seventeen.

"Up the Wando?" asked Scott.

She nodded. "That makes the most sense when we only have a couple hours."

They made the most of it. They gunned it up the river, passed under the tall expanse of the James B. Edwards Bridge, and cruised toward North Mount Pleasant, Awendaw, and Jane's family plantation, the Old Cannon. A youth baseball stadium nestled in one of the river's sharp curves. As they slowed in the no wake zone, cheering, chanting, and the smell of popcorn floated across the water.

As Scott had suggested, Tipsy relaxed. They didn't chat much, and that was okay. The scenery, sounds, and smells, were more important than idle small talk. She could be alone with her thoughts, which allowed her to let some of them go. Scott's boat play list rolled through beachy classics from Zac Brown to the Beach Boys. It was a gorgeous night, with flat glassy water and enough breeze to chase away the horseflies. She had a warm sweater and a cold beer. Scott's arm rubbed against hers. She admired his tan hands on the steering wheel, and his easy confidence. He'd taken to captaining immediately, and she already trusted his judgement on the water. His perfectionist nature wouldn't tolerate anything but complete mastery.

The river narrowed, so they spun around and headed south again. They dipped into skinny Ralston Creek, home of some of the most exclusive real estate on Daniel Island, and hence, in all of Charleston. They admired and critiqued the architecture and landscaping as they puttered along.

"I don't *love* that outdoor living space," said Tipsy, as they passed a pink stucco Italianate mansion. "They could have done so much more with it."

"I agree. Pool is too small."

"That archway...dated."

"Yup. Roofline is kind of weird, too."

"I mean, you *could force* me to live there."

He laughed and they clinked cans. "It's easy to have an opinion when we're not paying for it."

The boat was due back before dark, so after their armchair architectural reviews, they returned to the dock. They decided to have a drink at the Kingstide's second floor bar, where boating attire was welcomed. Wide windows divided the indoor bar space from a patio overlooking the park, the docks, and the river. They found seats at the outdoor side of the bar. On the other side of the river, towering metal quay cranes hoisted shipping containers onto another giant cargo ship. Little Ayers always said the cranes reminded him of AT-AT's from Star Wars, but to Tipsy, they looked like skeletal giraffes. Years ago, she'd said so out loud, and Olivia Grace had burst into tears over the poor dead giraffes. Since then, Tipsy stuck with Little A's version.

They ordered appetizers and a couple beers, and Tipsy told Scott about her attempt to make contact with the ghost across the street. Like Granna, Scott gently advised her to think twice about taking on another challenge.

"I appreciate you and Granna looking out for me, but I have to try." She explained her reasons: guilt, practicality, learning new tricks of the trade that might help Henry. "The ghost is only a kid, on the verge of being a teenager, like Little Ayers and Tris. From the looks of him, he's been all alone for at least fifty years. Like, *half a century*. By *himself*. Think about how much our boys need us these days, even if they think they don't."

"When you put it like that..."

"I knew you'd see it the same way. Ever since I met Henry and Jane, I've thought about helping ghosts just for the sake of helping. Helen Stokes inspired me. She sets ghosts free all over town. I'd love to be, like, her assistant. Together, we could take on some bigtime exorcisms!"

"Whoa, Egon Spengler. Don't get in over your head and end up with the Stay-Puft Marshmallow Man."

"Come on, Scott. These are *ghosts. Former people.* Not the evil manifestation of an ancient Sumerian god. That would be crazy."

"A couple years ago, the idea of ghosts was crazy," he said. "But seriously, baby, Helen has a lot more time on her hands. Philanthropic ghost-busting is the perfect retirement hobby."

She smiled. "So while you play golf someday, I'll look into the past, solve cold cases, and free trapped spirits?"

"Damn. Maybe I'll need a more meaningful hobby."

Her phone rang, and she held up the phone to show Scott a Facetime call from Mary Pratt. He nodded, and she answered it. "Hey, buddy," she said, "what's happen…"

Tipsy trailed off. Both girls' faces filled the screen. Four reddish, puffy eyes, and four shiny, tear-stained cheeks. Tipsy recognized the lovely marshside backdrop—May Penny and Tripp's dock on Conch Creek, a skinny outlet of the Intracoastal Waterway. May Penny always had dinner on at half past six, and it was quarter to seven. The girls were risking their grandmother's ire, and no one in the Collins family did so lightly. "Girls," said Tipsy. "Are y'all okay?"

"Daddy and Kate…" M.P. sniffled, and in the pause, O-Liv broke in. "They're getting divorced!"

"Oh, buddies. Can you tell me how you heard this?"

Out it came, in a rush of sniffing, nose-wiping, and frantic rambling. After school, Ayers had taken the kids to Ye Olde Fashioned Cafe for ice cream. In the booth, over a giant banana split and a brownie sundae, he informed his preteen children that he and Kate *couldn't make it work*. They didn't get along, because Kate was *unreasonable* and *angry*. She also *spent too much money*. She was *not the right person for him*, so they were getting divorced. He didn't know what would happen with his house, but Kate, Tristan, and Chloe would be staying there. The Collins crew would stay with GiGi and PopPop this weekend, and every weekend moving forward, until *everything got figured out*.

"We *just moved* into Daddy's house a couple years ago," said O-Liv. "Now we have to move again? It's not fair. We can't even go back to our old house, because other people live in it!"

"What if there's no house for him to buy in our neighborhood? He said he might move closer to Pinegrounds. I *want* to go to Pinegrounds, but I also want to stay in our neighborhood with our old friends..." M.P. sobbed noisily. "Oh, *Mooom!*"

Tipsy directed her questions at O-Liv, who was predictably calmer. "How did your brother take it?"

"He didn't say anything at Ye Olde Fashioned. He's been in the bunk room on his phone since we got here. Dad ordered pizza so Gigi wouldn't be up in our business about dinner. Everyone is kind of quiet. Dad went to the store. BopBop is reading a book. Gigi said she had a headache and went to bed. Maybe she's mad that we're staying here."

"No way," said Tipsy. "Gigi loves having y'all around. I bet she's giving everyone time to think."

"Ayers is staying in the bunk room because he's totally *P.O.'ed*. Especially because Daddy said we can't tell Tristan and Chloe."

"He said *Kate* has to tell them," said M.P., "but she's not ready to tell them yet. It's going to be *so weird*, since we're like, keeping a secret from them. This is literally the *worst!*"

"Okay, y'all, okay. I'm so sorry this was dropped on you. For now, please sit tight and...try to enjoy some time at GiGi and BopBop's. This kind of situation takes time to unfold, and we can't be sure how it will play out. I wish Dad had waited to tell you, but now that the cat is out of the bag, we have to make sure it doesn't run off and get hit by a car."

M.P. rubbed her face on her tee-shirt. "Since we won't be with Chloe and Tristan this weekend, we don't have to *lie* to them. But *next weekend* we'll see them with you and Scott, and—"

"What if they're mad at Dad?" asked O-Liv. "Then they might be mad at us, too, and they're our brother and sister. *Sort of.* They'll still be, even if Dad and Kate get divorced, since you and Scott are getting married—" Her lip trembled. "It's so confusing, Mama."

"I know, honey. Our family situation is unique. There are good things about it, and sometimes, there will be hard things. But I believe Tristan and Chloe love y'all. I can't imagine either of them will take this out on you."

"Okay," said M.P. Another swipe of her face with her tee-shirt. "Yup. Right."

"If it's easier, we'll do our own thing next weekend, and so will Scott and Chloe and Tris. We'll—"

"At least we don't have to move with y'all. We don't have to move, right?" asked M.P. "I don't *want* to move anymore."

"No, honey. We're staying at Miss Callie's."

"Thank goodness," said M.P.

"I'll call your brother when I get home. Try to be patient with each other, because everyone will be on edge, okay?"

They nodded, and exchanged *I love you's*, and the twins hung up.

"I don't think I have to repeat much of that," said Tipsy to Scott. "The girls were so upset, everyone on this patio knows the deal."

Scott gestured around them. The nearest couple's fierce whispering smacked of an argument, and the group at the end of the bar was taking shots. "No one is paying any attention to us. They got their own problems. Relationship problems. Drinking problems."

"I cannot believe Ayers dumped this on them. The divorce. Griping about Kate. She's no angel, but he's just as unreasonable and angry as she is, and he's far from thrifty. That man keeps Sportman's Warehouse and Home Depot in business. He has more power tools than Bob the Builder, and in a decade of marriage, I never saw him *build* a damn thing. He has a three-thousand dollar fishing rod, for the love of God. It's completely inappropriate to talk to the children about his personal problems with Kate. It's bad enough that he's using me as his therapist, but them—" No way to sugarcoat it; Tipsy was *pissed*. An uncharacteristic urge to confront Ayers seized her. "Do you mind if I call him? Will you try to ask Kate for an update?"

"I'll try, but she won't admit to me that things are bad."

"I know, but—"

"Call Ayers, and I'll try to call her."

"I'll be over by the railing, where no one can hear me if I lose my shit." She found a spot in the corner, beside an empty table. Below her, children were doing cartwheels in the grass. In her mind, she imagined they had simple lives, where their parents weren't bouncing between marriage and divorce.

Those kids may be in foster care for all you know, said Granna.

Tipsy opened her phone, then her "favorites" list (always ironic to see her ex-husband's name on that list, but that's co-parenting), and called Big Ayers. He answered on the second ring. "Yeah?" he said.

"Hello to you, too."

"I got a lot going on right now, Tipsy."

"The girls called me, sobbing."

His audible sigh made the phone static-y. "I had to tell them. I had to—"

"Kate hasn't told her kids. Now you've put ours in the middle of this."

"We'll be staying with my parents for the time being. They need to understand why."

"There are some things they do *not need* to understand, Ayers. Like your *financial complaints* about Kate!"

"Little Ayers asked why we're breaking up, so I—"

"Whatever! If he asks why, you tell him those are adult matters he shouldn't worry about! Why tell them *any* of this, when you have no real plan? They have so many questions we can't answer, like what will happen with your house. What to say to Tristan and Chloe—"

"I thought about it a lot before talking to them. I'm not hiding shit from my kids. When you and I got divorced, we didn't keep it a secret, and they were much younger."

"You have a selective memory. We didn't tell them anything until you and your furniture were in the apartment, and we *certainly* didn't give them details about our relationship problems. It wasn't ideal, but—"

"None of this is ideal. I feel awful that I'm…putting them through… *this* again." He sounded like he might be crying himself. "But I have to be upfront with them. My parents never talked to me about anything. I never knew what was happening in our family."

"I'm all about open communication, and I know May Penny and Tripp are a bit repressed. But you're not thinking clearly."

"They *know*, Tipsy! Can't take it back now. Will you please stop riding me? I'm in hell and I'm doing the best I can."

"I know, but—"

A shrill female voice in the background. "*Come back inside, Ayers! Stop hiding. It's ridiculous.*"

"I'll be there in a second! Keep your voice down. Your kids will hear you!" he called back.

"Did you go *back* to *your* house?" asked Tipsy. "Our kids need you right now—"

"If I hadn't come over here and left them with Mom and Dad for an hour, Kate would have shown up and raised hell at their house. I'll head back to Sullivan's soon. Now I gotta go. Get off my back, Tipsy. If you're not going to be helpful, butt out."

"Ayers, I—"

He hung up. Tipsy watched the quay cranes swinging their metal gorilla arms above a rusty, gray-black container ship that desperately needed a paint job. Unlike the rainbow of Chicklet containers she'd observed during her walk with Helen, these tin cans were brownish orange, sickly yellow, and pea green. The industrial eyesore of the port was like Big Ayers's divorce. Looming over everyone and sullying a gorgeous view of the future.

"From the look on your face," said Scott, as she sat beside him again, "that wasn't a productive conversation."

"No. How did yours go?"

"Surprisingly, she answered the phone. I asked her if there were problems in the house since your kids felt some tension. She insisted there's nothing wrong. I *tried* to ask if our kids are okay. She suggested I take an elevator straight down to hell and then hung up on me."

"She had to get off the phone to scream at Ayers before he slinks back to his parents' house." Tipsy took his hand. "What are we going to do?"

"Be there for our kids. What else can we do?"

It could take a year or more for Ayers and Kate to finalize their divorce. Kate would never leave that house willingly, and Ayers wouldn't give her one cent unless ordered to do so by a judge. Her kids would be bunking up with their grandparents and their increasingly frazzled father for months. Would it be better for her to take over until he stabilized?

"I don't know," said Tipsy, as she pictured LeeLee Moretz in her polished courtroom attire and her pink flip-flops. "But I need a professional opinion."

~

As Tipsy was blow drying her hair on Saturday evening in preparation for the see-and-be-seen scene at Hall's, she got a text from Lindsey via the girls' group chat.

LINDSEY: Y'ALL...SOOOOO SORRY TO CANCEL, BUT WE HAVE TO TAKE A RAINCHECK. LATE BIRTHDAY CELEBRATION SOON? XOXO

Tipsy and Shelby immediately sidestepped the group chat to speculate about Lindsey cancelling her own birthday party. Halls booked up months in advance, so by the time they secured another dinner reservation for six, they'd be celebrating Lindsey's next birthday. Lindsey didn't give much detail; only referenced an "issue" she and P.D. needed to address. Tipsy and Shelby decided to postpone Hall's, as it seemed inappropriate to celebrate Lindsey's birthday, at Lindsey's favorite restaurant, with no Lindsey.

Instead, the remaining Saturday night warriors upped their hipness quotient by popping around the neighborhoods on the upper peninsula. Tipsy was never sure where Hampton Park Terrace ended and Wagener Terrace began, nor did she know the exact boundary between North Central and Westside. When she first visited Charleston with Ayers twenty years ago, those neighborhoods were predominantly African-American, with the exception of the Citadel faculty homes surrounding Hampton Park. Some deep-rooted residents were holding on, but the streets were distinctly whiter and younger these days. Black folks still called out to family and friends from their porches, and escorted children to school, and attended churches founded by their great-great-grandparents, but they were outnumbered by bearded brewery bros, emo chicks with blue hair and tattoos, and jogging moms pushing expensive strollers.

It started when the growth of the College of Charleston pushed students north of Harleston Village and Radcliffeborough in search of affordable apartments. They discovered a plethora of comparably inexpensive options, and kept going past Septima Clark Parkway, also known as the Crosstown. Many graduated and stuck around. Typical of gentrifying neighborhoods, as young white people found starter homes and investment properties, property values increased and the long-term residents were priced out.

As Scott trolled for a parking space around the eight-hundred-block of King Street, Tipsy observed the neighborhood's gritty vitality through the windows of his Yukon. Block after block of early twentieth century colonial houses in various states of disrepair and rejuvenation. Dive bars and gastropubs, convenience stores and yoga studios, spas and basketball courts, nonprofits and tech startups. Sprawling condominium complexes towered over narrow, pinched off roads. The William Enston Home, a historic retirement community turned subsidized housing, sat behind an elaborate stone gate leading to cobblestone streets and roundabouts. With its unusual uniform red brick Victorian homes, the Enston Home reminded Tipsy of monopoly houses huddled in a storybook village. Outside the gate, repurposed warehouses accommodated breweries, distilleries, and spin studios. At a rundown gas station on the corner of King and Huger Streets, metal bars separated the staff from their patrons.

If Big Ayers had the foresight to buy property on the upper peninsula fifteen years ago, it would have been a hell of a boon to their marital estate. On the other hand, if people like her ex-husband—and Tipsy herself—kept buying everything up, where would the original residents go? Too much of the Lowcountry had already been taken from those who built it.

What did Henry call you a couple years ago? asked Granna, as Scott squeezed the Yukon into a parking space on Race Street. *You remember. Talkin' about how you always look at every side of an issue until you spin yourself dizzy.*

Intellectually ambidextrous? offered Tipsy. She opened the car door and stepped onto the sidewalk in a pair of high-heeled ankle boots she'd inherited from Pamella Brewton.

That was it. Now don't be spinning yourself dizzy in those boots on these cracked up sidewalks.

Tipsy blew Granna a kiss in her mind as she slid her arm through Scott's. The two couples had dinner at Little Jack's Tavern, then walked a few blocks to one of Charleston's favorite dive bars, Faculty Lounge. The narrow, lopsided one-story building resembled a ramshackle single-wide trailer with a solid wooden door. No obvious signage, and they had to ring a doorbell to be buzzed in. Tipsy and Shelby sat at a rickety table while Scott and Brian grabbed drinks.

"I feel like I'm in a submarine in this place," said Shelby, as she pointed out the lack of windows. "So what's *really* going on with Lindsey?"

"*Something* is definitely up in the Starkey household. Lindsey was so looking forward to dinner tonight, and P.D. takes advantage of every chance to get out of the house."

"I'm getting legit worried about them. Having baby number two when they're struggling with one…"

"Another infant is not going to increase their conjugal felicity."

"Conjugal felicity?" said Shelby, with a snort. "Okay, Jane Austen."

"Jane Austen was too proper to use the word *conjugal*," said Tipsy. "Don't judge me. Scott loves my use of anachronisms."

"What do spiders have to do with your weird vocabulary?"

Tipsy laughed. "Not arachnids. Anachronisms—"

"You throwing some sexy lingo around?" asked Scott, as he sat beside Tipsy.

"Y'all's version of *sexy lingo* is very different from ours," said Shelby.

"Some things should stay between a man and his wife, Shelby." Brian, an unthreateningly cute New Englander who was contentedly embracing his dad bod, draped an arm over the back of Shelby's chair.

Tipsy leaned into Scott's shoulder. "I like to throw around a few archaic phrases to mix things up."

Scott kissed her. "Hottie."

"Y'all are too much." Shelby rolled her eyes.

"We haven't been married *that* long," said Brian, with a teasing smile. "You're not down with PDA anymore?"

"It takes more than words to turn me on."

"I'll get up with Baby B tonight if he wakes up."

"*Now* you're talking," said Shelby.

"I'm so glad the baby days are behind us," said Scott.

"Y'all don't want to create a little Tipsy-Scott hybrid?" asked Brian.

Tipsy and Scott looked at each other, and both laughed. "Hell *to* the *no*," she said.

"Five kids are plenty," agreed Scott.

The unisex conversation meandered from children to home improvement to vacation planning, until football distracted Scott and Brian. Scott was a diehard Tennessee fan. Brian grew up in Connecticut, but he attended the University of Michigan. Even in the springtime, those two fanbases never ran out of commentary.

Shelby listened for about two minutes, then turned to Tipsy. "How are Little A and the girls holding up?"

"Mimi and her kids are at May Penny and Tripp's, so they're having fun. They're distracted."

"Has May Penny talked to you about what's happening with Ayers?"

"Not yet. Nothing from Mimi, either. They'll reach out soon, and they'll expect information. You know May Penny and Mimi's early support of our relationship—" She pointed at Scott. "— came with a price."

"Right. An ongoing agreement to exchange Ayers intel," said Shelby. "I do *not* envy you, being in the middle of this battle. I mean…*so many armies*."

"Ha. Let's take a moment to explore all the potential armed conflicts." Tipsy counted off on her fingers. "Ayers and Kate. Ayers and *me*. Ayers and *my kids*. My kids and *Scott's kids*. Scott and Kate. *Me* and Kate." She took a long, dramatic breath. "*Ayers* and his parents. *Kate* and his parents—"

"Stop, stop," said Shelby. "That's, like, poisonous Dijon gas—"

Tipsy swallowed beer and laughed at the same time. She coughed and her eyes watered. "You mean *mustard* gas?"

"Whatever. It's giving me a headache."

Tipsy's phone buzzed in her purse. She'd kept it on vibrate in case any of the aforementioned children, ex-husbands, or former in-laws texted her. She had a message from Little Ayers, and as she swiped, a text from Big Ayers also came through.

LITTLE AYERS: WE WENT TO YOUR HOUSE TO GET MY SKATEBOARD I USED THE HIDDEN KEY TO GET IN BUT THERE WERE CRASHES UPSTAIRS AND IT FREAKED ME OUT

BIG AYERS: HEY. WE STOPPED BY YOUR HOUSE TO GET A'S SKATEBOARD STUFF. HE RAN UPSTAIRS TO GRAB EVERYTHING FROM HIS ROOM AND CAME RUNNING OUT ALL SCARED. SAID SOMETHING CRASHED. HOPE U DON'T MIND I WENT INSIDE BECAUSE HE WAS ALL WORKED UP. WENT UPSTAIRS AND I HEARD A SOUND LIKE SOMETHING BREAKING IN A BEDROOM AT THE END OF THE HALL BUT THE DOOR WAS LOCKED. U MIGHT WANT TO CHECK IT OUT.

Tipsy thanked both of them for letting her know and promised to look into it, but her chill Saturday evening mood immediately shifted. Wherefore a crash in her house, there went a disgruntled Henry Mott. As Brian and Shelby answered a Facetime call from their teenaged babysitter, Tipsy's phone dinged again.

LITTLE AYERS: OKAY MOM CHECK IT BECAUSE IT WAS REALLY LOUD. LIKE SOMEONE WAS BLOWING THINGS UP IN THE SPARE ROOM AND WHY WAS THE DOOR LOCKED? His follow up message incited mild alarm. SOMETIMES I THINK OUR HOUSE IS HAUNTED HAHA BUT SERIOUSLY SOMETIMES I DO NO CAP

TIPSY: HAHA RIGHT, DON'T SCARE YOUR SISTERS OR CHLOE AND TRIS! She added a ghost emoji, then leaned over to show Scott the texts.

"Hmm. You think we need to check it out?" he whispered.

"Yeah. This has Henry written all over it in permanent marker." She added her son's Gen-Z-ism for *that's the truth* for emphasis. "No cap."

"No cap, huh? That's serious."

"We gotta wrap it up," said Shelby, as she plopped her phone into her bag. "Brandon woke up and the sitter can't get him back to sleep. Ugh. Why does my mom have to have her own life sometimes?"

They got the check, gave out wishes for a peaceful night and a cooperative baby, and split up to retrieve their cars. It had started raining while they were encased inside Faculty Lounge, and lightning flashed on the Mount Pleasant side of the Ravenel Bridge. Tipsy's anxiety increased with each rotation of the tires. Neither Little Ayers nor his dad scared easily, and Tipsy had never locked the spare bedroom door. Henry must have used his telekinetic powers to lock it. She'd have to pick the lock, or ask Henry to telekinetically open it.

They arrived at the house, and Scott followed Tipsy up the front steps. She unlocked the front door and they stepped inside. She fumbled with the light switches until she found the one that turned on the foyer's ancient brass chandelier. Wet footprints lingered on the hardwood floor. Big and Little Ayers had come in without wiping their feet, as if his father's presence caused Little A to forget her house rules.

"You want me to come upstairs with you?" asked Scott. He eyed the floor. "Or…I can clean this up."

"Probably best I deal with Henry alone. And floorcare is your area of expertise."

"I'll leave the ghosts to you. You leave the Swiffering to me."

She flipped more light switches as she climbed the stairs and turned left when she reached the landing. During their lives, Henry and Jane's bedroom and dressing suite had taken up half of the second floor, but a subsequent owner had reconfigured their spacious retreat into two small bedrooms and a bathroom. Tipsy had found Jane in one of those bedrooms on the day she moved into the house. As their friendship blossomed, Jane revealed that the bedroom had been her personal grooming area, and she felt at home there.

Tipsy opened the door to the first spare bedroom and saw nothing out of place, but when she tried the door to Jane's former dressing room, she found it locked. Perhaps Henry was inside, mourning his lost wife. He might feel closer to her in this room.

"Henry, you in there? Can I come in?" she asked.

His muffled voice through the door. "Tipsy is here," he said. "Remember Tipsy?"

He was talking to himself. Not a good sign, but at least it sounded like he recognized her this time. She knocked again. "Can you unlock the door?"

"Wake up. Please," said Henry.

Maybe Henry was asleep. Having a nightmare. She knocked a third time. Henry was still talking, but she could only make out phrases here and there.

"Don't worry," said Henry. "Everything is…you know…Proctor…it's *Tipsy*."

He's talking to Proctor, Granna. Shit, he's truly lost it.

He's got to open up.

She gently rattled the doorknob. If she startled him, the door might blast open and knock her upside the head. "Henry, please let me in."

Henry's voice through the door again. "Come." To her relief, the knob's internal workings mysteriously clicked, and the handle turned in her hand.

Henry sat on the bed with his back to her, but the curtains were drawn back from the window. Several empty drawers had been wrenched from a bureau and tossed across the room. An old fashioned standing oval mirror—the kind that hung in a wooden frame on pedestal legs—had tipped over. Bits of shattered glass on the rug sparkled in time to the heat lightning that pulsed outside the window.

"Henry?" Tipsy approached the bed. She called Henry's name again, but he didn't turn. Her brows came together as she tiptoed toward him. There was something on the bed. At first, she took it to be a pile of rumpled bedding, but no. It was a *human* shape.

Tipsy peered over Henry's shoulder. He was stroking something on the pillow. Something dark and shiny.

A flash of lightning revealed Jane Mott's delicate features and bone-white skin. Tipsy gasped and clapped both hands over her mouth. "Jane," she whispered. "Oh, good lord. *Janie?*"

But Jane didn't stir. Her light blue eyes were closed. Her long lashes, still. Her jaw clenched, unmoving.

Jane's presence went against everything Tipsy had learned about ghosts. *Tipsy's First Rule of Supernatural Mechanics: When a ghost moves on, there's no coming back.* Yet there was Jane, with Henry's hands roving over her black hair.

How could she be here, and equally important, *why* was she here? Was she asleep? Sick? Comatose?

"Henry, buddy." Tipsy addressed Henry using her favorite motherly endearment. "Can you tell me—"

"Sometimes I take my repose here," he said, his eyes trained on his wife's face. "I fool myself that I can smell her freshly washed clothes and her perfume. This afternoon, I came here to nap, but thunder woke me as the sun set. I rolled over, and her…*hair*. I saw her hair first, on the pillow beside my face. I thought I was dreaming. It was too painful to let such a lovely dream continue. I had to wake myself up. I'm sorry, but…I…"

"You knocked over the mirror and ejected the drawers."

He nodded. "That sound didn't wake me, or Jane. I heard one of the children running down the hallway, so I locked the door." He looked up at Tipsy. "You see her, don't you?"

"I see her clear as I see you."

Outside, the skies grumbled their confusion over this unexplainable turn of events. Henry parroted Tipsy's thoughts. "How? Why? I don't *understand*."

"It must have something to do with whatever has been ailing you. You've been having a hard time, and you were worried about her, and here she is."

"*No.* I *never* intended to drag her back *here*."

"You didn't do it on purpose, but maybe—"

"She *moved on*. If my illness, or whatever it is, brought her back, I'll never forgive myself!"

"Henry, stop. Something *really* strange is going on here, with you *and* with Jane. Remember the message? Jane said there was something more to *y'all's* story. That the *two of you* would never truly be at peace."

"That doesn't explain Jane coming back after she *already* moved on. But now that she's here, why won't she wake up?" He waved Tipsy toward the bed. "Will you speak to her?"

Tipsy sat on the edge of the quilt. She leaned toward her old friend. "Jane? Honey, it's Tipsy. Henry and I are so happy to see you. Can you hear me?"

She didn't move.

"Sweet Jesus and all the suffering martyrs," said Henry. "She's not asleep. She's…dead."

"Of course she's dead. You're *both* dead."

"What is this is a…second death? A fate worse than normal death!"

Tipsy had never considered that the dead could die again. "Is *that* possible?"

"I don't know!" His voice crept up in volume and hysteria with every word. "Janie, my love. *Please wake up!* You must! Please don't be doubly dead—"

"Do you want her to wake up to you freaking out? She might be as scared as you are."

"You're right. What can I do…what can I say to her—Ah. I know. I'll *read* to her. On the bookshelf, downstairs in the parlor. There's a copy of *Wuthering Heights*."

The parlor was the largest room on the first floor, and the bookshelves took up the room's longest wall. "Do you know where it is on the shelves?" asked Tipsy.

"No," he said, and he went back to stroking Jane's hair.

With that helpful response ringing in her ears, Tipsy went downstairs to the parlor. Scott was sitting on the sofa beside the bookshelf with his phone in his hand. "All okay?" he asked. "I didn't want to disturb you, and I didn't hear any more crashes—"

"*Jane* is upstairs."

"Jane as in Henry's wife? The ghost who *used* to be here, and then *wasn't*, is *back*?"

"Apparently."

"Is that normal? In the context of this kind of normal."

"I have no idea. Right now, I need to consult Heathcliff and Catherine."

"Huh?"

"There's an old copy of *Wuthering Heights* on the bookshelves," said Tipsy. "We have to find it for Henry."

Scott looked at the shelf. "There are about five hundred books on these shelves."

"Then we better get our browse on." Tipsy started on the end of the room by the fireplace, and Scott started on the end by the hallway.

"Bunch of classics over here," said Scott, after ten minutes of searching. "Austen. Dickens. Ah—ooops, *Jane Eyre*. Wrong Bronte. Hawthorne. Whitman. How about—bingo!" He held up a slim black book with a gold leaf design on the cover. Tipsy read the gold lettering embossed on the spine. *Wuthering Heights.*

She kissed Scott, ran back upstairs with the book, and burst into the Jane's old dressing room. "I found it!"

"Shhh," said Henry, in a mansplainy kind of voice. "You'll frighten her. Please remain calm."

"Hold up. I just told *you* to—" Given the circumstances, she decided to let both his condescension and his hypocrisy slide. "No problem," she said, as she approached the bed.

"Jane and I loved *Wuthering Heights*." He held out one hand, and Tipsy felt a gentle tug on the book. She released it, and it floated toward him. "Jane used to teasingly call me Heathcliff," said Henry. "Back then, neither of us realized the tragic appropriateness of that comparison."

"When I met Jane's great-niece, Billy Childress, out at the Old Cannon, she called y'all her family's Heathcliff and Catherine." Tipsy sat in the club chair beside the bed.

Henry released the book, but it hovered before his eyes. The pages turned, and he started reading. "*1801...I have just returned from a visit to my landlord—the solitary neighbor that I shall be troubled with. This is certainly a beautiful country! In all England, I do not believe that I could have fixed on a situation so completely removed from the stir of society. A perfect misanthropist's heaven...and Mr. Heathcliff and I are such a suitable pair to divide the desolation between us. A capital fellow! He little imagined how my heart warmed towards him when I beheld his black eyes withdraw so suspiciously under their brows, as I rode up…"*

His deep voice lulled Tipsy. He intended to wake Jane, but he might put Tipsy to sleep.

"*…Wuthering Heights is the name of Mr. Heathcliff's dwelling. "Wuthering" being a significant provincial adjective, descriptive of the atmospheric tumult to which its station is exposed in stormy weather….*"

Rain pinged against the windowpane. Tipsy wondered if Cathy was outside. Floating by the window. But Cathy…no, *Jane*…was right there. A ghost, certainly, but not a banshee wailing across the windswept moors.

Tipsy squinted at her friend's calm face. She detected a fluttering of her eyelids.

"*…among a wilderness of crumbling griffins and shameless little boys, I detected the date 1500, and the name Hareton Earnshaw…*"

Jane rolled toward Henry. He stumbled over a few words, and then kept reading. "*…he has an erect and handsome figure; and rather morose…*"

His wife sighed and tucked her hands under her cheek. Tipsy had a brief glimpse of her engagement ring—a rather small, purplish-blue sapphire surrounded by tiny diamonds—and her simple wedding band. Both were set in rose gold.

"*…He'll love and hate equally under cover, and esteem it a species of impertinence to be loved or hated again—*"

"*Henry*," said Jane, and her eyes opened.

The book hit the quilt with a muffled thud. "Jane? Janie?"

"Where are we, darling?" she asked.

"Oh, sweetheart. We're in…*our house*. You came back here. I don't know why. I'm so sorry—"

"Shhh. I'm tired. So *terribly* tired."

"I know, my *dearest* wife. I've felt the same way—but no. I won't bother you with that now. I won't—"

"Will you lay beside me? Even if I can't feel your arms around me, when I open my eyes, I'll see your hands." She smiled at Tipsy. "*Tipsy,* my friend, how *good* to see you. I'm sorry I'm so sleepy…" She blinked languidly, and her eyes closed. "Rest with me, Henry."

"Yes. Whatever you want." He looked up at Tipsy. "I'll…I'm going to…"

"I'll check in with you two tomorrow morning. Warning, it will be early. I'm not going to sleep tonight."

"I don't want to sleep. I want to watch *her* sleep." He lay down beside Jane and wrapped an arm protectively around her. Big spoon, little spoon. Jane snuggled against him and sighed again. Henry's big hand engulfed her small slender one. Their misty fingers wove together. His plain gold wedding band beside her equally understated jewelry.

Tipsy glanced down at her own modest emerald ring, surrounded by tiny diamonds, and set in rose gold. During her first marriage, she'd had a typical twenty-first century diamond bauble. A large round stone flanked by two not-quite-as-large-but-still-pretty-big baguettes, in a platinum setting. When she and Scott talked marriage, she told him she wanted something different. Something special. Something just for the two of them. Now, looking at the ring she and Scott had selected, it dawned on her that she'd been inspired by Jane's ring.

Her eyes went back to their pale hands, and her mental camera clicked.

Hand studies were notoriously tricky. The fact that Jane and Henry's fingers and palms and wrists were semi-translucent would make it even harder, but she would give it a go. As she had the first summer she knew them, Tipsy found artistic inspiration in the eternal quandary of Jane and Henry Mott's love.

Chapter 5

Over the next few days, Jane slowly emerged from paranormal hibernation. First, she sat up in the bed in her old dressing room, and then she moved to the sofa in the parlor. Eventually, she tolerated a rocking chair on the front porch. She recognized Henry and Tipsy, but sometimes she forgot she was dead, or that she'd ever moved on. She asked after her parents, her sister, the date, and the state of the world. Sometimes she laughed for no reason. Twice, Tipsy found her staring silently at her own hands while tears streamed down her cheeks.

Henry forbade Tipsy from pestering Jane about her return. "I also want to understand why she's here," he said, "but if we're patient, she'll tell us whatever she knows."

Tipsy promised to give Jane time and space. To mollify her curiosity, she spent all her waking kid-free moments engrossed in painting. She wanted to get some projects off her plate and start on Henry and Jane's hand study. On Wednesday, she put the finishing touches on two gallery pieces—her red parrot, and a large landscape she'd been working on for weeks. On Thursday morning, after she dropped off the girls at their elementary school and backtracked to take Little Ayers to Pinegrounds, she transported both pieces to the GQB.

As Tipsy had told Granna, Shelby had expressed doubt about Tipsy's new infatuation with the fantastical, but once she put eyes on the parrot, Shelby chuckled and said, "You did it again, sister. What's the other one?"

"Another creative anomaly. I literally dreamed it up."

"You're all imagination lately. Giving Walt GD Disney a run for his money." She lightly punched Tipsy's arm. "I like it, even if I usually think of you as a realism gal."

"Most of my work *is* based in reality." *My reality, anyway.* Shelby had no idea that ghosts had inspired several of Tipsy's best pieces. "But for this one…I had *such* a vivid dream. It's like a scene from *once upon a time.*" Tipsy removed the tarp from the landscape. The tones were mostly dark, so the eye had to adjust to the shadows. As his or her vision sharpened, the viewer would pick out rolling hills, low stubby trees, and jagged mountains in the distance. Heavy rainclouds hung like gray water balloons hugged the edges of the tableau. A foggy, chilly place; foreign and rather desolate. Not unlike the moors of *Wuthering Heights.*

A herd of horses galloped across the foreground. Against the gray-brown-black background, their brilliant white coats seemed to reflect the streaks of yellow lightning.

Shelby leaned in closer. "Wait—they're not horses. They're unicorns!"

"Told you. Once upon a damn time."

"They're outrunning a storm!"

"That's the idea."

"Is there a metaphor there?"

"Maybe. Or maybe my subconscious reminded me that Little Tipsy used to *loooove* her some unicorns."

"All little girls love unicorns." Shelby smiled. "It's a true original. All hail the fairy-core, Mother Goose."

Shelby hung the unicorns on Tipsy's display wall, where they joined a detailed study of the Dr. Rene Bonneau House's intricate front gate, a dolphin pod surfacing in Shem Creek, and a portrait of her twins in mirror profiles on her front porch loveseat. Shelby propped the parrot on the easel in the gallery window. He glared out at passersby with his astute yellow eyes.

Birds can't truly laugh. Even parrots can only mimic human chuckling. They can't understand the joke. Still, this one looked like he would cackle hysterically if someone tripped on the uneven sidewalks or got a parking ticket. He looked like he, himself, had a *fabulous* sense of humor.

It's my fairy-core world, she thought. *If I want my parrot to be an avian standup comedian, why not?*

She had to get back to her sketchpad and her plans for the hand study, so she hugged Shelby and bid a fond farewell to her feathered Monty Python and her tempest-tossed unicorns. She left the gallery and stood beside her car, answering texts from Scott and Pamella. As she typed, Mimi's name appeared at the top of the screen. She swiped over it.

MIMI: HI, CAN YOU STOP BY MOM'S BEFORE YOU GET THE KIDS?

Tipsy did a quick check of her mental task list. She didn't want to waste her valuable workday hours chatting with Mimi and May Penny, but she didn't have much choice, given their pact to share information about Big Ayers. She had to tell them what she knew, and hopefully, they'd reciprocate.

TIPSY: SURE. I HAVE TO BE AT PG CARPOOL BY 2:30 SO I CAN SCOOP LITTLE A AND MAKE IT BACK TO MT. P TO GET THE GIRLS AT 3:45. DOES 1 WORK?

Mimi sent her a thumbs up emoji. Tipsy plopped her phone in her purse, and then dug around inside it like she was reaching into Mary Poppins's magic satchel. She muttered to herself "Keys…where the hell—"

"Tipsy?"

It was LeeLee Moretz, in a long brown floral dress. The pattern of gold blossoms and green and gray leaves complemented her multicolored hazel eyes. Her unique beauty once again struck Tipsy. Olive skin, high cheekbones, and unusual eyes framed by darkly dramatic brows and lashes.

"Hey, LeeLee." She followed up with the first thing that popped into her head. "You look so pretty."

"Gosh, thank you. I was just thinking the same thing about you."

Tipsy looked down at her workout clothes. "Thanks, but I haven't showered and I probably have paint in my eyebrows."

"Seriously. Mimi described you as *so pretty*, but she didn't do you justice."

"You're sweet. Is your office around here?"

LeeLee pointed down State Street. "Yes. Near State and Chalmers. I'm going to get some decent coffee. You…want to join me?"

"Ah…let me think…" *Of course* Tipsy wanted to join her. Here was the woman who had subtly called out her clairvoyance with an obscure poetry reference, but if she got coffee with LeeLee, she wouldn't have time to work before she met Mimi and May Penny. Practicality had to trump curiosity. "I'd love to, but I have to get home and start drawing." She pointed toward the gallery window. "Just dropped off that piece. Finish one, move on to the next."

LeeLee smiled at the parrot. "That bird wants to tell me a secret. A *funny* secret."

"That's the feeling I'm going for. I still owe you a text about getting the boys together. It's on my to-do list. You know, the one that's always running through my head and never gets shorter."

"Oh, I know it. *The Mom List.* I have one myself."

"Coffee another time?"

"Definitely." Tipsy added a new line to that mental to-do list. *Coffee with LeeLee. Confirm Madam Sosostris reference.* She pressed the unlock button on her car clicker, but LeeLee grabbed her arm as she started to walk around to the driver's side.

"Tipsy, wait." LeeLee squeezed gently. "There's a secret, *inside* the secret."

"Pardon?"

"The issue…that you and your friend are trying to solve. Your ginger friend."

"My *ginger* friend?"

"Yes. I think he's…" She let go of Tipsy's arm. "…*dead.* Is that possible?"

"How do you—what—"

"The problem has nothing to do with how he died. It's about the secret *inside* the secret."

"I don't understand what you're saying. I mean…I do…sort of. But how do you know about my…dead friend? And what you mean by *a secret inside a secret*?"

"I'm sorry I can't give you more details. These things are not always clear to me."

Holy shit, Granna. How does she know about Henry?

"His name is Henry?" asked LeeLee.

"Hold up. Did you just read my mind?"

LeeLee stepped away. "I felt like I had to tell you. It seems important to you…and Henry. When I met you, I realized you're…*different*. Like me. But we're *different* in different ways."

"How are we different in different ways?" Tipsy stepped closer to LeeLee. "Are you some kind of *Madame Sosostris* yourself?"

Tipsy, give the woman some breathing room! said Granna.

"Ha, right. Madame Sosostris. There I go, blabbing away. I'm sorry to confuse you, but I…I have to go." She smiled brightly, but given her quivering voice and the shaking hand she ran over her hair, she looked like she might faint. "Text me about the boys!"

With that, LeeLee Moretz resumed her quest for good coffee.

Tipsy was now certain that LeeLee Moretz had strange abilities of her own. She had recognized Tipsy's supernatural power, knew about her private interactions, and accessed her very thoughts. She pushed this fascinating new development to the back of her mind during her morning drawing session, as Jane and Henry's hand study (*The Hand Study* in her mind, as if it were the only hand study in the world) required absolute concentration. As soon as she hopped in her Tahoe to drive to May Penny's house on Sullivan's, she started chattering away with Granna in her head.

Seems like LeeLee is a clairvoyant horse of a different color, she said. *Like, an Appaloosa to my palomino.*

I've always said there must be other supernatural forces in this world.

Yeah, but it's super creepy to believe someone can be all up in my thoughts.

Tiffany Lynn, said Granna. *You got a lot of nerve, judging anyone else's abilities as creepy. You pretty much read thoughts when you're spying on dead people's memories.*

I know, but…they're dead. And it all happened a long time ago!

That's less creepy *than hearing a living person's thoughts in the here and now?*

Irk. You're right. But now I want to know more about what she can do, and what she knows about me, and Henry. Damnit. Why did she run off like that?

You can ask her over that cup of decent coffee.

You know damn well I will. Sooner rather than later. Although…she did seem freaked out. Maybe I'll let her stew a few days. She might reach out to me.

Yup. Let that Crock Pot simmer.

By 1:03pm, Tipsy was sitting on the Collins's dock overlooking Conch Creek and the Intracoastal Waterway. She joined Mimi and May Penny in Adirondack chairs under the covered pierhead that served as an outdoor living room crossed with a fish cleaning station. Tripp had hung old buoys and fishing lures from the rafters, and May Penny had countered with twinkly white lights and a sign from Hobby Lobby. *What Happens on the Dock, Stays on the Dock.*

Garnet Wave III, Tripp's center console Contender, was tied up below them. The glare off the pristinely maintained boat's pale blue hull, white Bimini hard top, and four shiny white 350-horsepower Yamaha engines made Tipsy's eyes water. In a salute to the garnet wave, a University of South Carolina banner flew from the dock's flagpole.

Tipsy looked past the plastic coyotes and the spinning silver fans that deterred pelicans and sea gulls from pooping on the dock. The Collins's house sat on the northern end of the island, close to Breach Inlet. To Tipsy's left, the Ravenel Bridge and the Old Village, and to her right, the Isle of Palms connector. Straight ahead: Conch Creek, the wider main channel of the Intracoastal, and approximately a mile of open marsh. At high tide, smaller boats crept through the narrow creeks that crisscrossed that expanse of green and brown. The resulting optical illusion made it seem like they were motoring through tall grass.

Even on an early Thursday afternoon, the Intracoastal bustled with boat traffic. Sailboats. Fishing trawlers. Jon boats. Kayaks. Many center consoles of various makes, models, and sizes. Some captains and their passengers seemed intent on catching fish, but more appeared to be out for afternoon pleasure cruises. They sipped beers, laughed boisterously, and blasted music from Pitbull to Prince to Patsy Cline. Tipsy wondered what those people did for a living, to have so much free time.

Low tide had exposed the oyster beds, as if nature was encouraging the three women to discuss the sharp edges of Ayers's marital problems. Mimi and May Penny wore their weekday afternoon casual attire, i.e., designer workout clothes. May Penny sported a white Athleta tennis dress and clunky Hoka running shoes. She removed her hot pink visor and propped her matching oversized Gucci sunglasses on her head. All her colored accents matched: visor, shades, bright coral lipstick. Mimi had pulled her blonde hair back in a smooth ponytail and she wore solid black yoga ensemble. Poufy fuchsia bows on her flip-flops highlighted her bright pink toenails. As always, Mimi and May Penny complemented each other, even if they were worlds apart in personality.

They discussed their latest workout routines (May Penny had taken up pickleball and Mimi joined a new barre studio) before they got to the meat of the conversational sandwich.

"Tipsy, do you know why we asked you here today?" May Penny sounded like a cross between Sherlock Holmes and Jerry Springer.

"I assume it's related to Big Ayers's tackle box in the foyer. I'd make him store that thing in the garage. You give him an inch, and you'll have a cooler of night crawlers on your dining room table."

"I figured you knew what's going on," said Mimi. "After all, you've been his therapist for the past couple years."

Before Tipsy replied, May Penny heaved a sigh and tossed her bobbed blonde hair. "I *cannot* believe it's come to this. My *only son*. Divorced, *again*. My, my, my. Where did I go wrong? I loved him, cherished him, and gave him every little thing he ever wanted."

She answered her own question with that last bit, said Granna, as May Penny went on.

"All I have *ever* wanted is my son's happiness. Yet somehow, happiness eludes him." Her voice trembled, as if on the verge of tears, but once she delivered her soliloquy, she turned to Tipsy with dry, discerning eyes. "Tipsy, there was a time when I believed you abandoned him because you were a terrible person."

"Mama!" said Mimi.

"I…Ah…I never meant to—"

May Penny held up one hand toward Mimi, and the other toward Tipsy, as if casting spells over them. "Wait now, ladies. Let me finish. I'm not *wrong* often, but when I am, I admit it. I wanted to blame you, but Ayers's behavior when y'all were in the thickest part of the divorce bramblebush forced me to accept some harsh truths about him. I know you put up with…*a lot*…during your marriage."

As May Penny talked, Tipsy's hackles settled. "Thank you," she said, and Mimi reached over and squeezed her shoulder.

"We acknowledge that Ayers is difficult," said May Penny.

"He absolutely is," said Tipsy, "but Kate is equally challenging. They both need to be handled with kid gloves, and neither one wears them."

"It seems like Ayers has been *trying* to compromise," said Mimi.

"He has, in his way, but he's still Ayers," said Tipsy. "Blunt. Short fuse. Stubborn as a herd of mules. Based on what Ayers has told me and my observations of Scott's dealings with Kate, she's just as ornery."

"Do you think they *should* split up?" asked Mimi.

"No. If not her, it will be someone else. At least she's a known entity. I don't want Ayers condemned to a lifetime of misery, but I'd rather they both try harder to work it out."

"We agree," said May Penny. "That's the message we're sending, but he seems hell bent on rejecting the delivery. He spoke to a realtor about selling their house, and he paid a retainer to Clark Middleton. Clark is drafting a divorce settlement."

"He's already told the kids they're getting divorced," said Tipsy. "They're freaking out. I've spoken with the girls, but Little A won't discuss anything. He's…pissed. At his dad. At Kate. At me for pestering him about it. At the world."

"Good gravy," said Mimi. "We all know Ayers blows hot, then he blows cold. He blows the wind right up under your skirt, and then just as quickly, things blow over. Next week, he might be madly in love with Kate again. He should *not* have dragged the kids into it."

"So what are you planning to do about this distasteful spectacle in the making, Tipsy?" asked May Penny.

"*Do* about it?"

"You're a mama bear. There's no way you'll take this threat to your cubs lying down."

"I *have* considered...keeping the kids with me. Not forever, but until things calm down for Ayers."

"Aren't you getting married soon?"

"Yes. Memorial Day weekend."

"Ayers has gotten used to the idea of you and Scott," said May Penny. "He even tentatively likes him. But he won't be usurped."

"I don't intend anything like that," said Tipsy. "It would be *temporary*. And of course, I'd bring the kids over here to see all of y'all."

"I won't support you taking my son's time with his children. Not when we don't know how long this will go on."

"That's the point. We're facing months of him lugging all three kids over here every other weekend. They love hanging out with y'all, but they need a home."

"Kind of like the *home* our family has provided for *you* all these years," said May Penny, her voice dangerously hard. She didn't need to elaborate. Miss Callie's house might belong to Mimi's husband's family, but Tipsy had long understood that she and her kids had moved in, and stayed there, due to May Penny and Tripp's influence.

An unpleasant tingle at the base of her neck reminded her of her old fear of May Penny's wrath. Over the past few years, she'd come to depend on her former mother-in-law's support and assistance with the kids, and she'd even grown fond of her. She hated to sacrifice their relationship, but May Penny was right. Mama Bear had to look out for her cubs. "May Penny, I haven't decided on any course of action. I don't even understand what's possible."

"I'm glad you and your new husband are buying that house, but you've got your own changes coming, so let's not blame all the instability Ayers."

May Penny's observation annoyed her. She may have a valid point, but notwithstanding the increasing ghostly complications, Tipsy and Scott had been methodically planning this transition since they began discussing marriage a year ago. Leave it to Ayers to upend his own life just when she was solidifying hers.

"I will do everything in my power to make this a smooth transition for them. Like I have with every other transition we've faced." Tipsy looked at her phone. "I have to go. Got to get in carpool line."

She stood, and both Collins women stood with her. May Penny stepped back and crossed her arms over her chest, but Mimi hugged her. "I'll keep you in the loop if Ayers talks to me."

"I'll share whatever he tells me, too." Tipsy turned to May Penny. "Thanks for having the kids here last weekend."

"They're *always* welcome. As often as necessary."

"For the record, we all agree that the best outcome would be Ayers staying married," said Mimi. "Yes?"

"*Agreed*," said May Penny.

"Agreed." Tipsy felt like they were creating a new Fellowship of the Ring. She wasn't sure who represented the graceful elves, or the precocious hobbits, or the race of mortal men who above all crave power, but as she looked down at May Penny's jutting chin and stubbornly furrowed brow, she knew where the dwarves stood.

"I ran into LeeLee Moretz at Pinegrounds the other day," said Mimi. "She said she met you!"

Tipsy turned from May Penny's scowl to Mimi's perky smile. "Yup. She seems really cool."

"Oh, she is. She's—"

"The young woman who works for *Darlene Donnelly's* law firm?" asked May Penny.

"Right," said Mimi.

"Hmmm. Darlene and I went to school together. She's a tough cookie. I assume she's tough in the *courtroom,* too." May Penny eyed Tipsy as Mimi's phone rang.

"My barre instructor," said Mimi. "Trying to reschedule my private session tomorrow." She answered the phone and walked toward the porch railing.

"Like I said…I gotta…" Tipsy pointed at the door.

"I know you'll explore your options, Tipsy," said May Penny. "Let's keep those options *out of the family court.*"

~

When Tipsy thought back on the precarious early days of her post-divorce life, she hardly recognized herself in her own memories. A frightened, lonely woman who had discovered two frightened, lonely souls in her new home. Tipsy's life had evolved in ways she couldn't have imagined back then. Her relationships. Her career. Her understanding of herself and the world around her. At the beginning of their friendship, Jane was in an even worse position then Tipsy. The woman was dead, crazy, and trapped in a house with the husband she detested. Jane had leapt all those hurdles and sprinted the last leg of the race, only to trip after crossing the finish line. She'd landed flat on her face and knocked herself out cold. When she woke up, she was right back where she started—stuck in Miss Callie's house, a ghost without substance or purpose, with only Tipsy and her questionably sane husband for company.

After her stressful meeting with May Penny and Mimi, Tipsy needed chill time. Once the kids settled into their post-dinner and homework wind down activities, she retreated to the front porch with a glass of sweet tea. Happily, she found Jane had the same idea. "Hey, friend," said Tipsy, as she sat in the rocker beside Jane. "How are you holding up?"

"As well as can be *expected,*" said Jane, in her fey voice. She blink-blink-blinked at the dying sunlight and tucked her small, pale feet under herself. Tipsy smiled at the familiarity of it all—Jane's musical accent, her habit of curling her slender limbs underneath her like a cat, and her incessant blinking. It seemed no time had passed, and in the long span of Jane's existence, the four years she'd spent away from this house were a single blink of her pale blue, almond-shaped eyes.

"I wish I could put a blanket over you. You look so cold and fragile."

Jane gave her a weak smile. "I'm far from *fragile*. On the contrary, I seem frustratingly indestructible."

"I can't imagine how frustrated you must feel. I'm so sorry."

"You still apologize for things that are wholly *not* your responsibility."

"Sorry isn't the right word. It's kind of a catchall for commiseration. So…*I empathize*."

"That's better." Jane's smile widened, until she looked almost normal by deceased standards.

"I've been working on my excessive apologizing. It's easier now, since my fiancé doesn't intimidate me, or make me feel like I'm unreasonably demanding."

"I've seen your betrothed around the house. Remind me of his name?"

"Scott."

"Henry said he's a doctor. The kind who helps those whose minds are disturbed. That's a true calling. He seems kind, and he's always laughing. He's tidy! He's even handsome."

"He is all of those things. I'm very fortunate."

"So is he, my sweet friend. He has you, and your *darling* children. Y'all are a proper big family."

"We're getting there. He has his own son and daughter. Blended families are challenging—"

"Blended families?"

"Scott and I are both divorced with our own kids. We're getting remarried and combining into one unit. Voila, *blended family*."

"Sounds like y'all are *ingredients* in a favorite *cake* recipe."

"That's a nice way to put it. Makes it seem less intimidating! Anyway, it's not always easy, but we're making great progress."

"Little Ayers and the twins have grown *so much* since last I saw them. Even Mary Pratt and Olivia Grace are taller than me. Although, with my stature, that's to be expected. Are they doing well in school?"

"Oh, yes. Mary Pratt sometimes gets in trouble for her sassiness—"

"A child after my *own heart*."

"But they all make very good grades. Olivia Grace reads like a young Henry. Little Ayers is at Pinegrounds School now."

"John Huger went to Pinegrounds. Connie and I attended Cooper Hall. It was the only option for young ladies. We girls visited Pinegrounds for dance lessons, and the boys came to Cooper Hall for socials, like high tea."

"Henry went to boarding school, right?"

"He attended Catholic school when we were young. Frederick Mott was raised Catholic," said Jane, and Fred Mott's clandestine reverence for the Catholic cathedral in Henry's memory suddenly made sense. "Patience grew up in some *backcountry* church on Edisto Island. They gave all that up and joined St. Philip's. Papists and snake handlers weren't well tolerated in my parents' circle. The Motts cared more about the opinions of their neighbors than their eternal salvation."

"From what I've learned about Fred and Patty over the last few years, that doesn't surprise me."

"Given Henry's *odd manner*, they thought he needed a firm hand. When those *monstrous* Dominican priests couldn't tame him, they sent him to Woodberry Forest School, in Virginia. He only came home during the summer."

"Not even for the holidays?"

"No. The Motts didn't want the *embarrassment* of him at Christmas Eve service."

"It's a wonder Henry turned out as normal as he did, between his screwy family and his secret, solo clairvoyance. I met his mother a couple years ago. Her ghost, of course."

"That doesn't surprise me one skinny bit. I imagine Patience kept on existing out of *pure stubborn spite*. Henry told me y'all found her haunting her old house on Bull Street, and that she made amends with him before she moved on."

"She did, but that doesn't change what happened in the past. I've seen how she treated him in his memories. You stuck up for him. To her, and everyone else."

"We stuck up for each other."

"You just said you were sassy, like my M.P. I can't imagine you needed people to stick up for you very often."

"It's easier to stand for others than for yourself. You know I dabbled in acting in my youth."

Tipsy nodded, and Jane went on.

"When Henry returned from Europe and we...*you know*..."

"Started courting? Dating? Hanging out? Fell madly in love?"

"All of the above, I suppose. Anyway, in those first...passionate months, Henry *loved* watching me on stage. He was so proud of me, but my parents wanted me to quit. All that nonsense about being a proper lady. Scaring away husbands. Scandalous costumes and vulgar language."

"Ugh. I would *not* have done well in those days. I love scandalous costumes and vulgar language. Thankfully, my preferences didn't scare Scott away."

"It didn't scare Henry, either. He went to my father and spoke on my behalf. Daddy could be *mighty intimidating*, and he was already hesitant about Henry and me. I worried Daddy would drop kick Henry right off our piazza for running his mouth, but Henry somehow convinced him, and my parents relented for a few years."

"And Mr. Robinette gave y'all his blessing to get married?"

"Eventually. Henry's *gumption* actually *convinced* him. Afterward, he told me that Henry's great love for me shone through in his argument."

"That's so sweet. It seems like y'all were destined for one another."

"There was always *something* between us. When we were children, I found him...*fascinating*. I don't know how else to describe it. All the other boys were so simple. Henry always lingered in the back of my mind."

"In his memories, he showed me how he clung to that connection even when y'all were apart for years."

"I did, too, in my way." She smiled. "I remember how he'd *pop* into my mind like a bubble, at the *strange*st times...once I...would you like to see?"

Tipsy looked over her shoulder. Knowing Henry, he might be lurking in the bushes. "I promised Henry that I'd let you rest. Not bug you about returning from the dead and seeing memories and what not. Are you strong enough?"

"I believe so. Henry told me how he's shown you pieces of the past by thinking hard on a special memory. I'd like to try it. Perhaps it will be helpful as we try to understand what's happening with us. As I said in my message to the young woman with the pretty auburn hair—"

"Catherine Porcher."

Jane nodded. "Yes, her. I said we must *both* understand our story—our whole story—to find peace. It took two of us to live and die as we did, and now it will take two of us to set things right."

"I can't argue with that." Tipsy held up her hand, and then lowered it. "It's so good to hear you talk about Henry…nicely."

"Given what you witnessed between us when you moved into this house, I understand why simple niceness would be a relief." Jane looked down into her lap. Her fingers twirled among themselves, solid and then translucent and solid again. Before she moved on, Tipsy often caught Jane engaged in this kind of fidgeting. She thought of it as Jane knitting with invisible needles. "He's been *so kind* the past few days. So attentive," the ghost said, with a sweet smile. "Perhaps this time together in our old home will be an unexpected gift."

"The chance to be a normal couple." Tipsy raised her hand, palm out, as if offering Jane something sacred, like a communion wafer.

Jane's smooth palm met Tipsy's. "I don't know if I'd ever describe Henry and myself as a normal couple."

The bedroom Tipsy stands in is gloriously girly, with pale blue walls, lacy curtains, and a thick lavender and periwinkle quilt on a cast iron bed. All the furniture is white, including the bedframe, the carved armoire, and the tea table set with pink China. Dolls and worn stuffed animals are piled on a white hope chest, and a white curio cabinet contains porcelain animal figurines. On the white nightstand: a pile of books, and a framed black and white photograph of two dark-haired little girls in pale dresses.

Tipsy recognizes little Jane and Constance Robinette, so this must be one of their bedrooms, at the Robinette House on Water Street. On the other bedside table, a Tiffany lamp casts weak yellowish light over the room. Whatever the date of this memory, Pierre and Theresa Robinette have already invested in some electrical wiring.

A scratching sound draws Tipsy's attention to the far corner of the room. Young Jane sits at her dressing table and rakes a brush through her long black hair. It's angry brushing, and Tipsy knows it stings, but Jane doesn't care. She should be celebrating, and instead, she's staring at her own bloodshot eyes and about to pull her hair right out of her head.

Paintings of purple flowers adorn the wall—violets, tulips, hydrangeas. The biggest piece features clusters of delicate purplish-blue and pinkish blossoms on long stalks. Tipsy can't put a name on them, but similar frond-like blooms burst from a vase on Jane's nightstand. She approaches the big painting, and reads the spidery writing underneath the blossoms. The text under the purple-blue flowers reads, Baptisia Australis, or False "Wild" Indigo. *Under the pinkish ones,* Indigofera Tinctoria, or True Indigo. *Tipsy looks closely at the flowers in the vase. They appear to be the indigo blooms of the false variety.*

The door opens and Jane's sister, Constance, enters. She tiptoes toward Jane and her vengeful hairbrush, and hovers behind her, wringing her hands.

"Janie, be gentle," says Connie.

"If I'm to be hidden away in a kitchen for all eternity, why should I care if my hair is ragged?"

"You're being dramatic. You're also about to knock over those flowers with your flailing elbows."

Jane slides the vase across the desk. "I'm an actress. I'm supposed to be dramatic. Didn't I just play Juliet?"

Connie sits on the edge of the bed. "You did, and you were lovely. Everyone thinks so."

"Everyone but Mama and Daddy."

"They're proud of you."

"So proud they've decided this is my last performance!" Jane's eyes sting, but she refuses to cry anymore. At almost seventeen, she's already learned that

no one takes a woman seriously if she cries, and tonight, she's shed enough tears to float that great ship that everyone is talking about, the Titanic. The one that's supposedly unsinkable, and is crossing the Atlantic on its way to New York city at this very moment. She's heard there is all manner of entertainment on such ships. Perhaps they need Shakespearean actresses. Maybe she will run away to New York, join a traveling theater troupe, and sail around the world.

As soon as she thinks it, guilt and fear wash over her. She could never leave her parents, whom she adores, or her beloved Connie. She also knows down deep that she doesn't want to live up north, where it's frigid cold and people have harsh accents and poor manners. She needs the salt air and sunshine and the soothing familiarity of her hometown. She fancies herself more independent than the average girl, but she isn't that brave. Still, she's angry, and she plans to let her family know it.

"I'm a good girl. I do what I'm told—"

"Like when you climbed Grandmere's tree at the Old Cannon and hung upside down with your skirts in your face and your bloomers showing?"

"I was seven, *Connie. No one had told me not to hang from the tree—"*

"That's a given for young ladies." She pointed at the vase of flowers. "You're as wild as that indigo."

"— and I got down as soon as Daddy hollered at me. I don't understand why they're hollering at me now. They always encouraged me to act when we were children. You remember all the plays we used to make up."

"That was different. We were small, and they were amused when we dressed up in their clothes and told our silly versions of bible stories. It's different now that we're near grown. I'm surprised they've let you take it this far. Only you could convince Mama to convince Daddy to let you prance around on the stage at the Dock Street Theater."

Jane stares at her own puffy face in the mirror. Her eyes, which she knows are her best feature, stand out from her face. Red lines radiate from her blue irises like the stripes in a warped American flag. She pulls her purple housecoat tighter around her shoulders.

Connie takes the brush from Jane and gently runs it over her head. As she brushes, the tension runs out of Jane's shoulders. "I wish they understood how much I love *acting," says Jane. "Especially Mama. I always thought she understood."*

"Mama is so dedicated to her family that she thinks of nothing else. She can't fathom how any other woman could think of anything else, either. She loves nothing more than recipes and making the house pretty and—"

"And finding husbands for her girls." Jane glowers at her reflection.

"Is she still on about Johnny?"

"Not lately, praise the lord."

"She'll drop that hot potato eventually. Deep down she knows y'all are only friends."

"Can you imagine marrying Johnny? It'd be like marrying our brother, if we had one."

"Besides, you know how he is." Connie blushes.

Jane nods. She loves Johnny as a member of her own family, but even she questions his moral scruples when it comes to young ladies. Just last year, a rumor had flown around church that John's parents made him seek the counsel of Proctor James, the junior rector, after they found him in an indelicate position with a pretty barmaid from one of the taverns on the wharf. He'd had the audacity to sneak the girl into the Huger's house at the corner of Meeting Street and South Battery. He tied sheets together and tossed them over the second floor piazza. The girl tied the sheet-rope around her waist, and Johnny hauled her right up to his own bedroom. Thank goodness his knot held and his arms were strong, for Mr. Huger would have been rightfully embarrassed if the girl had plunged to her death from his piazza after an indecent liaison with his sixteen-year-old son. It was rather hilarious at the time, but when Mrs. Robinette and Mrs. Huger got together and started hinting that maybe what Johnny needed was a wife from a good family to settle him down, the situation lost its humor.

"Oh, I certainly do know," says Jane. "I'd marry the Reverend himself before I married Johnny."

"Now there's *an ironic statement," whispers the unseen Tipsy.*

"You'd make a poor preacher's wife," says Connie, "with your acting and your hanging upside down."

Jane leans against her sister. "You don't have to worry about Mama trying to marry you off. You already made her happy with Andrew."

"I feel fortunate. Andrew has been my sweetheart for so long, I don't know how to love anyone else."

"I don't know how to love anyone at all."

"Your great love is out there, Janie. You can have your pick. All the boys in town have always been in love with you."

Jane responds with a pretty snort. "They don't love me. They love the pretty picture Mama turns me into."

"I don't think that's true."

Jane doesn't argue with her. She adores her sister, but Connie is only fifteen, and her straightforward romantic life has made her naïve. Connie taps Jane's head with the brush. "All you do is break their hearts, anyway. You're only in love with the stage."

"I'll be quite lonely when Mama and Daddy take that away from me."

"Give them time, sissy. I bet they'll come around. I'll talk to Mama, too."

"Will you?" Jane reaches up and grabs Connie's hand. It's no small thing for her sister to question her parents. Unlike Jane, she doesn't have it in her to make demands or thumb her nose at convention.

"Sure will. We'll be practicing your lines in the parlor in no time."

Her sister's support buoys Jane, and she squints at herself in the mirror again. She opens the drawer to her dressing table, selects a cotton square, and dabs it in the dish of lemon water beside the mirror. Hopefully she can stave off the puffiness before it spreads to the rest of her face. Her daddy likes her to be pert and positive, not bedraggled and glowering. If she wants to convince him to let her audition for the Dock Street's summer productions, she needs to charm him.

She and Connie chat about Andrew and his family, and speculate on how long it will take him to propose once he finishes his studies at the Citadel, and where the two of them might live. The Bishops and the Robinettes will provide for the new couple to set up their first home, and Connie is already following in their mother's elegant footsteps. She spends most of her time thinking about wallpaper and draperies and perusing sewing patterns. Jane envies her sister's simple happiness. Connie doesn't question her role in their family's planning, and she loves Andrew with a sweet dedication that Jane might have found contrived if she didn't know that Constance had been in love with Andrew Bishop since they played Mary and Joseph in the St. Philip's Christmas Pageant.

As Connie chatters, Jane thinks about the role she just played. The star-crossed relationship of Romeo and Juliet could not be less like Connie and Andrew's slow, lifelong romance. Connie and Andrew's stars had aligned perfectly before they were old enough to know it. As for Jane, she will never fulfill her mother's dream and marry John Huger, who is fixing to be an even more eligible bachelor than Andrew Bishop. Andrew is handsome and charming, and his family is old and rich, but the Hugers are even older and richer, and as for looks, no one outshines Johnny. Theresa and Pierre will think themselves highly successful parents if they marry off Connie to Andrew and Jane to John.

No matter what her parents want, Jane will not marry John. And despite Connie's speculation that all the boys in town are in love with her, she doesn't think Johnny wants to marry her, either. He flirts with her endlessly, but he flirts with all the girls. He flirts with Mrs. Lamboll, the eighty-something-year-old Sunday School teacher.

Jane dabs cold cream on her eyelids and laughs to herself, as she remembers Johnny handing Mrs. Lamboll a bunch of flowers he'd picked from her garden, at the old lady's seventy-fifth birthday party, so long ago. Even then, Mrs. Lamboll was too dotty and enthralled with John to realize he gifted her with her own camellias. That was after they cut the cake—but she remembers feeling unsettled by something…what was it?

A face swims into her mind. Henry Mott—that odd boy they'd grown up with, with the fiery red hair, dark blue eyes, and gloomy manner. Henry's mother had given him a slice of cake, but he sat on a bench and stared out at the garden, with the plate untouched on his lap. She remembers wondering if he was still upset by Johnny and the other boys teasing him. Something about the way he sat there silently while everyone else chatted and ate sweets had both intrigued her and pulled at her. She had wondered what Henry Mott was thinking. She had felt bad for him. He seemed so lonely.

Not long after the party, Henry's parents had sent him to boarding school. She's heard nothing of him in years.

She stands to get dressed in something her father will like—her lavender striped dress will do. Daddy bought it for her, for he knows she loves purple, so it will make him smile to be reminded of how well he knows his little girl. As she removes the dress from the armoire, she feels a little like Juliet, longing for Romeo. Jane's longing is for a person who doesn't yet exist, or at least, hasn't yet shown himself in her life. It's only a vague longing for some imagined sentiment, or kinship, or comfort. But he has to be out there, somewhere, the man who can provide all that. After all, Juliet stumbled upon Romeo in the most unlikely of places. For a moment, as she unbuttons the purple striped dress, Jane wonders if Henry Mott is still lonely.

Chapter 6

M.P. and O-Liv voluntarily kept Tipsy informed of their feelings about their dad's predicament. They described the situation as *lowkey so annoying*. At first, her children's use of *lowkey* had confused Tipsy even more than the typical generational miscommunication. When a storm knocked over her potted plants on the front porch, Little Ayers had informed her that the flowers got *lowkey massacred* by the wind. Why combine such a forceful verb as *massacre*, with a descriptive that indicated casualness? The girls sometimes referred to an ugly outfit as *lowkey hideous* or their GiGi's meatloaf as *lowkey gross*. It seemed to indicate that something was serious, but also not *that* bad, or perhaps it was a Gen-Z way of softening the blow. As in, *her dress is lowkey hideous, bless her heart.*

Tipsy's interpretation of *lowkey so annoying* gave her the sense that the girls were frustrated, trying to make the best of it, and felt sort of sorry for their father. They clued her in on their plan to ask GiGi to move them out of the bunk room and into one of the spare bedrooms (Mary Pratt: "There's like *five* other bedrooms! Why should we have to listen to Ayers and his friends arguing about video games? Boys are lowkey so dumb."). While they hadn't seen Chloe, she didn't seem upset with them (Olivia Grace: "She's still texting us like normal, so I think she's lowkey clueless."). Little A, however, remained uncharacteristically glum and taciturn. He resisted her gentle questioning about his state of mind. For the first time, he was shutting her out. It was lowkey heartbreaking.

On Saturday of Tipsy's kid weekend, the girls had all-day volleyball clinic, but Little Ayers had nothing on his agenda, so she dropped him off at a friend's house. Now that he attended private school, his friends lived all over town. Mount Pleasant, downtown, James Island, the Isle of Palms, even far flung Johns Island. A happy coincidence that his chosen Saturday hangout was happening in I'On, Scott's neighborhood a few miles from the Old Village.

No kids to monitor, so she planned a productive afternoon. She hit the gym, worked on *The Hand Study*, caught up on business and social media stuff, and made it in and out of Target without purchasing any candles, coffee mugs, bathing suits, or beach chairs. Tipsy and Scott planned to eschew weekend get-togethers with the children until Scott's kids were in the know, but she missed him, so she dropped in on him before picking up Little Ayers.

When she arrived, he was sitting at his kitchen table with his laptop in front of him. Tipsy encouraged him to avoid work on Saturdays, but as he'd taken on more administrative responsibilities, it was harder for him to get away from it. He glared into the computer and typed ferociously.

He hadn't trimmed his beard, and his hair stuck up in the back like Dennis the Menace. He clearly rolled out of bed and opened his computer.

"Where are the kids?" she asked him.

"Uh…Chloe's at Town Centre at the movies with friends. Tristin is…ah…skateboarding in the neighborhood." *Type-type-type-type.*

"Hmm." She stood behind him and rubbed his shoulders, then got him a fresh glass of iced coffee, but there would be no distracting him until he put out whatever fire was blazing through the hospital's psychiatric ward. She leaned down and whispered in his ear. "I'll leave you to it."

He rubbed his eyes and grabbed her hand. "I'm sorry. It's these emails about the physician payment restructuring. And then stuff about Medicaid reimbursement—"

"It's okay, baby. You'll feel better once you've addressed it."

"I know, but my grumpy ass is ignoring you on a pretty Saturday—"

"Shhhh."

"Maybe I should really consider private practice. But it would be a leap of faith." He looked up at her with tired blue eyes. "It freaks me out."

"I know. Have you done any more research?" They'd been tossing the idea around for a while. Private practice could eventually be more lucrative for Scott, but she knew he worried about stepping off the predictable track of academic medicine.

"Going to call a guy back in Nashville who recently made the jump and bounce ideas off him." He rubbed his eyes. "I have to get all those documents to the closing attorneys about the house."

"Buying Miss Callie's house, or selling this one?"

"Both."

"And Tristan is so damn moody, and his grades are slipping—"

"Tris? He's always been such a good student."

"He inherited my math brain, and hence, he's no Ernest Hemingway. Crappy grade on his last paper, so his English grade fell. Last week he bombed a history test. Kate blames me. Says I'm not monitoring him enough over here."

"Can I do anything to help?"

"No. I'm fine. There's just a lot going on right now."

The anxiety in his eyes and his uncharacteristically disheveled appearance reiterated that she had to get Jane and Henry sorted out soon. Jane seemed perfectly fine after showing Tipsy the memory of her teenage angst, so it was time to start pushing, whether Henry liked it or not. Work, kids, the move—Scott truly had enough to worry about.

"It *is* a lot, for everyone," she said. "I'll support whatever you decide to do, work-wise, and if you make a change, we'll figure out the details together."

He squeezed her hand. "Team Scipsy."

"Rahrahrah." She smiled and kissed him. "Now finish up before you get Chloe."

"They'll get TCBY after, so I have time." As soon as he faced the computer, the scowl returned. His fingers flew over the keys, and two more emails popped up in his inbox.

She returned to her truck, drove a few blocks to Little A's friend's house, and texted her son. He came out with his skateboard under one arm.

"Hey, buddy," she said. "Did y'all see Tristan while you were skateboarding? Scott told me he was out in the neighborhood, too."

"Yeah," said Ayers, as he closed the door.

"That's fun. Did y'all skate together for a while?"

"Yeah."

"Did you get ice cream at the Square Onion?"

"Uh huh."

"Everything okay?"

He shrugged.

"You know you can talk to me, right?"

He nodded, and looked out the window. She didn't turn on the radio, so he couldn't hide behind music. The wheels in his head finally rolled to a stop and he spoke. "It was weird seeing Tristan when I have to lie to him about Dad and Kate getting divorced."

"Ah. I see. You're not really lying to him, are you?"

"Not regular lying. But it's still a kind of lying, since I know something he'd want to know and I'm not telling."

"That's called lying by omission."

"Like a secret mission?"

"Sort of."

"Are we going to have to stay with GiGi and BopBop every weekend with Dad?"

"I don't know, honey. We have to see how things play out."

"I don't want to. GiGi makes us all sleep in the bunkroom. Me, and the girls. It's, like, embarrassing when I'm playing video games with my friends. Them blabbing away in the background. They lowkey never shut up."

"Yeah. The girls aren't crazy about that arrangement either."

"Plus Gigi wants us to go to bed at, like, eight. It's, like, ridiculous. She treats me like a baby."

"Hmmm. Ayers, I know you're upset, but—"

"I'm *sorry* I'm being *mean* about Gigi and BopBop and the girls. I love them all."

He didn't say he *lowkey* loved them all, but he didn't sound genuine, either. In fact, he sounded a little condescending. For the first time, Tipsy sensed her son placating her.

"I should hope so."

He sighed, and her sincere little boy was back. "I *am* sorry, Mom. But it sucks—er…stinks."

She let the suckiness slide, because he was twelve, and it did suck.

"I understand. I wish there was something your dad could do, or I could do—"

"Can't we stay with you? Please?"

She clenched the steering wheel. She couldn't look at him—his big gray eyes, so like her own—or her resolve to co-parent in a healthy way with proper boundaries would dissolve into a puddle of his unshed tears. "Buddy, I would love that. But that's not how we do things in our family. We have a schedule, so Dad and I both have time with y'all, because you have two parents who love you, and two parents that y'all love."

Out of the corner of her eye, she saw him swipe his. "Fine," he said. "Whatever."

"Ayers—"

"*Whatever,* Mom. Let's go home. That's what I want. *Home*," he said.

Tipsy drove on in silence, but she was thinking about coffee with LeeLee Moretz. When they pulled up to the house, Ayers immediately got out of the car. Tipsy followed him inside. He didn't stomp, nor did he slam any doors, but it wasn't far off.

As he disappeared upstairs, Tipsy set her purse on the console table. She sent Scott a text. LITTLE AYERS FINALLY TALKED TO ME. SORT OF. THERE WAS A LOT OF UH HUH AND FINE AND WHATEVER.

She opened a text from Lindsey. Tipsy had sent her a gif earlier that day: the teacher from *Ferris Bueller's Day Off,* endlessly repeating the absent Ferris's last name and getting no reply.

LINDSEY: I'M SORRY I'VE BEEN SO MIA. I'VE BEEN HAVING MORNING SICKNESS, ALTHOUGH IT'S REALLY ALL DAY SICKNESS. PAUL HAS BEEN WAKING UP IN THE MIDDLE OF THE NIGHT AGAIN. I'M SO TIRED I CAN'T THINK STRAIGHT, SO PARDON IF THESE TEXTS ARE INCOHERENT.

TIPSY: IT'S OKAY. JUST A LITTLE WORRIED ABOUT YOU. ☺ CAN I HELP?

LINDSEY: CAN YOU MAKE P.D. CHOOSE HIS FAMILY OVER FLOUNDER GIGGING? Another message came through immediately. HAHA.

Tipsy took a moment to reply. A *haha* ending in a period. The second text was meant to mask the truth in the first one.

TIPSY: I WISH I COULD, HONEY. AYERS WAS THE SAME WAY. IT CAN MAKE A MAMA FEEL LONELY.

LINDSEY: HE IS WHO HE IS, AND IT IS WHAT IT IS.

That kind of gloomy resignation was unlike Lindsey. Tipsy's worry kicked up a notch.

TIPSY: HAVE Y'ALL TRIED COUNSELING? THE TIME TO GO IS NOW, BEFORE YOUR RESENTMENT–Tipsy almost wrote *becomes insurmountable,* but instead, she typed—KEEPS BUILDING AND EXPLODES.

LINDSEY: IT ALREADY EXPLODED LAST NIGHT. P.D. SLEPT ON THE SOFA. ALTHOUGH HE PROBABLY DIDN'T MIND BEING AWAY FROM ME TOSSING AND TURNING WITH HEARTBURN. AND BEING OUT OF RANGE OF PAUL'S FUSSING. NOT THAT DISTANCE MATTERS. HE ALWAYS SLEEPS THROUGH THE CRYING.

TIPSY: MEN HAVE SELECTIVE HEARING. BUT SERIOUSLY, THERAPY?

LINDSEY: MAYBE. I GOTTA GO. EMMA NEEDS HELP WITH A HISTORY PAPER. THANKS FOR LISTENING. LOVE YA.

TIPSY: LOVE YOU! HANG IN THERE.

Tipsy took a moment to consider all the disgruntled souls in her life. Lindsey and P.D. Big Ayers and Kate. Henry and Jane. All three of her kids. Even her stressed out Scott. One of those intense rushes of gratitude hit her. As she opened a text box to remind him how much she loved him, she received a message from him.

SCOTT: ALL YOU CAN DO IS KEEP TRYING TO GET THROUGH TO LITTLE AYERS. IF YOU CAN REACH ME WHEN I'M IN THE 7TH CIRCLE OF EMAIL HELL, YOU CAN GET THROUGH TO ANYONE. THANKS FOR YOUR PATIENCE. AND YOUR SUPPORT. SOMETIMES IT FEELS LIKE I'M STILL GETTING USED TO IT.

TIPSY: IT'S SO EASY TO BE PATIENT WITH YOU. WE'LL FIGURE OUT THIS WORK STUFF. LOVE YOU SO MUCH. CALL ME LATER.

Pounding feet on the stairs behind her announced Little Ayers. He scooted around her, basketball in hand. He muttered something about going to a neighborhood friend's house.

"We just walked in the door, buddy," she said. "How about you chill out and have a snack."

He turned and said, with his uncanny maturity, "I'd rather go shoot baskets than sit around in my room. The more I sit, the more I'll think about Dad, and the more annoyed I'll get."

Tipsy ran a hand over his forehead. His hair was still damp from his skateboarding adventures. "Get a glass of water from the kitchen and drink it before you go."

His mouth twitched in a smile. "Water. Mom's famous medicine."

"You know it. Take a granola bar, too."

"Yes, ma'am," he said.

Once he walked out the door, rehydrated and with granola bar in hand, Tipsy walked out onto the front porch herself. She had a couple hours before she had to get the girls. Weird to be in this position, where no one needed her. Maybe she could get another memory out of Jane.

"Jane? You around?" She tried a few more times, but Jane didn't appear.

Maybe that last memory took more out of her than you thought, said Granna.

Hmm. Tipsy didn't love that idea, as it would slow her down, but Granna may be right. If she couldn't get anywhere with Jane, she might as well make more progress on the hand study. She stretched her arms over her head and flexed her neck to work out the kinks. As she rubbed her achy right wrist, she noticed the ghost boy with the birthmark standing on a mound of fill dirt, watching her.

How opportune, Granna. A conveniently located ghost has a mystery that needs solving, and here I am with my jacked up wrist. A sign to give the painting appendages a rest.

I can't argue with your taking care of your arm any more than a baseball coach would argue with his star pitcher.

Tipsy looked up and down the street. Pretty deserted on a late Saturday afternoon. The neighbors had finished their daytime plans, or they were preparing for their evening plans. She waved to the ghost boy. He looked over his shoulder, as if the construction team had returned and Tipsy had waved to one of them. When he realized no one else could be the target of her salutation, he tentatively waved back. He shifted from one foot to the other, and the purplish-blue light around him changed hue as he fidgeted. Dark, then light, then an in-between shade when he stood still. Tipsy thought of the flowers on the teenage Jane's wall—false indigo. No, *wild* indigo. Wild indigo seemed more apropos for this flighty, reclusive spirit.

She walked to the edge of the property and beckoned to him. He vanished and reappeared under an oak tree near the sidewalk. She put her phone to her ear as she walked toward him. "Hi there," she said.

He looked between her eyes and the phone. "Are you speaking to me?"

"Yes. Don't mind the phone. It's a prop to fend off gossipy neighbors." She held it away from her face for a moment. "You know what these are, right? Our fancy modern phones?"

He nodded. "The men who are working here have them. They speak other languages into them."

"Probably Spanish," said Tipsy.

"They're from Spain?"

"Mostly Mexican, I assume. Some Central American."

"They work very hard. For hours. No matter how hot or cold it is."

"A lot of them have families in their countries to support."

"Huh." His eyes roved from the top of her head to her toes. "We're talking, so you can see me."

"I can. My name's Tipsy, friendly neighborhood clairvoyant." She looked the boy up and down as well. He had gangly long arms, and those big feet he hadn't had a chance to grow into. His sweater and shorts had the threadbare look of a hand-me-downs, but his neatly trimmed and combed hair meant someone cared about him. His dark brown eyes stood out against his pale skin and the red birthmark. His teeth were crooked, but looked strong enough to chew a tough hunk of beef. Other than the birthmark, and his status as a ghost, he appeared to be your standard blue collar, mid-century teenage white boy. "What's your name?" she asked.

"Stephen Ramsey."

"It's so nice to meet you, Stephen—"

"Don't look at me so…hard."

"Pardon?"

"You're looking *right at me*. I ain't…can't…" The indigo light darkened around him, as if to defend his face from his own embarrassment. "People always look at me funny because…" He pointed at his cheek. "When you first saw me, you looked like…they used to look."

"I'm sorry, sugar," she said. "I was surprised—"

"It doesn't *hurt*. People used to ask me, *does that thing hurt?* But it never felt like nothin'."

"I'm glad it doesn't hurt, but there are other types of pain." She tapped her head, and then her chest. "Like, in here. Or here."

He scowled. "That's not pain. That's being a sissy. Like a little crying girl. I ain't a sissy. Don't ever cry. I don't even remember crying, in my whole life. Not ever."

"Got it."

"I wasn't a sissy in life. Now that I'm dead, I'm just as tough. I ain't even afraid of my own dead self! I'm not afraid of anything. Nothing…" He covered the birthmark with his fingers, then whipped his hand away again. "But I can scare you. Boo!"

Tipsy didn't bat an eyelash at his ghostly kookiness. "It's pretty hard to scare me, given what I've seen in my day."

"You see the dead. *I'm* dead. Dead as Washington, Lincoln, and Theodore Roosevelt."

"And you're stuck here." She pointed at the house. "Was this your home?"

"S'pose. I lived in it."

"With your family?"

"No."

"Who then? You couldn't have been more than fifteen when you…passed on—"

"Fourteen."

"So how did you live in this big house, if not with family?"

"I come to live here when I's eight. My mother couldn't keep me. She had to work at a…a tavern. The lady who owned *this house*, Pearl Fischer, she took care of children for women like my mother. Mama paid her money for my keep. I called her Mother Pearl, but she wasn't really my mother."

"Sounds like what we'd call a foster care situation," said Tipsy. "This Mother Pearl had a few kids living here?"

"Yes, ma'am. Five or six at any given time."

"Did she have her own children, or a husband?"

He shook his head. "She said she never met a man she could suffer, so she ended up an old maid. After her daddy died and left her the house, she started taking in wards to keep that big place running smooth. There was a garden out back, and she had chickens and a cow for milking. We fixed things and tended the plants and the animals."

"You talked about your mother, but where was your father?"

He shrugged. "Never knew him. Him and my mama wasn't never married. She was fifteen when I was born and he was past thirty. Story goes, he took one look at my marked-up new baby face, walked out the door, and she never heard tell of him again."

"Did your mother visit you?"

"Once a month or so. She was a good lady. Hard, but good. Mother Pearl said the world made her hard."

"Was Mother Pearl…a…good lady?"

"I reckon she was. She was a hard one, too—maybe that's why she understood my mama's ways—but she kept us fed and clothed up. She didn't suffer fools, or sissies. But she taught me how I was supposed to act and how to be a proper man. Just like she taught the girls how they were supposed to act and be good women. In the kitchen and all. None of us would have known nothing without Mother Pearl." He smiled for the first time. "Mother Pearl was skinny as a fishing pole, but she was strong. Once she caught a half year pig that me and Eldridge Crowder had been trying to corner for an hour. Scooped him right up, mud and all. We all had a good laugh about it. Mother Pearl laughed something fierce when things were funny. Sounded like a cock crowing. Sometimes she laughed so hard, she'd spit right on top of a kid's head, but no one cared. It was a good sound."

"Sounds like you had a short life, but an interesting one," said Tipsy. "Do you…know when you…died?"

"'Course. 1929. I's born in 1915. Came to Mother Pearl in 1923."

"What about *how* you died? I assume you *do not* remember that."

"No," he said. "The last I recall, it was springtime. Then I's dead."

"You never heard anyone talking about it in the house?"

"No. My good pal Eldridge was gone, and Mother Pearl started moving the others out not long after. Within a year, it was only her in this big place. She didn't have much to say, or laugh about, all on her own."

"How did she maintain it with y'all gone?"

"Not too well. A few years went by—I think a few—and she had to sell. She had other ways of making money, but never enough to hire hands to help her. It also seemed like the neighbors didn't like her anymore after I died. They stopped coming to buy her other…trades."

"What other trades?" asked Tipsy. "How else did she make money?"

"She made homemade tonics and salves for people who was feeling poorly. And she was…a…seer."

"Like me?"

"No. Never said nothing about ghosts. More like she *knew* things. Things that happened in the past and might happen in the future. Sometimes things that were happening right there in someone's head. People paid her money to tell them such things."

"Wow." LeeLee Moretz immediately popped into Tipsy's head. "I recently met some—"

"Hey, Mom?"

Tipsy turned at the sound of Little Ayers's voice. Beside her, Stephen Ramsey flickered like an agitated blue lightning bug.

"Hey, buddy," she called out. "What's up?"

"I'm lowkey starving. I *need food*. Please."

Tipsy laughed. "I told you that you'd get hungry! Go inside and make popcorn. I'll make you a sandwich when I come in."

"I always burn the popcorn."

"Use the popcorn button on the microwave."

"Popcorn button," he muttered, as he headed for the house. By the time Tipsy turned back to Stephen, he was gone.

That was a lot to digest, said Granna.

Thanksgiving meal-sized, agreed Tipsy. *So…Stephen Ramsey. Died at age fourteen. Foster child born out of wedlock. Mother was a barmaid. Deadbeat dad who would have been convicted of statutory rape by today's laws. Lived with a pig-wrestling woman named Mother Pearl, a Great Depression eccentric cat lady, who sounds like an early model LeeLee Moretz. Hearing thoughts and telling the future.*

Just as interesting—young Stephen arrived at this house in 1923.

Henry and Jane died the same year. Tipsy thought for a moment. *But they died in February. They could have easily missed each other. Still, I'll ask them if they knew this kid.*

Her phone dinged as she walked toward the house. It was Helen Stokes. FINALLY GOT A HOLD OF AUNT TALIA! SHE'S HAPPY TO TALK TO YOU. SHE'S HARD OF HEARING, SO BEST TO MEET HER IN PERSON. CAN YOU RIDE OUT TO HER PLACE ON JAMES ISLAND?

TIPSY: ABSOLUTELY. LET ME KNOW WHEN SHE CAN SQUEEZE ME IN TO HER BUSY SCHEDULE!

Tipsy had her own busy schedule, and it seemed to keep getting busier. Now she planned to uncover more about Stephen Ramsey *and* this exciting new form of clairvoyance that kept turning up. Still, Aunt Talia had been freeing ghosts for at least eighty years. If she had the opportunity to speak with such a person, she'd find time.

Where there is a will, there's always time.

After a quick artwork sesh, it was time to pick up the girls from volleyball. On the way, Tipsy and Little Ayers ran into Harris Teeter for a rotisserie chicken, a bag of salad, a couple boxes of Kraft Mac-n-Cheese, and a half-gallon of ice cream. After a quasi-homemade meal, she set her progeny up with bowls of cookies and cream and the latest Marvel movie (*Thor and the Somebody Scary of Someplace Imaginary*) in the den off the kitchen. She retreated to the parlor—the room where Jane and Henry lost their lives—and turned on the television above the fireplace. Like talking into a cell phone, CNN was part of her ghost-convo camouflage. The pundits' squabbling was like white noise machine static.

"Hey," she said. "*Y'all.* Any Motts in the house? Mr. and Mrs. Mott?"

Henry appeared first on the sofa across from her, and Jane materialized beside him as he crossed one leg over the other. She tucked her bare feet under her.

"Evening, Tipsy," said Henry.

"And how *are you* today, dear?" asked Jane, in that way that simultaneously channeled best friend and mother.

"I'm good," said Tipsy. "Busy day. Running kids around. Painting. Soothing Scott when he wants to throw his computer out the window."

"Does he have writer's block?"

"Nope. Unfortunately, nothing is blocked on his computer. It's more like a deluge. Of emails—"

Henry turned to Jane. "That's how they send letters. Email. *Electrical mail.* Isn't that clever?"

"Very. How does it work?"

He frowned. "I don't know. Tipsy?"

"Even I can't explain it. In modern life, we push a button. Take it for granted that if it doesn't work, we can hire someone to fix it."

"How *fascinating*," said Jane, with a bright smile.

"Yes, it is," said Henry. He cleared his throat and folded his hands in his lap.

Tipsy glanced between the two of them, side-by-side on the sofa. Closer than she'd ever seen them prior to Jane moving on, but there was something sort of...*American Gothic* about it all. Their ramrod straight backs, and the foot of empty space between them, belied none of the tender affection and familiarity of their initial reunion. The beautiful scene that had inspired *The Hand Study*.

Their stiffness didn't sit well with Tipsy. "How are y'all doing?" she asked.

"We're well," said Henry, as Jane said, "Just fine."

"Did you want to speak to us about something?" asked Henry. "I know Jane is tired."

"Henry, I appreciate your concern, but as I said, I'm fine."

"I'm only trying to—"

Tipsy only had so much time before a kid called for her, so she jumped in. "I wanted to ask you about the house across the street. The one they're rebuilding—"

"Pearl Fischer's place," said Jane.

"Yes, *exactly.* Did y'all know Pearl?"

"Not well, but she was our neighbor for years. The Fischers came from up north. Massachusetts, I believe. Maybe…Rhode Island? *Somewhere* like that. Her father moved down here after the War."

"Which war?" asked Tipsy. "The First World War?"

"She means the Great War," said Henry to Jane.

"Oh, no. Not the *Great* War. The…*War*. The War Between the States," said Jane, as if it were the only war that mattered. "He was a Quaker. He taught at the orphans' schools, and not only at the white children's schools. The schools they set up for the colored children, too. Everyone said he was a *lovely* man, but by the time we moved into our home, he was long dead. He left her the house, but not much else. She was a spinster, so she took in children from unfortunate backgrounds."

"The parents paid Pearl Fischer for their keep," said Henry, "and did what they had to do to survive. Sailors. Fisherman. Traveling performers. Women who…did disrespectful things."

"Like work in taverns?" suggested Tipsy, thinking of Stephen Ramsey's unnamed mother.

"Yes, but there were other more disrespectful things a woman could do," said Henry, with a smirk.

Jane swatted him, but happily, Tipsy detected playfulness in her gesture. Her hand went right through his thigh. "Henry Mott, that's not polite conversation. Besides, I feel for those women. Their lives must have been terribly hard, if they chose to leave their children with Pearl!"

"Always so compassionate," said Henry, and the fondness in his voice was also a relief. "Now, Tipsy, why are you asking about Pearl?"

"Did you ever look out your window and see another ghost? In Pearl's house?"

Henry shook his head, and Jane said, "No. Never."

"Well, there *is* one. A fourteen-year-old boy named Stephen Ramsey. Died in 1929."

"Damnation," said Henry. "Wish I'd known. I'd have appreciated a dead neighbor. Someone to chat with when Jane and I were estranged in this house. Might have buffered my insanity."

"He's always stayed inside, but the construction noise forced him out. I want to help him."

"How honorable," said Jane. "What do you know about him?"

Tipsy gave them the information she'd gleaned about Stephen. "… and he has a birthmark on his face. Do y'all remember a kid like that? He said he came to live with Mother Pearl—that's what he calls her—in 1923. The same year y'all died."

"I don't recall such a child," said Jane. "Seems like a face one would remember. Perhaps he arrived later that year, after we died."

"Yeah. I didn't get a chance to mention y'all to him. Little Ayers came strolling up and he disappeared." Tipsy shifted on her chair. "Did y'all know much about this Mother Pearl? That boy died under her watch. She might have had something to do with it. Sad to say, but it's not terribly uncommon for children to die in foster care."

"I don't really know *how* to describe Pearl Fischer," said Jane. "She was…skinny as a porch rail."

"Stephen said the same, but he also said she was tough and strong."

"I'm sure she was, running that big house and caring for all those children on her own. She had mousy gray hair and dark eyes. Rather prominent nose, wouldn't you say, Henry?"

"Hmmm. Yes. Hooked like a coat hanger," said Henry. "She always seemed to be yelling at the children, but it was more boisterous than cruel. They were her battalion of little soldiers. They appeared healthy enough. Hand me down clothes, but that's to be expected. Nothing fancy about any of it, but nothing alarming."

"Remember how Pearl used to wear men's pants and coats?" Jane chuckled. "And she chewed tobacco! She grew herbs and sold homemade medicines. She even claimed she could predict the future."

"Stephen said people paid her for her predictions."

"A lot of hogwash," said Henry.

"Tipsy sees ghosts," said Jane. "You saw them in life. Here we sit, dead and talking to her. Most would say *hogwash* to all of that."

"I suppose when you put it like that…" said Henry. "Still, she was indeed the village oddball."

Tipsy took all this in. A spinster who wore men's clothes, treated the children who lived with her like her personal platoon, was an amateur pharmacist, and claimed prophetic powers. "Did she only take in white children?"

"Yes," said Jane. "The colored orphanage was a few houses down. Y'all—the *modern* y'all—would see it different, but no one would have thought to mix them."

"Stephen said she had about half a dozen kids living there at a time."

Jane nodded. "It seemed as if most of them turned up around age six, and stayed until they were about the age of your Stephen. Then she hustled them out into the world, and a new one showed up."

"I recall some of them," said Henry. "A girl named Maudie. She had such sweet curls. At least two Jacks! A rotation of Jacks in that house!"

"What about the siblings? The towheads," added Jane.

"Oh, yes! Hannah and Eldridge."

"Stephen mentioned a boy named Eldridge," said Tipsy.

"It must be the same child," said Jane. "The boy was a year or two older than the girl. I believe their mother died, and their father worked on a farm south of here. Colleton County, maybe?"

"Hmm. Yes. Colleton. Or Hampton. Adorable children. Like little Viking fairies. Huge blue eyes. White blonde hair," said Henry. "So you're going to try to figure out how this lad died, and set him free?"

"Hopefully. In all my *spare time.* If you remember anything else, let me know."

"Certainly," said Henry. "And now, I shall try to write, since I don't feel particularly crazy this evening. Will you ladies excuse me?"

"Of course," said Jane.

"I'll be in our bedroom, sweetheart," he said. "The computer is up there."

"I'll be up shortly, too."

"Don't pester her, Tipsy."

"I won't!"

"Go on now," said Jane. Henry disappeared, and she turned to Tipsy. "He's a dear, but why don't you go ahead and start pestering?"

"You're that anxious to show me another memory?"

"I don't have much choice."

"You have something in mind?"

"Nothing specific. Can we chitchat, and see if it sparks anything?"

"I love a good chitchat."

"Let's see…when are you and the dear doctor getting married?"

"In about a month."

"What church will host your marriage? Christ Church is lovely. We passed it on the way to the Old Cannon. Or St. Andrews, around the block."

"Ah, no. We're doing something simple. Close friends and family, here in our yard. Not everyone gets married in churches these days."

Tipsy expected Jane to be surprised, but she simply nodded. "Standing up in a church isn't the most important thing. Henry and I had a beautiful ceremony at St. Philip's. It lasted over an hour. Choir. Communion. All of it. Proctor stood there like St. Peter himself, blessing our union." Pain flickered over her face. "You know how that turned out."

Tipsy opened her mouth to say something, then closed it. She searched for a tactful way to ask Jane about her adulterous affair with her own murderer. The noise that ultimately came out of her flapping jaws sounded like, "*I-uh-so-yeah…*"

"Go *ahead*. Ask me about Proctor," said Jane, with a hint of a smile and a few good blinks. "Your *curiosity* is written all over your face."

"I mean…if you want to talk about it."

"I don't know if *want* is the correct word, but we never had a chance to discuss him before I sashayed off into the afterlife. I've *wondered* what you thought of me. A woman who steps out on her husband with the minister she's known *all her life*."

"I'm not judging you, if that's what you mean. You were in a terrible situation. But I do wonder...did you love him?"

Jane blinkety-blinked as she collected her thoughts. "In a way, but it was the kind of love that seeps into being. I needed to fill an empty space, like water rising from below to fill in a hole in the dirt. All I did was *take* from him."

"I think he loved you so much that he didn't care if you gave anything back."

"So he would have kept endlessly pouring his soul into the leaky bucket of mine? Even the most ardent lover will eventually run dry. At times, I *believed* I truly loved Proctor. Maybe I take some selfish comfort in that now."

"When you're in a bad place, all kinds of feelings can seem like love. Take my ex-boyfriend Will Garrison. You remember him, don't you?"

"Oh, yes. Henry told me he turned out to be quite a *peach*. As in, he looks nice and juicy, but he's actually smushy and bland and terribly disappointing."

"Now *there's* an accurate analogy. I thought I was in love with Will, but in reality, I loved the false sense of security he gave me. Our friends, our kids. I felt like I belonged somewhere."

Jane nodded her understanding. "When it seemed like Henry didn't want me, it made sense to be with Proctor. I didn't know I had put myself and Henry in terrible danger."

"You weren't thinking clearly, even when you thought you were. There were multiple points along my divorce timeline where I thought, *I'm good. I'm over it.* But now I understand that the only way to get over my life falling apart is to accept that I'll *never* be completely over it. I had to come to peace with the choices I made during my first marriage, and after my divorce, when I *thought* I was okay. Sometimes it feels like I lost my mind, then recovered, then lost it again."

"That's a sensation both Henry and I can relate to."

"I look back at the agony I went through with Will, and while our relationship had good points, I clung to it for all the wrong reasons. Sounds like you did the same with Proctor. You cared about him very much, but you didn't love him truly, madly, deeply. Not like I love Scott."

Jane looked into the foyer and up the staircase. "Henry was my true, deep, mad love."

"I believe you, but…y'all were kind of a…hot mess."

Jane smiled. "*Hot mess.* Burnt scrambled eggs? Bubbly porridge? My mother's hair when she left her curling tongs in too long?"

"All of the above," said Tipsy.

"It certainly wasn't a *perfect* love, but it was my *greatest* love."

"You told me once that you realized you shouldn't have married him. That your love should have been allowed to burn bright and fizzle out."

"That's accurate, if I wanted a *peaceful* life. A much *longer* life, given how things turned out. He's still the only love I ever knew. A *hurricane* that blew into my life from across the Atlantic Ocean. When he came home from overseas, it was…I can still remember—" She smiled. "Would you like to see?"

"Yeah, but Henry wants you to rest, and I don't want to piss him off."

"If he grumbles, I can manage him. I managed him for a long time. Now…let me think for a moment..." Her smile widened. "Better to start with beautiful treasured memories, and work our way toward the unpleasant forgotten ones."

Before Tipsy argued with her, Jane reached out and touched Tipsy's knee.

Tipsy wakes in a room she's never seen, but it's not wholly unfamiliar, because she's spent enough memory time in old Charleston mansions to

recognize their cavernous yet cozy spaces. No beds, so it's not a bedroom. Not enough books to be a library. No outdated appliances, so it's not a kitchen.

Flotillas of spindly furniture drift on blue and green seas of heavy oriental rugs. The fireplaces at each end of the room are ports of call. Heavy green draperies line a single wide bay window. On the walls, paintings of hunting dogs, tall ships, and elegant ladies in tightly cinched gowns. It's a parlor.

Jane perches on a settee beside a crackling fire with a book in her hand. On the table beside her, another Tiffany lamp casts its soft golden glow. Her feet are tucked under her, and a knitted blanket covers her lap. As she turns the page, her sister Constance peeks into the room from the foyer. "Janie," says Constance. "I'm helping Mama with the mistletoe and Patience Mott is sending over their donation today. Her note said it's an especially large one this year. Can you meet Mr. Mott in the carriage house?"

Jane looks out the bay window. It's chilly for a Charleston December day. She was up before the sun to make Christmas wreathes from magnolia leaves (straight from her parents' front yard) and spruce sprigs (Mama orders them from a farm in the North Carolina mountains every year). Her fingers are raw from pine needles and sticky sap, so she stole time after lunch for a cup of hot tea and some reading. The idea of leaving her novel and the fireplace's warmth to stand in the wind and wait for Fred Mott is unpleasant, but her discomfort will be for a good cause: her parents' annual Christmas toy and clothing collection for the Charleston Orphan House. A significant donation comes with an invitation to the Robinette's holiday soiree. Three days before the party, their carriage house is filled with gifts. The Motts always try to outdo their neighbors, so Jane might need to move things around to make room.

"I will. When is Mr. Mott due to arrive?"

"Two o'clock."

"What time is it now?"

Connie grimaces. "Five after."

"Goodness," says Jane. "Fred Mott will be banging on our door any minute and I don't fancy listening to the dogs bark their fool heads off. Did Jackson open the gate?"

"He did. He's already helping Mr. Mott unload."

Tipsy follows as Jane stands and walks into the foyer. She dons a lavender coat trimmed in white fur and tugs a white wool hat over her dark hair. Black fur-lined gloves and she's ready. New Yorkers and Bostonians might laugh at her attire, for she looks prepared for a blizzard, but Jane Robinette is a Charlestonian through and through. She cannot tolerate a chill.

She walks onto the piazza and down into the garden. She can see her breath, and her cold cheeks tingle as she approaches the carriage house. Jackson, the Robinette's groundskeeper and handyman, stands beside a tall man in a burgundy overcoat and a bowler hat. The man's back is to her, but Jane immediately surmises him to be too svelte to be the middle-aged Fred Mott.

Jackson, a stocky black man in his fifties, waves as she approaches. "We got these boxes and packages down from Mr. Mott's motor car, Miss Jane. I'll help him get them into the carriage house, but first I need to make room. How's that sound?"

"Thank you, Jackson," Jane says, but the man in the dark red coat doesn't move at the sound of her voice. She clears her throat. "And thank you…ah, sir, for helping Mr. Mott with his delivery…"

The man removes his hat and turns slowly. As she gets a good look at his face, Jane trails off. She can't help it. Frankly, she's never seen such a man.

He's well over six feet tall with broad shoulders and a wiry build. Pomade has darkened his hair to auburn. He has high cheekbones, full lips, and a dusting of freckles over his rather strong nose. Thick reddish brows, and dark blue eyes. Curling russet eyelashes.

He twists his bowler hat in his big hands. He isn't wearing gloves. She notices the smattering of ginger hair on the back of his exposed wrists. He wears a small silver ring on his right pinky finger.

Jane isn't sure why all these minute details leap out at her, nor does she have any idea who he is, but she can't take her eyes off him.

Tipsy knows exactly who he is. She's spent hours talking to a version of him that's about a decade older, and she knows what it's like to be drawn to that same serious, elegant face.

"Miss Jane?" says Jackson.

"Oh, yes. Yes, please. Make room in the carriage house."

Jackson nods and disappears into the carriage house. If he notices her gawking like a child at the circus, he's too tactful to call attention to it.

"Hello, Jane," says the red-haired man.

"Hello." She gives him a tentative smile. "I'm sorry, I expected Mr. Mott and—"

"So you have him." He smiles back at her.

"I don't understand, I—" The image of the odd little boy, miserable at Ms. Lamboll's birthday picnic, pops into her mind, and hence, into Tipsy's. "Wait…are you…that is…Henry?"

"Indeed. The third Mr. Mott, after my father and my older brother. At your service."

Jane exhales nervous laughter, and her breath floats around her face in a white cloud. "My goodness. I'd never have recognized—Oh, lord. That sounded terrible."

Henry chuckles. "No, I've grown considerably taller since the last time you saw me."

"Have you just returned?" She tries to remember what she last heard about Henry Mott, probably when Patience Mott cornered her own mother after church. "You were in Europe, weren't you?"

"Yes. England, mostly. But I spent time in France."

"Is Paris as lovely as I imagine it?"

"Lovelier."

"And what about London?"

"It's also lovely, although it's a bit cold and wet for my tastes."

"No wonder you're not wearing gloves or a scarf. It must seem balmy here to you."

"Let's just say it's good to be home." He watches her with those deep blue eyes, like the dark edges of the indigo flowers she loves so much. If her face burns any hotter, she might contract a fever and need to be put to bed.

"What is it your mother sent?" she asks.

"The smaller boxes and parcels are my mother's gifts. Clothes. Useful things. This big box is my donation. It's not as practical, but I love it, anyway."

"Might I see it?"

Henry pulls at the crate's lid. He fishes around, removing soft layers of cloth. He gently lifts a wrapped rectangular object and sets it on the cobblestone drive.

"Go on," he says. "Open it. Perhaps you can tell me if you think the girls at the orphanage will like it."

Jane feels as if she's a child on Christmas morning herself. She tugs at the cloth until it falls away.

"Oh," she says. "How lovely."

It's a wooden dollhouse. It has three stories, and nine rooms. The walls of each room are hand painted, as are the flowers that cover the white exterior walls and burst from painted window boxes. It even has piazzas on the left side. A perfect replica of a Charleston home.

"Where on earth did you get this?"

"I commissioned it from a craftsman in London." He points into the box at more wrapped packages. "There's furniture, and a family. A large family, with six children, grandparents, and a few aunts and uncles. I didn't want the girls fighting over the dolls."

"You had it sent all the way to Charleston for our party?"

"My mother has kept me in the know over the years, so to say."

"This is wonderful!" says Jane. "It will be perfect for the school room in the Orphan's Home." She beams at him. "It's so thoughtful, and generous."

"I have years of missed donations to make up for."

"Will you be coming to the party then?"

"I'd like to, if I'm invited."

"Of course you are. After this gift, you might be crowned Santa Claus himself. The Christmas King!"

"I've heard you're the queen of this event. Should I be crowned king, nothing would make me happier."

The back of Jane's neck tingles. Is he flirting with her? Silly that she should feel so giddy. She tries to focus on pleasantries. "What do you plan on doing with yourself now that you're back in town?"

"I'm working on a novel."

"That's wonderful. I love to read. I abandoned my book to come out here and meet you."

"What are you reading?"

"Oh, Pioneers. *I'm barely able to put it down."*

"There are women who spread ruin through no fault of theirs," *said Henry,* "just by being too beautiful, too full of life and love. People come to them as people go to a warm fire in winter."

"Goodness. You have a fine memory."

"I envy Ms. Catha's prose. But also, that line stuck with me. I knew such a lady once."

"In London?"

"No. Here in Charleston. Although she was a girl when I knew her."

Now the hair on the back of Jane's neck is crackling, like she stuck her finger in one of her parents' newfangled electric switches. Can he mean her? But they'd known each other so long ago, and had hardly been friends. "Charleston is *known for pretty women."*

"Perhaps. But from what I remember, there were none like this girl. I haven't met her like, in Canada or France or England."

"She'll be a woman now, not the girl you remember."

"Yes, she is. But she's just as beautiful. And just as compelling, from what I've seen of her since I've been home."

"Have you seen her?"

"Yes."

She waits for him to say more, but he simply watches her.

Oh, lord. He *is* talking about me.

Many men have flirted with Jane Robinette. They've spilled flattery and innuendo and given her gifts. But no one has ever spoken so few words that said so much.

"Ah. Um. Well." She suddenly has to get away from him, before she says something wholly inappropriate or completely ridiculous, or worse, says nothing meaningful at all, and stands there mumbling nonsense. She takes two steps back. "Jackson will help you with the dollhouse. Thank you so much, again."

His face falls, just enough for her to understand that his own feelings are tampering with him, no matter how collected he appears on the outside. "I hope I haven't said something to offend you."

"No. Heavens, *no." She gives him a wide smile this time, for she already can't stand the thought of wounding his poetic heart. "I'm…I'm happy you're home, Henry."*

He exhales, and smiles back. "I'm happy to be here. I'll help Jackson, and then I'll be on my way."

"I'll see you on Friday evening, at the party."

"That evening can't come soon enough."

She turns and walks back toward the house. She fights the urge to run up the stairs to the piazza. To take them two at a time, as she did when she was a girl. She opens the door and steps inside.

Connie walks through the foyer with a sweetgrass basket containing sprigs of mistletoe. She pauses at the sight of Jane, leaning against the door with her hands in her pockets and her chin tucked into her coat. Jane stares at her own flushed reflection in the hallway mirror.

"Janie, are you alright?" Connie asks. "You look like you've seen a ghost."

Jane grins at her. "Maybe I have, Connie. Maybe I have."

Chapter 7

On Monday morning two days later, Tipsy parked in front of LeeLee Moretz's office on State Street, a couple blocks from the GQB. She'd gotten up before the kids to shower and make herself presentable. She wore one of her long prairie chic dresses and dressy flat sandals. Her hair was swept up in a non-messy bun and she'd swiped mascara over her lashes. Her easel was calling her, but she would not be that tacky person who showed up to a legal consult in paint-splattered yoga pants and beat up running shoes.

According to the Charleston Historical Society plaque, the three-story stucco building that housed Donnelly Family Law, LLC was built before 1775. She opened a wrought iron gate and walked down a narrow passageway between the law office and its next door neighbor. There was no piazza, just a simple door along the side of the building, so she stepped directly from the flagstone path into the dimly lit foyer. The house had the layout of a true Charleston single: one room wide and several rooms long with a central staircase. Some long gone artisan had painted a pattern of golden stars on the wooden floors, but they had faded as the wide planks warped. It smelled like coffee and dusty paper.

The conference room on the first floor overlooked the street. The lumpy plaster walls were burgundy; the heavy drapes, hunter green with burgundy stripes. Rusty, cobwebby fireplace tools sat beside a hearth that looked as if it hadn't seen flames since Henry and Jane's day. A stuffy painting of Rainbow Row above the carved wooden mantle faced off against framed eighteenth century French political cartoons on the opposite wall. Tipsy took a seat at the shiny mahogany conference table. State Street got a lot of foot traffic from nearby Market and East

Bay Streets, so she listened to the chattering of tour guides and tourists through the thin window glass as she waited for LeeLee.

The lawyerly lady in question squeezed between the conference room door and the foyer. She asked the paralegal to hold her calls before turning to Tipsy with a smile. "Heyyyyyy! Great to see you!" She closed the door behind her, pulled out a chair, and smoothed her camel-colored skirt underneath her as she sat.

"Hey," said Tipsy. "So good to see you, too—"

A high-pitched *yip-yip* from the direction of the fireplace interrupted their greetings. A fluffy orange floor pillow…*moved.* Four scrawny legs unfurled and two beady black eyes blinked at Tipsy.

"Hush, Sandra," said LeeLee. "Go back to sleep."

"*Sandra?* Is that a dog, or someone's grandma?"

"She's named after Sandra Day O'Connor."

The old dog turned in a slow circle, groaned, and settled her bones onto her doggie bed. She promptly went back to sleep as LeeLee arranged pens around her legal pad. "She's mostly deaf and snoozes all day. The other three are up in Darlene's office."

"Three more? That's a lot of fur," said Tipsy.

"Yup. Darlene loves her Pomeranians. She's got Ruthie, Sonia, and Elena. The younger ones jump all over clients and piddle everywhere, so they stay upstairs." She straightened the collar of her green silk blouse. "So, what can I do for you?"

"I'm trying to understand my options. If I have any, and if I should exercise them."

"From your text, it sounds like your ex is moving toward a second divorce, and you're worried that he's not stable enough to have the kids right now."

"Right. He's having inappropriate conversations with them about his personal life, and he's planning to stay with his parents every weekend—"

LeeLee jotted a few notes. "Where do his parents live?"

"On Sullivan's."

She looked up from her legal pad. "Within walking distance to the beach?"

"They're basically on the Intracoastal, so they have a deep water dock. They usually take the golf cart to the beach, but it's walkable."

"Hmm."

Tipsy read the room. "I acknowledge that it's a beautiful house. There's a pool, and they go out on their grandparents' boat—"

"Doesn't sound terrible."

"It's not *truly* terrible." *It's lowkey terrible*, she thought, but she said, "It's the psychological element. They're freaked out by the thought of Ayers moving. They want to be in their own rooms. My former mother-in-law adores them, but she's a tough cookie. Like stale Oreo tough. It's a really difficult dynamic—" She corrected herself again. "Maybe *difficult* isn't the right word. This sounds ridiculous, but my kids would say—"

"It's *lowkey* difficult."

Tipsy chuckled. "Exactly what I was thinking. No cap," she added.

LeeLee squinted up at the ceiling and pursed her lips. "It's giving… childhood trauma."

"We are definitely Gen-Z moms," said Tipsy. "Look, it's not trauma like my childhood—"

"You had a rough childhood?"

"Yeah. My parents are not the most upstanding people. My grandmother pretty much raised me, upstate. It was always a struggle, financially and emotionally."

"Huh. My early days were lacking in sunshine and roses, so I get it." LeeLee tapped her pen against the table. "Actually, I can relate enough to have a hypothesis about you."

"What's that?"

"Maybe your own upbringing makes it harder for *you* to handle this turn of events."

Tipsy considered it, and then shrugged. "Probably. I've always wanted my kids to have an idyllic childhood. They've already been through a divorce. And Ayers—he's hard to deal with, for me and the kids. Even his own parents acknowledge it. He's going to be pricklier and more demanding than ever."

"So what would you like to see happen?"

"What if he didn't have them overnight until this is all sorted out? They can stay with me, and he can see them during the day, or something. I'm not trying to keep them from him. I just don't want to expose them to more conflict and instability..." Tipsy trailed off at the appraising look in LeeLee's eyes.

"I've had people be straight up with me when I needed it," said LeeLee, "and I try to do the same."

"Okay," said Tipsy, as Sandra the Geriatric Judicial Pomeranian squeaked and chirped in her sleep.

"The standard for the court to modify a custodial timesharing arrangement is a substantial change in circumstances affecting the welfare of the children. Two prongs. Number one, *substantial.* Number two, *affecting the welfare of the children*. In your situation, you've got a change in circumstances. But does it arise to the level of a substantial change that negatively affects your children?"

"It feels substantial to me."

"You have to consider what we see in the courts every day. Your kids are staying with their grandparents in a mansion while their dad figures out some things in his personal life. I'm not saying it's ideal, but if this is the worst thing that ever happens to them, they're doing pretty well."

Tipsy sighed, and Sandra sighed right along with her. LeeLee went on. "I believe you when you say that you're not trying to take the kids from him, but his time with them is already limited. A judge isn't going to further reduce that time."

"I guess that makes sense."

"Post-divorce custody actions are our most complicated cases. If you're back in court, then you've been through the entire agonizing process and you're *still* going at each other."

"Ayers and I aren't like *that*."

"You say that now, but you'd be opening a ten gallon jug of nightcrawlers. These things can drag on for years and put your children through hell. I've seen people go into it with the best of intentions and reasonably well adjusted kids. Eight years later, they come out the other side with teenagers with permanent emotional damage. They pay at least a hundred grand for all that fun."

Tipsy recoiled. "I thought it might be a simple thing—you know, the court giving me full custody on a temporary basis—"

"No, my dear. It is not simple. In the end, you married this guy and had kids with him. Is it surprising that it's going down like this?"

"No, but it's so hard to know when and how to intervene. I've been struggling with this ever since we got divorced. I thought we'd come to a pretty good place. Between me, his mother, and his sister, it felt like we had him on a smooth path. Even the new wife—I'm no big fan—"

"Mimi told me you're marrying her ex."

"Yup. Crazy, I know."

"It is a little odd. I'm sure you get that a lot."

"Most people do a quadruple take. Some assume we're swingers. I have to assure them that both original couples were divorced before either new couple got together. Anyway, Kate might be unpleasant, but she keeps a firm hand on him. Firmer than I did when we were married. He needs that. But their relationship has gotten more volatile over the past year. He can only be stable for so long, and she's got her own issues."

"Some people are destined for turbulence."

Tipsy thought of Henry. "Feels like I know a lot of men like that."

"Men. Women. Whether they're gay, straight, or none of the above. Some people always find their way back to rough water."

"It sounds like I have to ride it out. So do my kids."

"That's what I'd advise, unless something drastic happens. A DUI. Suicide threats. A physical altercation with the new wife. That's when we do can something."

"Jeez. You sound so matter of fact."

"I have a lot of compassion for people, but I'm doing my clients an injustice if I get emotionally involved. And nothing surprises me anymore. I've *seen it all*."

Sandra abruptly sat up. Her cloudy left eye winked and she let out a raspy yip, as if encouraging Tipsy to seize the conversational moment.

"*Riiiiight*...when I ran into you on the street by the gallery," said Tipsy, "I got the impression you can truly *see it all*."

"Ah...sure—that was—"

"I heard an interesting story the other day. About a woman who was a sort of...*seer*. An oracle. She's been dead a long time, but supposedly people paid her to tell them about the future.

"Where did you hear that, if she's been dead for a long time?"

Tipsy looked her right in the eyes. "From the ghost of a boy who knew her. He's my neighbor across the street."

"A ghost neighbor, huh?"

"I have ghost *roommates*, too. You mentioned one of them the last time we met. Remember the red-haired guy? Looks...dead?"

"I did mention him, didn't I." LeeLee rested her elbow on the table and her chin on her palm. "Can you *really* see ghosts?"

"I can. Can you *really* read minds and make predictions?"

"Seeing ghosts sounds straightforward. They're either there, or they're not. My abilities are less black and white." LeeLee looked at her phone. "I could talk about this stuff for hours and still not explain it all, but I'm running up against my next appointment."

"You gotta give me *a little* more insight. Did you read my thoughts about ghosts? Is that how you knew that I'm a clairvoyant?"

"No. I had a...vision. You on the porch of a white house, talking to a red-haired man. He seemed...otherworldly. Pale. Sort of transparent. Old-fashioned. Like a moving antique photograph. Then he vanished. I figured he must be a ghost."

"I've had a million interactions like that with Henry over the past few years."

"I assumed that vision was something from *your* past. This Henry guy seemed like the past come to life. So the whole thing...had a *past within the past* feel to it."

"Speaking of *things within other things,* what's up with this idea of a *secret within a secret*?"

"I sensed you had a conundrum with some dead people, and the voice in my head spoke up with a solution."

"Find the *secret within the secret*. Not much of a solution."

"My visions of the future are always confusing. The past is usually easier to understand."

"Whose future are you talking about? My future? Henry's future? Or his wife, Jane? She's also dead, and stuck haunting my house."

"All of y'all. Maybe. Probably. Possibly."

Tipsy chuckled. "A lot less black and white than seeing ghosts."

"I'm sorry I freaked out. I have these…insights...sometimes, but I usually keep them to myself. I only spoke up to *you* because I sensed you have your own supernatural powers."

"Can you tell me anything else?"

Sandra got up from her pillow, hobbled across the room, and leaned against LeeLee's leg. LeeLee reached down and scratched the dog's head. "All I can say is…death is usually your focus, and I can see why. But this is different. It's about their lives. Something that haunted them *before* they were ghosts."

There was a knock on the door. A cute blonde woman stuck her head inside. "Lee, your next appointment is waiting. Darlene is coming down."

"Thanks, Britt." The paralegal disappeared, and LeeLee turned back to Tipsy. "Darlene wants me to meet with her and a new client. I wish I could be more help."

LeeLee stood, and Tipsy followed her. "Maybe something else… supernatural…will come to you."

"If it does, I promise I'll let you know. I definitely want to get coffee. I've never met someone who sees ghosts before."

"Yes, definitely. If we're going to discuss our freakish supernatural powers, maybe a beer is in order."

LeeLee smiled. "That would be great."

They walked into the foyer. LeeLee's boss, Darlene, a sixty-something, bleached-blonde lady wearing a bright blue suit, stood at the foot of the staircase. In the waiting room behind her, a man with curly blonde hair was leaning over a box of files. He was obviously agitated. He loudly rustled around in the box and dropped a pile of folders. They landed on the floor with a splat.

"Hey, Lee," said Darlene. She smiled at Tipsy. "Nice to meet you, Ms. Collins."

"Nice to meet you, too."

The man spoke loudly over his shoulder. He sounded like a whiny child. "The papers must be in here *somewhere*. The process server dropped off a packet. Damnit. All these bank statements and mortgage documents and—"

"Take your time," said Darlene to the back of the man's head. She looked at Tipsy again. "As you can see, we're always busy around here, but I don't mean to seem like we're chasing you out."

"No problem. I have to get going." Tipsy said goodbye and put a hand on the doorknob as the blonde man straightened. He turned toward LeeLee, and Tipsy's eyes flickered over his annoyingly familiar profile. She had one foot out the door, but she recognized his nasally, ingratiating voice.

"*Sooo* nice to *meet* you, LeeLee. I'm Brad Humphries."

There were few people in Charleston whom Tipsy detested more than Brad Humphries, a colleague of Big Ayers. Several years ago, Brad had cheated on his wife with the equally married Mimi. Once Mimi pressed Brad to leave their respective spouses to legitimatize their true love, he unceremoniously ditched her with sanctimonious *yada-yada* about God and family, and promptly moved on to his next adulterous fling. To add to Tipsy's ire, it was Brad who broke the news to Ayers that Tipsy was seeing Scott, after they saw him entertaining his young, pretty co-worker at a downtown bar. Ayers and Kate had gone ballistic.

"Of all the people to run into," Tipsy said to Scott over Facetime that evening. "I peeled out of there like Lightning McQueen, so I think I got away before he got a look at my disgusted face. His wife must have finally wised up and served him with papers. I hope she takes him to the cleaners."

"If he recognized you, he's going to wonder if you're *returning* Ayers to the cleaners. Unless that law firm does other kinds of litigation?"

"Nope. It clearly says *Donnelly Family Law* on the sign. Ugh. If he *did* recognize me, he's going to tell Ayers he saw me there."

"Maybe not. He'll have to tell Ayers why *he* was there, too."

Tipsy felt a glimmer of hope. Despite Brad's philandering, he fancied himself a well-respected family man. He probably believed that everyone else agreed with his delusional self-assessment.

Over the next few days, she relaxed as she detected no difference in Big Ayers's mood. He was grumpy and uncommunicative, but he didn't direct his ire at her. By Friday afternoon, she felt tentatively confident that Brad hadn't recognized her, or his humiliation was keeping him quiet. As a bonus, Big Ayers was participating in a long-planned three-day fishing tournament, so Tipsy had another weekend with the kids, who were thus spared a stint at their grandparents' house with said disgruntled father.

She said as much to Henry as she prepped for Taco Night after picking up M.P. and O-Liv from volleyball practice. The girl's feet thudded above them as they ran down the second floor hallway. Little A was spending the night at a friend's house, and Tipsy heard water start running upstairs. One of the twins would be in their bathroom; the other, in Tipsy's, so she spoke to Henry without worrying about anyone overhearing. "Big Ayers hasn't said anything alarming in our text exchanges, so I don't think he knows I ran into Brad. Ayers will be offshore and out of text range most of the weekend. If Brad saw me, and texts Ayers, Ayers won't get the message."

Henry sat at the kitchen table, methodically shredding bits of iceberg lettuce via telekinesis and adding them to the bowl in from of him. "I agree that this Brad person has not yet dumped that pot of beans on Big Ayers's head. If he did see you, let's hope he forgets by the time Big Ayers can receive texters again."

"How is Jane today? I haven't seen her since I left the house this morning."

"She's resting, but we walked around the garden at midday. The sunshine seemed to do right by her, even if she can't feel it."

"Good. Should I look into her memory again?"

Henry scowled, and bits of lettuce floated around his head. "I don't appreciate the two of you looking into my past without me. Especially after I asked you to let Jane rest."

"I already told you. She *insisted*. You know how persuasive she can be."

"Hmph. At least y'all confessed your treachery to me."

Tipsy ignored his Henry-hyperbole. "No way I could keep that memory to myself. I've been waiting for a chance to discuss it with you. Your romantic meet-cute in her parents' driveway when you came home from Europe."

"Meet-cute? What a saccharine phrase. It's so sickly-sweet that I don't even have to clarify what it means."

"Don't rain on my romance!"

"I suppose it *was* all *rather* romantic."

"She was so smitten by you," said Tipsy, as she sliced tomatoes. "You *were* swoon-worthy. Cool, calm, and collected, with just the right amount of angsty arrogance. The perfect tragic hero."

He shook his head, but Tipsy knew her words pleased him. "Eh. The self-importance of youth."

"She was so happy in that memory. It was refreshing, since so many of the memories I see in ghosts' heads are torturous."

"I was happy, too. I almost ran the car off the street on the way back to my parents' house."

"Soo…what happened next?"

"Do you *truly* want to know all that ancient history?" He looked up at Tipsy from under one raised eyebrow.

"Reviewing ancient history is literally the most important part of—"

"If you insist! Now…where to begin?"

Tipsy smiled down at the tomatoes. Clearly, Henry was eager to talk about his early courtship of Jane, but he wanted Tipsy to think she had to drag it out of him. She humored him. "The more detail, the better."

"By the end of her parents' Christmas party, I was more in love with her than I imagined possible, and I'd been imagining for years. What a night…" He stared dreamily out the window, through a cloud of tossed confetti lettuce. "We danced, and laughed, and talked about everything under the sun. She dragged me from room to room and reintroduced me to people I hadn't seen in a decade. From that evening on, we saw each other as often as propriety and the winter weather would allow. Tea by the fireplace in the parlor at the Robinette's house, sharing books and poems. I walked her to and from church every Sunday. As springtime warmed up the world, it was picnics, strolls around town, garden parties, and evenings on her parents' piazza. We rode horses at the old Cannon, and rowed around in my old canoe at the Pond—er, Colonial Lake—near Broad Street. She made sure I was invited to every social event, and you know…I actually enjoyed myself. Such a joyful time."

"I'd like to see that joy from your perspective."

He smiled. "It's hard to pick a single memory…but…I think the best night was…Wait! This is the perfect chance to show you…"

He disappeared, and Tipsy scowled. She set down her knife. "What the hell? Lowkey annoying."

She dumped the sliced tomatoes into a bowl and gathered up stray bits of lettuce. She was about to start simmering ground beef when Henry returned to the kitchen. A lumpy gray object floated in front of him. "Apologies for my abrupt exit, but I found something quite wonderful a few days ago. In Miss Callie's curio cabinet, in the sewing room."

The sewing room was behind the den, catty corner to the cramped laundry room. According to Henry, the den, laundry room, and sewing room had once been his study. Upon the automizing of laundry, the study had been divvied up. The fireplace area had become the den, the washer and dryer were installed in the annex near the kitchen, and the sewing room was simply…leftover. Miss Callie had set up her sewing machine in there, but it also served as her oversized junk drawer, where she deposited old furniture, boxes of books, and a 1980s stationary bike.

Tipsy and Scott wanted to reconfigure the sewing room into a modern mudroom and laundry space as part of their long term renovation plan. Until that happened, Tipsy had little reason to go into the sewing room, but she remembered the curio cabinet. A spindly glass and wood structure that looked like it would collapse under the weight of one more knickknack. The shelves were crammed with decorative boxes, figurines, little clocks, and tiny vases and glassware.

"I've been thinking about the early days since Jane told me she showed you our cute-meet. I remembered Miss Callie finding *this* in the attic, years ago."

The object swirled in front of her. As it settled on the kitchen table, she recognized it as a polished oyster shell. She picked it up. The smooth side was pearl white with a dark purplish splotch in the center. The rough back side, gold-plated.

"I wondered if she kept it, so I looked everywhere. The bookshelves in the study. The China cabinet in the dining room. All the bedside tables in the spare bedrooms. I finally found it, on the bottom shelf of the curio cabinet."

"It's pretty," she said, as she held it out toward him. "But what—"

"I'd much rather show you." He closed his own hands over the oyster shell. As he did, his fingers curled over hers.

Tipsy opens her eyes to the dim yet warm light that only exists right before dawn, or right after sunset. She's standing on a sand and gravel path beside an oak tree of substantial girth. She peers around the tree at a bandstand, and the grandiose piazzas of South Battery. The air is fishy, and across the harbor, effervescent light radiates beyond the tree line. The sun is making a stand over James Island, southwest of the peninsula. It's the end of the day, not the beginning of a new one. She's in White Point Garden, the park that has long buffered the Battery from the encroaching ocean.

Henry stands in the grass under an oak. His hands are in his pockets, but spring has arrived in Charleston in all its pollen-drenched enthusiasm. Tipsy knows Henry isn't cold. Far from it. He's sweating and his collar feels like it's strangling him. His hands are in his pockets for two reasons. First, to keep from raking them over his neatly pomaded hair. Second, to keep a tight hold of a wooden box and the precious gift it contains.

Everyone has cleared out of the park except a man and woman walking their collie dogs. It's May, and the days are lengthening, but even though it's not yet fully dark, he feels guilty asking Jane to meet him after supper. Rather scandalous, but it's hard for her to get away during the day. Her mother and sister keep her busy with their charitable and social endeavors, and she insists on spending time with her niece, Louisa. It warms Henry's heart to watch her affectionately attend to the child. He knows she will be a wonderful mother. The Auntie Em to Patience Mott's Wicked Witch of the West.

Henry stares into the dying sunlight and pictures what his and Jane's children might look like. Hopefully, exactly like their mother, although if they are boys, his height will be a blessing. He turns at the sound of light footsteps, but it's a boy with his baseball mitt in one hand and the remains of his sack lunch in the other. Henry wants to look at his pocket watch, but that would mean letting go of his box or potentially ruining his hair. He's about to start hopping in place when a soft hand touches his back.

"I'm sorry I'm late—"

He spins around and scoops Jane into his arms. He kisses her, almost frantically, and she kisses him back. Her hands go to his hair, and he no longer cares if it stands straight up from his head like the flames of a brush fire.

He slowly lowers her to her feet, and rests his chin on the top of her head. She rests her head on his chest. "Darling," she whispers. "Your heart is beating like mad."

"Excitement mixed with terror will do that to a man."

"Is something wrong? I wondered why you insisted we meet this evening." She smiles. "Although I'm so happy you did. Someday we won't have to arrange such meetings. We'll meet over our own dinner table."

"Jane, do you mean that?"

"You know I do. Everything we've talked about. Our future." She touches his cheek. "I love you, Henry."

"I love you, too. And I—" He steps away from her and takes a deep breath. The clashing scents of jasmine and pluff mud are suffocating.

Am I truly going to do this? Does she truly want me? *His own conscience has an English accent. It almost sounds like Anne Boleyn.* Am I sure I can make her happy?

Henry has never understood the idea of happiness very well, but he knows that for the past six months, Jane Robinette has made him feel more hopeful and content and full of life than he's ever felt before. She makes him as happy as he's capable of being. He vows that he'll do his damndest to make her happy, even if another red-headed Henry failed the love of his life four hundred years ago.

I have to do it now, before I scare myself off.

With that thought, Henry falls to one knee.

"Henry! Goodness. Did you trip—" She takes his arm.

He digs around in his pocket, and for a moment, he can't find the damn box. He's about to turn the pocket inside out when his fingers close on it. He presents the box to Jane.

She puts one hand over her mouth. He prays to God, or fate, or the ghost of Anne Boleyn, that her wide eyes are a good sign.

"Jane, I love you. I loved you when we were children. I loved you when all I knew of you were your eyes staring out at me from Mother's newspaper clippings. Staring at me... like you saw me. Like you were trying to tell me something. Like maybe you needed me." He opens the box, and Tipsy peers over Jane's shoulder. Inside is an oyster shell resting on a bed of pine needles.

Jane squints at it, then smiles up at him curiously.

"It's from your parents' oyster roast on New Year's Day," he says.

"The day of our first kiss."

"Mr. Croghan shined it up for me and applied the gold leaf."

"Mr. Croghan?"

Tipsy recognizes the name. Even in her day, Croghan's Jewel Box on King Street is the finest jewelry store in Charleston. Scott bought Tipsy's engagement ring at that shop.

"I had other business with him as well." Henry points at the shell. "Look underneath it."

Jane gingerly lifts it and gasps. Henry picks up something tiny. Tipsy scoots as close as possible to see it. The dark purple stone—the tiny diamonds. It's Jane's engagement ring.

Henry holds the ring toward her. "Jane, sweetheart. Will you marry me?"

"Oh, lord. Yes!" Jane jabs her finger at him and he pushes the ring past her knuckle. She throws her arms around his neck. He falls over backwards and they tumble onto the damp spring grass. He lands on his back with her sprawled across his chest.

"Damn. Are you alright?" he asks, as he slides the box containing the oyster shell back into his pocket.

"Yes. Yes, darling."

"My ass is wet. Not the most dignified proposal."

Jane laughs. She holds up her left hand. "Oh, the ring. I want to see it in the sunlight."

"It's a deep blue sapphire," he says. "Almost purple. It reminds me of your wild indigo bushes."

"I do love them. They're just reaching their peak."

"So am I, since you said yes to me."

"Silly. We have years ahead of us to grow and flower."

He takes her hand and kisses her ring finger. "I had Mr. Croghan find the stone especially for you."

"Not a typical engagement ring."

"You're not a typical girl. I thought you could set the oyster shell on your dressing table. Place your ring in it when you're doing your little lady things."

"I will do exactly that, and think of this night every time I look at the ring or the shell." Jane props herself on her elbows and looks down at him. Strands of dark hair fall around her face. "I love it."

"Let me ask you again, just to hear your reply," he whispers. "Will you marry me, Jane Robinette?"

"I will, Henry Mott."

She leans down and kisses him again. He wraps his arms around her.

"Good heavens," says a female voice. "Young people have no shame."

They glance up at the elderly collie walkers. Jane giggles and buries her face in Henry's chest.

"Ah, Mildred," says the old man. "You weren't opposed to a roll in the grass in your day."

"Mildred, you hussy," Henry says in Jane's ear.

She covers her mouth with her hands and he sniggers into her hair. She rolls onto the grass. "I'm crushing you," she says.

He turns toward her. Tipsy looks down on them as they hold hands with their noses touching. "Never. You're so tiny. The only way you could ever crush me is by not telling me exactly what I must do to make you happy for the rest of your life."

"This," says Jane, as she kisses him again.

The memory fades, but Tipsy knows that they will eventually make it home that night. Henry will walk Jane back to her house, and promise to visit the next morning to speak with her father. Neither will think about the fact that he's done the asking in reverse by talking to Jane first. Henry has never been a man to worry about such things, and Jane is too happy to care.

Tipsy's physical reaction to her memory time-hops seemed to be settling into a predictable pattern commensurate with her level of ghost-busting experience. After she witnessed Henry's moonlight proposal, her shoulders and joints ached for the rest of the evening. A headache gently thumped in time to her footfalls as she plodded up and down the stairs with baskets of laundry.

In her experience, the best way to cure a hangover, whether induced by alcohol or supernatural forces, was to sleep it off. After a successful Taco Night, she crawled into bed as soon as the kids were settled, but to her chagrin, she was like a hound dog with a stuffed up nose. The sweet scent of sleep eluded her. She tossed and turned. She sent Scott an extra goodnight text and checked on the sleeping children three times. She felt chilly, and then overheated. When she rested on her right side, her wrist throbbed and her sciatic nerve seized up.

Her overtired brain produced clipped, repetitive thoughts. She pictured Jane and Henry in White Point Garden, and for the millionth time, wondered how two people who were so in love could have ended up being one another's kiss of death.

It sure seemed like Henry put a lot of thought into that ring, said Granna. *He was right pleased with himself.*

I can see why. Jane loved it, and it couldn't have been easy for him to purchase a special sapphire on whatever allowance his parents gave him. The oyster shell was another pretty little touch. Tipsy watched the ceiling fan spinning over the bed. *He's keeping it on the vanity table in Jane's old dressing room. Right back where it belongs. He said he hopes it brings her comfort to see it there.*

That man can be damn thoughtful.

No kidding. So much effort. Then he lets her slip away as easily as me dropping my cell phone overboard on P.D.'s boat last summer.

Henry had worshipped Jane from across an ocean for years, and done everything possible to convince her father of his spousal suitability. He even agreed to work at his father's dry goods store, a choice that suffocated his creative dreams under sacks of salt and flour. After all that, he shoved her right into the arms of another man. Had he lost his mind during his life, then lost it a second time as a ghost? Or was he truly that self-centered? That ungrateful for his amazing good fortune?

He lost everything in the end. Some might say, serves you right, Henry Mott.

How many times do I have to remind you, sugar? asked Granna. *Plenty of people deserve a dollop of fresh cream, and get spoiled milk instead. Vicer-verser, too.*

Regardless of Granna's rationale, Tipsy would never take her own blessings for granted. She lay in bed, feeling intensely thankful for her children and Scott. For her friends, living and dead. For a career that allowed her to follow her passions and put food on the table. For the beauty of the Lowcountry. For her health. Even for Big Ayers, who had given her those children. She'd had challenges, but these days, life was *so good.*

She scrunched her eyes shut and tried to send positive energy out into the universe, or karma, or *Our-Father-who-art-in-heaven*. Whatever force controlled fate and life trajectories. The afterlife, too, since she knew it existed. Surely something out there had a plan. She longed to tap into it and know everything would be okay; that she wouldn't lose this beautiful life that she feared she'd simply stumbled into. She channeled her gratitude into the ether, and finally fell asleep.

She dreamed she was falling down a flight of stairs. She grabbed for the railings, but her hands were sweaty and she wore slippery silk. She couldn't stop herself. Faces flashed past her and she screamed for help, but no one reached out and grabbed her flailing hands. They all stared at her, and even though she couldn't see their features or hear their voices, she knew they were judging her. She tried to yell for Scott and her kids, but she couldn't remember their names. She couldn't remember her grandmother's name. There was nothing but this endless falling, like Gandalf tumbling into the chasm at *Khazad-dûm* after the fiery Balrog.

What kind of mother was she? What kind of person can't remember the names of the most important people in her life?

I do know their names Ayers-Mary-Pratt-Olivia-Grace-Scott! Estelle Myers McNair known as Miss Stella at the Martinville Piggly Wiggly wake up wake up wake up Tipsy!

Unlike in the movies, Tipsy never screamed when she woke from a nightmare. She didn't sit up or flail around. She simply regained consciousness. She tried to open her eyes, and for one terrifying second, her eyelashes stuck together. She'd been crying in her sleep. Her heartbeat slammed in her ears. Dream emotions are spring water pure, and shame and fear swamped her. She blinked, and some of the emotional detritus washed away with the tears.

She sat up and wiped her face. She had to lay eyes on her kids, so she clipped down the hallway and peeked into their bedrooms. She returned to her own room and picked up her phone. It was three in the morning. The worst time for insomnia to strike. By the time she fell asleep again, it would be time to get up. Scott would be down for the count, but she sent him a text, anyway. I HOPE THIS ISN'T WAKING YOU. BAD DREAM AND I HAD TO TOUCH BASE. CAN'T WAIT UNTIL THAT WILL ONLY REQUIRE ROLLING OVER.

"Back to bed," she whispered to herself. "Going to count sheep. Say the alphabet. Count to ten thousand—"

"I used to sing nursery rhymes to myself when I couldn't sleep," said a soft voice.

Tipsy hadn't noticed the blue light wafting from under the bathroom door. Jane passed through the door and into the bedroom. "In my last few years of life," said the ghost, "a good night's rest was *hard* to come by."

"Do you still have that problem as a ghost?" asked Tipsy, as she sat on the edge of the bed.

Jane disappeared and reappeared beside her. Tipsy tucked her legs under the blanket to shield herself from Jane's chill.

"Never," said Jane. "As a ghost, any time I close my eyes, I drift off into a state of…*something*."

"Do you dream?"

"No. I miss it."

"I usually look forward to my dreams. Maybe it's my artistic nature, but they tend to be dramatic. Sort of adventurous. Worlds I can't explain. Creatures I've never seen. Things that seem like magic but make total sense. But what just happened in my head…" She rubbed her hands over her face. "No thank you."

"Henry described his dreams like that, so it must indeed be the creative in you both. Mine were more *practical.* I forgot to pick up a package from the post office. I kept going back, but every time I leave, I forget it again. *That* sort of thing."

"Scott always dreams he's back in college and forgot he had a test. Why are so many dreams about forgetting things?"

"Perhaps because when we're awake, it can be *so hard* to forget. I'm sorry to bother you—"

"You're not bothering me! This reminds me of our old chats on my bed. Remember?"

Jane smiled and nodded. "How we laughed! And *you* ate those strange orange squares."

"Cheez-its. Still love 'em." Tipsy snuggled into the covers. "I want y'all to move on, Jane. But I'm glad I'm getting extra time with you."

"So am I, my friend." Jane lay down beside her, like they were two girls telling secrets at a sleepover. "Thank you for looking after Henry for me."

"He looked after me as much as I looked after him. Just like you asked him to. He's been an amazing friend to me." Tipsy bit back tears. "I don't know what I would have done without him."

"I suppose I don't know what I would have done without him, either."

"Maybe lived a lot longer. Sorry, that was harsh."

"Our lives ended harshly, but…could I have made *other* decisions? Not married Henry *at all*? Not turned to Proctor? *Perhaps*." Blink, blink, blink. "But I *did*, and here we are."

"Can I ask you…"

Jane smiled again. "You can ask me anything. So don't ask if you can ask. Just *ask*."

"How are you feeling about Henry…right now? You said you're appreciating the time together but…I imagine it must be kinda weird. Ninety years estranged. Y'all find out how y'all died, then you move on right away. A few years missing each other from two opposing planes of existence and now you're back together and—"

"I understand what you mean. We're *trying*, but sometimes we look at one another and…there's so *much* to say, but neither of us know where to start. So we merely…"

"Y'all what?"

"We…*stare* at one another. Like two alley cats walking on the same fence, trying to scoot around each other."

"Hmm." Tipsy thought about LeeLee Moretz's hypothesis that Jane and Henry's current conundrum was about their *lives* rather than their deaths. If that was true, they needed to start talking, but it was a lot to expect of them. No matter how much they loved one another, they were still products of their own time. A time when children were seen and not heard and adults were supposed to suffer in noble silence.

Jane and Henry needed intense post-mortem marriage therapy. Henry, a male specimen of the Lost Generation, would be particularly ill-equipped for such an emotional deep dive.

Well…I've been Big Ayers's unofficial therapist for two years, and I'm marrying a mental health professional.

Still a tall psychological order for someone with a fine arts degree, said Granna.

"The conversation has been…*ungainly*…at times," said Jane, "but I still love him, and he still loves me. Despite all the naysayers who said we wouldn't last a year."

"Who were the naysayers, other than your parents?"

"There were a few. Some louder with their opinions than others, like…one *special someone*. He was as opinionated and pushy as Henry, and as stubborn and sentimental as me. Even if he tried to hide the tender part of his nature, or didn't understand it."

"John Huger."

"Yes. The *brother* I never had. Sweet Johnny."

"I'm so happy I got to meet him, Jane. He was an amazing guy."

"And I'm glad he found love with Miss Ivy. I always knew he was waiting for the right one. Even before he knew it himself. As a matter of fact, I questioned his romantic life even as he questioned mine."

"Really? When?"

"How about another practice memory?"

The flashing yellow lights that often mark the transition from present to past dissipate into regular old sunshine. Tipsy stands beside a barn, close to the edge of the woods. Down a dirt road lined with picket fences, she sees a brick and clapboard house. It's Jane's mother's family farm, the Old Cannon Plantation. The leaves haven't turned yet, but they have a lackluster, faded look that means they're considering it. The sky is as bright as the leaves are dull. In the Lowcountry, the leaves usually don't fall until late November, and the last quarter of the year brings some of the most brilliant skies. Tipsy guesses it's autumn.

She turns toward the sound of humming. Jane sits on an overturned feed bucket in front of a cramped paddock. She wears dusty old-fashioned jodhpurs and muddy paddock boots. Her black hair is braided and hangs down her back. Tipsy notes her sapphire ring on her left hand. Seems she should have removed it for farm work, but maybe it's still too novel. Too precious to let it off her finger for a split second.

She's rubbing a fat white Shetland pony's leg. The little animal nibbles at her sleeve and snuffles her boot. Contentment oozes off her as she whispers to the pony.

"Shh, shh, Snowflake." The pony puffs in her ear and Jane gently pushes her head away.

Jane's happy thoughts and emotions waft over Tipsy. Jane loves all the animals at the Old Cannon. Chickens, ducks, geese. The three saddle horses, quarter horse geldings named after local rivers: Stono, Cooper, and Ed (short for Edisto). She loves the herd of six goats, the farm's crafty, gluttonous busybodies. She has a special fondness, however, for Snowflake, the best Christmas gift Jane and Connie ever received. The girls were only five and three, respectively, on that long gone Christmas morning. They had named her for her shiny white coat, even though they'd never seen snow and couldn't know that the stocky pony was as far from a delicate snowflake as a horse could be. They'd outgrown Snowflake within a few years. Their father considered selling her to the family at the next farm over, who had a passel of grandchildren. Jane and Connie had been mortified, and Jane made her parents promise to keep Snowflake forever, in the hope that someday their own children might ride her. Connie's daughter, Louisa, had already brought Snowflake out of her repose, much to the pony's annoyance. She preferred to snooze under an oak tree and eat until she was as wide as she was tall.

Jane knows she's a poor singer, but she keeps up her tuneless humming as she picks burs out of Snowflake's thick mane. She's thinking about the arrival of her friends and family, as well as Henry and his family, later that afternoon for two days of engagement festivities. Hopefully, she and Henry will sneak in some alone time. The hayloft might do nicely. Scratchy, but it offers some privacy. Her own nerve impressed her. "I've become so brave in my womanhood, Snowflake," she whispers, with a conspiratorial smile.

"Daydreaming as always, aren't you?"

She turns at that familiar voice, shades her eyes, and looks up at the dear face of John Huger.

She stands and hugs him, although her head barely reaches the middle of his chest. "Johnny! Y'all aren't supposed to arrive until supper. Mama will be mortified if the house isn't just so."

Tipsy wishes she *could hug John Huger, who will end up as a dear ghostly friend, even if this living version of John wouldn't know who the hell she is. Instead, she has to content herself with admiring him. His NBA-player height, and broad chest swelling against his white cotton shirt. The straight blonde hair that falls across his forehead. His bright blue eyes and square jaw covered in sandy five-o'clock shadow.*

"It's only me and my good pal Bullet." John points at a tall chestnut horse with white stockings. Bullet's rein is draped over a fence rail beside the barn. He nibbles at a few leftover dandelion stalks.

"Y'all rode over from Merrimac?" John's family plantation is about two miles away. A series of woodland paths connect the two farms and the others in the area.

"It's a fine day for it. Bullet needed to stretch his legs, and I wanted to catch you alone. Before you're drowning in good wishes and I can't get a word in edgewise."

Jane steps around Snowflake, who has returned to nibbling the laces of her boots. "What words do you have to get in? You have opinions on the flowery China my mother selected for me?"

"Too fussy for my tastes. You and Henry plan on doing a lot of entertaining?"

"No more than any of our friends."

"Henry doesn't strike me as an eager host. He's a bit…uneasy with others."

Jane stiffens. "You've come to discuss my fiancé's flaws."

"No. But I want to discuss your choice."

She sits again as Snowflake wanders toward her water bucket. "My choice is made, and I'm happy with it. Why can't you be happy for me, too?"

"Janie, I want *you to be happy. Even if my mother's great dream of our marriage will die when you and Mott say I do in June."*

"Haha. My parents feel the same way. Even if you and I never did."

"I've told them that it would be like incest for me to marry you, or Connie. Plus neither of you would tolerate my antics."

"That's true. All the women might chase after you, but woe be to the one who actually catches you."

"You mean my philandering ways?" He rubs his fuzzy chin with one big hand.

"That, yes. But also your high and mighty opinion of yourself." She grins and throws a piece of carrot at him.

"Can't help it. My parents raised me to be arrogant."

"We all did, with the way we all love you."

"And I love you. That's why I want to make sure you want to do this. Y'all got engaged after courting for what, four months—"

"Nearly six, Johnny, and by the time we walk down the aisle, it will have been well over a year since Henry came home. We'd like to get married sooner, but my mother is set on a June wedding. I'll be twenty-one, and Henry, twenty-two. We're not children."

"Even if you're not racing to the chapel, there's still the matter of—"

"I hope you experience this someday. But it's true what they say. When you know, you know." She holds up her ring finger, and points at her sapphire. "Like Henry knew exactly what kind of ring I'd like. Didn't even have to ask me."

"That was nice of him, but there's more to it than picking out jewelry. So what is it? I don't understand. None of us do, frankly. He's always been so odd—"

"Y'all were mean as snakes to him! You don't know whether he's truly odd, or he was simply cowed by you and Reed and Tradd, not to mention Cam Brewton. That child was like a hungry horsefly on Bullet's behind."

"We weren't kind to him. I'll give you that. But don't you remember how he was? Staring into space? Talking to shadows?"

"He's not like that anymore. He's a grown man, and he's traveled the world, and he's nothing like the boy you remember. Sometimes he's shy—"

"That man has never had an opinion he didn't want to express, and most condescendingly."

"Y'all don't have much in common. Henry is a man who lives in his mind."

"And I'm a big stupid oaf. That's what he thinks of me, anyway."

"He doesn't," she said, but she didn't sound convincing.

"I'd love to be proved wrong about Henry, if the man ever lowers himself to have a conversation with me. But I'm worried. Y'all are happy now. But what happens two years from now? Five years? When the bloom is off the blossom? Do you want to be married to melancholy?"

"He's not always melancholy. It's more like…" She loved Henry more even as she struggled to describe him. "Other men are defined by action, but Henry is all thoughts. I've never met a man who thinks so much, so deeply. And he loves my *thoughts. You don't know what it's like to be a woman, where your face on the front of your skull matters more than what's happening inside it."*

John grimaces. "That's morbid."

"But it's true. All I've heard my whole life is how pretty I am. How with my looks and my last name, I can have my pick of men. But that's not really true, is it?"

"It is true, Janie." He smiles. "Except me. But we've already established that's mutual."

"See—that's what a man might think. A pretty woman—and one with family money, to boot— picks and chooses. But what you don't understand is that a man might see me and think, that's the girl for me. *Then he gets to know me and finds I'm not so appealing."*

"Don't be silly. All the boys in town are after you."

"You sound like Connie! Some might think *they're in love with me, from a distance. I'm the ideal of what their parents have told them they should want, but it's not as if I had other serious suitors. No one beating down my door to marry me."*

"I suppose when you put it that way—"

"I'm twenty years old. *I know how men think. I'm a woman with too many opinions. To many hopes and dreams of my own, beyond a family and a pretty house."*

"You're getting married. Y'all are moving into that pretty house in Mount Pleasant after the wedding, and I assume you're not planning to live like a Papist priest and nun."

"Of course not. I want children. A whole slew of them. So does Henry. But he sees me as more than a pleasant face and a bank account and a baby

factory! He loves me for all the things another man might merely tolerate in me."

"I suppose so, but—"

"He's the one who is *beating down the door for me. Despite all my unwomanly thoughts and opinions. When Daddy finally approved our marriage he said to Henry,* you want to take her on, she's yours now.*"*

"He may have said that when you and Henry were both harassing him day and night, but he's worried, too. You ever considered that your mama wants a long engagement to give you time to change your mind?"

Jane glares up at him. "No, I have *not, and I* will *not. Y'all need to trust me. Besides, who are you to talk? I don't see you skipping down the aisle. I know you. You're waiting for something special. Something beyond what our parents imagine for us."*

"We're talking about you, not me."

"Aren't you though?"

"I don't know. Maybe…I…" He throws up his hands, but he smiles. "Always gotta be putting uncomfortable ideas in my head, don't you? No wonder Henry Mott, who loves to fill up his brain with confusing notions and impossible questions, is the only man who can tolerate you."

"But he doesn't just tolerate *me, John. I* just said *that. He loves me for all the reasons I want to be loved."*

"Alright, alright. I can tell you're not going to waiver. Maybe I even admire you. So overrun by passion and so damn sure of yourself."

"That will happen for you someday. I know it will. In the meantime, will you at least try to get to know Henry? Maybe y'all could be friends. You may not share a love of hunting and baseball, but you're not true *opposites."*

"We both admire strong women. And we share that insufferable arrogant streak."

"You might even bring out the best in one another."

"I'll try if he'll try. We have one other commonality. We both want you to be happy."

"We will be, Johnny. I'm sure of it."

Chapter 8

On Wednesday evening, Big Ayers ran the volleyball carpool and Tipsy scooped up Little Ayers from lacrosse. As she crossed the Ravenel Bridge, she noted that it was almost 7:00pm. She was bone tired from lack of sleep, painting, taxiing kids and monitoring the end-of-the-year academic crunch, and the never ending grind of organizing everyone's lives. Two supernatural memories in twelve hours pushed her over the edge. If she tried to cook anything, she risked burning the house down.

"How about Chick-fil-A, buddy?" she asked Little Ayers.

"*Dude,"* said Little Ayers.

"Is that dude good, or dude bad?"

"Chick-fil-A is always good. Chick-fil-a is *fire*."

"'Kay, you got it. But I'm not your dude, remember? Nor am I your *bruuuuuh*."

"Sorry, Mom. Sometimes it's easier to use one word that says it all."

At the stoplight, Tipsy sent Big Ayers a text. I'M GETTING CHICK-FIL-A. WILL GET THE GIRLS THEIR USUAL ORDER UNLESS I HEAR DIFFERENT FROM YOU. BTW, A IS STILL DRIVING ME NUTS WITH ALL HIS DUDE TALK! PLEASE REMIND ME HE'LL GROW OUT OF IT, BRUH!

They hit the drive-thru and headed home. Immediately upon entry, she sent a muddy, grass-stained Little Ayers up to take a shower. She looked at her phone. Nothing from Big Ayers. They had a rare running joke about their son's bro-speak, so she figured he'd reply.

Big Ayers isn't known for his sense of humor, said Granna. *Maybe the joke got old.*

He didn't reply about Chick-fil-A, either.

The girls always get Chick-fil-A sandwich meals, no pickles, with a Dr. Pepper. No need for him to reply.

You're probably right, said Tipsy, as she put the food bags in the oven to keep them warm and stuck the drinks in the fridge. She texted Scott.

TIPSY: FINALLY HOME, BABY! WHAT A DAY. I WORKED ON MY TO-DO LIST FOR HOURS, CHECKED OFF TWO THINGS, AND ADDED FIVE. DID YOU PICK UP T & C?

SCOTT: HEY BABY. NO, I DIDN'T. KATE SENT ME A TEXT SAYING SHE WANTED TO KEEP THEM TONIGHT. NO REASON. NO RESPONSE TO MY TEXT SAYING I PLANNED ON HAVING THEM AND HAD DINNER WAITING.

TIPSY: IRK. THAT'S ANNOYING.

SCOTT: SHE'S HOARDING THE CHILDREN, A SURE SIGN THAT SHE'S MISERABLE WITH AYERS. NOT SURE HOW TO HANDLE IT. SHE CAN'T KEEP SWITCHING PLANS AT THE LAST MINUTE WHEN THEY HAVE HOMEWORK AND STUFF.

TIPSY: IT'S A HARD BALANCE, AS WE BOTH KNOW. DO YOU WANT TO COME OVER LATER SO WE CAN TALK ABOUT IT?

SCOTT: YUP. I'LL HIT THE GYM FIRST. IF I DON'T HAVE KIDS, MIGHT AS WELL GET IN A WORKOUT.

TIPSY: K. LOVE YOU.

SCOTT. LOVE YOU, TOO.

The front door opened and Mary Pratt and Olivia Grace ran inside. "What's for dinner?" asked M.P. "We were bugging Dad to go faster because we're lowkey starving to death."

"Chick-fil-A," said Tipsy. "Didn't Dad tell you?"

"Yay!" said O-Liv. "Nope. He didn't tell us. Where is it? I'm, like, dying."

A freshly scrubbed Little Ayers walked into the kitchen. "Y'all go up and shower first."

"Moooommm. We're wasting away." M.P. sucked in her cheeks.

"I had to shower first," said Ayers.

"You're smellier than us," said O-Liv. "Boys are naturally stinkier."

"Ayers, you were covered in mud from being outside," said Tipsy. "The girls are sweaty, but—"

"We're still sweet!" M.P. grabbed the bag from the oven while O-Liv retrieved the drinks and a bottle of Chick-fil-A sauce from the fridge.

"I don't know about all that," said Tipsy. "I was going to say, it's almost eight. Dirty or not, y'all have to eat."

"That's unfair," said Ayers. "It's discrimination, bruh."

"No, you refuse to wear deodorant!" said M.P.

"Whoa, y'all. Chill out, okay? Sit and eat, then the girls are going right up to shower."

"Great," said Little A. "I'll watch TV while you dudes remove your own stink."

"I am *not* a dude, Ayers," said O-Liv.

"Oh, Mom, Dad wants to talk to you," said M.P. "He's waiting outside. He asked us to tell you, but I forgot because Ayers is being so annoying."

"Watch out. Dad's in a grumpy mood," said O-Liv, matter-of-factly.

"Huh. Okay. Can I leave y'all in here for five minutes without someone getting a chicken nugget shoved up their nose?"

Little Ayers pretended to jab himself in the eye with a waffle fry, and the girls cracked up. Their arguments over stink factor and the unfairness of shower order were temporarily forgotten.

Tipsy walked out the front door and put eyes on Big Ayers in his truck. When he rolled down the window, she noted uncharacteristic silence. He usually blasted music, and she never knew what tunes DJ ALC IV would be spinning. Artists from Johnny Cash to Lady Gaga had a spot on his iTunes library's bookshelf. He wore his black and orange NASCAR driver shades.

"Hey," said Tipsy. "Sorry the girls were hustling you. I texted about Chick-fil-A—"

"You trying to take me back to court, Tipsy?"

"Uh—" She instinctively answered his question with a question. "Why do you ask?"

"Brad Humphries is a fountain of knowledge. First, he exposes you and Brandt. Now he's filled me in on your visit to Darlene Donnelly."

"I didn't meet with Darlene. I met with LeeLee Moretz."

"You're airing our dirty laundry to our son's friend's mother."

"It's not our dirty laundry, Ayers."

"Right. It's only mine. Every problem in this family is the result of me spilling chocolate milk and red wine and ketchup all over our lives."

"That's not what I'm saying—"

"You couldn't *come* to me, Tipsy? We've been getting along and I've been cool about you and…*him,* and you still sneak around behind my back and see a lawyer. A lawyer who happens to be the secretary of the Pinegrounds PTA!"

"You've snuck around talking to lawyers plenty over the past four years. I wanted to see if I should be doing anything, *legally*, to provide stability for our children."

He removed his sunglasses. The bags under his eyes reminded her of Little A's wet socks. The graying blobs of cotton that were probably congealing on the bathroom floor. "You don't give *a shit* about me, do you?" he asked.

"Don't be ridiculous. I've always hoped you'd find happiness. But you're not…we're not… I'm not your *best buddy*. I'm the mother of your children. If your wellbeing aligns with theirs, and I can help and support you, I will. But I'm not putting your wellbeing before theirs."

"And *this bullshit* is supposed to benefit the kids? Taking me to court and riling things up again? I'm existing in a damn pressure cooker. Like batter in a waffle iron!"

"I didn't say I'm taking you to court. I was just exploring my—"

"*Fuck* your options, Tipsy. You come after me right now, and I swear, we'll never recover."

"We've recovered from worse than this."

"*Nothing* has ever been this bad. I can't—the past few years—things were getting better and now—"

He abruptly jammed a finger on the stereo system. The Notorious B.I.G. blasted through the speakers. Biggie lamented that it was all a dream, but for Big Ayers, the dream had become his nightmare reality. He dug his fists into his eyes.

"Ayers," said Tipsy. "Are you okay?"

"No!" he shouted. "I'm not goddamn okay! I'm about to get divorced for the second time and you're taking me back to court on top of it!"

"I'm not—"

"Stop it. *Stop talking*. Stop—" He gasped, and his eyes rolled back in his head. He smacked the console, and inadvertently whacked his phone. The stereo skipped, and Biggie started crooning about how Miami and DC prefer Versace.

"Are you having a panic attack? *Ayers!* You need to breathe—"

At that moment, Scott's Yukon pulled into the driveway beside Ayers's Sierra. Scott killed his engine and got out of his truck. Tipsy motioned to him. "Scott, can you please—there's something wrong with Ayers. I don't—"

"No, no, no." Ayers gasped it out. "Don't bring him—can't see—"

"Ayers, hey," said Scott. He was wearing gym clothes. Still sweaty from his workout, but mild compared to the sweat dripping down Ayers's forehead. "You okay, man?"

"Not fucking okay!" barked Ayers.

"Tipsy." Scott waved toward the house. "Give him space."

Tipsy backed up as Scott calmly spoke to Ayers. Tipsy couldn't make out his words, but Ayers's breathing slowed. He covered his face with his hands, but Scott kept talking. Ayers's music library moved on to Puff Daddy/P Diddy, who didn't know what anyone wanted from him, but he had a lot of money and a lot of problems.

As Ayers got a grip on himself, he leaned back against the head rest. "Can you drive, man?" asked Scott, more definitively. "You want to come inside?"

Ayers opened his bloodshot eyes and grabbed the gear shift. "No. Yes. Uh, I'm fine to drive. Not coming in. Kids are there. I'll go."

"Ayers," said Tipsy, as she crept closer. "Please don't be embarrassed about this—"

Scott tried to hush her, and from the look on Ayers's face, she knew she'd said the wrong thing. Ayers's lip curled. "You gonna run to LeeLee and tell her I'm having a nervous breakdown? Take my kids from me? Ruin my life for the second time—or maybe it's the third time. Hell, I can't keep track of all the times you screwed me over."

"No, I'm not—"

He cranked the engine. "I'll fight you. If I have to fight you and Kate at the same time I will."

Scott rested his hands on the window. "Come on, dude. No one wants to fight anyone—"

Ayers shoved his glasses onto his face, although the sun was setting and the streetlights were on. He cackled hysterically. "Ah-hahaha! That's where Little Ayers gets it. All the *dude this, man that.* Y'all trying to replace me as his father?" He pointed one finger at Scott. "I always knew your Mr. Nice Guy routine was bullshit."

He slammed the truck in reverse and sped down Bennett Street. He wore his sunglasses at night, like a redneck Corey Hart.

"What the hell just happened?" asked Scott.

He looked truly bewildered, so Tipsy gave him a complete explanation. "Brad finally told Ayers I met with LeeLee. He had a panic attack over me taking him back to court. Your soothing Dr. Brandt voice talked him off the ledge. Now he's enraged with both of us for seeing him in a vulnerable state."

"That clears it up."

"Apparently, he's also paranoid that you're trying to replace him, because our son is using mannerisms common to all male persons over the age of ten, including Ayers himself."

"Not all of us. I still haven't picked up *bruh*. But sorry if I'm spreading *dude-man* to Little Ayers."

"Ayers himself used to refer to me as *dude* when we were married. He seems to have forgotten we've been joking about Little A's bruh-isms for months. You could have called him a jolly old chap, or Comrade Collins, and he still would have taken offense. *Shit.* I never had a chance to tell him that LeeLee advised me *against* taking him to court, or that I'm following her advice."

Scott shook his head. "Dude."

"Bruh," said Tipsy, because as Little Ayers had pointed out, sometimes one word sufficed.

She pictured Ayers, frantically taking lefts and rights in the Old Village with Cypress Hill blaring from his speakers. Insanity had infiltrated his membranes. Maybe he'd switch to Wu-tang Clan as he peeled across the Ben Sawyer Bridge. He'd speed down Middle Street, and hopefully avoid running over a jogger or rear ending a golf cart. He'd wheel into his parents' driveway like a bat out of hell heading into another level of the inferno.

When one is seeking an escape, there are endless roads to take. Highways, wooded paths, country lanes.

Long, straight, dirt driveways in little upstate towns.

Tipsy is fourteen, and she's standing on the cement front porch of Granna's house. In the four years since Daddy took her to get new shoes at Clodhopper's, he's switched from an old pickup truck to an old van. It's tan with brown and orange stripes around it and looks like something Scooby-Doo and the gang would ride around in. The Martinville Mystery Machine. Daddy is sitting in the driver's seat. There's stuff piled all around him, so Tipsy can hardly see him. It's a good thing Mama is small, because she'll be squeezing in there.

Tipsy already said goodbye to Daddy. It was uncomfortable, like their interactions always are. Now she's saying goodbye to her mother. She's about eight inches taller than Denise Denning, so even though Denise is the parent, she's looking up at Tipsy with wide gray eyes like a child trying to explain away her own naughtiness.

"You know Daddy has always had trouble finding work around here. The Denning name won't get you far in this town."

"Right," says Tipsy. She knows that her grandfather on Daddy's side, who died of liver failure before she was born, was a legendary town drunk. His son had taken over that illustrious title, albeit with better looks and more charm. His charm had worn thin on the people of Martinville as Randy stumbled through his twenties, getting fired from job after job and racking up a bunch of DUIs. She'd heard the ladies at church saying that it was lucky he'd never killed someone, although it might be good riddance to bad company if he ran into a tree. Something that absolved the world of him, but didn't do anyone else harm.

"It's a blessing that he's found work in Charlotte," says Mama. "If he gets some good training, maybe we can move back."

"I know," says Tipsy.

"You're better off here with your Granna. Who wants to move to a new school in ninth grade?"

"Not me."

"Course not. You don't want to leave all your friends."

Tipsy's mother doesn't realize she doesn't have many friends these days. Tipsy almost corrects her, but it seems pointless, so she says, "Uh huh."

Granna opens the screen door and steps onto the porch. "Did you sign that document from the lawyer?"

"We both did. It's on the counter. You got full custody."

"I have to get it filed with the court first."

"Call us if you have any problems."

"You'll need a give me a number."

"I'll call as soon as we get settled in the new apartment. Phone ain't hooked up yet."

"Right," says Granna.

"We better get going!" Mama hugs Granna, who stiffly pats her back. Then Mama looks at Tipsy. Her stare makes Tipsy feel like a strange species of bird that should be living in the tropics. Not here, at the edge of the mountains. She suddenly grabs Tipsy and hugs her, too. Tipsy freezes, and even though she isn't trying to imitate Granna, she ends up giving her mother an equally stiff pat on the back.

"Y'all take care! I hope this nice fall weather sticks around!" Denise runs to the van. She hops in and slams the door. The vehicle is in reverse before she's fully settled in the seat.

Neither Denise nor Randy wave. They back down the driveway in a cloud of dust, turn onto the state road, and disappear.

Tipsy exhales when Granna puts a hand on her shoulder.

"You doing all right, sugar? You haven't said much."

"Ain't much to say."

"Not *much to say."*

"You say ain't, *Granna."*

"You ain't me, Tiffany Lynn." She points down the driveway. "And you sure ain't them."

"No. I'm not." Tipsy looks down at Granna, who is about the same height as her mother. "You think they'll stay married?"

"They're thirty-three years old, and they've been together since they were fifteen. If they've stuck it out this long, I assume they'll keep at it."

"I think Daddy screws around on Mama."

"I won't ask why you think that, unless you want to tell me."

Tipsy thinks about Marnie from the shoe store. She wonders if her father had called her. "I don't want to talk about it."

"That's fine."

"You think Mama knows?"

"If her fourteen-year-old daughter knows, pretty much everyone knows."

"Why does she put up with him? And why doesn't he leave her, if he doesn't want to be married?"

"As to your first question, people will put up with a whole lot out of fear of the unknown. As to the second, maybe Randy Denning has his own fears of the unknown. Or maybe he's just an asshole who was blessed with a handsome face."

Tipsy sighs again. "I got chemistry homework."

"I got chicken to fry."

"Sounds yummy."

So on the day her parents leave her, Tipsy and Granna go back to their usual routine. Over the years, Tipsy will wonder why her parents never got divorced. In the end, Granna's answer seems the simplest, and the most accurate.

The day after Big Ayers's meltdown, Tipsy was on her front porch, squinting at an alligator. Not a real one, fortunately. Gators rarely turned up in her neighborhood. They preferred freshwater ponds like the ones in I'On, not the salty expanse of the harbor surrounding the Old Village. As for this guy, he originated from the wet end of Tipsy's paintbrush, not from a leathery egg.

Despite her many depictions of Lowcountry fauna, she'd never tackled a gator. Her quirky new clients had asked for *something like a psychedelic Chinese tapestry*, and she'd come up with this beast. The electric green gator was bottom up. His tail at the top of the narrow canvas; his frontend, southbound. The perspective made his powerful jaws seem to loom out of the stark white background. Except for his neon beer sign coloring, the gator was eerily realistic. Dozens of shiny teeth and thousands of rough scales. Vacant yellow eyes with a black slash down the center, like the Eye of Sauron.

I've had Lord of the Rings on the mind lately, Granna.

Maybe that's where you're getting inspiration for those fantasy pieces.

Tipsy considered the idea, but it didn't seem quite right. *Something like that. To quote Tori Amos, a sort of fairytale.*

That scaly fellow would do well in Mr. Tolkien's world. He's more dragon than gator.

Yes, replied Tipsy. *Some world, or another.*

Henry and Jane strolled right on through the closed front door as she dabbed white and yellow paint on the gator's prehistoric chompers. They exchanged good mornings all around, and Jane peered closely at the canvas. "That's a *strange* painting, if you don't mind me saying so. I never saw a gator like *that* in the pond at the Old Cannon."

Tipsy straightened out of her hunch and nodded. "The couple who commissioned it, Richard and David, are renovating a house downtown on the Eastside. They moved here from New York and have eclectic taste."

"Modern parents give their children the oddest names," said Henry. "Who is the man, and who is the woman?"

"Neither," said Tipsy. "They're both men."

Henry frowned. "You said they're a *couple*."

"They are. They're married." Tipsy tilted her head to the left to stretch the right side of her neck. "Men can marry men, and women can marry women."

"That's the most bizarre thing I've heard in one hundred and thirty years."

Jane frowned right along with Henry, but she recovered her manners faster than he did. "Well, I *never*...but...that's...so *interesting*."

"Some people still don't agree with it—"

"I second their disagreement. That's quite unnatural."

"You might think so, H.M., but gay people are people, too."

"Surely they can be *happy* with a proper spouse."

"Huh? Oh." Tipsy chuckled. "Gay doesn't mean happy in this context. It means...men who love men. Women who love women. Then there are people who love *everyone*, or no one—"

"Psst. That's too much for me, Tipsy. It's all...how do you say it? Beyond my outhouse."

"You mean *outside your wheelhouse*. I won't try to convince you of anything more than the reality of the situation. Gay people exist, and they always have. They're *normal people*. They have lives and families. They're sons and daughters and siblings and parents. And they commission expensive artwork, so here I am with this *fabulous* gator."

"Parents? How is *that* possible?"

Jane hushed Henry, and beckoned him to the loveseat. As they sat, she said, "We heard rumors about people like *that*, even in our day. So much has changed in the world. Who are we to judge?"

"But...but...that's simply...two men...I...and look at that painting! Eclectic taste? More like *terrible* taste."

"Do you remember Blaine McLeod? He worked for my father at the bank." Jane's voice dropped to a whisper, as if Blaine McLeod, who must be long dead, might hear her questioning his intimate proclivities. "Such a nice man, but there was something *different* about him."

"I suppose he walked more like a...and his laugh..." Henry sighed. "But he was a decent fellow."

Tipsy left them to their palavering and returned to her work. Jane's open mind and kind nature would beat Henry down. Henry had accepted many aspects of modernity, from emails to women in obscenely tight pants to improved racial harmony. She figured he'd eventually accept gay people, too. He knew what it was like to be pushed to the outskirts of society due to a trait over which he had no control. The man *was* a clairvoyant.

Tipsy's phone dinged, giving her the one hour warning before she had to pick up the kids. She plopped her paintbrush into a cup of murky water, and pushed her hands into the small of her back. She raised her voice to be heard over Jane and Henry's chattering. "I'm done in, y'all. I can't tell which is more exhausted, my body or my brain." She paused. "Is it rude to say that, when y'all don't have either?"

"It's simply our ghostly reality. *Ghostly reality*. How silly." Jane looked Tipsy up and down. "You're perspiring, dear. Get yourself a *cold* drink. I still can't feel a thing, but I imagine it's getting quite warm."

Henry squinted into the afternoon sun. "Is it too bright out here for you, Jane? Tipsy, she gets fearsome headaches."

"No," said Jane. "One has to be able to feel *something* to have a headache. But it's true; I did have terrible headaches during my life. They were worse at a certain *time of the month*."

Tipsy thought Henry's red hair might combust with embarrassment. "Jane, come now," he said. "Men aren't meant to speak about, or even hear about, *such things*."

Tipsy saw an opportunity to gently chastise Henry's repressed nature. "Men can talk about the same things that women talk about. Natural bodily functions. Feelings. Intimate relationships."

"I have no desire to speak about the natural functions of my former body, or anyone else's, but I always speak freely about my feelings," said Henry. "Too freely, if you could ask those who knew me in life."

"That's quite true, Tipsy," said Jane. "John once described Henry as a pickle jar full of fermenting feelings."

"Did John say that?" Henry looked mildly offended, then reconsidered. "Surprisingly poetic."

"I know you do, but…" Tipsy wasn't sure how to explain what she meant. Henry had lived his life wrestling openly with existential philosophical questions, grand romantic notions, and his own personal Southern Gothic tragedy, but Tipsy sensed he and Jane needed to fully and genuinely address a century of guilt, shame, embarrassment, regret, and jealousy. If they were going to uncover the *secret within the secret*, they would have to flail around, undignified and exposed, in sour, vinegary vulnerability. That was quite a different jar of pickles.

"Husband, *such things* are as much a part of life as…how would one make a comparison for a man, let's see…" Jane's face lit up. "A swift kick in the balls?

Henry snorted a laugh; his embarrassment briefly forgotten. "I'm glad Pierre Robinette isn't here to hear that kind of talk from his sweet daughter."

"I've done plenty of listening in this house. One thing about being dead, you hear all manner of things you'd never hear in life. Look at us today, talking about men and women marrying…men and women."

"Men say a kick in the balls is as bad as childbirth, but I've done that three times, and I don't believe it," said Tipsy.

"I wouldn't know," said Jane.

Tipsy realized she had inadvertently taken a bite out of her own foot. "Oh, gosh. I'm sorry. I wasn't thinking."

"It's all right," said Jane. "It's no secret that Henry and I never had children."

"You wanted kids, though, right? Did y'all ever—" She paused on the wobbly tightrope between intrusive and encouraging. "I don't want to bring up things y'all don't want to think about, but maybe it's *good* for y'all to discuss these private issues."

"It's not a good time," said Henry. "Jane still hasn't fully recovered—"

"Darling, this isn't a *head cold*, where I'll return to fighting form with a few days of rest. I'm still dead." She gave him a patient smile. "Tipsy is right. It's been so long since we spoke about those…struggles."

Henry squirmed with discomfort, as if Jane had brought up homosexuality again, but he didn't contradict her.

"Yes, we wanted children," Jane continued. "I thought of *little else* for years. So many ups and downs. High hopes. Dashed expectations. I had several…losses."

"Oh, Jane. That must have been so difficult," said Tipsy.

"It was hard on the *whole family*. For years, my parents *pestered* us about children. They had only Louisa, and they wanted a passel of grandchildren. I believe my mother eventually sensed things were not right, and she made my father stop asking. But I felt like a failure."

"The failure surely originated with me," said Henry. "I'm *certain* everyone else thought so. They laid the blame on my…suspect masculinity. Perhaps they thought me one of your…*happy men*."

"No, darling," said Jane. "History always blames the womb."

"Science has proven it's just as likely to be a problem with the man as the woman," said Tipsy. "Henry, look at your girl Anne Boleyn's husband. Henry VIII had six wives and a bunch of mistresses. He only produced a few children. Somehow *all those women* were at fault? Hell, no. The crown jewels were tarnished, if you get my drift. Nowadays doctors can help people with fertility issues. Y'all had the bad luck to be born too early to benefit from any of that."

Henry looked at his wife. "I never blamed you, Janie. Did you *think* I blamed you?"

"My feelings changed from day to day. To tell you the truth, those time of the month *headaches* might have been time of the month *heartaches*. I don't recall feeling that you *blamed* me. Perhaps you stopped caring, but I'll never forget how loving and kind you *could be* in those situations. Do you remember the first loss? We can show *that memory* to Tipsy."

"I never *stopped caring*, even if it seemed I did. And of course I remember, but—" Henry's fidgeting had become a seated jig on that loveseat. "This is all so *personal*."

"What about all the memories I've seen?" asked Tipsy. "You showed me your wedding proposal, from *your* perspective."

"I know I did, but this is even more—"

"She saw us both die a *gruesome death*," said Jane. "There's nothing more *personal* than that. Tipsy needs to understand us. Not only the *us* she saw in this house before I moved on. These memories are the only way to figure out what's gone wrong with you and me and…and… eternity."

"That's exactly what I've been thinking," said Tipsy. "Scott always says true self-reflection is by its nature uncomfortable—"

"That's a lovely philosophical sentiment, but Tipsy has to pick up her children, and—"

"I have thirty minutes before I have to leave. I'll pop some Advil and drink a Coke on the way if need be."

He knew enough that the combination of Advil and Coke didn't need explaining, and if Jane didn't, she didn't care. "Let's show her, Henry."

Jane's openness and enthusiasm heartened Tipsy, but Henry kept babbling excuses. "It might be too taxing on you. You've already pushed yourself too much—"

"I'm strong enough. But if we show her *together*, that will make me stronger."

Henry couldn't refuse that request. He sighed, and held up one hand. Jane and Tipsy followed suit. Three hands met over the glass-topped coffee table, like dancers around a century-old May pole.

Tipsy's house on Bennett Street looks larger, because the trees surrounding it are smaller. She knows the magnolia tree in the corner of the yard as a gorgeous woody matriarch, but in this memory, the tree is only about twelve feet tall, and it's as skinny and knobby as a ten-year-old girl. It seems embarrassed by its prominent setting, as if it isn't ready to be the center of attention.

The house's wood planked siding is white, and the shutters are Charleston green. The same color scheme as in Tipsy's when, but in the twenty-first century, the double front doors are also blackish green. Jane and Henry have a single door, and it's painted red. A white picket fence surrounds the yard. It can't be the same fence Tipsy knows—no wooden fence could last that long—but she can't pick out any differences. Picket fences are as timeless as the American family dream of a happy couple, a few adorable children, and a dog. Only the variety of dog changes. In Jane and Henry's when, perhaps it would have been a collie or a beagle. The subsequent decades had many canine fads: cocker spaniels, Irish Setters, toy poodles, black and yellow and chocolate labs. Tipsy and Scott make fun of Mount Pleasant's current doodle craze. She's never heard Jane or Henry reference a dog, but they should have had one. A neutrally loving and loyal ball of fur may have buffered the tension between them.

"Ouch! Damnation."

Tipsy turns toward that harried voice, and sees Jane leaning over a flowerbed. She's wearing a straw bonnet and a dark purple, calf length dress. Her feet are bare and covered in dirt, like the ghost of Stephen Ramsey. Perhaps acceptable for teenage boys, but it can't be the norm for the lady of a house like this.

Jane straightens, and shakes her hand. She looks at her finger—perhaps examining a cut or a bruise—and wipes it on her skirt. The white ribbon that's supposed to secure her bonnet has come loose. It dangles below her chin, and the bonnet is cattywampus on her head. It's pre-flapper era Jane, so her hair is still long. It's braided, like it was in her memory of John at the Old Cannon, but even from a distance, Tipsy sees that this braid is a haphazard attempt to tame hair that hasn't been brushed in a while. Frizzy strands float from under her hat and stick to her sweaty face.

In her other hand, she holds a trowel, and she wipes that on her skirt, too. She presses her free hand into the small of her back, like Tipsy after a long painting session, then grimaces and transfers that hand to her midsection. Another swipe of the trowel on her skirt, and she's on her knees in the dirt amidst a cluster of purple flowers.

A horn toots twice. Tipsy turns to see a black Model-T type car pull into the drive. It stops before a smallish brick building that no longer exists in Tipsy's when. Perhaps a carriage house. A remnant of those days when the residents of this house kept horses instead of Fords.

Henry peers out the car's window as he drives onto the property. He cranes his neck in Jane's direction, and his face registers increasing alarm. He kills the engine, hops out, and slams the door. He's wearing a gray suit, a white shirt with a high collar, a dark tie, and a straw boater hat with a blue band. He removes his gloves as he strides across the yard.

"Jane!" he says, and then he glances over his shoulder at the neighbor's house. He lowers his voice. "Janie."

Tipsy joins him in approaching Jane, but Jane doesn't look up. She keeps messing with the flowers.

"Janie?" Henry says again, to the top of her head.

She pulls on some weeds. Henry squats before her, so Tipsy joins them. The three of them hunker in the grass. Jane yanks on stalks and plucks dead blossoms and turns over wet dirt. The tense air around Jane is heavy with the scent of spring mud and crushed flowers.

"What are you doing, sweetheart?" asks Henry.

"The wild indigo has finally settled in!" she chirps, but her eyes are on her busy hands. "I'm making sure the weeds don't overrun it. This shade of purple is so vivid—"

"It's lovely, but—"

"You know, they also call these flowers false indigo! *So silly. False or true, it's all* indigo. *So what if it wouldn't make a perfect dye if I squeezed these leaves to a pulp? They're just as lovely. Did you know that the true indigo plant usually has pink flowers? How* true *is it, if it's not even purple? Pink is nice, but these deep colors are so much prettier."*

"I agree, Janie. Like I said, they're lovely—"

"So why call it false? What is true *and what is* false, *anyway? Flowers, families…happiness?" Her voice is more harried with each word, and tears track through the dirt on her face. "We think our happiness will come about in this way, or that way. Just plant the seeds, and it will grow. But will it be true indigo, or false indigo?"*

"Jane. Shhh," says Henry.

"These flowers are also called wild *indigo, Henry, so it makes no sense that they would be* false. *Wildness is much truer that whatever human beings create in our futile…fruitless…attempts to be happy."*

"My wild girl," says Henry, with a patience Tipsy has never seen from him. "You should be resting. Are you in pain?"

She finally looks up at him, and her eyes are bloodshot and swollen. "Pain?"

"Yes. The doctor said you'd have pain. Here." He makes a band around his stomach and his back. "Is it bad?"

"That pain. *Oh, I forgot about it. I suppose there is some."*

"Let me take you inside so you can nap."

"No, no, no. I have so much to do out here." She smiles, but it doesn't touch her bruised-looking eyes. "So much to do, if I'm to make this garden bloom like the gardens at Versailles. See? See all I have to do?"

"I see what you're trying *to do. You're trying not to think about what happened yesterday morning. But we have to think about it sooner or later. Best to get the thinking over with, yes?"*

She abruptly stands, and Henry follows her as if she's jerked his marionette strings. She sways on her feet and drops the trowel. Her hands go to her belly.

"You must rest," he says. "Let me help you."

"I couldn't hold on to our baby, Henry."

He grips her arm to steady her. "Don't talk like that, like you dropped a basket of eggs—"

"But I did, didn't I? I dropped the most precious basket." She takes a stumbling step toward him, and cries out. He looks down at her pale foot against his dark shoe. To Tipsy's horror, there is blood on Jane's foot. "I wanted so badly to hold on, but I couldn't—"

Henry scoops Jane up in his arms. Her bare feet peek out from under her skirts, and the blood drips off them onto her false indigo flowers. She sobs against his chest.

Tipsy follows as he strides toward the house. He keeps up a constant stream of comfort as he takes the steps two at a time, kicks the front door open, and makes for the staircase. "Shhh, sweetheart. I'm here. I'm here with you."

He goes upstairs to their old bedroom—the room that in Tipsy's when is two small bedrooms. He elbows the door open and eases through it sideways. The curtains are open, and the afternoon sun strikes a four-poster bed covered in the same lavender and blue quilt that Tipsy once saw in Jane's bedroom on Water Street. He lays Jane gently on the bed and drapes a fuzzy blanket over her shoulders "Hold on, sweetheart. Let me get…"

Tipsy stands helplessly by the bed as Henry races downstairs. Jane huddles under the blanket, crying in soft hitching breaths. Henry reappears with a pile of soft towels and rags and a basin of water. He sets the basin on the bedside table and then carefully administers to his wife. Tipsy moves away, so she can't see what exactly is happening. The Henry of her time was right about this part—this is too personal a moment to watch in detail. From the quiet whispering, it seems Henry wipes Jane's legs clean, gets her fresh undergarments from the chest of drawers on the other side of the room, along with some kind of period protection belt that must have been a precursor to pads and tampons, but looks to Tipsy like a torture device. He finishes his ministrations by helping her into a lavender robe. The entire time, they whisper to one another, and at one point, Jane reaches up and touches Henry's face, perhaps to wipe away a tear.

When he seems satisfied that she's comfortable, he removes his jacket, vest, suspenders, tie and button-down shirt. His white undershirt clings to his chest and his neatly pomade hair flops into his eyes. He walks around to the other side of the bed, removes his shoes, and lays down beside her. He pulls the blanket over her shoulders and wraps his arm around her.

"Can I tell you a story, sweetheart?" he asks.

"Please do," she says.

"Once there was a man named Heathcliff. He was a gloomy, unpleasant fellow of no fine pedigree, but he somehow won the heart of Catherine, a most passionate, vivacious, beautiful lady. Some questioned her sanity for falling in love with him."

She chuckles. "Even if you have a gloomy streak, only you could make me smile on this day."

"You smiled today. You will smile again tomorrow. Not only for me, but for yourself. Someday, for our child."

"Do you believe that?"

"It's only one…loss…" He says it as if the words are difficult to form. "We have endless time ahead of us to try again. And again. And again. Until it happens."

"If you say so, but I'll always mourn this loss."

"As will I." He squeezes her. "I love you, my wild indigo girl."

"And I you. If all else perished, and he remained, I should still continue to be; and if all else remained, and he were annihilated, the universe would turn to a mighty stranger."

He brushes her hair from her ears and kisses her neck. "If you ever looked at me once with what I know is in you, I would be your slave," *he says. "So you did, and so I am."*

Tipsy recognizes the lines from Wuthering Heights from her eleventh grade English paper on the Bronte sisters. She wipes at her own cheeks, which are suddenly wet.

"Sleep, sweetheart," says Henry.

"I will," says Jane, with the utmost trust. And then Tipsy wakes up to the sound of her own sobs.

When Tipsy looked into Jane and Henry's pale faces, her sobs became the braying of a donkey. "Oh, *good lord,* y'all. I've seen some sad memories in ghosts' heads. I've seen violent deaths and vicious murders and star crossed lovers and abusive parents. But I've never seen anything as sad and beautiful…beautiful and sad…" She thought of Henry kicking down the door, and Jane's tiny bloody foot, and him dabbing at her legs, and her wiping his cheek. She covered her face with a paint splattered rag. "I can't *take* it!"

"I told you, Janie," said Henry. "Tipsy has done much creeping around in our heads, but that was *too much.*"

"No." Tipsy waved a hand. "I'm glad I saw it. I'm so…it was…*whoa.* Okay." She sniffed and tossed the rag on the nearest rocking chair. "You had *how* many miscarriages…er…losses?"

"At least three, maybe four. With the last one, the symptoms started, but they ended after only a week. The doctor told us that my *monthly visitor* had simply arrived late, but I was *sure.*"

"What year was the memory you just showed me?" asked Tipsy.

"It was April of 1917," said Jane.

"I'm sorry, y'all, but I *don't get* what happened over the next few years. I've never seen two people more in love. What changed?"

Henry silently fidgeted, but Jane spoke up. Hesitantly at first, then she seemed to catch her stride, like a lame but spirited racehorse who realized she could still run. "After the first…miscarriage…we started drifting apart. Perhaps it was my fault. With each one, I found it harder to recover. Not physically…but spiritually. Oh, everyone's expectations and disappointment! As soon as we walked through my parents' door, our entire family and all our friends were staring at my belly over their tea cups. I don't know what was worse, their questions, or them silently evaluating me like a prize cow. Even Johnny! I once overheard him and my brother-in-law Andrew speculating over whether I'd gained weight. I missed everyone, but sometimes, I didn't want to visit with any of them. With Henry and I barely speaking at home, I was…*so lonely*."

Tipsy remembered a memory she'd seen several years ago: Jane tentatively expressing that loneliness to Henry, and him blowing her off. Although, it was more than just *blowing her off.* More like blasting her out of the water by giving her "permission" to turn to another man.

Jane looked at Henry. "I'm sorry if that sounds…*harsh*."

"That truth is a harsh winter," said Henry.

"This is *good*, y'all. Jane, you're telling Henry how you truly felt, and Henry heard you," said Tipsy, the armchair therapist. "Now Henry, your feelings are important, too—"

"Why does it matter how I felt?" asked Henry. "I became more reclusive. More disagreeable. Meaner." He crossed his arms over his chest, a gesture of annoyance and self-defense. "It wasn't only the…losses. It was everything. Working for my father. My writing. Living in a backwater village. We already *know* I was a proper ass. Must we rehash all this?"

"If we're trying to figure out what frame of mind y'all were in during that last week, it's helpful to talk about the status of your relationship at that time."

"Our status is well known. I became a martyr to the written word and drove my wife into another man's arms." He stood.

"Henry," said Jane. "I believe Tipsy's right. You and I have spoken about the happy times since I returned. But not about the bad days—"

"I don't want to speak of them, Jane. I have accepted that I caused our deaths."

"Darling, put aside our deaths for a moment. It's our *lives* that need rehashing."

"Even if you were a total ass for years," said Tipsy, "y'all's deaths are not entirely your fault. Proctor pulled the trigger, *twice*, and Jane was a grown woman who made her own decisions. It's not a simple matter of fault or innocence."

"True indigo, or false?" He laughed, but there was something frantic about it. "All right. You want to talk about our lives? I'll tell you. Each time…every loss…was worse than the last. The last one happened about a year before we died, around Christmastime. I arrived home for lunch and the house smelled of gingerbread, and Jane was in the kitchen with a bloody towel, sobbing. I couldn't stand it because I couldn't do anything to fix it or even ease her pain—"

"Your tenderness *always* eased my pain, Henry."

"But I had no tenderness left! I'd used it all up. I turned around and went right out the door. I went for a walk along the harbor and we both cried about it on our own. I couldn't keep…*trying*…because I couldn't stand to see her go through that pain again while I stood by, useless to help her!"

Jane stared at him incredulously. "That's ridiculous. I wanted nothing more than to have a child. I never understood why you pushed me away that last year."

"I was trying to protect you!"

"You couldn't make that decision for me. Not without *discussing* it with me!"

"How could I discuss it? I failed at everything. Writing. Being a good husband. Being a good friend and a good son. I couldn't even sire a child, something buzzards and rats and gators manage quite easily!" He stormed around the porch. The furniture rattled against the floorboards. The screens peeled away from the window panes and waved like dark mourning banners.

Jane looked at Tipsy, and then back at her husband, with growing alarm on her face. "Darling, please. If that's how you *truly* feel, all the more reason for us to discuss it now—"

"There's *nothing* to discuss! I ruined our lives. You wanted to leave me. You *should* have left me. I was terrible. *Terrible.* You add this shame…and…" His face darkened to the purplish blue of a hematoma. A blood blister on the verge of popping. "I have to leave before something explodes."

He spun around and walked through the wall. The furniture stopped moving and the screens flopped against the wall like blackened banana peels.

"At least he stopped himself before he did too much damage." Tipsy pointed at the screens. "Scott and I are planning to remove those, anyway. When you look out the window from inside, they make everything look dingy."

Jane wiped her own sparkly eyes. "Is that what it's like to observe Henry and me? Dingy on the inside."

"Maybe I shouldn't push y'all to talk about that stuff."

"No. We have no choice. We must talk about these unresolved issues between us."

"Was he really *that bad* about the miscarriages?"

"As he said, each time it happened, he grew a little colder. Angrier. Less attentive. I can't say all our problems would have been solved by having a child—"

"Believe me, there's nothing like raising children to increase marital stress. Having kids only exacerbated the problems between Big Ayers and me."

"Still, those struggles placed a wedge between us. Henry retreated further into himself. I would spend a week hibernating in my sadness, and then emerge and pretend I didn't have a care in the world. Ignore everyone's questions and staring eyes. Cheerfully drive myself mad looking for some purpose." She shrugged. "While I envy you ladies your independence and your passions, once I was married, I didn't have much to look forward to beyond raising a family. I couldn't even do that. If I stopped running around like a decapitated broody hen, I felt hopelessness gnawing at me."

"I wish we'd talked more about this a few years ago. Everything that happened—you and Henry and Proctor—makes even more sense now."

"Henry and I barely spoke of these failings when we were alive. I didn't discuss it with my mother, or my sister. Not with John or Proctor."

"We *need* to talk about it now. We have to fully understand all the dynamics. Find the secret within the secret."

"Thank the good lord I have a friend with whom I *can* speak of it." She smiled sadly. "A hundred years after the fact, but better late than never."

Chapter 9

Saturday marked a second attempt at celebrating Lindsey's birthday. With no reservations available at Hall's, and Lindsey in need of an early bedtime, she requested a daytime get together on the Isle of Palms. Shelby and Brian met Lindsey and P.D. at their boat for the cruise up the Intracoastal, but Tipsy had to work on Richard and David's gator, and Scott had emails to answer. They decided to arrive by land rather than sea, so Tipsy offered to drop off kids' stuff at May Penny and Tripp's on the way. She gathered M.P.'s phone charger, Little A's favorite hoodie, and O-Liv's latest dystopian YA book.

"It's great that O-Liv is such a bookworm," said Scott, as they drove over the Ben Sawyer Bridge onto Sullivan's Island.

"Agreed," said Tipsy, "even if these stories are all the same. Let's see…" She turned the book over and pretended to read the blurb on the back. *"Filigree Mistletoe, the chosen one who doesn't realize she's a fairy princess, must save the world from the Superpox, while choosing between two hot guys who are both vampires. They're both madly in love with her even though she is socially awkward and only* slightly *pretty."*

Scott laughed. "I see the appeal to the target readers."

"She *tore* through three of these books during Ayers's last weekend. She left scorch marks on the pages." Tipsy sent the kids a text notifying them of her imminent arrival. "An acceptable excuse to hide in the bunkroom and avoid Gigi's mystery meatloaf."

Scott pulled into May Penny and Tripp's driveway and Tipsy got out of the car. Ayers's truck sat in the driveway beside May Penny's Mercedes sedan. A few beach chairs, a sandy boogie board, and damp towels were piled on the family's garnet and black Gamecock-themed golfcart. The front door opened and all three kids descended the front porch steps in bathing suits. Scott waved to them, then he buried his nose in emails on his phone.

"How's it going, buddies?" she asked them, as she shut the car door behind her. "Y'all went the beach today?"

They responded with shuffling feet and shifting eyes, until Little Ayers said, "Everything's okay. Yeah. The beach."

She ran a hand over M.P.'s wet hair. "Y'all having fun in the pool?"

"Uh, huh," said M.P.

"Going on the boat today?"

"Yeah," said O-Liv. "When BopBop gets back from golf."

At least O-Liv had given her a complete sentence.

"That will be fun," said Tipsy.

A stretch of quiet from the kids. Up north, one might reference crickets, but on a warm Sullivan's Island afternoon, the uniform harmony of a million cicadas provides the rattling backdrop to uncomfortable silences. They droned and paused. Droned and paused. Droned and paused.

More fidgety feet and restless eyes. Predictably, M.P. spoke up first. "Can we come back to your house tonight? We've been with Dad for two nights."

The other two looked at Tipsy hopefully. Despite the pang in her heart, Tipsy said what needed to be said. "No, y'all. This is Dad's time with you."

"But I'm sick of GiGi and BopBop's," said M.P. "It's fun to visit them and stuff, but living here is…" She put both hands on the sides of her head and squeezed. Her eyes bugged and she stuck her tongue out.

"They always say we're on our phones too much," said Ayers.

"And GiGi made me try *mushrooms*," said O-Liv.

"Did you like them?" asked Tipsy.

"They're not as gross as I always thought they would be, but I still don't like them. And she's making *mystery meatloaf* tonight!"

Tipsy smiled at the running family joke. "Ah, mystery meatloaf! I thought you might—"

O-Liv wasn't finished. "I'm ten. Why do I have to eat something I don't like because GiGi says so? Mushrooms *or* mystery meatloaf. It's *so annoying*."

"Careful, honey, you're stompin' on thin ice in steel-toed shoes. Be respectful." It was unlike O-Liv to be the stridently frustrated. "What does your dad do when y'all have these…disagreements?"

"That's the most annoying part," said O-Liv. "One minute he's telling us we have to do what GiGi says because it's her house."

"Then the next minute he's like, *they're my kids, Mama! Damn!*" said M.P., in a passable impression of her father.

"M.P., do not say *damn*."

"We want to be at home," said Ayers. "At your house. Or Dad's *real* house. Why do Tristan and Chloe get to stay there and we have to leave? It's so *unfair*."

"This isn't about fair or unfair. It stinks, but there are grown up dynamics at play here that are affecting y'all."

"I *hate* this," said M.P. "Why did Dad marry Kate, anyway? We don't need her to have Tristan and Chloe as stepsister and brother now that you're marrying Scott."

"How was Scott ever married to her?" asked O-Liv. "She's such a jerk. She's so mean to Dad."

"Y'all," said Tipsy. "I feel like Dad is telling y'all too much—"

"At least I know who *not* to marry," said Little A. "Anyone like Kate the Opp."

The girls laughed, but Tipsy held up her hands. "Okay, enough now."

"Can't we—your house—please Mom—" The chorus came from all three voices. Tipsy wanted to throw them all in the car and get them away from this toxic ass situation, but she couldn't. If she gave in this time, she'd get pushback every time Ayers had the kids. Still, she feared whatever was happening here would damage them forever.

Tipsy, said Granna. *Your kids ain't got nothing like your childhood challenges. Or Scott's, with his drunk daddy who knocked him around and went and got himself killed when the man was four. I ain't trying to make light of the situation, but remember what Lawyer LeeLee said. If this is the worst thing your kids go through, they're doing pretty well.*

Right. It's either this, or drag them through court, which will mess them up more.

You're better working Big Ayers from the inside.

But how? Now he's so pissed at me.

Deal with that later. Deal with the kids now.

She took a deep breath and spoke over them all. "Listen. Listen, y'all! I'm sorry, but as I said, this is Dad's time. I know it's hard. But y'all are strong, resilient kids, and this too shall pass."

"What does that mean?" asked O-Liv.

"It means good times come and go, but so do bad times. You feel frustrated now, but this situation isn't forever, and in the end, it's not that bad, is it?"

"It's like, literally, *the worst*…but we have a pool," said M.P.

"Y'all remember that. Plenty of people in a lot more misery who *don't have a pool.* I'm not making excuses for Dad. He made his decisions, and now everyone has to deal with the consequences. But I hope y'all can learn some lessons from these challenges."

"Like Ayers not marrying someone like Kate?" asked M.P.

Before Tipsy answered, O-Liv said, "Kate is a pain, but Dad can be a pain himself."

"They say it takes two to tango," said Tipsy.

"That's the dancing they do on *Dancing with the Stars*, Ayers," said O-Liv.

"I know what the tango is," said Ayers. "Dad and Kate step on each other's feet the whole time."

"Y'all go back upstairs, okay? Text me if you feel especially frustrated. I'm always here to listen, even if I can't offer a quick fix."

They exchanged hugs and kisses, the kids ran back up the stairs, and Tipsy returned to Scott's truck. She filled him in on the conversation as Scott drove toward the Isle of Palms.

"You handled it well," he said. "My kids still don't even know what's going on, but when they do, I'll have a good script ready."

"Have they been asking questions?"

"Nope. She's telling them that Ayers and the kids are staying with their grandparents again. This is the second weekend, so they may start to get curious."

"Are you sure I handled it okay? Part of me wants to drive back there and get them out of there." She chuckled. "Out of that waterfront mansion where all the adult inhabitants love and spoil them."

"You just answered your own question. We can't save them from every hurt and discomfort, as much as we want to. Like you said, a lot of lessons to be learned in these tough-ish times."

Tipsy squeezed his hand. "Lowkey tough," she said.

He smiled and squeezed back. "No cap."

Despite being condemned a few years ago, the rambling structure at the intersection of the Intracoastal Waterway and Morgan Creek had not tumbled into the Intracoastal. Through vacillating tides and tropical storms, it clung to its pilings like a giant barnacle. After months of renovations by dedicated local restauranteurs, locals and tourists alike had rejoiced at the restaurant's reincarnation as Islander 71 Fishhouse and Deck Bar. Once again, that patch of dockside dry land was a happily chaotic destination for soaking up sunshine and beer. Several levels of elevated decks and a screened in rooftop bar and dining room provided marshy vistas in all directions. For the less adventurous, the interior's wide-paned glass windows separated diners from the mosquitos.

Outside, kids ran amuck on an Astroturf yard in front of a covered stage, panting dogs hid under chairs and slurped up stray French fries, and harried teenage food runners sprinted between tables with platters of fried seafood. Vessels of all shapes, sizes, and methods of locomotion came and went between IOP, Goat Island, the ICW, and Morgan Creek. An opinionated Dad squad supervised the boat ramp beside the IOP Marina Store and judged other dudes' trailer-loading and unloading skills. Salty ladies waved wine glasses and frozen cocktails over their heads as they danced to the band's not-terrible cover of *Brown Eyed Girl.*

Everyone was spring-time happy, with the exception of Lindsey Starkey. She sat between Tipsy and Shelby at the cabana bar while the guys tossed beanbags into a Clemson cornhole board on the Astroturf. P.D.'s twangy voice carried over the music, a toddler's screechy meltdown, and the *fwump-fwump-smack-fwump* of multiple cornhole matches. He loudly entertained Scott and Brian with a raucous concert story—maybe Phish '04, or Dave Matthews circa 2011. It involved taking shots, smoking weed, and making quite the fool of himself.

"I'm *so proud,* y'all," said Lindsey, and rolled her eyes.

"I sense sarcasm," said Shelby.

"You prefer straight talk? Sure, why not. I'm dangling on the edge of the Cliffs of Insanity. With no Fezzik to carry me to the top."

"Princess Bride analogies don't count as straight talk," said Tipsy.

"It's *that* bad?" asked Shelby.

"P.D. *does not* get it. *Yes,* he's busy at work, but his job mostly involves visiting corporate clients and then schmoozing them up on Clarice's boats. I'm at home with Little Paul all day, then racing to pick up Emma and dealing with her activities all afternoon. Then I make dinner and clean up, get Paul to bed, and do homework with Emma. Oh, and there's the endless laundry."

"Don't say the L word," said Shelby. "I've got three loads waiting on me."

"Now that I'm pregnant again, I'm so exhausted I can't see straight. When P.D. *is* home, he's no help. He riles up Paul so he can't settle down for bed, which pushes *my* bedtime back. P.D. wants me to leave Paul with Emma and go out, or God forbid, stay awake till Emma is asleep and have sex. I just want to sleep myself."

"At least when my kids were little and helpless," said Tipsy, "everyone went to bed early. I got a couple hours to myself."

"If it wasn't for my mother's help, I'd have completely lost my mind. She's keeping Paul overnight tonight and Emma is at a sleepover. I'm glad I'm out in the sun with y'all, but I'm already counting the hours until I go home and pass out."

"When I was pregnant with Brandon, I could barely function," said Shelby. "I don't know how Tipsy managed being pregnant with twins while Little Ayers was a toddler."

"I don't really *remember* how I did it. It's like I blocked out a few years of my life," said Tipsy. "Survival mode."

"Can't P.D. work from home a couple days a week?" asked Shelby. "Clarice should understand. He was a dad."

"Still am a dad, from what I can tell," said a deep voice from behind them. Tipsy looked over her shoulder and right into Clarice Andrews's bluesish hazel eyes. "What's up, ladies?" he asked.

"Clarice! Heeeyyyy!" Lindsey was too chipper, as if she feared he'd overheard her bitching about P.D. "What are *you* doing here?"

"Same as everyone else. Pretty day, cold beer, boat, and music." He turned back to Tipsy. "Hey, there, TC. Long time, no text."

"Hey," said Tipsy. "It's been a while. Good to see you."

"I heard you got engaged to a shrink."

"Wow. Word sure does fly."

"Like a hungry seagull after a fishing trawler. Congrats. Where's the lucky guy?"

"Over there, beside P.D. The one with the dark hair and the beard."

As if sensing her eyes upon him, Scott turned. He smiled and waved. As always, his handsomeness struck Tipsy like a four car pileup. She returned his smile, then blew him a kiss for good measure.

Clarice was a rancher sizing up a head of prime cattle. He nodded. "That makes sense."

"I'm not sure how to take *that* comment."

"It's a compliment. Y'all make a fine looking couple. A lot of hearts broke the day he popped the question. But you know how it is. People snooze, they lose."

"Uh, thanks." Tipsy had no interest in Clarice, but she squirmed, anyway. A couple years ago, he'd expressed his hope that she'd be available when he finally tired of his bachelor life.

"So what's your complaint about my best salesman, Mrs. Starkey?" he asked Lindsey.

"Probably the same complaints your ex-wife had about you," said Shelby, before Lindsey could reply.

"Works all the time? Not enough help with the kids?"

"Sounds right. But don't forget the Peter Pan syndrome and an overactive libido—"

"We were hoping you'd give P.D. a little flexibility," said Tipsy.

"Maybe show him the error of his ways before he ends up *divorced* like you," added Shelby.

Lindsey scowled and took Shelby's frozen margarita from her. "Shelby tends to be blunt when she's hanging out with *Senor Patron* and *Senor Cuervo*. Everything is…fine."

"Just family growing pains, right, Linds?" asked Tipsy.

Lindsey smiled stiffly and stood. "Yup, that's it. I have to go to the bathroom. Again."

"I'll come with you to make up for my big mouth." Shelby cut her eyes at Tipsy as she got to her feet.

Tipsy wanted to kill Shelby for leaving her alone with Clarice. She couldn't resist stirring up drama. As her friends headed for the potty, Tipsy felt around for a safe topic. "Sooo…how's work?"

"Busy. Isn't that the only correct answer? But it's Saturday, so I have a few hours off the clock. Perfect day to meet a friend here for drinks."

"*Right.*" Tipsy knew all about Clarice's friends, who were usually female, pretty, and came with a lot of benefits.

"Not *that* kind of friend. One of my high school buddies is in town. He's staying on the island with his family."

"Oh, that's nice. Sorry I jumped to conclusions."

"No worries," he said. "Those convos we had a few years ago stuck with me. I haven't gotten involved with anyone who doesn't want what I'm interested in."

"Most women don't, even if they say they do."

"I learned that, too. So thanks. Now that I've been divorced for a few years, I'm open to something significant. Not sure I want to get married again, but I don't want to be *that guy* at the bar forever. You hit fifty, and it gets downright creepy."

"P.D. needs a reminder of that fact."

"Huh. It's legit bad?"

Tipsy nodded. "If you and P.D. have a good relationship, you may want to encourage him to tone it *down* with the partying. And *up* with the fathering and husbanding."

"Will do."

Tipsy's curiosity got the better of her. "So you're looking for a real relationship?"

"If I can find a good one. Seems like a certain *head doctor* reeled in one of the prime catches before I could cast my line."

"Haha."

"I'm happy for you. You deserve it. If he deserves *you*, then he must be a good guy. Y'all take care of what you've got."

"We will. I hope you find someone awesome."

"There's my buddy. Good catching up with you."

"You, too." Clarice walked off toward a balding, pot-bellied middle aged guy, and Tipsy took a few seconds to acknowledge that Clarice wasn't a total womanizing creep.

Or I guess it's more accurate to say that he was a womanizing creep a few years ago, but he isn't now. Maybe he wasn't before, *either. Before his divorce screwed him up.*

Divorce makes everyone go off the deep end for a while, said Granna.

I certainly did. Like I told Jane the other day, I was sooooo not okay. Two years in a parallel dimension, where Tipsy Collins was a hot mess inside a dumpster fire inside a trainwreck. Thinking about it all made Tipsy's toes curl in her flip-flops. Terrible dating choices had resulted in endless gossip, lost alimony, text meltdowns, cringy run-ins, the public throwdown of the Windjammer incident, and the worst hangover of her life. Multiple heartbreaks—including a self-imposed one when she freaked out and temporarily dumped Scott. *Who the hell was that person, Granna?*

You learned so much, sugar, and you found yourself again, said Granna. *Scott had his own post-divorce crisis in dating Whitney, then he came back to earth. Maybe Clarice had to find his way back to his true nature, too.*

"Hey, baby," said Scott, as he appeared behind her. She turned in her seat, slid her arms around his waist, and squeezed.

"Hey." She looked up at him. "I love you."

"Love you, too."

"I really, really do." She squeezed tighter.

He tapped her nose. "Same. You a little tipsy, Tipsy?"

"I'm always Tipsy," she said. "Just ask Lindsey." She pointed at Lindsey and Shelby, who were on the return leg of their potty break. Shelby whispered in Tipsy's ear before she slid into her chair.

"*Gossssss-iiiip*," she said. "You're not going to believe this. Seriously."

"Oh, boy," said Tipsy, but she followed up with, "What happened?" Even if she didn't like being the subject of gossip herself, it was hard to resist Shelby's suspenseful delivery.

Shelby wagged her eyebrows at Scott, who was getting himself and Tipsy another beer. "Hold please," Shelby whispered.

Scott handed Tipsy her beer, kissed her again, and returned to the guys. As soon as he was out of earshot, Lindsey leaned in. "We ran into Julia."

"Will's Julia?" asked Tipsy. "Or his *former* Julia?"

Julia was Lindsey's longtime aesthetician, a pretty brunette who wasn't quite thirty. She had the dubious honor of being the next notch on the belt of Will Garrison, Tipsy's squishy peach post-divorce relationship. According to Lindsey, Will had broken it off with Julia when she pressured him to get married and have kids. The downward spiral of *Wulia* started slowly, with Will commencing the same hokey-pokey, in-and-out routine he'd pulled with Tipsy. After jerking Julia around for a few months, he abruptly ended it and immediately moved on. His newest conquest: Brittany, a divorced mom in her early thirties with one child. After several years of experimentation with different models of women, Brittany and her single offspring were a happy medium between Tipsy and her boisterous brood of three, and Julia and her anxious ovaries.

"Yup. It's so awful. I feel so bad for Julia," said Lindsey. "You know he's already got a new chick. Brittany Woods or Woodley or Wooten. Something like that. He did work in her kitchen—"

"Maybe in her bedroom," said Shelby.

"Julia hadn't talked to him in a while... *until* this morning. She ran into them at brunch—"

"Oh, *good lord.* Not at Red Drum?" The very spot where Tipsy had discovered Will was seeing Julia.

"Yes! *Lit-er-ally*!" Shelby shook her head. "Will is *so predictable*. The man can't even have an original run in with an ex-girlfriend."

"At least you kept it together when you discovered him with Julia. As for Julia..." Lindsey grimaced.

"She went ballistic and dumped a pitcher of Bloody Marys on his white shirt," said Shelby. "It looked like a murder scene. Olives and celery everywhere. The manager kicked her out."

"Wow," said Tipsy. "I don't even know what to say."

"Don't say anything," said Lindsey. "There she is."

Tipsy glanced over her shoulder. Julia had approached P.D. at the cornhole court. Tipsy felt awful for her. She'd lost so much weight on her heartbreak diet that her butt was barely holding up her jeans. Her eyes were puffy from a recent cry. She tried to talk to P.D. but he didn't pay any attention to her. He kept swigging his beer and laughing, even as Julia wiped those tear-swollen eyes. She finally gave up and walked off.

Lindsey's own eyes narrowed as she watched her husband. "What a *jerk*. He's got all the sensitivity of a mouth full of Novocain."

"Come on, Linds," said Shelby. "Maybe he doesn't want to get caught in the rumor mill—"

"*Shelby.* You know P.D. cannot keep his mouth shut about gossip any more than we can. He's just drunk, and being an asshole."

As she finished that sentence, the asshole in question approached the bar. "Hey, hottie!" he yelled. "There's my *gorgeous* wife. How you doing, honeybunch?"

Lindsey ignored him and sipped her Sprite.

"Uh, oh. What did I do *now*, ladies?" he asked Shelby and Tipsy.

Shelby shrugged and Tipsy muttered something about pregnancy and tiredness. P.D. leaned over Lindsey's shoulder. "What's up, hot stuff? Come on. You want something to eat?" He patted her stomach. "Feed the little monster?" His smile became a grin. "And the baby?"

Lindsey's head slowly turned, like the possessed girl in *The Exorcist* facing down an ineffective servant of God. She didn't levitate, or projectile vomit on P.D., but her voice was hellfire. "Get your *boozy breath* out of my *face* before I *punch* you in *yours.*"

Two random women to Lindsey's left looked at each other with wide eyes. The guy standing behind them muttered, "*Damnnnnn.*"

"Whoa!" said P.D. "I was joking—"

"Joking? *Joking?* Do I have to explain the difference between a *joke* and an *insult*? Are you forty years old, or fourteen?"

"*Okay*! I'm sorry—"

"You're *always* sorry. Did you tell Julia you were sorry for ignoring her when she was crying?"

"Julia…*what?* She's worked up about Will and Brittany—"

"You hung out with Julia regularly for *three years*, but you won't look away from your cornhole for five minutes and give the poor girl some comfort. No wonder you can't give *me* any comfort! You're like… an *emotional epidural*! A great big *needle*, right in my *ass*!"

Lindsey's ranting so enthralled the bartender that he overpoured a draft Westbrook IPA. As he grabbed a rag to sop up the mess, Tipsy almost gave in to nervous blabbing. *She means a needle in her spine, not her ass, every pregnant lady knows that! Nothing to see here!* Anything to discourage the eyeballs that were now staring at Lindsey and PD from all four sides of the rectangular bar, including Clarice and his friend, who observed the spectacle over their cheery yellow frozen Painkillers.

P.D. glared at Lindsey. "You need to *calm down*," he said. As every woman knows, that is the *worst* thing a man can say in the pursuit of said result.

"Don't you tell me to calm down! Don't you—"

"You're not making any sense! How did we go from me not talking about my best friend with his old girlfriend to me being a terrible husband?"

"You *weren't* a terrible husband until we had a *baby*!"

P.D.'s mouth fell open. "Am I a terrible father, too?" he asked, when he got over his shock. "Are you saying I don't love my son? Or the child you're carrying?"

"I'm *not* saying that." Lindsey started crying. "I know you love them, but—"

"What about Emma? *Your daughter*, who spends more time with *me* than your old geezer of an ex-husband?"

"It's not that…that's not what I mean—"

"What the hell do you mean, Lindsey?"

"I've been trying to say all these things in a *nicer way* and you never listen and now it's all coming out wrong because I'm so… *tired*… and so… *sad*… and—" She collapsed onto Tipsy's shoulder, sobbing.

"Hoppin' hell. What is *going on* here? Linds?" P.D. touched Lindsey's shoulder but she shrugged him off.

Shelby stood and whispered to him. "Y'all got to get out of here, P.D."

P.D.'s tortured expression combined growing hurt and confusion with lingering anger. "But I wasn't planning on driving the boat yet…I took a couple shots—"

"Argh!" Lindsey slid off her barstool. "I'll drive it."

"You shouldn't be driving across the harbor—"

"The harbor is as flat as two-day old spiked seltzer this time of day, and I've been driving a boat since I was ten!"

"I'm trying to look out for you and the baby—"

"Whatever! You love it when I'm *knocked up* and I can drive you everywhere, by land or sea—"

"Linds," said Tipsy, in her ear. "You gotta stop. People are staring."

"I don't care anymore. Can y'all get our tab? I'll Venmo you."

"Yes, sure—"

"Are you coming with me?" Lindsey asked P.D.

Tipsy held her breath. If P.D. decided to stay and drink and play cornhole, Lindsey would probably make an appointment with LeeLee Moretz on Monday. Thankfully, for the sake of the entire Starkey family, P.D. sighed. "Let's go."

Lindsey stalked off toward the dock with her huge husband lumbering after her.

"Jesus, Mary, and ever-lovin' Joseph." Shelby waved at the gawkers around them, both behind the bar and in front of it. "Show's over, people! Go back to your Fireball shots and crab dip." She waved at the bartender. "Can I get a Mich Ultra, draft?"

"Gotta change out the keg," said the bartender. "Is a can okay?"

Shelby nodded and retrieved a BROCo koozie from her purse.

"Whoa," said Tipsy. Between her children's angst, running into Clarice, watching Julia boohoo over Will, and that performance from Lindsey and P.D., she needed downtime. "This has been a long ass day, and it's not even five o'clock somewhere yet. I'm as tapped out as the Mich Ultra keg."

"Same," said Shelby. "How about we retreat to the cornhole court and sit in silence?"

Tipsy nodded, and they found Adirondack chairs near the guys' cornhole game. Scott and Brian were still tossing beanbags. "What happened to Starkey and Starkey?" asked Scott.

"Lindsey was feeling…a bit off. They went home."

"I'm surprised she could drag P-Daddy out of here," said Brian. "He was in rare form."

"That's not *rare* form with P.D., unfortunately. It's his everyday form," said Shelby. She lowered her voice. "That's the problem," she said to Tipsy.

Tipsy nodded her agreement and clapped for Scott as he tossed his third straight bag into the hole. "Nice one, handsome!"

"I'll never stop trying to impress you," he said, and flexed one bicep.

Tipsy laughed, and settled back into her chair. She held her beer in her lap, slipped off her flip-flops, and tucked her bare feet underneath her, Jane style. She thought about P.D. and Lindsey, and how he'd clearly stopped trying to impress her. Or maybe he'd stayed true to his nature. If Tipsy and Scott's true nature led them back to family-oriented stability, maybe P.D.'s would keep him entrenched in the opposite mentality. That didn't bode well for his own family life.

It remained to be seen if P.D. could adjust his nature enough to save his marriage.

~

Once Lindsey and PD left, the afternoon mellowed out. The remaining foursome stuck around Islander 71 until sunset. Shelby, once the queen of the late night rallying cry, sounded an early retreat, since she'd be getting up with her babies when said sun resurfaced. Tipsy and Scott returned to Bennett Street and watched Netflix for an hour. They were in bed by eleven, which was how she liked her Saturday nights these days, but once again, she couldn't sleep. She stared at the ceiling long after Scott had fallen asleep. Around one in the morning, she sat up and swung her legs over the edge of the bed.

Scott rolled over and ran his fingers down her arm. "Where y'going?" He blinked against the moonlight streaming through the open window.

"Can't sleep. Going to see if Jane is up for a girls' chat."

"Come back soon. I'll get cold without you."

"You throw off more heat than a bottle of Texas Pete, silly."

"Come back soon, anyway," he said, and rolled back onto his side. She patted his shoulder, donned her USC hoodie and her taco print pants, and crept downstairs. She flopped onto the sofa in the sitting room and covered her legs with a blanket. "Jane? You around?" She gave it a few seconds, then tried again. "Janie?"

Jane materialized on the sofa beside her. She rubbed her eyes as if just waking up, but as usual, she had no sleep-puffed face or pillow-messy hair. Probably no cotton mouth or dragon breath either. "Goodness. You're up late again."

"Can't sleep. Got a lot on my mind."

"Offload your crates onto my railcar, honey. That's what friends are for."

So Tipsy described the day's drama, with her kids and with Lindsey and P.D. She told Jane about running into the infamous Clarice Andrews, and Will's disgruntled former flame. Jane wrinkled her nose the mention of Will. "I'm still so disappointed in that man. He seemed like a fine fellow when y'all started courting."

"Sometimes you gotta get past the courting stage to know who someone really is."

"Are you and Dr. Brandt passed that stage?"

"Oh, gosh, yes. He's the only man I've ever loved *more* after that first blush of romance wore off. I've never been more certain about anyone in my life than I am about Scott."

"It sounds like your friend Lindsey isn't so sure. And as for the elder Ayers…"

"I don't know if he's capable of being truly sure about anything or anyone. I can't help but feel sorry for him. I even feel bad for Julia. Now she's almost thirty, and she's wasted three years with him. She might end up marrying the first guy that comes along. Some women don't want kids, and that's the right thing for them. But if you do want them, the biological clock's ticking can be more like a gong. I remember Shelby—" Tipsy noticed a thin line had formed between Jane's eyebrows. "Damn. There I go again," she said. "Goin' on about biological clocks after everything you went through."

"*Biological clock.* I've never heard that, but it makes sense to me. The farther Henry and I drifted apart, it felt like my clock's springs were rusting and seizing up. Tiiiiickkkk…toccccck….tiiickkkk…toccccck… *Sproing!*"

Tipsy pictured a cartoon clock, like the ones in old Looney Tunes cartoons, exploding. "Henry sure didn't help matters. When the three of us were talking the other day, I remembered a memory you showed me years ago. The one where Henry suggested you go elsewhere after you… you…" Tipsy sighed. There was no way to tiptoe around it. "This might sound blunt, but in modern lingo, we'd say you propositioned him."

"He clearly recognized it as a proposition, and just as clearly rejected it." Jane lowered her voice and elongated her vowels. *"If this is about conceiving a child, Jane, you can say so."* She shivered with embarrassment. "I felt ridiculous. Other women hinted around about how they had to beat their husbands off with a stick, and mine...you saw how it was."

"I *also* saw y'all both about combust with passion."

"We certainly put in enough effort to conceive an entire classroom of children." She chuckled. "Sometimes I can't believe I speak this way, about these things! In my day, women never spoke of our intimate lives in any detail. My friends hinted about their men's unquenchable appetites and animalistic nature..."

Tipsy thought of Lindsey's pre-marriage romps with much younger men. "It's not only guys who have unquenchable appetites. Henry lost his though, huh?"

"He didn't *lose* it. It went into hibernation. When he was in a good mood, he'd suddenly sweep me off my feet, and we were madly in love again. I'd feel hopeful that things would change. The next day, he'd want nothing to do with me."

"That must have been so confusing," said Tipsy.

"In so many ways." Jane rested her chin on her elbow. Tipsy sensed memories flittering around in Jane's head, but she didn't raise her hand and offer to share them.

"Was it like that up until the end?"

"Hmm? Ah, yes. Yes, it was," said Jane. "I'm feeling tired myself now, dear."

Tipsy hadn't clandestinely peered into a ghost's memory since her adventures with the psychopath Thomas Bonneau two years ago, but Jane's hesitance piqued her interest. Perhaps the memories she was reliving were important.

"Go rest. Let's reconvene tomorrow," said Tipsy. She inched toward Jane and picked up her phone. "I'll stay down here for a while and scroll through social media."

Jane smiled. "Whatever *that* is."

Tipsy shifted even closer. "Social media? It's mostly photos. My photos, and other people's photos. *Famous people* that I don't even know. Right here on my phone." As Jane leaned in for a glimpse of Instagram, Tipsy braced herself for supernatural impact. "So many memories."

~

The room is bigger than Jane's childhood bedroom. A flimsy wooden door with a crooked knob is sandwiched between two windows. The door leads to the piazza. Tipsy has no faith in that door's ability to keep out either drafts or intruders. At the far end of the room, a carved wooden mantle embraces a fireplace. A dying fire glows in the hearth, and one of those bedside Tiffany lamps is the only other source of light. Tipsy makes out walls covered in blue and gold fleur de lis *paper. Beaded tassels dangle along the edges of the gold brocaded drapes.*

Across from the fireplace, there's a bed with a carved wooden headboard. A mishmash of gray and tan blankets are piled atop the navy blue quilt. A man's wool coat is draped over a chair, beside a desk covered in books and paper and correspondence. Tipsy inhales the scent of burning wood and citrusy perfume as she walks toward the bed. A pink lady's woolen bucket shaped hat and a pair of white fur-lined gloves sit on the bedside table. Given the fire, the extra blankets, and the outerwear, it must be winter. She peers out one of the windows into a dark night light by gas street lamps. The trees are indeed bare. It's Water Street, near the corner of East Battery. She's back in Jane's parents' house.

Rickety-looking cars line the street, so it's not a memory from Jane's early childhood. Tipsy turns toward the interior door as boisterous voices echo down the hallways. Laughter. Pounding feet.

The door flies open and Henry and Jane catapult into the bedroom. They're dressed to the nines—Jane in a black beaded dress that ends below her knees and long black gloves. Her bobbed hair is styled in neat finger curls that are pinned back from her face by a diamond hairpin. Her lipstick is bright red. The whole look compliments her fair skin. Henry is equally fancy in a black formal suit with tails, a high collar, a white bow tie, and glossy black shoes. His hair is slicked to his head. His straight middle part is an arrow pointing to his piercing eyes.

Jane is giggling, breathless, and Henry slams the door behind them. He grabs her from behind and wraps his arms around her. He kisses the back of her neck.

"You must be freezing, sweetheart," he says.

"I'm not! I haven't danced like that in years. I'm still perspiring!"

"Still, this room gets so drafty. I'll stoke the fire."

"Go on. It is frightfully cold out this evening." She waves at the fireplace before sitting at the vanity desk to remove her gloves and earrings. "I'll never understand why my parents got married in January. Still, thirty years is quite impressive, isn't it?"

"It is. And a splendid party to celebrate."

"We have so much to celebrate! Especially your story being considered for The Evening Post*!" Their eyes meet in their reflections and Jane smiles again. Her pretty dimples dig deep into her cheeks. "Maybe Mr. Rockwell will base his newest cover on your story. A painting of your fictional heroes, Mr. and Mrs. Dupre, and their macabre mystery."*

"That would be something, wouldn't it? I doubt Mr. Rockwell has ever painted a Charleston piazza scene. He could come here, and we could serve as his models. Or you *could. No one wants to looks at my gloomy mug while reading the paper."*

"Silly. You're the most handsome *man in this town."*

"More handsome than Johnny?"

Tipsy wonders if Henry is being passive aggressive, but he's smiling. Jane stands and walks toward him. "No matter how many times you ask me that, my answer is always *the same."*

He slides his arms around her waist. "Tell me you only have eyes for me."

"John Huger and Tradd Hamilton and Rudolph Valentino *himself have nothing on my husband. I've only had eyes for you since the day you turned up in our drive for the Christmas party."*

"I've only had eyes for you since you rescued me at Mrs. Lamboll's birthday party. You've always rescued me."

"We rescued each other. You rescued me from marriage to some boring, not nearly handsome enough husband."

They kiss, and Tipsy feels uncomfortable watching, as she did when she observed the memory that started in the garden and ended in their bedroom. She reminds herself that the intimacy is necessary, ignores her own discomfort, and focuses on the unpleasant emotions coming from Jane.

Guilt. Confusion. Torn loyalties.

Thoughts of Proctor flit around in Jane's mind. She feels like she's betraying her lover by being with her husband. An awful conundrum, but her confusion doesn't last long. In Henry's arms, Jane forgets Proctor pretty fast. Despite Proctor's hypocrisy, and his responsibility for Jane and Henry's deaths, Tipsy feels sorry for him. For Jane, Proctor was indeed a temporary panacea. A distraction from her heartbreak. Henry always held sway over her soul.

Henry abruptly pulls away from their kiss and looks down at her. "Do you really think my story stands a chance? As you said, it's rather macabre."

"It's amazing. I'm so glad you let me read it! It's been years since you let me read your work."

"It's only a short story. But if I can have this success, perhaps it will provide inspiration for my novel." He frowns. "I worry that it's too dark for the readers of The Saturday Evening Post.*"*

"It will be a smash. Perhaps instead of the next Fitzgerald, you'll be the next Edgar Allan Poe."

"You know Poe spent time in Charleston, don't you? He was posted at Fort Moultrie in the 1820s."

"I do recall you telling me that years ago."

"He signed up for the army under an assumed name and lied about his age to get away from his overbearing father. What a rascal. Not his true father, mind you. His true father was a drunken actor who abandoned his wife and children. Then his actress mother passed away when he was a young child, and his adoptive mother when he was a young man, and his wife died early…so much tragedy!" He chuckled.

"Poor man. Yet you're laughing!"

"I just realized that Edgar had many more reasons to be solemn than me, yet still I brood." He laughed harder, and she joined him.

"It's so good to see you laughing and smiling, darling."

"It feels good. Like holding you feels good." He rubs her back. "This story could be the opportunity I've needed, Jane."

"I'm sure it will be."

"If I can finally be recognized...truly recognized, I'm sure I'll be able to complete THE GREAT STORY.*"*

"You will. I know you will."

"I'll be able to write full time."

"Yes! No more warehouse."

He kisses her again, as if the idea is turning him on. She kisses him back, and once again, Tipsy feels uncomfortable. She wishes she could hide behind those shiny golden drapes. They stumble back toward the bed, but Henry stops and stares down at Jane again.

"If I can be proud of myself, I can be the husband you want. That you deserve. I promise. I love you so much."

"Then show me, Mr. Mott."

Again they're heading for the bed, and Tipsy turns away, ready for the memory to end. Thankfully, the golden drapes begin to fade. As she wakes up, Tipsy thinks that Henry's story must not have made it into the Saturday Evening Post. *If it did, it certainly hadn't been the marriage cure all they were both hoping for.*

Chapter 10

Tipsy didn't see Jane much over the next few days, a disconcerting development. Since she thought of herself as Jane and Henry's unofficial mental health treatment provider (no licensing needed when one is counseling the dead), she channeled Scott's informal process for analyzing clinical scenarios. On Tuesday—her third Jane-less morning—she sat at the kitchen table with a pen poised over the blank pages in the back of her day planner. As she'd seen Scott do a thousand times, she jotted notes.

SCENARIO 1: JANE SUSPECTS THAT TIPSY LOOKED INTO HER MEMORY, AND FEELS ANNOYED, EMBARRASSED, BETRAYED, OR ALL OF THE ABOVE, AND SHE IS HENCE AVOIDING TIPSY.

SCENARIO 2: THE RECENT DEEP DIVE INTO JANE'S DISASTROUS FAMILY PLANNING EFFORTS HAS PROVED OVERWHELMING, HUMILIATING, DEPRESSING, OR ALL OF THE ABOVE, AND SHE IS HENCE AVOIDING TIPSY.

SCENARIO 3: ALL OF THE ABOVE, COMPREHENSIVELY.

She tapped her pen against her chin as she reread.

Henry has been keeping to himself, too, she said to Granna. *I hope they're not growing apart again.*

They're around all day and you're not, said Granna. *Maybe they're having those long, deep conversations you want them to have, but in private.*

I can't see Henry talking about any of this stuff without me or Jane holding his feet to the fire. Now that the initial happy reunion has passed, being trapped in this house cannot be good for them. It's got to be triggering, being stuck in this place again where they were so miserable, with me pressing them to talk about the origins of all that misery. I need to figure out this secret within a secret before their relationship is destroyed for like the third time.

You're doing the best you can, said Granna. *You've already seen a whole slew of memories, and you're playing marriage therapist. Too bad Scott can't take over that role.*

I wouldn't ask him even if he could see them. He's already got too much stress.

And you don't?

I'm used to stress involving ghosts. He's not.

If he's going to be with you, paranormal stress is going to come up from time to time. He wouldn't want you to keep things from him.

Who says I'm keeping things from him? We're speaking hypothetically. He's never going to see ghosts, so we don't have to worry about him doing marriage therapy with the Motts.

I know, but…Proctor said Jane always had a protective streak. So do you. I don't want that streak to start running amuck. Y'all are in this together. He wants to support you. Team Scipsy, remember?

I know that, Granna, said Tipsy, annoyed.

I'm just saying, don't be afraid to let him. He can handle it. Rahrahrah!

I'm not afraid! And I know he can!

I said my piece, now let's take a breather. In Tipsy's mind, she saw Granna's version of taking a breather. Sucking on a cigarette followed by a long, slow release of smoke. She used to do that when the teenage Tipsy got feisty. *So…anything new from Big Ayers?* asked Granna.

Nothing much. He's avoiding me, too. It's a little alarming.

An ironic thought, since she'd eschewed any unnecessary interactions with Big Ayers for years, even before they divorced, and now she anxiously awaited his every text or phone call. She hated being in the dark, but the kids were so happy to be home with her, they had no interest in discussing their dad's situation. She refused to push them to talk about it.

She reread her notes once more, decided that Scenario 3 was most likely, and got about the rest of her workday. The alligator was nearing completion, so she gave herself a couple hours to work on *The Hand Study*. After about fifteen detailed practice sketches, she'd chosen a final layout and moved from her sketchpad to a 24 x 30 canvas. She'd taken inspiration from the gator's psychedelic Chinese tapestry layout. Jane and Henry's intertwined hands were in the forefront of the piece, so they seemed to reach for the viewer. Behind their fingers and wrists and forearms, almost fading into the background, their peaceful faces. Jane, eyes closed, her cupid's bow mouth turned up at the corners in a small sleepy smile. The first curves of her dimples were faded footprints on her smooth, pale cheeks. Henry, as the big spoon, wrapping himself protectively around her. His square jaw fit neatly into the crook between her neck and her shoulder. Through his thick lashes, his eyes were slightly open. He was keeping watch.

Tipsy was still working on the pencil drawing on the canvas, which required greater detail than the sketchy swooping backgrounds of her acrylic paintings. She'd decided on watercolor for this piece. She didn't often work in watercolor, but she instinctively knew it to be the best medium for capturing the unusual light composition of ghostly blue effervescence and flashing nighttime heat lightning. As she followed the lines of Jane's elegant fingers and her engagement ring in her mind with her charcoal pencil, splotches of color bloomed like indigo flowers inside her head. Lilac, lavender, plum, violet, wine, cobalt, navy, sapphire, azure, haint blue, periwinkle. A golden haze around it all. That warm yellow was comforting, even though it originated in lightning's potentially destructive electrical crackle.

There is no such thing as a false color, she thought. *All are wild. All are true.*

On Wednesday evening, instead of giving their mother insight into Big Ayers's latest activities, the children provided an update on another vexing former romantic partner.

"Guess who we saw at the beach last weekend, Mama," said O-Liv, as they finished up dinner.

"Mr. Will and his kids," said M.P.

"Now Mom isn't *guessing*, big mouth," said Little Ayers.

"Ayers, quit it," said Tipsy. She turned to her daughters. "That's nice. Did you say hi to Ella and Rosie?"

"Yeah. We haven't seen them in a long time, so it was sort of cringe at first," said M.P. "But then it was cool. They were kicking a soccer ball around and they're pretty good."

"That makes sense. Their big sister Isabel played a lot of soccer."

"They said Isabel is driving now."

"Time flies," said Tipsy.

"Mr. Will was there with a lady who is, like, his girlfriend."

"Maybe mom doesn't want to talk about her ex, M.P.," said O-Liv. "Do you want to talk about Mason?"

M.P. made a face and gagged. "Ew, no. He's such a *simp*."

Simp was in Tipsy's adolescent dictionary. A person who was desperate, romantically speaking. Someone like…Proctor James.

"M.P., that's not nice," said Tipsy. "Mason is a sweet kid."

Little Ayers couldn't resist a dig at his little sister's romantic life. "Mason was M.P.'s boyfriend for three days. He doesn't count."

"You've never had a girlfriend for *one day*," said M.P., digging right back. "*You're* a simp!"

"Yes, I have! And I am *not* a simp!"

"Haley doesn't count. She's been our neighbor at Dad's our entire lives. She's like our other sister, or our cousin."

O-Liv laughed. "Ew! Ayers is trying to riz up his cousin!"

"Enough, y'all," said Tipsy.

What in the world is she talking about now? asked Granna. *Raisins?*

No, riz, said Tipsy, like a Gen-Z version of Google translate. *Short for charisma. As in, despite being perpetually glum and arrogant, Henry Mott has a certain unidentifiable riz.*

"Mr. Will was with his new girlfriend, and his kids, and *her* kid. The girlfriend is short and blonde and has big—" M.P. grabbed two apples from the fruit bowl in the center of the table and held them to her chest. She shimmied, and her siblings cracked up. Tipsy took the apples.

"It's true, Mom," said O-Liv. "She sure doesn't look like you."

"She's kind of *mid*, not gonna lie," said Ayers.

"I'm sure she's very pretty," said Tipsy, in response to her son's assessment of Will's new girlfriend as not particularly attractive. She assumed his comment originated in a wholly unnecessary effort to make Tipsy feel better. "People talk about having a type, but Scott doesn't look like Daddy. I shouldn't have to remind you that's it's what's on—"

"—the inside that counts," said M.P. "We know. Anyway, Ella said that lady and Mr. Will are going to get married."

"That's great! I hope it works out for them."

"Hopefully better than it worked out for Dad and Kate," said Ayers.

"No one gets married thinking they're getting divorced," said Tipsy, as she took her plate to the sink, "so I hope everything works out for *all* of them."

"I hope it works out for you and Scott," said O-Liv. Tipsy finished rinsing her plate, and turned around. All three children were staring silently into space. She returned to the table.

"I love Scott, y'all. We've known each other for several years at this point, and we've talked about everything two people can talk about before getting married. We both take it very seriously, because it affects five kids. I firmly believe we will be together forever. He's my best friend."

"Better than Aunt Shelby?" asked M.P.

"It's a different kind of friendship. But in many ways, yes. He's my partner in everything in my life. Aside from y'all, there's no one I want to be with more than Scott. Every day, all day."

"That's kind of gross," said Little Ayers, but he smiled. "Y'all are *both* simps."

"Gross, but cool," said O-Liv, and M.P. nodded.

They finished eating and left the room, and Tipsy wrapped up her tidying. Jane spoke from behind her. "It makes me happy to see how your children speak so freely to you. Even if their modern talk is even harder to understand than yours."

Tipsy turned around. "I've always encouraged it. I'm happy they're comfortable expressing themselves. As for *riz* and *mid* and *simp*, et cetera, sometimes I still need clarification myself, not gonna lie." It was time to fess up. "Jane…I saw into your memory the other night—"

"I suspected you did. You fainted. Once you started waking up and I knew you were safe, I left."

"I saw you and Henry. The night of your parents' thirtieth wedding anniversary."

Jane colored. "Oh, dear. That's *exactly* why I left."

"It ended before I saw anything too private."

"Thank goodness. That night was… it was…*well*….very…"

Tipsy let her off the hook. "You thought of Proctor for a moment. I felt bad for you. And for Proctor, weirdly."

"Even I sometimes feel bad for Proctor."

"You were so happy that night. But I assume things didn't get any better between you and Henry."

She shook her head. "He got word that his story was rejected a few days later. That damn magazine took him to cloud nine and then shoved him off it, all within a week. He was inconsolable."

"You died when you were twenty-eight, and that was your parents' thirtieth, and it was winter. Makes me think it was close to the end."

"It was about a month before we died. After, I tried to reclaim the joy we felt that night. Encourage him. Commiserate with him. But he would have none of it."

"Big Ayers was like that sometimes. I kept filling balloons with positivity, but as soon as I released them, he shot them down with his snark arrows."

A deep voice entered the conversation. "Now I'm no better than Big Ayers."

Tipsy looked around, and found Henry standing beside the refrigerator with his arms crossed over his chest.

"I told you that night that I'd be the husband you deserved," he said. "Just like that gum-chewing buffoon, I never succeeded. I never succeeded at *anything*."

Tipsy felt a hint of annoyance. "Dude, this martyr routine is getting old. Instead of self-flagellating, let's focus on—"

"I was the worst husband in history! Worse than the great decapitator, Henry VIII!"

"Henry," said Jane. "That's ridic—"

"I can't believe you stayed with me as long as you did!"

He kicked the fridge. His foot passed through the door, but Tipsy heard a few bottles inside explode. Water blasted into the sink, and the bookshelf in the corner teetered. A few cookbooks skidded off the shelves and hit the floor with a smack.

"Mom!" yelled one of the girls from the TV room. "What was that?"

"Nothing, honey! Butterfingers in here, dropping cookbooks!" She leaned down to grab the books, but they shot into the air, narrowly missing her nose. With a *skrish-skreet*, covers and pages ripped from book spines. Paper sprayed across the room.

"Henry!" hissed Tipsy. "Damnit, get it together."

"Tipsy's right, Henry," said Jane. "You must control—"

"I could never control myself! No wonder you wanted to leave me!"

He stormed straight into the refrigerator and disappeared. Tipsy and Jane were left staring at a splotch of slightly shimmery air. Tipsy half expected Henry to reappear, but as the air smoothed itself out, he stayed gone. "*What* just happened?" she asked Jane.

"Henry," said Jane, as if that said it all.

"I can see how that man gave you emotional whiplash," said Tipsy. Before Jane asked, Tipsy said, "Like, he spun you around until your head about came loose."

"*Indeed.*" Jane blinked even harder than usual. The kind of blinking that held back tears.

Tipsy wished she could offer her a tissue. "I don't know how you did it day in and day out, for years." As Tipsy bent to pick up the scattered papers, a girlish voice spoke from behind her. Always hard to tell which girl until she laid eyes on the twin in question.

"Mama?"

Mama meant Olivia Grace. Tipsy looked at her first daughter—older by seven minutes—from under her armpit. She straightened up with a smile plastered over her face. "Hey, honey! What's up?"

"Uh…getting a snack. What's up with…" She pointed at the shredded books. "And the water is—"

Tipsy sidled over to the sink and turned off the water. "Just washing some crusty dishes!"

"You arguing with someone? I thought I heard you say...*Henry*."

"I...was on my phone. With a client. Henry. I'm painting something for him and he...hasn't paid me yet. We sorted it out."

"Oh. Okay."

"And I was doing some meal planning and these cookbooks are so old they...fell apart."

"Oh, *dear*," said Jane, unseen and unheard by O-Liv. "An argument with a cheapskate is believable. That one, not so much."

"Go ahead and get your snack," Tipsy said to O-Liv. "I'll clean this up."

O-Liv grabbed an ice cream sandwich out of the freezer, opened it, and dumped the wrapper in the trash. She exited the kitchen with one skeptical eye on her mama.

"Shit," muttered Tipsy. "That was so sus." Before Jane asked, Tipsy explained. "Little Ayers-speak for suspicious. Meaning, O-Liv was not buying it."

"Terribly sus," said Jane. "But what else could you say? Three heavy books exploded in your kitchen for no reason."

"Jane, what am I going to do? Henry has been having these episodes more often. Soon Scott will be living here with his kids. It will be hard for everyone to settle in, even without poltergeist activity. I'm getting more worried by the day."

"I don't blame you," said Jane. "We are quite a handful, especially for one living person. But at least this time, when we go insane, you and Scott can manage us together."

Quick as a self-righteous cat scooting up a vindication tree, Granna spoke up. *See. Miss Jane agrees with me—*

If Jane is already planning to lose her mind, too, I'll take her wisdom with a grain of salt. Tipsy said goodnight to both her dead grandmother and her dead girlfriend, and called her kids to get ready for bed.

Helen Stokes's Aunt Talia lived at the end of a half-mile dirt road on James Island, the unincorporated town across the Charleston Harbor from Mount Pleasant. The City of Charleston included James Island, the downtown peninsula, the swath of suburbia known as West Ashley, and even Daniel Island. To locals, however, those communities were as different in character as the cast of *Friends*.

If West Ashley bespoke the post-World War II era, and Mount Pleasant exemplified the region's current robust growth, James Island seemed to have peaked in the 1980s. A dearth of homeowners' associations meant rambling lots, comfortable split level houses in various states of repair, chain link fences, and boats parked in driveways. Strip malls bumped up against outdated public school campuses, where trailer classrooms surrounded the main educational buildings like scattered LEGOS. Lutheran and Presbyterian and Methodist parishes had lost the majority of their congregations to a few slick mega-churches. Only the egregious traffic on Folly Road, a smattering of trendy restaurants and Crossfit gyms, and the aggressive construction of new housing developments and apartment complexes brought James Island into the twenty-first century.

While most of JI was an ode to Gen-X childhoods, the southern end of the island, near Folly Beach, had significant swaths of undeveloped land. It was here that Helen's relatives were making their stand, on land inherited from her father's ancestors. Helen had referred to it as her *family land*, and from what Tipsy could garner, the family land was a parcel of *heirs' property*. A familiar concept, as her Appalachian upbringing had brought her into contact with these informal family compounds. In rural areas, isolation and distrust of the legal system led landowners to eschew wills and other estate planning devices. All direct descendants of the original landowner had the right to use the land, but as a result, title was never clear. An entire branch of law had developed to help heirs manage the conflicts that inevitably accompanied mass ownership.

Tipsy almost missed the informal street sign announcing Abraham Parker Lane—a half mile dirt road that wound past a few houses, mobile homes, and a warehouse. Abraham Parker's several-hundred-acre legacy abutted the Stono River, and perhaps by virtue of seniority, Mrs. Talia Parker had situated her small yellow clapboard house in a prime waterfront location. Tipsy parked on the driveway beside Helen's Cadillac, an old red pickup truck, and a well-maintained early 2000s silver Buick. Two blue bottle trees framed the short cement staircase leading to Aunt Talia's front porch. A healthy population of ceramic gnomes and stone woodland animals resided in the garden beds, amidst real flowers and faded silk ones. Although Tipsy, like most people under the age of seventy, disdained artificial flowers, Aunt Talia's fake daffodils and tulips and daisies were cheerful and springy. The stone bunnies and ducks made the yard feel like an Easter basket.

At Helen's direction, Tipsy walked around the house. She passed a screened back porch, a cement patio, and an old meat smoker. A rolling lawn dotted with oak trees and crepe myrtles led to a stunning view of the wide, winding Stono River. Tipsy couldn't help comparing the empty expanse of the Stono with the nautical hubbub of the Intracoastal behind May Penny and Tripp's house. Out here, on a Thursday morning, only one center console fishing boat cut through the glassy water. A single camouflage-colored jon boat sat in the marsh. The man onboard stood silent sentry over his fishing pole. He turned in Tipsy's direction, as if he felt her eyes on him. Her mental camera clicked, and she crammed the image into her mind's crowded file cabinet. He didn't know it, but he'd eventually be part of a gorgeous landscape painting. The marsh and the river would be the main show; the man on his boat, a small side attraction in the bottom right corner.

Tipsy loved the Collins's place, but at that moment, she preferred the wild solitude of the Stono. Even as she admired Aunt Talia's spread, she feared for it. Across the river, on Johns Island, the outlines of half-finished, cookie cutter houses broke up the line of trees. The developer had crammed them in to eke out every last dime from waterfront views. In twenty years, the Stono might be as busy as the ICW around Sullivan's Island.

She hoped the Parker Family would get along well enough to hold onto this artist's dream. Even Henry's stubborn writer's block would have to bow to such bittersweet beauty.

"Tipsy! Here!"

Two women sat in rocking chairs on a short, dilapidated dock. Helen stood and waved as Tipsy crossed the yard. The dock reached out over a small tidal tributary of the larger river. The dock's warped boards wobbled under Tipsy's flip-flops as she crossed fifteen feet of marsh. It was low tide, and snails had crawled onto the blades of marsh grass, where they hung like tiny Christmas ornaments and waited for the water to return. She stepped out of the sun's glare into the relative dimness under the pierhead. The darkness under the wooden ceiling only brightened the green grass, blue sky, white clouds, and gray-green water.

She inhaled the scent of marsh muck and damp wooden pilings as she smiled down at Mrs. Parker. Aunt Talia was a predictably tiny woman with bright dark eyes, luminous brown skin, and short white hair. She wore a pink and green Alpha Kappa Alpha sorority sweatshirt and matching green sweatpants. Tipsy clasped Aunt Talia's hand in greeting, then leaned down to make sure the old woman heard her. "Mrs. Parker, thank you for having me. Your home is gorgeous."

"My pleasure, sugar," said Aunt Talia, and Tipsy's heart swelled at the lady's use of Granna's favorite Southern endearment. Despite her advanced age, Aunt Talia's astute expression indicated that she was as sharp as a wasp sting. "We don't meet too many like-minded souls, do we? It's a good thing to share our knowledge with our own."

She spoke with the musical quality that would make out-of-towners wonder if Aunt Talia haled from the Bahamas or Jamaica. If she overheard Aunt Talia speaking to her family and friends, Tipsy would have trouble understanding her, as she had with the enslaved man in Henry's childhood memory. She figured Aunt Talia was used to code-switching from her unique Geechee language to standard English. She waved Tipsy into the rocking chair beside Helen.

"Do you live out here alone?" asked Tipsy, as she sat.

"Um, hmm," said Aunt Talia. "Since my husband Burton died, going on twenty-six years ago."

"Her husband and my daddy were brothers. Bundy and Burton Parker married Tessie and Talia Green."

"Sisters marrying brothers!" said Tipsy. "That's like a fairytale."

Aunt Talia laughed. "Sometimes it was, but Tessie and Bundy lived two houses down. Could get a little crowded on these hundred acres when we all started riding each other's nerves."

"So you grew up out here?" Tipsy asked Helen.

"I did. Me and my two brothers. My oldest brother lives in my parents' old house."

"And my oldest son next door to him. I had five boys and a girl. They help me keep my place spick and span. But I do all my own gardening."

"It's lovely," said Tipsy. "I can imagine y'all got into spats living so close to one another, but I always wanted a big family. Having cousins and aunts and uncles within a stone's throw sounds like heaven to me. Especially for the likes of us. Clairvoyants, I mean. How awesome, to grow up with lots of people who understand you."

"In our family, there are a few of us in every generation," said Aunt Talia. "We don't sprout like sunflowers all over this land, but even the normal folks accept it. We are fortunate, unlike your ghost friends who haunt your house." She shook her head and tut-tutted. "Sounds like they're having quite a time. Quite. A. *Time*."

"I gave Auntie the basics about your friends' tribulations," said Helen. "Both the husband and the wife."

"What tribulations they are!" said Aunt Talia. "Um, hmm."

"I told her he's trapped in his haunting, *again*, and that his wife returned unexpectedly, and now they're both re-stuck."

The dock's tired floorboards squeaked for mercy under Aunt Talia's rocker. "Lord help 'em."

"Auntie has a story that may help you understand what's happening," said Helen.

"I'm here to listen," said Tipsy, "and I love a good story."

"I'm no preacher, but I've been known to tell a tale or two." Aunt Talia's rocking chair went still, and it seemed the floorboards sighed in relief. Her jaw worked and her fingers tapped as she considered where to begin. She stared across the Stono River, once again reminding Tipsy of Granna. Granna used to watch the mountain skyline when she wanted to sort out her own thoughts. Helen was raised with pluff mud sucking at her shoes, and Tipsy's Granna grew up shaking granite dust from hers, but Tipsy recognized a great Southern storyteller when she saw one.

"I have to start where it all ended," said Aunt Talia.

"Where's that?"

"With a pecan tree and a grapevine."

"I don't—"

Granna interrupted in Tipsy's head. *Let the woman talk, Tipsy.*

"Okay, okay," said Tipsy. "Sorry. My deceased Granna is hushing me in my head."

Aunt Talia didn't ask for clarification, thus confirming her status as an unflappable paranormal professional. "So…up in Orangeburg—where Helen's mama Tessie and me were raised—my grandparents had a small farm at the intersection of two dirt roads. They grew or raised up all the things we needed on that farm. From chickens and cows, to vegetables and nuts, to muscadine wine. Down near the road stood a big pecan tree. On the other side of the drive, my daddy's muscadine vines. People used to pass the house to get wherever they were going. Walking, riding a horse, or sitting in a cart. Sometimes driving a car, if they were high class. Me and Tessie used to play down by the road and talk to folks who passed. Gather stories about what our neighbors were up to. We'd tuck those stories into our pockets like we gathered pecans as they fell. Take them back to the house so Mama could cook 'em all up in a pie." She laughed at her own wit. "Whether black or white, rich or poor, nothing Southerners love more than a hot slice of gossip fresh from the oven."

"Amen," said Tipsy.

"My mama *knew* everyone, of course, so she pretty much let us *talk to* everyone. Everyone who looked like us, that is. Nothing would send us runnin' back to the house faster than the sight of a white man coming down that road. Mama wouldn't have us putting ourselves in that kind of danger."

"I'm sure she had her reasons," said Tipsy.

"She certainly did. But it wasn't only the white men we were supposed to avoid. Can't forget about the Quincy Brothers. Earl was the older, and Ted the younger."

"What was up with them?"

"They lived down the road a ways. They inherited their daddy's land and neither of them ever married. Terrible drunks, both of them. Good for nothing pretty boys who were slowly running their father's legacy into the ground. Their only talent was making moonshine. They'd get all liquored up and come high steppin' down the road. Sometimes they were laughing. Sometimes they were fighting. But Mama didn't want her girls anywhere near those men with their wandering drunk eyes and their heavy drunk hands. One summer evening, me and Tessie were down by the road. We were older than ten and younger than twenty, so Mama trusted us to sit at the end of the drive with okra and eggs and carrots and honey. See if any passersby wanted to buy 'em. We were enjoying ourselves, talking about boys we liked and ghosts we'd seen, when Teddy Quincy came runnin' down the street like the devil was nipping at his heels."

"Let me guess. The devil took the form of his big brother."

"You are correct. Young Teddy was faster, but he tripped over his own long feet. He fell on his face, flat as a bike tire with a nail in it. Earl was on him like an owl on a lame mouse. They went rollin' right into our yard. Tussling and yellin'. Somehow Ted stabbed Earl, even as Earl strangled the life out of Ted. Earl held on to Ted's neck while he, himself, bled out beside my mother's tomato plants. Me and Tessie didn't even run back to the house. We screamed for our father. He came running out of the barn, but it was too late. Ted was already dead with his throat crushed, and Earl's life was draining away into the dirt. My father yelled into Earl's face. *Earl Quincy, what happened? Huh? Why'd you and Ted go all Cain and Abel on each other?*"

"Who was Cain, and who was Abel?" asked Helen.

"Only the Lord knows," said Aunt Talia. "Before he died, Earl said something about them arguing over their mother's wedding ring and gold crucifix. One argument, after a lifetime of living together, and they're dead right there on my parents' land."

"Must have been quite an argument," said Tipsy. "But lucky them for dying in front of *y'all's* house."

"True. Three clairvoyants under one roof. Mama, me, and Tessie all had this gift. About ten days later, Tessie and me see Earl and Ted, dead as flattened roadkill, wandering our yard. Mama went right out there and told those men what happened. That they'd been fighting something fierce when they were drunk, and Earl strangled Ted, and Ted stabbed Earl. Mama gave them all colors of holy hell. *Now wouldn't your mama be proud? Her two sons killed each other over her jewelry! Shame on you both!* They both recalled what happened, and they were able to *move on*. Earl left with no fuss, but Ted wasn't ready. He chose to stay."

"I'm sure your parents loved that."

"Mama was fit to be tied. She didn't want her two girls, who could see ghosts, exposed to Ted Quincy's slick talk. She tried for years to make Ted go on, but he wouldn't. He sat on the edge of the yard himself, by the pecan tree, and watched people come and go. He lost his senses, as most spirits do. Talking to the crows in the pecan tree, day and night. Otherwise, he seemed content with his lot. Until…"

"Let me guess," said Tipsy. "Until he suddenly *couldn't* move on."

"Exactly. One day Ted came running up to me and Tessie, yowling about how he couldn't move on anymore. He was truly stuck, so naturally, he decided he wanted to go. He begged us to help him. We told our mother, but she'd never heard of anything like that, so she didn't know what to do. Things got even stranger when *Earl* Quincy turned up again."

"No way."

"Yes, indeed. One day Mama looked out the window, and there went Earl Quincy, sitting beside the muscadine vines."

"Were they happy to see each other?"

"Maybe at first, but that didn't last. Soon they were arguing away in my parents' yard all hours of the day and night. My father couldn't hear anything, but us three women couldn't sleep at night."

"Did y'all try to help them move on?"

"We did, but we could never figure out why they were stuck, or why Earl came back. Eventually, Earl and Ted *hated* one another. Ted stayed under the pecan tree. Earl sat by the grapevines. My family called them Pecan Ted and Grapevine Earl."

"Jeez. When was this?"

"Oh, maybe late 1930's. Or early '40s. During the wartimes, me and Tessie went to Claflin University to become teachers, then we both moved to Charleston to teach at the Avery Normal Institute on the peninsula. We met those charming Parker brothers, and here we all are." She smiled. "My parents sold the farm in Orangeburg not long after and moved down here to be close to us and our children."

"Do you know what happened to Pecan Ted and Grapevine Earl?"

"I assume they're still there, even if the tree and the grapevines were bulldozed to make way for a strip mall."

"That *is* a crazy story. So…it's not out of the question for a ghost to get stuck again, nor out of the question for one to be pulled back. But that doesn't help us with the why, or how to move them on again."

"I see commonalities between the Quincy Brothers and your Mr. and Mrs. Mott." Aunt Talia eyed Tipsy like the retired teacher she was. "Do you?"

Tipsy thought for a moment. "Both twosomes had a very close relationship in life. Brothers. Spouses. It sounds like the Quincy Bros had a love-hate thing going on. Jane and Henry were—are—pretty turbulent, too. Both were intricately involved in one another's deaths, and they died in the same place. One moved on, one stayed."

"Good job," said Aunt Talia. If she'd had one, she might have given Tipsy a gold star sticker.

"I recently met a woman who is…I *think*… another form of seer—"

"Future? Past?" suggested Aunt Talia. "That manner of seeing?"

"Yes, actually," said Tipsy, surprised. "I never knew people like that existed."

"Sure they do. They're less common than us ghost-seers, but they're out there."

"She told me that Henry and Jane's current problem is not about their deaths. It's about something that happened before they died. She called it a *secret within a secret.*"

"Ah," said Talia. "Like the layers of an onion. Or flower petals, depending on whether that secret smells rank or sweet. It wouldn't surprise me if the Quincy brothers had a secret within a secret, too. Lord knows they were strange ducks. After all, why were two grown men fighting about their mother's jewelry? Their daddy left them a decent amount of money. They were slowly throwing it into the privy, but they weren't desperate. Not yet."

"It's a relief to know Jane and Henry's problem isn't some… paranormal mutation," said Tipsy. "But I still have to figure out their extra secret. Hopefully, once we understand, they'll regain the ability to move on."

"How are the memories coming?" asked Helen.

"I'm definitely getting a better sense for what went wrong in their relationship. It wasn't so simple as Henry being a jerk, and Jane disillusioned with their marriage."

"Tell me more about your friend who sees the future," said Talia.

"I just met her, so I don't know that much," said Tipsy. "She's a little hesitant to talk about it all. I understand *that* feeling."

"Talking to you reminds me how lucky I was," said Helen. "Having my mother, and grandmother, and auntie. Plus two first cousins and one second."

"Remember when your cousin Delphine got a crush on the ghost that haunted Carl Brown's junk yard?" Aunt Talia twittered. "I about split myself laughing. There went my husband, standing on a pile of old tires, trying to defend his daughter's honor from a dead man he couldn't see."

"Ah, yes! Tell that story, Auntie. Tipsy, you want to hear it?"

"Definitely! I knew a girl who had a crush on a ghost, too," said Tipsy, thinking of Sophie Yates' infatuation with the psychopath Thomas Bonneau. "It freaked me out. The guy was dangerous."

"This spirit was handsome enough to tempt a saint, but otherwise harmless. He must have been a pure fool during life, because he was dumber than a box of rocks as a ghost. Still, Delphine was all cow-eyed over him. So Burton went down the junkyard with a baseball bat—as if that would do a thing!"

"He was the first spirit my cousin Delphine ever freed," said Helen. "She looked into that empty head of his and saw him get crushed when a car slid off the jack and squashed him like a slow palmetto bug."

"A *bug* indeed," said Mrs. Parker, with a *tee-hee-hee*. "But not a roach."

"It was a Volkswagen Beetle," said Helen.

Tipsy listened for the better part of two hours to Aunt Talia and Helen's ghost stories. She heard about easy cases (Helen's uncle, who turned up dead after choking on a chicken bone in his own kitchen) and the impossible ones (the sad little girl who haunted the woods near Helen's childhood school). She listened with the rapt attention of a law school student studying the technique of seasoned trial attorneys, or a medical resident observing a master surgeon. Through it all, Helen and Aunt Talia exuded pride in their accomplishments, even the efforts they made on the part of ghosts they couldn't help. She eventually had to bid them farewell to pick up Little Ayers at school.

As she drove back down the dirt road, she took comfort from the lessons learned during her visit to the Parkers' family land. Helen and Aunt Talia's collective supernatural satisfaction cemented her intention to take up the Parkers' altruistic outlook on ghost management. As for her immediate paranormal puzzle, she could now be sure that Jane and Henry's mobility problems were no spiritual aberration. From her experience, that meant that there had to be a solution.

Chapter 11

The morning after her visit with Aunt Talia, Tipsy pulled into her driveway after dropping the kids at school and went to her mailbox. Several of her elderly commission clients disdained Venmo, and she expected a big check via Ye Olde United States Postal Service. She opened the box and sorted through a bunch of junk mail. No check, so she made a mental note to follow up with her client. Via telephone, because said client also poo-pooed texting.

The idea of making an unnecessary phone call vexed her. *Texting is so much faster, Granna. I don't have thirty minutes to spare for Linda Bertolli from Minneapolis. She might be a retired English teacher, but every convo with her is one long run-on sentence, and I know her daughter bought her an iPhone. The woman can respond to a text if she wants to.*

I've always found Midwesterners to be overly chatty.

As a Southerner, that generalization recalls the old adage about soot-smeared pots and kettles. Tipsy tucked the junk mail under her arm. *I'll add Linda to my call list. Along with the bakery. They still haven't confirmed my cupcake order for the wedding. Those new paintbrushes I ordered haven't come yet, so I have to track the shipment. I told Scott I'd follow up with the home appraiser, and the fence guy. Scott wants to replace the fence as soon as we sign the closing documents. All three kids need updated sports physicals if they're going to participate in swim team at Tripp's country club this summer, and I haven't posted any new artwork on Instagram in three days—*

You better start writing this down, sugar, said Granna.

I will. I'd rather be painting on the porch than inside dealing with the Tipsy-do list. It's such a pretty day. Tipsy looked up and down the street. *Kind of quiet around here this morning, isn't it?*

'Tis. The construction vans haven't arrived yet.

Yeah. They're usually here by now.

Tipsy considered the half-finished house across the street. It looked more sheepish than ever, as if it had grown accustomed to hiding behind vans and pickup trucks and the occasional forklift. Helen's uncle and his lethal chicken bone popped into her head. Maybe young Stephen Ramsey had a similarly simple story, and one peek into his memories would set him free.

I'm a dizzy hamster on my to-do list wheel, said Tipsy. *If I luck out and send Stephen on in one shot, I'll accomplish something today!*

You seem set on ignoring my advice about chomping more candy when you're already chewing a mouthful. Might as well take a victory lap on the ol' hamster wheel.

Tipsy stuffed the junk mail back in the mailbox and crossed the street. She paused on the edge of the sidewalk, looked around for curious neighbors, and then stepped onto the overgrown yard. Damp blades of grass tickled her toes around her flip-flops.

If someone asks what I'm doing, I'll say I'm looking for my... cat.

You always rely on cats, said Granna. *Maybe try another animal, to mix it up. How about one of them hamsters?*

Cats eat hamsters. I can't regress on the food chain.

Tipsy recalled her first feline scapegoat, on Sullivan's Island, as she poked around for the ghost of John Huger. A nosy neighbor called her out, and she'd instinctively claimed a missing cat. Then there was Peach, the resident kitty at Henry's mother's place on Bull Street. That chubby furball's friendliness had given her a good excuse to plunk her butt down on the sidewalk in front of the house. *Cats make sense for clairvoyant adventures, Granna. Something witchy about them.* Tipsy thought of Granna's rangy, cross-eyed, perpetually yowling Siamese cat. *Remember Gin Rummy?*

My sweet Gin-Gin. He's here with me now.

Aww, it's nice to know the rainbow bridge is really a thing.

Course it is. Animals are truly pure spirits—

"Your lips are moving," said a crackly voice. Stephen Ramsey had appeared on the pile of fill dirt beside the addition.

"Hi, Stephen." She retrieved her phone from the pocket of her leggings. Once she had it beside her face, she went on. "Sorry. I was talking to my grandmother. She's dead, but she exists in my head."

"Your head is too small to have another person inside it."

"Ah, well. It's hard to explain, but take my word for it. She's there. So, how are you?"

"You don't care how I am." A pouty statement, as if he *wanted* her to disagree with him. A familiar strategy with Tipsy's kids (especially the contrarian yet clingy Mary Pratt), so she obliged him.

"I *do* care. I wouldn't be over here risking the other neighbors thinking I'm snooping, stealing, or crazy if I didn't care." She walked toward the house and peeked under some half-dead shrubs.

"What are you doing now?" he asked.

"Looking for my imaginary cat."

"You *sure* you're not crazy?"

"I feel pretty sane, but ask my children what they think. They're getting to that age where kids start to question parental sanity."

"You have kids?"

"Three. Not much younger than you."

"You look young, and you don't seem tired enough to be a mother."

"I'm plenty tired, but life in your day was harder on a woman's face We have better moisturizers, and I broke down and started getting the occasional Botox." She chuckled at his quizzical look. "You ghosts! I always have to explain myself." She raised her voice as a woman in a floppy straw hat biked down the street. "Here, kitty, kitty, kitty!"

"Mother Pearl had three cats. Spring, Autumn, and Winter. Winter was white and Autumn was orange."

"What color was Spring?"

"Dark gray with black stripes."

"Not very springy."

"Made more sense than summer. Cats don't come in green."

Tipsy wanted to cut to the chase before the construction crew turned up. "Listen, Stephen. I know you've been stuck here for a long time, all alone. Would you like to move on?"

"What do you mean, *move on*?"

"Think about it. Everyone *dies*, but *not everyone* sticks around as a ghost. Most people *move on* to the next plane of existence—"

"Or maybe people just…*stop*. Maybe it all ends."

"I see why you'd think that, but they don't. A few people remain trapped in our world, like you. *Everyone else* moves on to the next one."

"How do you know?"

"Like I said, I can still talk to my Granna in my head, and she passed away a long time ago—"

"Like *I* said, maybe you're crazy."

"—and what's more, I've sent several ghosts on to the next plane. We have to understand how you died, and then you can move on."

"What does my death have to do with it?"

She explained the mechanics. Tipsy looking into his memories; Stephen coming to grips with the reality of his death; etc., etc. "So I need to touch you. Maybe once if we're lucky, but it could require a few tries. It all depends on what your memory shows me."

"Ehh…no, thank you. What if you *believe* those ghosts moved on, but instead, they're just gone? If they *do* move on like you said, what happens when you get there?"

"I don't know. Granna can't explain it. It's something you have to experience—"

"I don't believe in God, so I *definitely* don't believe in heaven."

"I don't know exactly what I believe in, either. But it's also hard to deny the existence of *something* divine. I see evidence of it every day. You, yourself, are evidence that there's more to our existence than just…this."

"What if you see into my memories, and then I disappear—*vamoose*—and I don't exist anymore? I don't like *that* idea. I'd rather stay here, where I know that I'm *something*. I'd rather be something than nothing…" He trailed off. His brow wrinkled as he stared past Tipsy's shoulder. Tipsy turned to see Henry walking toward them.

"Where did *that man* come from?" asked Stephen. "Is he dead, like me? Is he…who…*ohhhh*…" He abruptly vanished in a spurt of indigo flame. He reappeared on his pile of fill dirt and watched as Tipsy closed the distance between herself and Henry.

"Henry, what's up? I'm kind of in the middle of something."

"Is that the boy who lived with Pearl Fischer?" asked Henry.

"Yes. I'm trying to convince him to let me see into his memories, but he's not buying it. He thinks he'll disappear into a black hole if I touch him—"

"A black hole like a sewer drain?"

"No, it's a thing in space…gravity…" Henry stared at her blankly, so she said, "Sure. The sewer drain of no return. So *what's up*?"

"I had a little accident in the house."

"Oh, good lord. What now?"

"I was thinking about Jane and Proctor, and how I pushed her toward him, but then I reminded myself that he's a devious, lecherous, evil—"

"Right, right."

"I felt distressed and you *know* how *things happen* when I'm distressed—"

"Henry! Spit it out!"

"The television! It *activated.* I wasn't even handling the control remote."

"*Remote control.* Okay, so the TV came on and—"

"It's showing the most upsetting film. About a man with razors on his fingers who stalks people in their dreams."

"Ah. *A Nightmare on Elm Street.* Yeah, it's pretty awful. Can you ignore it?"

"I *can't.* It's so loud, and disturbing, and I'm *already* disturbed."

She sighed. Last thing she needed was an increase in Henry's disturbance level. "Go back to the house and sit on the porch. I'll be back soon."

Henry disappeared. Tipsy turned around and returned to Stephen. She was about to tell him that they'd have to continue their existential discussion another time, when he spoke up.

"That man. He *is* a ghost. He must be."

"Yes, he is. Like you. Would you like to talk to—"

"I know him."

"Pardon?"

"I *know* him. Or *knew* him. When I was alive."

"So y'all *did* meet. I asked him, but he didn't remember you—"

"I remember *him*. I only met him once, not long after I moved into this house. Mother Pearl made me promise to never forget him."

"Why would she make you promise that?"

The boy shoved his hands into his pockets. He stared at the grass between his sandy feet.

"*Stephen*," said Tipsy. "Please answer me. Why would Mother Pearl make a little boy promise to remember a random neighbor?"

He looked up at her. "Can you see any memory I want to show you?"

"Usually. Unless there's something blocking it. But this is something you *already* remember? From long before you died?"

He nodded.

"Then yes. If you think about it, I should be able to see it."

"Then I'll show you this one memory. If I still exist afterward, I'll think about letting you look for my death. That's my deal."

"That's a *great* deal," said Tipsy, sensing an opportunity to kill two mysteries with one memory. Or at least make progress on both of them.

"How does it work?" he asked.

"I have to touch you, but…" She looked around. "Here on the sidewalk isn't the best location. Can you go around to the back of the house? Will your haunting allow you to go that far?"

"Yes. And yes."

"I'll meet you back there."

She trotted around the house to the backyard, where a collapsing wooden deck overlooked a cement patio and an overgrown yard. The house had a water view, but it wasn't truly *waterfront* anymore. Arbitrary zoning had allowed someone who owned it after Mother Pearl to sell the slice of land directly abutting the harbor. A large house with 1990s vibes stood between Tipsy and the choppy, whitecap dotted harbor. A tall privacy fence encircled the newer house. Unless the owners peered out their second story windows, they wouldn't see Tipsy sitting amidst the weeds behind the unoccupied renovation project.

She gave a fire ant hill wide berth, and lifted her feet to avoid any baby copperheads that might be curled in the grass. Said grass was a foot tall in some spots, and patchy brown in others. No way she could avoid all the biting creatures residing in that pigmy jungle, so she sat on the cool edge of the cement patio. Stephen Ramsey appeared, seated, beside her. He tucked his bare feet underneath him and shifted his weight onto one hip, reminding her of Jane. "Tell me what to do," he said.

She took in his tense posture. "It will be easier if you close your eyes. Think about what you want to show me. I'll do the rest."

She touched his forehead, like she might wipe Little Ayers's sweaty hair out of his eyes after lacrosse. His hair didn't move when her fingers brushed what appeared to be blue-white skin. It was like holding her hand before an air conditioning unit. The chill seeped up her arm and wrapped her mind in a cold sleep.

Tipsy stands on a narrow porch and looks across a dirt road at her own house. During her last historical viewing (in what she thinks of as the Miscarriage Memory), she noted her house's unchanging color scheme of white siding and Charleston green shutters. In that memory, the paint had been fresh and shiny. In this one, both the house and the picket fence need some TLC. The shutters are faded. Gray mildew mars the siding. The fence posts are shedding paint like peeling albino snake skin.

Jane's magnolia has entered gawky arboreal adolescence, with long, skinny branches and foliage as sparse as a teenage boy's first mustache. Her wild indigo bushes have filled in since Tipsy's last visit, but they're brownish and cropped low to the ground. The deciduous trees are bare. Tiny orange oak leaves add texture to the sandy brown dirt road. Wind whips the palmetto leaves into a frenzy over her head and the sky is a steely gray, like the color of Tipsy's own eyes. It's definitely winter.

She looks around to get her bearings. This porch must be attached to Pearl Fischer's house. Don't forget, in Tipsy's when, Pearl's house is porchless and the front door opens onto a concrete staircase. Seems odd that any self-respecting Southerner would have ripped off a front porch, but when Tipsy looks up, she notices dry rot in the eves and the pillars, and the floor is warped and buckled. Perhaps the removal of the porch was a matter of safety, not aesthetics. Still, the space has a cozy, busy feel to it, as if this is a place to be productive, not just sit and watch the world go by. Potted plants, baskets of drying herbs, and gardening tools sit on a red wooden shelf. In the yard, wooden stakes hold up the crispy, twiggy remains of dead vegetable plants, like grisly crucified insects. A row of old sunflower stalks creates a brownish curtain between the house and the street.

A woman sits in one of the porch rockers. She has the look of someone who would be tall if she stood, with thin limbs and a long neck. She appears to be somewhere in her sixties, although, as Stephen pointed out, it's hard to ascertain years in a time when people aged differently. A grayish braid hangs over her shoulder. She has dark eyes and a markedly hooked nose. She wears a blue button down men's shirt, a pair of dark blue trousers, and brown boots. Mother Pearl, the woman who sometimes just knows *things.*

A sewing basket sits beside her; a small green dress is laid across her lap. A boy of eight-ish is rolling marbles along the cracks between the floorboards. Stephen Ramsey has straight brown hair, and he wears dark pants and a gray wool coat. The pants are too short, and the coat is too big. His brown boots have scraggly laces, but his hands and his knobby knees look clean.

"Is that dress for Hannah?" he asks.

"'Tis," says Mother Pearl. "I'm letting out the hem."

"What's that mean?"

"Making it longer."

"It's pretty. I like the flowers on it."

Stephen's boyish thoughts fill Tipsy's mind. Looking at those flowers warms up his heart on a winter day like this. He looks at his own plain brown sleeve and imagines it covered in pretty daisies. Red, white, yellow, with bright green leaves.

"They are *nice," says Mother Pearl. "Remind me of spring when the winter wind is blowing."*

"That's just what I was thinking!" says Stephen, with a smile. Tipsy is reminded that people like Mother Pearl and LeeLee Moretz sometimes hear people's thoughts as they are happening. "Why do girls get to wear pretty things like flowers and lace and ribbons, and boys' clothes are all plain?" asks Stephen.

Mother Pearl's busy needle slows. "The world cares more about how girls look than boys. Pretty dresses, with flowers and frilly what nots, make a girl herself seem prettier."

"You don't wear flowers and lace. There's no ribbon in your hair."

Mother Pearl stops rocking, and the boy's hands freeze on his marble. "Stephen Ramsey," she says.

He looks up at her, and Tipsy sees the birthmark on his face. His eyes are squinched up, as if he expects her to hit him. Sometimes his mama hit him, when she was worried or tired or hungry. Sometimes just because he was there. "I'm sorry, ma'am."

"Since you're new, I'll let that comment go. But it's not your place to ask me such questions."

"I'm real sorry. I just never seen a lady like you, who wears boy clothes."

"I'm different from most ladies."

"Can I be different from most boys?"

"What do you mean by that?"

He shrugs. "I don't know."

"Son, your life is already difficult, what with your mother's…situation. Don't make it any harder for yourself. Boys are boys, and girls are girls."

"But you—"

"No buts. I haven't had a lot of joy, being this way—" She points at her clothes. "—but it's easier for a woman to be ignored. Men who…don't… aren't…" She sighs. "You mind the rules. All of them."

"Yes, ma'am."

"It's for your own good. There are people in this town who have particular opinions about who is who, and what is what."

"When I grow up, I'll move far away to a big city where I don't have to care about anyone else's 'pinions."

"You do that, child, but for now, it's my job to keep you safe. Now, what have you learned in the past five days, since your mother brought you here?"

"Ummm. I learned how to feed chickens and not get pecked when I collect eggs. I learned how to see what's a weed and what's not." He smiles. "I learned the other children's names."

"Tell me their names."

"There's the brother and sister, Eldridge and Hannah. They're nice. And then Maudie. Jack and Rex. Peter—"

"Excuse me, Ms. Fischer?" It's a baritone voice that Tipsy knows well. She looks over the porch railing, and there's Henry, in a brown overcoat, brown trousers, and a tan bowler hat.

"Mr. Mott. Good day."

"Good day." Henry turns to Stephen, who is staring at his own boots. "Who's this young man?"

"This is Stephen Ramsey. He just came on as a boarder. Stephen, say hello to Mr. Mott. He and his wife, Mrs. Jane Mott, live in that big white house."

"Hello," says Stephen, but his eyes remain lowered.

"Stephen, a man looks another man in the eye."

The boy looks up. Henry's eyes dart over his marked face, but to Henry's credit, he doesn't flinch. More than Tipsy can say about herself. He smiles. "Nice to meet you, Stephen."

"Sir," says Stephen, and he looks at his clunky boots again.

"How can I help you, Mr. Mott?" asks Pearl.

"I know we don't speak very often. I'm sorry I'm not more neighborly—"

"I like to keep to myself as well. No harm done. Your wife passes words with me sometimes."

"Jane loves to talk. I'm more taciturn by nature. You know what they say about opposites and attraction."

"I do. Now how can I. . . ."

"Yes, right. I've heard. . .that you know things. Can help people." Tipsy has rarely heard Henry sound so flummoxed, but Mother Pearl is nonplussed.

"Have you now," she says. "Perhaps you're right. Depends on what you think I know and what you need my help with. And how you'd like to trade for my knowledge."

"I've come prepared to pay. Can I come up?"

She pauses for a moment, as if judging the safety of letting her rich but rather strange neighbor onto her porch. Money wins out over oddity, because she nods. Henry walks up the stairs and removes his hat.

"That looks like a nice game of marbles, son," Henry says to Stephen.

"It is." Then Stephen says, because his mama always says his mouth runs away from him, "Your head on fire, sir?"

"Stephen!" says Mother Pearl, but Henry laughs.

"It's alright. Thank you for giving me my first laugh in days. No, my head isn't on fire." He looks at Mother Pearl. "It's my heart."

"Go inside, Stephen," says Mother Pearl. "Let grown people talk."

"Yes, ma'am." Stephen opens the screen door to the house, but something about this man fascinates him. He wants to know what's wrong with the man's heart, and what he wants from Mother Pearl. He squats beside the door and peers through the screen.

"It's my wife," says Henry. "It's my Jane."

"Such a pretty lady. I came across her a few weeks ago, walking on the beach."

"I assume she struck up a conversation."

"She did. Walked right up to me and chattered away. She seemed… lonely. If you don't mind me saying so."

"I don't mind, and she probably was. I'm not always the best company."

"Hmmm." Pearl lets that sink in, like tea diffusing into hot water.

"Jane is not well."

"What ails her?"

"She's sad. She's tired all the time. She can't eat. She says her stomach can't tolerate food."

"Has she been this way before?"

"She's always had a tendency to lose her appetite when things are difficult. When her sister's husband passed away, or if she quarrels with her mother. But this time…it's about…we've grown apart. She wants a divorce."

"Ah. Tsk." Even if Mother Pearl has never been subjected to marriage herself, it seems divorce doesn't sit well with her.

"I don't want it. But she does, and it's my fault. She's in love with another man—"

"She seems like a lovely lady, but if she's running around on you, that's her sin, not yours."

He leans forward on his elbows, and looks down at his big hands clenching his hat. "It's difficult to say this, but…I…encouraged the affair. I pushed her toward it. Not only with my coldness and my foul temper. She came to me, wanting affection, and I told her to look elsewhere."

Pearl looks at Henry as if he's crazy. "You told you wife to—"

"Yes. Yes, I did. I was a fool. A moron. A jackass of the highest order. But she took my advice, and now she wants to leave me, for him."

"Mr. Mott, perhaps you need to see a man of the law, not me."

Stephen isn't sure what they're talking about, but if Mother Pearl is talking about a policeman, it can't be good. It doesn't much matter, because Mr. Mott isn't interested in men of the law.

"No! I told you; I don't want it. But I love Jane, and I'm trying to do right by her. I didn't even realize the magnitude of what I'd done until a few days ago. I'll do anything to keep her, but if this is truly the only thing that will make her happy, I'll move to New York and get a divorce there. I'll let her go."

"So…what is your question for me?"

"Can I make her happy?"

"Pardon?"

"I've heard rumors that you can see into…the future. So tell me, can you look into my future and tell me if I'll ever be able to make Jane happy?"

"Whatever talents I have, they aren't that simple. If they were, I'd be betting on the ponies and my porch wouldn't be falling off my house."

"I thought…if it's true about what you can do—"

"I do get bits and pieces of the future, and the past. Sometimes the present."

"That's exactly what I need!"

"But Mr. Mott, it's not something I can do on command, like a trained poodle."

"Can you try? I'll pay you. I've heard people sometimes pay you. They come to you for help, and—"

"They come to me for help with belly aches and rashes, mostly. But you're right. Sometimes they come to ask for these kinds of services, but I don't like to get people's hopes riled up. Most times, I don't get anything. Sometimes when I do, it doesn't make much sense to them. Even if nothing comes to me, it's a dollar for me to try."

"I'll pay you two, just to look."

She nods. "Sit here then, beside me." She points at the next rocking chair. "That is, if you're agreeable to passing time with the town oddball on her porch."

"I've never given much of a damn about appearances." He sits in the rocker. "You're a respectable woman, providing a respectable service."

"Don't know if your preacher would find it respectable," she says.

"My preacher, Proctor James, is a forward thinking man. He ruminates deeply on God's reflection in all of us. You'd be surprised."

Tipsy cringes at Henry's positive estimation of Proctor. If Henry hadn't even remembered meeting the boy with the birthmark on his face, this memory must be part of Henry's own lost week. He knows Jane wants to leave him, and it's winter. He can't be more than a day or two from finding out the truth about his philosophical theologian.

Pearl says, "Not much surprises me, for many reasons. But I didn't plan on a ginger-haired rich man on my porch, so I can't see all."

She holds out her weathered hands. Henry hunches toward her and takes them in his. She closes her eyes. Long seconds tick by, and Pearl makes no move as Henry stares at her. Finally, she releases his fingers and sits back in her chair. "I…well…"

"Did you see Jane and I in the future? Is she happy with me? Or did you see us getting a divorce? Jane with another man?" When she doesn't reply, Henry presses. "Who? Who is the man?"

"I'm sorry. I didn't see anyone, or anything."

He slumps in his chair. "Ah, hell. I suppose it was silly of me to try."

"Maybe it's better for you to think of how your wife is feeling right now. You said she's unwell?"

"Yes. Very tired, and not eating. Headaches, too."

"Has the doctor visited?" She touches her temple. "Doctor…what's he called…"

"It's Doctor Kellerman here in the village, although Jane usually sees Doctor Coming on the peninsula. But no. I haven't called either. She doesn't want to talk to anyone."

"Is she drinking water?"

"Some, in the morning. But by the evening, she can't even keep that down."

"Hmm. Let me see what I have in the house." She stands, and walks inside. Stephen scrambles out of her way. She returns with a small bottle. "This here is a peppermint tonic. It will help soothe her stomach."

"Thank you, but I have to soothe her heart. I have to know if I should leave her."

"Mr. Mott, I don't know you. I don't know Mrs. Mott more than our conversation on the beach. But I do recall she talked about how much she loved her family. Including her husband. She spoke of you being a writer, and sacrificing all that to have a home with her. How smart and thoughtful you are. How lucky she is."

"Did she truly say that? I'm a rotten husband. More than that. I'm a rotten person."

"Maybe you are, but if you want to be less rotten, show that woman you love her. Don't let her go so easy." She hands him the bottle. "And ask her *how she's feeling. She may have something she wants to tell you."*

"Yes. I will. Thank you." He takes the bottle and presses a five dollar bill into her hand.

"We agreed on two. I'm not a charity case."

"You have a lot of mouths to feed. I took both your insight and your tonic, so take the five dollars."

She nods. Henry walks down the stairs, and she sinks deep into her rocker. Stephen comes outside. Pearl looks down at him and smiles, but she wipes at one tear that tracks down her lined cheek.

"What's wrong, Ms. Fisch—" She's told him to call her Mother Pearl, like the other children do. He thinks of her that way, but his true mama's

rules about respecting his elders still rule his mouth. He corrects himself. "I mean, Mother Pearl?"

"That man pulled on my heart."

"That man with his head on fire?"

She nods. "The same."

"Why did he ask you all those questions? About seeing things, and knowing things—"

"If you're living here, you'll understand eventually. Some people have ways of seeing deep into the world. Places other people can't see. Things that happened a long time ago, and things that haven't happened yet."

"Oh. My mama told me about people like that. Fortune tellers. She said they're all thieves and liars. Making money off people's hurt."

"Some do. Hucksters are commonplace. Those of us who are true are rare."

"Can you prove to me that you're not a liar?"

She chuckles and strokes his hair. "For one so young, you're not afraid to speak your mind."

"If I don't speak it, no one else will."

"I can't so much prove it to you. But if you stay here long enough, you'll see proof yourself."

"I'll wait then…but…did you see something when you touched that man? I saw he paid you good. If you really see things, maybe what you saw about him was big and 'portant."

"Sometimes things I see are clear, like looking down into a still creek. But sometimes it's churned up like some big creature is thrashing around in the mud."

"Like the dolphins throwing fish up on the shore?"

"Just like that."

"Is Mr. Mott's creek clear, or muddy? What did you see about him?"

"I told him true. I didn't see anyone, or anything. But I did get a sense of something bad coming for that man, and his pretty wife."

"Did you tell him?"

"No. Sometimes I have to decide what people need to know. There's no stopping whatever is coming for them. They're better served by trying to cure

the ills between them right now." She purses her lips. "Enough of that. Never you mind about Mr. Mott."

"I won't but..." Stephen looks over at Henry's house. He pictures the man with his head and his heart on fire, sitting in his own house, in front of a real fire. All by himself, without his pretty, sick wife. "Now I feel sad for him, too."

Pearl rests her hands on Stephen's shoulders, and suddenly, she twitches. She looks down at the little boy's head. "Huh." She holds her fingers before her face, as if they're tingling. "Hmm. I wonder." She shakes her hand. "Stephen...I..."

"Ma'am?"

"If you ever see that man again, you help him."

"You mean like if he wants me to help him pull weeds? Or paint that crusty old fence?"

"I suppose, yes. If it doesn't interfere with your chores here. Or you might...see him...some other place. Some other time."

Stephen shrugs. "Sure thing. I finished all my own chores, and I'm getting bored with these marbles. Can I go to the barn and see if Eldridge is finished with the goats?"

"Yes. You two have a little bit of fun. But both of you have reading to do before supper."

"Yes, ma'am," says Stephen. He starts down the porch stairs, but pauses to smile at her. "I'm glad I live here now. I think I'll stay forever."

She smiles back. "Forever is a long time, son."

"So Mother Pearl sensed something coming for Henry and Jane," said Tipsy. She blinked, and her eyelids scraped over her eyeballs. Her tongue felt like a loaf of stale bread and her rear end had fallen asleep underneath her. Bits of gravel dug into her skin through her leggings when she shifted to get the blood flowing to her butt. Her sunglasses were perched on her head, so she slid them over her forehead and onto her nose. Once she put darkness between herself and the sun, her headache abated. "Something *bad.*"

Stephen nodded. "Every Sunday, Mother Pearl made us all go to church—the Presbyterian Church, just 'round the corner—and Sunday school, and then church dinner. When we arrived home from church on the day after Mr. Mott's visit, other neighbors were milling around in the street and talking about gunshots that come from the Motts' house. As soon as we heard tell of what happened, Mother Pearl plunked down on the porch and covered her eyes with her hands. 'Course, she knew that Mr. Mott and his wife were dead. I only remember Mother Pearl crying twice. Both times, she done it over those people. Maybe she felt bad she didn't warn them."

"If she didn't know exactly what was coming, she couldn't do anything to change it."

"That might-could be right. Everyone 'round here said Mr. Mott killed his wife, then killed himself, but Mother Pearl didn't believe it. She said more was going on in their house, and she hoped they mended their rickety picket fence before they died." He nodded wisely. "Not their *real* fence mind you, although that pile of sticks needed help, too. *You know* the saying."

"I do know it. And she asked you to help *him.* Henry."

"Yes, ma'am. I wonder if she knew we'd both be ghosts when I next laid eyes on him? If she did, a warning would have been nice." He pointed at Tipsy's house. "Just think. Me and him been across the street from one another, dead and gone but still here, all this time. As soon as I saw him, I remembered him. He's got that odd look."

"He does."

"I hope I did what Mother Pearl wanted by telling you what I know about him. Does he *need* help?"

"He sure does." Tipsy thought for a moment. "What did Mother Pearl give to Henry for Jane? A peppermint tonic?"

He nodded. "She had all kind of homegrown remedies. She swore by peppermint tea for a sour stomach. She gave it to mothers with sick children. People who drank too much booze and heard the whiskey thunder the next morning. Ladies who were with child."

Tipsy's brow furrowed. "Jane was sick to her stomach, and tired. Mother Pearl thought she might have something to tell Henry." This time, the lightbulb didn't just turn on in Tipsy's head. It exploded, like Miss Callie's old porchlights had burst when Henry lost his temper. "Oh, shit. Maybe *that's* how you're helping him."

"What do you mean?"

"I think Pearl knew something that had nothing to do with seeing the future. Just plain old country good sense."

Chapter 12

"You're telling me that I asked Pearl Fischer to predict my future?" asked Henry. He sat on the sofa in Miss Callie's parlor with one elbow on the armrest. Jane sat beside him with her feet tucked under her. That wedge of empty space still separated them. Tipsy sat across from them in a club chair, a position that exacerbated the therapy session vibe.

Tipsy nodded. "You were looking for information to help you make a decision about Jane's request for a divorce. You asked Pearl if she could see you making Jane happy in the future."

"I suppose that was a rather ingenious way to—" He shook his head. "No. Just recently, I told y'all how I felt about all that fortune telling hogwash. Maybe now, sitting here dead, I can give some credence to it. But the living me didn't hold with that sort of thing."

"And as *I* recently reminded you, you've always held with *exactly* that kind of thing," said Jane. "You saw ghosts."

"That's different," he replied.

"*How* is that—"

Tipsy cut her off before they started bickering. She didn't want either spirit to get ticked off and disappear. "I saw you, Henry. You went to her house and asked her. Paid her five bucks for the privilege."

"Given the circumstances, it's *possible* I had a change of heart about my neighbor's prophetic powers."

"Exactly. You were desperate to know what might happen, but Pearl didn't give you any predictions. Instead, she asked after Jane's health." Tipsy turned to Jane. "Henry reported that you weren't eating well, and you were very tired. Pearl gave him a peppermint tonic. For *you*."

"Oh," said Jane. "Peppermint?"

"Yes," said Tipsy. "Then she told Henry to talk to you. She thought you had something to tell him. A secret."

"You *did* have a secret," said Henry. "You hadn't yet told me the identity of your lover. I didn't know it was Proctor until he turned up at our house."

"Can we look into y'all's memories together?" asked Tipsy. "See if this new information reveals something?"

Henry shrugged. "I suppose, but from your vision into that boy's head, Miss Pearl *did* get a message from the universe that day, but she chose to not tell me. She sensed *something bad* coming for us. Obviously, our impending violent deaths can be categorized as *something bad*."

"But there might be more to it. Jane, what do you think?"

Jane bit her lip. "I…don't know *what* to think."

"I see no harm in exploring this new angle. Now that you told me I engaged the services of the local fortune teller, I'm curious about my state of mind." Henry held up one hand. "What should I think about to direct the memory?"

"Umm…concentrate on Pearl Fischer…and whatever you did after you saw her." She turned to Jane. "Janie, you focus on how you were feeling unwell at the time."

"I had many reasons to feel unwell, but….peppermint tea…" She looked up. "Whatever it is…I want to know. After all this time, I *must* know."

Jane's stoic resolve and Henry's relative cluelessness made Tipsy think she was on the right track, but she chose not to enlighten Henry. *Nausea, exhaustion, peppermint tea. Sadness and a secret.* She wasn't sure how Henry would take it if she was right.

For a moment, it's still dark, then Tipsy's eyes adjust to the dim light. She's back in Henry and Jane's bedroom. The door behind her opens, and Henry enters. He walks to the window and opens the drapes. Light leaks

through the widening space between the curtains. A pleasantly flowery smell emanates from a bowl of dried lavender on the nightstand. The Jane-sized lump in the bed shifts.

"Janie," says Henry. He waves his hands over the bowl of lavender, as if the scent might help rouse her. "Sweetheart. It's almost noon, and you've been asleep since yesterday afternoon. Don't you think it's time to wake up?

She rolls toward him. "I'm sorry, but I'm so tired."

"You haven't eaten anything. You're like our car, that time I ran out of gas on the way to the Old Cannon." He smiles. "Stuck on the side of a dirt road with no pep."

She smiles back, weakly. "Yes…I…but I can't keep anything down. Uh…you know, little Louisa had a similar ailment last week. Poor thing, sick as a pack of stray puppies. Didn't I tell you?"

"You did. Perhaps you caught it from her. Although it must be a mighty catching sickness, since you were at your parents' house for less than a day."

"Yes, it must be."

"I brought you some medicine." He holds up the bottle. "It's a peppermint tonic. Pearl Fischer across the street makes them herself. She said it works wonders on weak stomachs."

"Oh. How nice."

He approaches the apothecary cabinet in the far corner of the room. "Do you have a measuring spoon in here? It's—" He selects a different bottle from the cabinet. "It looks like you already have a peppermint tonic."

"That's a special medicine. Meant to help…when I was…before I lost the last baby."

He reads the label. "I see. Miller's Tonic for Expectant Mothers."

"The symptoms can be the same. When one catches a sickness from one's niece, or one is…has…"

He looks at her. "Janie, are you…but no." He chuckles. "That can't be. You happen to be sick to your belly. And exhausted…and…terribly sad?" Something clicks behind his eyes as he trails off in a question.

Jane bursts into tears. "Please don't be—I wanted to tell you—"

"Are you expecting? Jane? You're—" The bemused smile falls from his face. "You're pregnant? But we…this other man…Oh, no."

"Henry. I swear to you, it's yours—"

"Oh, Jesus. No."

"I swear to you!" She's almost screaming. "You have to believe me. My parents' party. That night—"

"Oh, yes. The party." His shoulders relax into a slump. "That night was…it was…"

"Yes! That *night. That's the last time—"*

His back goes ramrod straight again. "But you've been with another man—"

"Not for weeks before, and not since. I swear it to you."

"But… you can't leave me. Why have you been threatening me with divorce, when you're carrying my child?"

"Because…because…" She starts crying again. "I only realized it a few days ago. I thought I should tell you, but then…maybe I shouldn't. I just don't know! The night of the party, I decided to tell him*—the other one—that I was done with him. But you were so cold and mean after the* Post *rejected your story. Each time you opened your mouth, you spewed wasps. Every word stung me. You turned your back on me again and I…*couldn't. *Maybe he'll be a better father—"*

"Can it get any worse that this? Losing my wife, and now my child?" His mouth trembles and a strangled sob erupts from his throat. He turns to Jane's vanity table and picks up an embroidered hand towel. He buries his face in their monogram, HMJ, and his shoulders shake. Tipsy has seen Henry shed a few tears, but she's never seen him truly cry. These are the constricted sobs of a proud man who has long forgotten the freewheeling weeping of his young childhood. They are uncomfortable, alien, and terrifying.

"You haven't lost me yet," says Jane, as his crying trails off into sniffling. "If the pregnancy lasts, you can make *me stay with you. You can tell my parents and your parents, and everyone will make me stay."*

"I couldn't live with myself if I have to make *you stay with me, when you don't think I deserve to father your child. Our child. I—"*

"Henry, I only started feeling sick a few days ago, but I've done this enough times to know what it feels like. But it may not last. I've never gotten past the first few months—"

"You have to do whatever it takes to keep the child safe. Even…if that means…leaving me."

"I don't know what *to do! All I've ever wanted is for us to be a family, with our children. But are you capable of it? Do you truly want it?"*

"I do. I swear it to you. But if you need more time for me to prove it to you, I understand. Can we try that? Give me a trial run, to show you I can change?"

"I want that. But we've had so many trial runs. So many times when you were so wonderful, but then the darkness came back. It always returns, even when you try to shine light into it."

"You're right. But this time…" He sits on the edge of the bed beside her with the hand towel on his lap. "You swear it's mine?"

"I swear."

"Then I believe you. I'll do whatever I need to do for you, and for the baby." He runs a finger down her cheek. "I think Pearl Fischer knew all this. Whether from her special powers, or because a woman knows the signs that another woman is pregnant. She told me I had to listen to you. To be what you need. I'm trying to do that. Can I lay down with you. Like I did…that first time? You remember."

She nods. "I remember…and I suppose so."

He slips off his shoes, lays down beside her, and wraps his arm around her. Tipsy senses her tentatively relaxing. Feels her intense desire to trust him, to let down her guard, to feel safe. Equally strong, Henry's intense, almost elemental desire to protect her.

Then comes a knock on the front door. A terrible, fateful rap-rap-rapping against the fragile walls of the fortress Henry wants to build around them.

"Who the hell is that?" mutters Henry

"I'm not expecting anyone, and I don't want to see anyone."

"It might do you good to get out of this bed, sweetheart. Have a reason to stretch your legs and have a nice glass of tea and a slice of jam and toast. It's cold out, but we could open the doors and let the breeze blow through."

She sighs. "Mama always said it's best to balance rest and fresh air. Best for the baby."

"The baby," whispers Henry. In that moment, Tipsy knows how deeply he wants to change. How sure he is he can do it. He runs a hand over Jane's hair, and her elbow, and down her hip, but before he can put a sheltering arm over her belly, she grabs that wandering hand. She holds onto it, but she isn't ready to let him touch her there. That fleeting feeling of tentative trust is broken, because she's justifiably afraid of the person he may be when they wake up tomorrow morning. The person who might make her child feel the way he's made her feel. It isn't only about her. She can't let herself simply believe Henry, when he's hurt her so many times. What is truly best for this baby, if she can keep him or her alive for the next nine months?

Another knock.

"Should I see who it is?" he asks. "Or do you want me to stay here?"

The knock becomes a bang.

"Whoever it is, they must have a reason for banging away," says Jane. She thinks of her niece, Louisa, who has been sick. Perhaps it's a message from her parents. Louisa may have taken a turn for the worse. "Go ahead and answer it."

Henry kisses her cheek and gets up. He puts his shoes on again, for he's not one to answer the door in his socks. He picks up the tear-stained hand towel, dips it in the jug of water beside the bed, and presses it to his eyes. He looks in the mirror. As if his pride is in charge of his visage, there is no evidence that he's been crying. Not like Jane, who has cavern eyes. Tipsy watches Jane, who is watching the ceiling.

She hears Henry go down the stairs, and his warm greeting, to the man she knows must be Proctor. Henry calls out her name, and Jane sits up and swings her bare feet over the bed. She's too far down her sadness rabbit hole to care about trifles like shoes. She's wearing her lumpy purple and gray shawl. Tipsy despairs, because she's had so many visions like this. She knows Jane is about to follow Henry to their deaths, and there's nothing she can do about it.

"You were…expecting," said Henry. "Expecting a…child." He said it like Jane was the Virgin Mary and he was a moody ginger version of Joseph.

"It seems I was," said Jane. Her lip trembled, and she swiped at a tear. "I remember now. How I started feeling sick in those last few days. I was so tired. Hungry, but I couldn't eat. Everything smelled wrong. My…" She blushed and touched her chest.

"Your heart?" asked Henry.

"No. My…uh…"

"*Noooo*, Henry." His gestational naivete annoyed Tipsy. "Not her heart. She means her *breasts.* When you're first pregnant, they're tender—"

"Even if it had nothing to do with *your* heart back then, mine is breaking right now."

"Oh, darling," said Jane. "I feel the same way. I—"

"You can't feel the same way. Because you know this mystery child was *yours*. But me…how can I…was it Proctor's child, Jane?"

"No! I told you then. If there was a child—and back then I believed there was—it was *your* child. I'm absolutely certain."

"But how can you be?"

"Because I know how these things work," said Jane, incredulously. "It could *not* have been Proctor's. I'd been with only you. For several months. The night…the night of my parents' party—"

"But you lied to me about other things. Betrayed me!"

"Henry, this reminds me of how twisted things were when you learned about the affair," said Tipsy. "You'd *already forgiven* Jane in the past, but when things started coming back to you, you got all worked up again. In the memory, she told you the child was yours, and it seemed like you believed her."

"We've already established that I was grasping at straws. I would have believed her if she told me that a colored man would be the president of the United States—"

"Uh…that's already happened."

"—and I didn't yet know it was *Proctor*." His eyes widened. "That's why Proctor turned up at our house! He *knew*!"

"Proctor might have been a lunatic, but I don't think he would have killed Jane if he knew she was pregnant."

"Henry," said Jane. "I didn't have…Proctor and I…Oh, this is so uncomfortable to discuss!"

"Good lord, y'all, get over yourselves," said Tipsy. "You've known each other for about a hundred and thirty years and from what I can tell, you were pretty uninhibited in life during Henry's good moods. Just talk, for the love of God! It won't kill you! It literally can't!"

"She's right. We're grown people." Jane squared her shoulders. "Proctor and I didn't have the kind of relationship that you and I had. It was more like a friendship. He didn't know how to…and I wasn't…I didn't…"

"He didn't turn you on?" offered Tipsy. "He didn't make you all hot and bothered? He didn't know how to press your buttons?"

"Those all sound about right. Nothing like you and me. We were so passionate. The last few months before we died, I *was unsure* about Proctor. We weren't alone, and that was fine with me. We sent letters. Made telephone calls. And after my parents' party, I was sure you and I would made amends. That night was so…"

"Magical," said Henry. "And then I ruined everything, like I always did. So you went running back to Proctor—"

"I didn't run anywhere! Not truly." She threw up her hands. "I admit it. I *did* tell him I would leave you. He kept begging me and I finally agreed to do it. But I didn't…"

"She didn't *go there*, Henry." Tipsy held up one hand. "Remember what I heard from LeeLee. The divorce lawyer who has psychic visions like Pearl Fischer. LeeLee said it's all about a *secret within the secret*. This *must* be it. The pregnancy you both wanted so badly, that Jane had *just* discovered."

"That's all well and good, damnit, but Proctor—"

Tipsy didn't let Henry finish. "I haven't had a chance to tell you, but this situation y'all are in—Jane coming back, both of you being stuck again—isn't unique. My new clairvoyant friend Helen Stokes told me a story about brothers who had the same plight. They were close in life, involved in each other's deaths, and died in the same place. One *moved on*, but the other stayed. Then years later, the brother who moved on unexpectedly returned to the haunting, and they were both trapped again. Do you see the similarities?"

"Yes! How interesting! Now, how did they move on?" Jane sounded like a tea party hostess searching for conversational commonality among a bunch of guests who couldn't stand one another. "Henry, are you listening to Tipsy?"

"I haven't figured that out yet," said Tipsy, "but the point is, those brothers must have had their own *secret within a secret*—"

If Henry heard anything Tipsy or Jane said, he didn't acknowledge it. He dragged the uncooperative conversation back to his archrival. "In the memory, Jane said Proctor would be a *better father* than me."

"I said he *might* be a better father. I was *afraid*, Henry. You were so bitter after the *Post* rejected your story. When I finally told you that I wanted a divorce, you seemed to have a reckoning, but how could I be sure it would last? You say you can't trust *me*, but how could *I* trust that *you* wouldn't return to your old ways? At least Proctor was kind and gentle and steady."

"So you would have let him raise *my child*?"

"I hadn't decided! I was confused. I wanted *you* to raise the child with me—"

"If you were even *contemplating* that, it must have been Proctor's! Don't lie to me, Jane! Not after all this time!"

"Damnit all, Henry Mott. I'm not lying—"

"Y'all!" said Tipsy. "Enough! Y'all have to come to a resolution about this pregnancy, even if it's painful—"

"I'm trying, but he won't *listen* to me!" Frustration had replaced desperation in Jane's voice.

Henry covered both ears with his hands. "I can't *heeeeaaar* you!"

Jane's mouth fell open in outrage. She pointed at him. "See? See what I must tolerate?"

Tipsy leaned toward her as Henry spun in a slow circle with his hands clapped against the side of his head. "He's not in his right mind, Jane," said Tipsy. "Try again, please."

Jane took a deep breath. "Henry. Husband. My *dearest.* Can we please talk about—"

"About Proctor's child? Or…*my child*…that Proctor would have raised?" Henry's hands bore down on his skull, as if to squeeze the image from his brain. "I can't…this is too much…"

He vanished. No stomping through solid objects. No melting away into the floor. No combusting into a minty-scented cloud of ghostly detritus. Nothing exploded or tipped over or fell off the walls. Mercifully, Henry simply disappeared.

Chapter 13

No matter how Jane and Tipsy tried to draw him out, Henry refused to make himself seen for days. As Tipsy's kid weekend came and went, the strain between Henry and Jane seeped into her own bones. Fatigue and headaches. Constant low grade nausea, like being seasick on dry land. Her belly growled, but the thought of food repelled her. It was as if the symptoms of Jane's ill-fated final pregnancy had followed her through time.

Now that Tipsy knew how to manage her supernatural abilities, such symptoms were usually acute and mercifully brief. They came on after she looked into a ghost's memory, or engaged in some manner of paranormal intervention, like shoving Thomas Bonneau into the afterlife. She'd only experienced persistent malaise during the first summer she lived in the house with Jane and Henry. When she was new to otherworldly finagling, and Jane and Henry couldn't stand one another.

None of these developments struck Tipsy as positive, but life had to go on, whether her ghostly roommates were on good terms or not. She somehow managed to complete the psychedelic alligator, and *The Hand Study*. On a balmy late-April Thursday, after a week of no Henry, she delivered the gator to Richard and David's house, then drove *The Hand Study* to the GQB. Miraculously, she found a parking space directly in front of the gallery. As she thanked the Charleston parking gods for small favors, her dear friend Pamella Brewton texted.

PAMELLA: SISTER! WHEREFORE ART THOU?

TIPSY: HAHA! FORSOOTH, I AM SO BUSY. SO MUCH GOING ON. WITH LIFE... AND DEATH. IF YOU KNOW WHAT I MEAN! She added a ghost emoji.

PAMMY: GHOST DRAMA! I WANT TO HEAR. ANY TIME TO CHAT TODAY?

TIPSY: I'M AT GQB DROPPING OFF A PAINTING. CAN I CALL YOU AFTER?

PAMMY: I'M ON MY WAY TO A BOARD MEETING AT C OF C. I CAN STOP BY THE GALLERY!

TIPSY: PERFECT. SEE YOU SOON.

The gallery wasn't open yet, but Tipsy still had a key, so she let herself in and propped the door open behind her. She found an easel in the storeroom and set it up beside the staircase, then she returned to her truck for her painting. She removed the old sheets she'd wrapped around the canvas, perched it on the easel, and stepped back to admire her own work.

She'd written the painting's name on the back of the canvas in small block letters, as she did with all her pieces. *THE HAND STUDY.* A hand study it was, but it had become much more than a portrayal of intertwined masculine and feminine digits. She had never produced a more intimate piece. Jane's peaceful, dreamy expression. Henry's quiet, protective watchfulness and his lips brushing her jawline. Her delicate, slim fingers engulfed in his big hands. His thick wrists laced with prominent veins. Her small, sparkly blue engagement ring and his plain gold band. The painting simultaneously screamed wild romance and whispered about steadfast love and deepest trust.

The figures had soft edges and a gentle effervescence that was particularly true to life—no, death. Muted shades of watercolor paint, mostly along that purple-blue spectrum, made it seem as if they were sleeping at the bottom of a clear pond. They were both perfectly still, even as the bubble around them seemed to fluctuate. That impeccable translucency made Tipsy question why she hadn't used watercolor for every supernaturally inspired painting.

"I freakin' *love* this painting, Granna," she said out loud.

Have you thought about keeping it, sugar?

Before Tipsy could answer, the doorbell *cling-clonged* behind her. She turned with a smile. "Pammy!"

Pamella Brewton swept into the gallery like the unbothered queen she was. She wore a short floral skirt, a pale pink tank top, and bedazzled flip flops. Even in flats, she was six feet tall. Her dark hair was pulled back in a tight ponytail at the base of her neck and secured by a pink ribbon. Tipsy resembled one of the Founding Fathers when she tried the low ponytail and ribbon look, but it worked for Pammy. "Lady! So *glad* we have a few minutes to catch up!" said Pamella. She handed Tipsy a cup with a straw. "Pomegranate juice blend," she said.

Tipsy took a hesitant sip. Pamella usually adjusted her anti-oxidant packed potions to suit Tipsy's sweet tooth, but the kale, garlic, and spinach concoctions of old had traumatized her. This beverage had only a hint of ginger aftertaste. "Delish," she said.

"Whoa," said Pamella, as she peered over Tipsy's shoulder. "Is this your newest piece?"

"It is," said Tipsy.

Pamella pointed at the male figure. "Red hair. Lookin' a bit like Newt Scamander. Henry?"

Tipsy nodded. She'd tried to explain Henry's unusual handsomeness to Pamella by comparing him to an acclaimed British actor, the appropriately named Eddie Redmayne. "Yes. That's Henry. And that's his wife, Jane."

"It's…*stunning*. It's like…Mr. Darcy walking across the more to meet Elizabeth Bennett. You know, the movie version, with Keira Knightley."

"*You have bewitched me, body and soul, and I love…love…*"

"Love you," finished Pamella. "Literally the most romantic scene in the history of film."

"I think of the Motts as more Bronte than Austen, but I get it. I'm not one to toot my own trombone, but I love this painting, too. It might be my favorite piece of my own work. Like, ever."

"Then why is it here? You should keep it."

Tipsy laughed. "That's not how this job works. If I love it that much, and so do you, hopefully others will feel the same way. I should be able to get a fast sale and a good price."

Pamella fixed her bright green eyes on Tipsy. "*Come on*, lady. You're prolific. You're keeping up with commissions, while shipping work to multiple galleries in multiple states. Since I've known you, you haven't kept one piece of your own work. You have…what, like…*three* of your own pieces in your house?"

Tipsy thought of the pieces in her bedroom. An oil painting of a woman draped in a red blanket, two charcoal studies of appaloosa horses, and a self-portrait she'd completed at age fourteen. "Four," she said.

"That's ridiculous. You've earned the right to decorate your own damn house, especially since you'll be getting rid of all that *grandma's attic* stuff of Miss Callie's in the estate sale."

"Sounds nice, but we have a lot of costs coming up—"

"One painting, Tipsy. *One*. That I assume is pretty personal to you, given that it's this passionate, dreamy-ass painting of your two dead friends. When did you see them like this, anyway? Before Jane moved on?"

"That story is as long as the complete works of Jane Austen and both Bronte sisters."

Pamella sat on the spiral staircase leading to the second floor exhibit rooms, set her logo-covered Louis-Chanel on the step beside her, and took a long slurp of her own juice blend. "I have two hours before my board meeting, and nothing to do but go shopping, or listen to you. Start talking."

Tipsy filled her in: Henry's malaise, Jane's return, both ghosts stuck in the house again, LeeLee and Helen and Aunt Talia, *secrets within secrets*, Pecan Ted and Grapevine Earl, Mother Pearl and Stephen Ramsey, and Henry and Jane's increasingly re-strained relationship. By the time she finished, her mouth was dry, so she sucked down the last of her pomegranate juice before wrapping it all up. "So in conclusion, it seems Jane was pregnant when she and Henry died. Neither of them remembered it. After *years* of trying to have children. Henry was a really difficult person, but I think the fertility issues ultimately drove them apart."

"I had friends who went through that. Kids are hard on a marriage, but not having them when you want them is even harder."

"And back then, they had no way of understanding what was happening, or why. No medical options. They were both sad and disappointed and frustrated, and they didn't know how to support each other. It became, like, this *embarrassing taboo*. Even between the two of them."

"Awful," said Pamella. "Now Henry is pissed?"

"Seems like it. He doesn't believe it was his child. I hope he'll get past it if we let him ponder. He usually figures things out, if you leave him alone long enough—"

"Stop *psychoanalyzing me*!"

Tipsy jumped in place and spun around. That familiar resonant voice bellowing such a modern phrase didn't make sense.

"What's up?" asked Pamella. "You look like you saw a—"

"Tell me *the truth*, Tipsy." Henry stood on the staircase. Both hands gripped the carved antique railing.

"—ghost," finished Pammy. "Wait…*did* you see one?"

Tipsy pointed up the stairs. "It's Henry. He's here."

Pamella scrunched up her nose and looked over her shoulder, as if she'd see Henry if she squinted hard enough. Henry stiffly descended a few steps. "Get up, Pammy," hissed Tipsy. "He's coming down."

Pamella hopped to her feet as if the wooden step had turned into August-hot tarmac and burned her skinny behind through her pretty silk skirt. She scooted behind Tipsy and held her empty smoothie cup out before her like sheathed light saber.

Tipsy smiled up at Henry, then looked over her shoulder at Pamella. "Pammy, Henry said we're *psychoanalyzing* him. He's clearly been listening to Scott!"

"Don't patronize me," he said, with a sneer. "I know Jane told *you* the truth. You're her friend. She loves you as much as any friend she had in life."

"I love her, too. But she hasn't told me anything you don't already know."

"You *would* believe her. You *always* preferred her over me." He sounded like a jealous sibling confronting a biased parent.

"That's not true! I love you both, equally."

"You pity her for being married to me! You think I'm a jerk! A real loser! A total *creeper*!" Henry had clearly eavesdropped when Tipsy and Shelby complained about men over the years.

"What's he saying—"

Tipsy waved a hushing hand in Pamella's direction as Henry's hysteria increased with each word. "You think I'm *awful and grim* and she's *lovely and sweet and kind* and *poor Jane* married to *glum sourpuss* Henry Mott *coward-loser-creeper* who killed his wife and himself that's what *everyone* said—"

The wide planked floorboards beneath Tipsy's feet started vibrating. Frames rattled against the wall, and a few sculptures bounced on their pedestals. Tipsy steadied a brightly colored abstract painting and pointed across the gallery. "Shit, Pammy! The pelican!"

Pamella fixed on a life-sized pelican. It was made of thousands of pieces of driftwood, and worth thousands of dollars. It jittered precariously close to the edge of its pedestal. Pammy took three long strides across the room, gingerly lifted it, and set it on the ground.

Henry's hair stood up from his head as if his own power was electrocuting him. The lights flickered, and the chain dangling from the whirling ceiling fan snapped like Indiana Jones's bullwhip. Henry had wreaked havoc on Tipsy's kitchen. He had slammed doors and knocked over bookshelves and ripped up pillows. This time, he was fixing to channel a never-before-seen level of destructive rage.

"Damn!" said Pamella. "It's my Meemaw Ivy's house all over again!"

The easel holding *The Hand Study* teeter-tottered across the floor like a rocking horse. The painting slid from left to right. Tipsy lunged for it. Her clasping fingers closed around one corner. The canvas quivered in her grip.

"Henry, please. Be careful—"

"Tell me the truth, damnit! It was Proctor's baby! I know it!"

"She swore it wasn't—wait!" Inspiration struck. "Why don't you *ask him*? Proctor! You can go there now—"

"Visit the devil's henchman? Never! That fiend! Hypocritical false prophet!"

"*Listen to me*, Henry! You're still angry with Proctor, but he's the only person who can validate Jane!"

"You already made me visit him! It only made everything worse!"

"*Hold up!* It was *your* idea to visit Proctor—"

"So many hours we've spent together the past four years. All the times I tried to counsel you through your troubles with Big Ayers and Will-yum and Hottie Head Doctor Brandt! Yet still, you're *on Jane's side! Proctor's side!*"

"I'm not on Jane's side or your side. You're *both* dear to me. As for Proctor, I'm *definitely* not on his side!"

"You are! He cuckolded me in every way and yet you want me to talk to him—"

"You *wanted* to talk to him a few weeks ago! Now you *need* to talk to him!"

"I will not!" Henry bore down on the banister and the old wood flexed beneath his hands. Cracks appeared in a few of the balusters. At the bottom of the stairs, the edges of the rug *slap-slap-slapped* the floor like a pack of dog tails. Artists' business cards shot out of their little holders and flew around the room, a flock of angry white paper starlings. The bell above the door clanged hysterically, as if in warning of a four-alarm fire. The wind from the swirling fan blew strands of Tipsy's hair into her mouth and lifted Pamella's skirt. She grabbed for it like Marilyn Monroe standing over a subway grate. Painted wood chips from the straining banister peppered Tipsy's arms.

"Tipsy!" said Pamella. "Watch out for the cow. Grab the sailboat. The fat guy is going down!" In any other setting, none of that would have made sense, but one by one, the described paintings fell off the wall. Pamella sprinted around the gallery, picked them up, and lay them face up on the quaking floor. A crack like a spider web appeared in one of the front door windowpanes.

Tipsy felt breath rushing in and out of her lungs as panic set in. If she didn't stop Henry, he'd destroy something of real value in this place. Perhaps that beautiful painting of him and his beloved wife, or one of Tipsy's other pieces. Her parrot and her unicorns had already sold, but two Tiffany Denning-Collins landscapes clung to the gallery walls like the last survivors of a catastrophic earthquake. Let's not forget tens of thousands of dollars of other artists' work. Cows. Sailboats. Fat guys. Pelicans. The banister was a carved antique in itself.

Pamella fluttered around her and tried to stabilize the artwork. "Tipsy, is there anything you can—"

"Shh. I'm doing it right now." Tipsy closed her eyes.

She had sent Henry back to Miss Callie's when he appeared on the Ravenel Bridge. She also put him in his place when he failed to recognize her in the kitchen. On the bridge, she pushed him toward an intended destination, and in the kitchen, she held him down until she could safely release him. One supernatural first, and then another, and now she would attempt a third. She would remove Henry from the gallery, send him where he needed to go, *and* make him stay there.

She had *no idea* how to do it, but yet… she *knew how* to do it.

She reached out with her own power and gripped him by his shoulders. She could almost feel her fingers digging into his hard, wiry biceps. Impossible, but imagination is a powerful thing. Tipsy had always had an unusually powerful imagination.

Henry, you must speak to Proctor.

I won't I hate him he did this to me it's all his fault—

Stop it right now, and go to Proctor. Stay there and wait for me.

Nonononono

I will meet you there, at the St. Philip's graveyard. She pictured the graveyard, and Proctor's calm face. *You're going. When you get there, you're staying there.*

Tipsy pictured Henry's arms flattened against his body. She had done the same to Thomas Bonneau before Henry and Catherine forced him to *move on* to the fires of hell, or the endless empty abyss, or wherever that evil bastard went. This time, she was only sending Henry around the corner, but it was still easier to tie him up, metaphysically speaking. She wrapped her mind around him like a straightjacket. He fought her, but he couldn't flail.

Tipsy, let me go!

Nope. You're going, and then you're staying. Right. Now.

She pushed, and opened her eyes as Henry vanished. As quickly as it had started to quake, the gallery went still, but for Tipsy, the walls started spinning. She sunk onto the Oriental carpet. Rugburn stung her kneecaps. Her eyeballs throbbed like they were trying to escape her skull and her lungs screamed for more air.

"Mercy," said Pamella, as her skirt went still. She let go of a blown glass vase. "That put Meemaw to shame!"

"I'm going to be sick." Tipsy pointed around the gallery. "Can you put everything back where it's supposed to—" She covered her mouth with one hand, stumbled to her feet, and ran to the tiny bathroom.

When she emerged a few minutes later, all artwork was back where it belonged. *The Hand Study* and the driftwood pelican. Cows, sailboats, vases, fat guys. Pammy was organizing the business cards. "Lady! Are you okay? Is he…gone?"

"I *think* I sent him to Proctor. Which means I have to see if he's there."

"You're still as green as split-pea soup. Give yourself a minute."

"I already wasted too much time hurling," said Tipsy. "I don't know how long I can keep him there, if he even went where I sent him."

"Is he like that all the time?"

"It's getting worse every day," said Tipsy, as she hobbled to the door.

"Post-wedding, it will be you, Scott…" Pamella counted on her fingers. "Y'all's five kids. And *two ghosts*. One with serious anger management issues. Whew. That's a full house, lady."

Tipsy paused with her hand on the doorknob. She opened the door a crack, and the bell above her head gave a sympathetic little *clink*. "I *know* it's a potential disaster. As much as I'll miss him, Henry has got to move on. Both him and Jane. Permanently." Tears stung her eyes as she finally let the magnitude of the situation sink in. "It's been so stressful. This…*ire*…between Jane and Henry is making me feel like shit. Like, imagine terrible PMS crossed with a stomach bug."

"Oh, lady—"

"But that's not the worst part. I can't expect Scott to deal with the house being in a state of constant chaos. He's under so much stress already with work, and dealing with Kate—"

"What do you mean, *can't?* Y'all are *buying* the house."

"It's my responsibility to make sure things are smooth for everyone. Especially when it comes to ghosts."

Pamella raised an eyebrow. "Scott knew the house is haunted when y'all decided to buy it."

"But it was only Henry, not Henry *and* Jane, and we thought Henry would eventually move on. Besides, Scott signed up for a peaceful spirit, not an unstable poltergeist."

"He signed up for a *haunted house*. No one can predict what happens in a haunted house! Now y'all have to deal with it together. So what if you're the one that sees the ghosts? That doesn't make it all your problem. It's going to be *y'all's house*."

"I know, but—"

"Have you told Scott how you feel? How stressed you've been about this, and how worried you are about how he'll handle it? That you're physically ill?"

Tipsy shook her head. Pamella approached her and put a hand on her shoulder. "What do you think he'll say when you tell him?"

"He'll reassure me. He'll tell me we're in it together."

"So why won't you let him be in it?"

"You sound like my Granna."

"You've always said she's a clever old bird. Think about it, lady. What's really going on here?"

"Maybe I'm still afraid that all this ghost stuff will be too much for him. Maybe I'm afraid of...of...losing him."

"Now *there's* some progress."

"But he's under a lot of stress and—"

"You want to protect him, and I'm sure he wants to protect you, too. You've always told me that you and Scott are a team. That you deal with things together. *You* describe it that way."

"I know I do!" Tipsy ran a hand over her clammy face.

"I'm betting that whole *fear of losing him* thing is the real problem here." She patted Tipsy's arm. "Think about where that comes from. I'd guess it's buried pretty deep in your emotional suitcase. Like, maybe hiding in one of those little side-zip pockets."

"I will. I promise. But right now I have to—" She pointed at the spire of St. Philip's.

"Right, right. Go do your exorcist thing."

"Love you, Pammy."

Pamella blew her a kiss as Tipsy slipped out the door. She wouldn't call this current supernatural task an *exorcism*, but she couldn't expect Pammy to understand. Even if supernatural nuances were lost on her, Pamella always seemed to understand Tipsy's emotional baggage. Often better than Tipsy herself.

Tipsy alternated between a speed walk and a clunky jog—her tender tummy could tolerate no more—as she covered the two blocks between the GQB and St. Philip's. She stopped once and leaned against a blue stucco wall beside a window box overflowing with white petunias. Bees buzzed past her face as she waited for her stomach to settle. Down Church Street, the salmon colored steeple of Saint Philip's drew her like a beckoning finger. She pushed off from the wall and kept moving.

Once past the cemetery gate, she circumvented Calhoun's edifice and trotted toward Jane and Henry's grave. To her relief, she saw no other livings visitors, but she *did* see Proctor standing over a lump with red hair. Henry, curled into the fetal position with his eyes screwed shut. He groaned and coughed, as if the wind had been knocked out of him.

Proctor turned as she approached. "Welcome back, Miss Seer. Given Henry's incoherence and prostrate position, I assume his presence is your doing."

"He wasn't keen on visiting you," said Tipsy, "so I…uh…blasted him over here from my friend's art gallery on Queen Street.

"Impressive," said Proctor, as Henry moaned at their feet. "I'll take any company I can get, but I have to ask, why is it so important that Henry and I talk now?"

"She's back!" Henry's croaking voice from below them. "She's returned! You stay away from her!"

Proctor pointed at Tipsy. "You know I can't hurt her—"

Henry pushed himself onto his knees. "Not Tipsy, you irreverent charlatan! Jane! My wife!"

"Whatever do you mean?"

"Proctor, Jane has returned from eternity," said Tipsy. "She's back. Her ghost. In my house."

"No," said Proctor. "How can that be?"

"We don't know—"

"Don't you dare try to contact her!" yelled Henry.

"Henry, *he can't*!" said Tipsy. "You *know* that."

Henry tried to stand, but whatever Tipsy had done to him had tampered with his equilibrium. He flopped onto his stomach and buried his face in the grass. "I know it was yours. You stole everything else from me, why not this?"

"Pardon, but I'm confused....what was mine? And is Jane—"

"The baby. The *baby*, you despicable man."

"I'm not following you—"

Henry regained control of his limbs. He pushed himself onto his knees, lurched to his feet, and lunged at Proctor. A few years ago, when John Huger tried a similar attack tactic on Henry himself, Henry had gracefully vanished and reappeared several feet out of John's reach. Proctor did the same thing. Henry's clutching arms closed on nothing. He spun wildly and jabbed one finger in Proctor's direction. "*Admit it!* You owe me that much, you fiend."

"Let me explain everything to him, Henry," said Tipsy.

Henry kept swinging his fists and yelling, so Tipsy took a deep breath, and re-engaged her clairvoyance muscles. She swung Henry like a ghostly kettle bell. "You. *Sit.* Down!"

It was as if she'd clipped Henry's legs out from under him. He was on his butt in the grass again. He glared at her, but he didn't jump up and go after Proctor. He wrapped his arms around his shins and hid his face behind his knees.

For the second time that day, she told the story of all the recent paranormal craziness happening on and around Bennett Street. For Proctor's version of the tale, she finished with Henry visiting Pearl Fischer the day before the murders, Pearl's hunch that Jane had a bun in the oven, and memory-Jane acknowledging to memory-Henry that she'd started feeling pregnancy symptoms. She noted that both memory-Jane and present-day-Jane had insisted the child was Henry's, and that memory-Henry had believed her, but present-day-Henry didn't. "You're the only person who can vouch for what Jane is saying. That the two of you weren't...that is couldn't possibly be—"

"That it couldn't have been my child?"

Tipsy nodded, and Henry looked up at her. "Why should I believe *him*, Tipsy?"

"Why can't you believe Jane herself?" asked Proctor.

"She lied to me *then*. She lied to me for *ninety years*. I want to believe her, but I can't...my head." Henry started gibbering. "My head and my heart and whatever part of me is sitting here on this grass—my soul—it's all splintering—"

"Henry, let me show you," said Proctor.

"You have to touch him," said Tipsy.

"God forbid!" said Henry. "I don't want to see *you* with *her*—"

"You *will* want to see this." Proctor took a step toward Henry, but Henry scooted backward. He tilted his head toward the sky, gripped his shins again, and started rocking. He closed his eyes, and an insectile humming noise like the death throes of a cicada grumbled up through his throat and past his clenched teeth. His edges blurred, until he resembled a messy version of Tipsy's watercolor portrayal of him.

"Just do it," said Tipsy to Proctor. "I'm afraid for him."

Proctor stepped behind Henry. He rested both hands on Henry's shoulder, as if Henry were still a small boy who needed guidance and direction. Tipsy touched Proctor's arm.

Tipsy is inside a church, but not the kind of church she grew up in. This place has vaulted ceilings, pillars straight out of a Greek temple, and a gray and white marble checkerboard floor. The immobile pews are enclosed

by swinging wooden doors, like stalls for thoroughbred racehorses. At the rear of the church, a majestic pipe organ hugs the ceiling. At the front, a spindly spiral staircase ascends to an intricately carved wooden pulpit. Behind the pulpit, a comparably simple altar, and behind the altar, a gorgeous stained glass window featuring painted saints and angels. Along the side aisles, carved, wall-mounted sculptures memorialize the well-known surnames of deceased parishioners. There must be a few Robinettes and Hugers up there.

Tipsy sits on a crimson cushion in one of the enclosed pews. Henry is sprawled out beside her. He's staring at the ceiling with his mouth hanging open.

"Henry!" says Tipsy. "Wake up!"

His head flops forward and he looks around. "Saint Philip's. We're at our church."

Behind them, the massive front doors open with the groan of old iron trying to hold up heavy wood. Jane speed walks down the aisle in her winter coat, and Tipsy swipes at Henry. She can't actually strike him, but he flinches instinctively, and he looks a little more aware. Tipsy points at Jane, and his eyes focus as she passes them.

Jane is carrying a large floral arrangement of white camellias and magnolias. She looks over her shoulder, approaches the altar, and sets the arrangement on the floor. She spins around, as if she's in a hurry to be out of here, but a soft voice stops her.

"Janie." Proctor steps from behind one of the carved pillars. The way he says her name, it's like a prayer. It's Proctor's memory, and his emotions swirl around him like a cloud of sickly sweet yet toxic mist. Awe, tenderness, paranoia, jealousy, fear of rejection. Longing, longing, longing.

She jumps in place with one hand over her heart. "Proctor, you scared me."

"I'm surprised to see you here. Y'all missed church, so I figured everyone was resting after last night's festivities. That was some party, but then again, your parents have had quite a marriage. Much to celebrate."

"It was a splendid night, wasn't it? But a late one. We all had a bit of a lie in. Mama wanted to donate this arrangement for the altar. She said

it will be better appreciated here than at our house." She giggles nervously. "Our family penance for missing church this morning."

"Rather unkind of Miss Theresa to make you walk over here in this chilly weather."

"She was going to ask Henry to do it, but I woke earlier than him, so I said I'd take care of it."

As if drawn by the sound of his name, Henry stands, walks right through the closed pew gate, and steps into the aisle. "The morning after the party, she wasn't in the bed when I woke up," he mutters.

Proctor approaches her like a hungry cat, as if he might collapse on his hands and knees and twist himself around her legs. "I'm glad you did. We don't get many chances to be alone lately."

Henry's eyes narrow, and he glares at Proctor. "He's a greasy toad, sliding up to my wife in a trail of his own slime—"

That puts my hungry cat metaphor to shame, *thinks Tipsy.*

"— and how dare *he speak of being alone with her—"*

"We're not here for you to be pissed off at Proctor," says Tipsy. "We need to hear what they're talking about."

"Yes, but—"

"Just shut up!" Tipsy rarely snaps at anyone like that, let alone her good pal Henry, but Proctor and Jane are still talking, and they might miss something important. Her fierceness shocks Henry into silence.

"Henry was in an unusually cheerful mood last night," says Proctor.

"His new story caught the attention of the Saturday Evening Post,*" replies Jane.*

Proctor doesn't want to hear about Henry. Doesn't want to think about him. When he does, his own mind vexes him with images of a ginger-haired boy gazing up at him like he's King Arthur. Damn that child for turning into such a brilliant, handsome, charismatic jackass. Damn him and bless him, because if he'd turned out the way Proctor once hoped, Proctor would never have stood a chance with Jane.

He tries to change the subject, but somehow, Henry is still part of the conversation. "I hope your parents weren't upset with me for leaving early. It's difficult to be in his *presence, knowing how he treats you. I'm not a violent man, but sometimes I—"*

"They understood why you left. Service this morning and all."

He abruptly grabs her hand and drags her behind the column. Henry lurches toward them, and Tipsy steps in front of him.

"You can't do *anything to him!" Tipsy reminds Henry. "You can strangle him and he'll keep right on breathing. Listen to what they're saying!"*

Tipsy moves around the pillar so she can hear Proctor and Jane, and Henry follows her. Proctor tugs at Jane's hands and she tries to pull them from his grip. It's a cartoonish interaction, like Bugs Bunny and Daffy Duck fighting over a slippery bar of soap.

"Jane, my disdain for Henry isn't the only reason I had to leave last night. It's getting harder and harder to hide what's between us. Have you considered my…proposal?"

"I haven't had the chance—"

"Darling, I can't watch you suffer any longer. We're both suffering. It's been so long—"

He pulls her closer, but she slithers away. "Proctor! We're in the church. Lord have mercy."

Proctor considers not taking no for an answer. In the films, the women are always saying, no, no, no, *and the men don't listen. They steal their kisses anyway, and the women melt into their arms. Maybe that's what he should do. Man up. Make sure she knows how much he wants her. He grabs for Jane's hand again, and another tug of war commences. "Jane, a kiss—"*

The carved angel on the wall-mounted memorial behind them seems to be gasping at Proctor's impropriety. Jane stomps one small foot, and the sound echoes in the cavernous space. "No! Stop. Someone might see, and it's highly inappropriate in the house of God!"

Clearly when Jane said no, *she meant it. He's suddenly ashamed. "I'm sorry. I have no talent for romance. This is all new to me and I'm simply no good at it. Can you forgive me?"*

She sighs, but she's shaking. "Yes, but I—"

"It's been…over three months since…we were alone…together…"

"Yes, yes. It's been a long time. Shhhh. Please."

So that's *want Proctor wants Tipsy and Henry to see. Jane and Proctor discussing the fact that they hadn't been alone together in months. Since Proctor's angsty, anxious longing is splattered all over the memory like spilled communion wine, Tipsy knows they're speaking the truth. A long time; much too long for Proctor's liking. He's worried. He's afraid Henry has wormed his way back into poor Jane's head.*

Jane looks over her shoulder again. "We must not speak like this. I have to leave. Right now."

"Where are you going?"

"Back to my parents' house."

"When is Henry returning to Mount Pleasant?"

"We're both returning tomorrow—"

"Both? I had hoped you'd stay on with your parents for a few days. So we could arrange a…" He drops his voice. "A private meeting."

Jane looks like she wants nothing more than to run away from him. It's not Jane's memory, so Tipsy can't read her emotions, but she remembers Jane's happiness when she and Henry fell into bed together after her parents' party. It must feel awful to listen to Proctor's lovelorn talk, when she's so hopeful that Henry will finally turn a corner.

"I'm sorry, it's not possible right now."

"Why? Because of Henry? Because he was in good humor for once last night? You know that never lasts." Proctor's angst is turning to irritation. Frustration. He tries to smother it. He doesn't want to frighten her off. He won her heart in the first place by being kind and understanding and patient.

"No, not because of that. This…it's too dangerous. Maybe in the spring—"

"I'll wait for you, Jane. I'll wait forever, but if you don't want what I want, please put me out of my misery. Or allow me to do it myself."

"What does that *mean?"*

"I can't live without you. That's all."

"You wouldn't do anything…drastic?"

"I love you more than anything in this world. More than God or the church. I'll do anything you ask of me, as long as there's hope. But if there's no hope for us, then there's no hope for me." He gazes up at the stained glass window. For the first time, the painted angels look judgmental, not

benevolent, but he doesn't care. "People would wonder why I did it. I couldn't abandon the congregation without…explaining. In my journal, perhaps. You know how faithful I am to my journals. I write all manner of thoughts in those books."

Tipsy realizes that Proctor has already thought through his potential suicide plan. He'll leave his journal where someone will find all his scribblings about their affair. He'll add a farewell note. He'll reveal everything that happened between himself and Jane. "Do you understand?"

"Yes. Yes, and of course…there's hope." Tipsy hears panicked confusion in her voice.

"You still love me? As you said last fall?"

"I…yes. Yes."

"Can you say it again?" Proctor knows he's backing her into the corner, and he doesn't care. He'll take any reassurance she'll give him, even if he forces her into it.

"I love you," she whispers.

"Argh!" Henry balls his hands into his fists. "Arrrrghhhh…."

"Shh!" says Tipsy. "Hush!"

"Thank you, lord," whispers Proctor, as if Jane's words are his salvation. "I'm going now. I'll be in touch. I promise."

"I'll wait to hear from you, my love."

She turns and strides out of the church as fast as her petite legs will carry her. Proctor watches her go. Before the darkness falls, Tipsy notices a tick under his eye.

Tipsy opened her eyes in time to see Henry disappear. She turned to Proctor. "Did he say anything?"

Proctor shook his head.

"That memory made it pretty obvious you couldn't have been the father of Jane's child. This might sound harsh, but you came off as damn desperate." Tipsy heard Mary Pratt's girlish voice in her head. *What a simp.*

"I realized even then that she didn't truly love me. Not like she loved Henry. I was a balm on the wounds he inflicted."

"In this day, we'd say that she *used* you. That was kind of selfish of her."

"I didn't care back then, and I don't care now. Her love—whatever version of it that I had—was the one thing in my life that brought me true joy, despite its fleeting nature."

"It *also* sounded like you tried to force her to maintain the relationship."

"Yes," he said, matter-of-factly. "Easy to threaten to off myself and leave a note blaming it all on her. I played on her guilt and her fear of being discovered. I only wanted her to leave Henry and be with me."

"What if she had, and you'd discovered she was pregnant with Henry's child?"

He paused. "I honestly don't know. I've never thought about it until now."

"Could you have raised a little red-headed Henry clone?"

"I like to think so. I imagine Jane and I running away to a small town somewhere, maybe in the mountains, and raising the child. Perhaps had another of our own. But I can't say for sure what I would have done. Maybe I would have secretly despised the baby. An everyday reminder that she loved the child's father more than she ever loved me."

"You still hate Henry, don't you?"

"No. No matter what passed between the three of us—no matter my anger toward him and my jealousy—I never *truly* hated him."

"Your emotions toward him in that memory were pretty nasty, and you *did* blow his head off."

"Hate is relatively *uncomplicated,* and my feelings for Henry were anything but simple. As I've told you, I was very fond of him in my youth. Such an intelligent, sensitive child, as I had been. When he returned to Charleston, I admired the man he'd become. He was just about the most alluring and interesting person in town."

"More alluring than John Huger?"

Proctor smiled. "John's allure was straightforward. Henry's allure, as complicated as my own sentiments toward him, and all the more powerful. We spent many hours talking about the ways of the world. I considered him a dear friend, until his wife's love became a possibility for me."

"Then you lost your mind and your morals."

"To quote the old country adage—and pardon the pun—I lost my religion. When I learned how he'd hurt her, I was angry with him. What had been admiration became jealousy and a burning desire to move him out of my way."

"So you justified any means. Even killing them both."

"Goodness, Miss Seer. I never *planned* to kill Jane. It was the only truly impulsive act in my life, or since my death. I was always one to ponder. It's a trait Henry and I shared."

"I know you snapped that day. With so much pressure on the three of y'all, someone was going to blow." She sighed. "I should go home and see Henry. Hopefully he'll be willing to acknowledge that Jane is telling the truth. If he does, maybe they'll both be able to move on. Scott—my fiancé—and I are buying Jane and Henry's old house. Our beautiful new home is going to be a total disaster if Henry doesn't finally find some peace."

"Lack of peace always leads to disaster," said Proctor. "Whether in a home, a nation, or a torrid love triangle."

Tipsy called out to Jane as she entered the sitting room. Jane immediately appeared on the sofa with her legs already tucked underneath her, as if she'd been waiting there, unseen.

"Have you seen Henry?" asked Tipsy.

"No. I assume he's still angry with me." Worry etched lines on her otherwise unblemished white forehead. "Have *you* seen him?"

"Yes, and we both *know* you're telling the truth about the pregnancy, so if he's still mad, he's truly lost it."

"How could you know that?"

"We visited Proctor and he showed us a memory. You bringing flowers to the church the day after your parents' party."

"Oh, yes. I remember that morning, and that visit to the church." Her brow relaxed as she thought back on her own version of the scene. "I was *so nervous*, for so many reasons. When my mother mentioned asking Henry to take the flowers to the church, I immediately offered to do it myself. I imagined Henry walking in—so buoyant about his story—and giving Proctor some sense that we were happy. I wasn't sure what Proctor would do."

"Were you protecting Henry, or Proctor?"

"Both, and myself. By then I'd been deceiving everyone for months. I was exhausted by it all. I wanted it to stop, but I had no idea how to end it."

"Proctor threatening to kill himself probably didn't help."

She winced. "The rancid cherry on an ice cream soda made from spoiled milk. I cared about Proctor deeply, and I couldn't stand the thought that he'd hurt himself, or that he'd leave those journals lying around. Exposure of our affair would have hurt *everyone*. Henry, my parents, the church congregation itself. It was so *awful*, Tipsy. I left that church wanting nothing more than a way out—a way to return to Henry, and let Proctor go—but feeling so *trapped*. Then the *Post* rejected Henry's story and he stayed in his study for a week. He slept on the sofa. We've already discussed his demeanor when he finally emerged. He was so *mean*—"

"I said you weren't intelligent enough to understand my pain," said Henry, from the other side of the room. He'd appeared quietly, and Tipsy guessed he heard most of the conversation. "One among many cruel comments. Then I refused to eat. Refused to sleep. Refused to be comforted. Belittled all your attempts."

"Yes," said Jane, with quiet dignity. "You did all those things."

"So you went back to *him*, again."

"I finally accepted that you'd never change, so I told him I'd leave you, and I told you that I wanted a divorce. Don't you see? Your behavior only made Proctor seem kinder and more dedicated."

"He tried to blackmail you into being with him by threatening to kill himself," said Tipsy. "He wasn't *dedicated*, he was a psycho."

"I see that *now*. But at the time…Oh, it was so confusing. After I told you that I wanted a divorce, you seemed so genuine about saving our marriage, and then I realized I was…*late*…and started feeling sick. Once again, I didn't know *what* to do, and I never got to make a decision." Two fat shimmery tears plunked over her eyelids and slid down her cheeks. "But regardless of the turmoil in my heart, I swear to you, if there was a baby, it was yours."

"I believe you," said Henry. "You have no reason to lie to me anymore, and Proctor's memory *can't* lie. I'm so sorry I doubted you. Can you forgive me, for the thousandth time?"

Jane wiped her eyes and smiled at him wanly. "I want to, but please, let this be the *last* time."

"It will be. I swear. It will be the—"

"Shhhh." Jane covered her own lips with her pale left hand. Henry stared at her sapphire engagement ring like a desperate sailor seizing upon a lighthouse flame.

"The time has come for us to *talk*, darling," said Jane.

"Yes. Talk. About anything, sweetheart." He looked lowkey terrified, but he nodded. "*Anything*."

"And everything. Come with me?"

"I will."

She disappeared, and he followed her to the most private of places. Somewhere even Tipsy could not follow, where they might unload a century of troubles from their overburdened souls.

Chapter 14

On Monday following Big Ayers's kid weekend, Tipsy stopped by May Penny's house to pick up stuff the kids had left over there. She felt anxious, as her terse communication with May Penny the last few weeks had been reminiscent of their earlier relationship. When she pulled into the driveway and saw Big Ayers getting out of his truck, trepidation morphed into plain old dread. She had no interest in a double dose of Collins family angst, but Little A's skateboard helmet and kneepads must be retrieved. She put her truck in park and got out. Big Ayers stopped and waited for her.

"Hey," she said. "I'm here for the skateboard stuff."

"I asked Mom to put it outside for you." He retrieved a *Berlin's for Women* (*since 1883*) shopping bag from the staircase. "Some of the girls' clothes are in here, too. Washed. Folded. May Penny style."

She took the bag from him and backed up. "Great. I'm gonna head out—"

"Can't believe that truck is still hanging in there." Ayers pointed at Tipsy's ten-year-old Tahoe.

"I had that transmission issue a couple years ago, but since then, it's been chuggin' along. I plan to drive it until the wheels fall off."

"You were never high maintenance about cars. I always appreciated that about you, even if I didn't say it."

"Uh, thanks. I have to—"

"Sorry about my meltdown in your driveway. We've had some explosive driveway discussions over the past few years."

"Some more productive than others."

"Driveways are neutral ground. Makes for an easy getaway, too."

"Don't worry about the latest driveway drama. You're under a lot of stress."

"I wanted to let you know, I'm not, like, *pissed* at you," he said. "I've been a dick. It's not right for me to take everything out on you."

"Wow. *Okay.* Thanks."

"Pretty humbling to have Scott talk me down from my panic attack."

"He's an expert at that sort of thing."

"It's still embarrassing. I'm a grown man."

"He saw it as a biological reaction to anxiety, not some negative reflection on your masculinity."

"Hard for *me* to think of it that way."

"That's how you were raised. How *most* men our age were raised."

"I've never been good at showing my emotions."

"You *sure* about that?" asked Tipsy.

"What do you mean?"

"Men have somehow convinced women that we're the more emotional sex by removing explosive anger and sullen resentment from the lexicon of human emotions."

Ayers watched a line of pelicans float over his parents' house. "Guess you're right."

Tipsy was on a roll. "Let's not forget that famous male coping mechanism—running away from problems to hide in a deer stand or a duck blind. Or in a liquor bottle—"

"I get it, Tipsy. Hopefully Scott can be a better role model for Little Ayers."

"I'm happy that Scott is in our kids' lives, but *you're* their dad. They love you at their deepest core. Little A will model himself after you, and the girls will carry you into their own relationships."

The pelicans disappeared and he returned his gaze to his former wife. "A couple years ago, I asked Mimi why you left me. I provided us a good life, you know? Nice house and cars. Vacations. You didn't have to work—"

"I *wanted* to work. I just *couldn't* for a while. My painters' block. I tried to tell you—"

"I know. I didn't take it seriously enough. But if you'd gotten past it, you could have painted to your heart's content, and had an easy life."

Tipsy didn't tell him that she wouldn't have gotten past in if she'd stayed in the marriage.

"I wondered," he went on, "was our life *that bad*, that you had to blow it up? But Mimi explained that you weren't some total ingrate after everything our family had done for you. That you weren't trying to run around dating a bunch of guys and partying like a Shem Creek boat fly. That you did it *for* the kids, not in spite of them. To get them away from our problems and show them something different."

Tipsy chose to focus on the positive parts of that little speech. "That's basically accurate."

"Now you've done what you set out to do. You've got a healthy relationship. Great life ahead of you. Nice sensitive doctor with good hair. Gonna buy Jimmy's mom's old house. Maybe you'll finally trade in the damn Tahoe." His voice crept up in volume.

She backed away a few more feet. "I'll get the kids' stuff and go."

"Here I am, fucking up again!" He opened his truck's door and slammed it. "What the hell is wrong with me, Tipsy?"

"I can't answer that. You have to figure it out yourself!"

"I don't know how!"

"You could start with seeing a therapist, and you also saw a psychiatrist a couple times after we split. I'm not a mental health professional, but I am about to marry one. I've known you for a long time. You probably have a mood disorder. Untreated depression, or serious anxiety. Something like—"

"I'm not crazy!"

"What does that *even mean?* Everyone around here is at least a little bit crazy, me included. Mimi and Jimmy included. Scott and your parents included. There's no shame in it! Some people manage their own crazy. Some people need outside assistance. The ones who manage it aren't winning a contest, and the ones who need help aren't losing it."

"I don't know *what to do*. I don't want to get divorced again—"

"Then don't! Speaking of therapists, have you and Kate seen one together?"

"No. She wants to see one, but…she's *begging* me to come back. Says she'll do anything. But she's said that kind of thing before. Nothing ever changes."

"Can you at least try therapy? It's a relationship-saver for some couples."

"Maybe. I don't *know*. I just had to get out of there. Away from the pressure of being around her."

"So this house—" Tipsy pointed up at May Penny and Tripp's mansion. "—is now your deer stand? Your six thousand square foot escape pod? Look, this is a chance for you to make changes in your life. Changes don't have to include getting divorced. I don't want that for you, and I definitely don't want it for the kids."

"You sound like my mother."

"We both want the best for everyone in this family."

"But what if nothing changes?"

"At least you'll know you tried."

"Another line I've already heard from Mom."

"Think about it, will you?"

He retrieved a pack of gum and his dinging phone from his pocket. "I will. I'll—" He held the phone away from his face. "It's Dad. I gotta get to the office."

"Okay. I'm glad we had this talk. I hope whatever I've said is helpful in some way."

His phone dinged again, and he squinted at it before typing. Ayers still had too much pride for reading glasses, but maybe his overall pride was dwindling, because he said, "You told me shit I don't want to hear. It's not pleasant, but if I have to hear it from anyone, I'm glad it's you."

That comment made Tipsy's throat constrict.

"Don't say anything about me getting all—" He wiggled his fingers in front of his eyes, then swirled them beside his temple.

"Got it," she said, and swallowed the throat lump. He got into his truck, popped a few pieces of gum into his mouth, and turned on the radio. Taylor Swift's ten-minute version of *All Too Well* floated through the open window. Tipsy had been casually cruel in the name of being honest, and Ayers had, for once, heard her.

As he drove away, May Penny's front door opened. The lady herself stepped onto the porch and descended the stairs. "I didn't have to come out here and stop another scream-off in my driveway."

"It was going in that direction, but we salvaged it."

"Did you tell him to move back into his house and work on his marriage instead of running away from his problems?"

"Something like that. I recommended therapy, too."

"We're on the same page."

"According to Ayers, yes."

"Funny how you and I seem to agree on most things these days. Who would have guessed that five years ago?"

"Not me," said Tipsy. "Although, from our last conversation, we're not *always* in agreement."

"I'm sorry I gave you grief about taking him back to court. I'm afraid for him if things get more complicated. He's standing at the crossroads of Rock Bottom Boulevard and Redemption Road."

"Meaning he could go either way."

May Penny nodded. "It's a chance for him to make lifechanging progress, or descend into chaos. I don't want to add to the strain between those choices. The thought of losing the kids would do that to him."

"I already met with a lawyer."

"*Really*." May Penny's jaw clenched.

"She gave me all my options. Legally, they're not good. Psychologically, for the kids and for Ayers, they're even worse. I'm not going down that path."

May Penny exhaled in a long blast. "Thank you, Jesus."

"But you couldn't strongarm me into not *exploring* those options, May Penny. I have to do what's right for my kids. Especially when Ayers is going through a major crisis."

"I understand that. I'm glad you went to an ethical attorney who didn't waste your time, money, and goodwill. I *do* care about you, Tipsy, and I respect you. But *I* won't be strongarmed into not protecting my son and my grandkids, either."

"I can't imagine anyone strongarming you."

May Penny smiled. "You don't give yourself enough credit. You're a formidable adversary these days. Although, I don't *want* you as an adversary. We've done a pretty good job as a team the past couple years."

"The crew of Starship Ayers, navigating through time and space."

"Dodging meteors and black holes."

"Ayers himself knows we're a force to be reckoned with."

May Penny squeezed her arm. "May the force be with you, honey."

As Tipsy got back into her car, she couldn't help but marvel at the changes in her relationship with May Penny. Ayers, too, given their relatively peaceful driveway convo. Those changes in Ayers might seem insignificant to some observers, like Shelby. Tipsy imagined her dear friend's commentary. *So what, Tipsy? He didn't scream in your face or leap into his truck and race away with Barbara Streisand or Blind Melon or Black Sabbath blasting from his speakers. You gonna give him a cookie? Bake him a batch of his favorite snickerdoodles?*

The imaginary Shelby was right in many ways. Ayers had been so difficult for so long, even a reasonably civil conversation and display of minor self-awareness seemed like great progress. Still, when you start face down in the dirt, rising to your elbows is cause for celebration. She hoped that Ayers would finally raise his head, and take a deep, clean breath. He'd been choking on mud for years.

It's an unusually hot and steamy January morning, and Tipsy has just dropped the children off at school for their first day back after winter break. She's exhausted, and despite the recent holiday season, she's lost ten pounds. The past six weeks have been one long, agonizing blur.

Around the beginning of the school year, she'd started enlightening Ayers as to her true feelings about their marriage. After a decade of him complaining about his unhappiness, and vaguely threatening divorce if she didn't fix some nebulous, unnamed problems, she'd finally raised her own issues. Nothing nebulous about Tipsy's complaints. They were as fixed as cold concrete, or scorch marks on silk, or dried Gorilla Glue. His temper. Their lack of emotional connection. The feeling of walking on eggshells around him. Her fears over the ramifications of their stilted, tense relationship on the children. His lack of presence in their lives and preference for hunting and fishing. His constant discontent and her despair at ever being able to make him happy.

When she first started speaking up, he blew her off. He flat out denied her objective observations. According to the man himself, he didn't yell. He rarely went hunting. He was perfectly happy, thank you very much. He insisted she was crazy, demanding, needy. All the while, his own rage increased with each expression of frustration on her part. Days before Thanksgiving, he called her an entitled diva, and reminded her that every woman wanted her life, with their pretty house and beautiful children. He informed her that he was a fine catch. He made damn good money and his parents helped them out with everything from vacations to vehicles to mortgage down payments. What the hell else did she want?

In one of her only shows of temper in their entire relationship, she'd slammed her fists on the granite kitchen countertops and yelled that she couldn't stand to listen to his voice for one more second. She told him to get out of her sight before she lost her mind.

The look on his face—flabbergasted—told her that she might have finally gotten through to him. The detailed explanations that she'd spent weeks calmly delivering had fallen on deaf ears, but those few hysterical sentences somehow resonated.

He'd spent the holidays alternating between being angry with her and telling her he'd do anything to make things right. He loved her; he'd change. She was breaking his heart. The kids would never recover if they split up.

She only sunk further away from him. She somehow made it through the Collins Family Thanksgiving, Christmas Eve (including a two-hour long church service with May Penny and Tripp), Christmas Day (Mimi asked if she was sick because of her weight loss), and a painful New Year's Eve party in their neighborhood. Now the kids were back at school. Only

Tipsy at home, with Ayers lingering around the house when he should be at work, trying to convince her they could work it out. That morning, he texted asking if she'd get breakfast with him, so she met him at the bagel shop in Belle Hall Shopping Center, not far from their house.

He seems to think it's going to be a pleasant post-holiday catch up. She isn't hungry, but he orders food for himself, and then sits across from her at a high top table. The busy shop is cramped and loud, and she already has a headache at half past eight in the morning. The smell of frying eggs nauseates her, and the sight of Ayers's greasy sausage and cheese bagel sandwich doesn't help.

"Everyone get to school okay?" he asks, after swallowing a bite.

"Yes."

"They seemed ready to go back. It gets boring being home for two weeks after Christmas."

"Probably."

"I…uh…Dad put me on a new project at work. Parking garage downtown."

"Great."

"That's it? Great?"

"I'm sure it will go well. Y'all have done lots of parking garages."

"I'm trying to make conversation, Tipsy."

"I'm sorry." Her mind starts to elaborate, to make more excuses, but in the end, that's all there is. She's sorry for the way things are between them, but that's about it.

"I've been trying—"

"I know you have."

"—but you're determined to be miserable."

"You've been determined to be miserable for years."

"Bullshit. I mean…I've been trying to figure out what I want. Career-wise. Like what will actually make me happy—"

"Ayers, you've told me yourself that everyone wants our life. Yet you're acknowledging that you've been trying to find some magic mushroom to make you eternally happy."

"We need to talk about you, not me. How you're *acting, when our marriage is falling apart."*

"I've been trying for years. Years. *You never paid attention."*

"So it's all my fault, right?"

"I've never said that. I should have been more forthcoming about my concerns—"

"You know what? Forget this. I've done everything I can to fix things. Maybe I'm *the one who is done now. Maybe* I *want out." He leans toward her, as if waiting for her to gasp in horror. "Maybe I should just...*move... out... of the house."

Here it is. The chance Tipsy has waited for. It's a bit of a cop out, but she's wanted him to be the first one to say it, and now he has. "Yes," she says. "That's a good idea."

He looks as if she slapped him. He doesn't say anything else. He stares out the window for thirty seconds or so—half a minute, after sixteen years of a shared life—and then he stands. He leaves her with his unfinished coffee and half eaten bagel sandwich.

Tipsy sits there in the bustling café and watches people collect their food. Old men with newspapers, moms with toddlers, a trainer from the gym on the other side of the shopping center. Bizarre feelings swamp her. Simultaneous relief and dread. One weight is lifted, and another slams into the back of her aching head. She notices that other patrons are hovering over her, waiting for a table. She gathers the remains of her husband's breakfast, dumps it in the trash can, and walks out the door. Hot muggy air hits her face. She glances up at the gathering dark clouds. A thunderstorm, on a January morning. As Granna would say, who woulda thunk it?

She looks left, and then right, and decides to go to Harris Teeter. Her kitchen is low on necessities. Milk. Bananas. Kraft Mac-n-cheese and chicken noodle soup. It might be warm, but it's still winter. The kids will enjoy some hot chocolate. Strange storms are brewing. Tipsy has to prepare.

As each of her previous supernatural mysteries had rumbled, tumbled, and bumbled toward a frustratingly changeable finish line, Tipsy had looked forward to the satisfaction of a definitive conclusion. The revelation of Jane and Henry's *secret within a secret* brought no such feelings of gratification. If Tipsy had truly freed Jane and Henry, she faced the bittersweet finality of them moving on. Both of them. *Permanently.* Of course she was happy for them, and relieved that she and Scott would have peace as they started their life together. As much peace as a couple with five adolescents could expect, anyway. At the same time, the idea of losing Jane *again*, and dear, constant, kooky Henry for the first time, filled her with dread. So much so, that she found herself avoiding them. She didn't call out to them when she entered or left her house, and they remained out of sight for days.

Maybe Jane didn't forgive Henry, Granna.

Is that a bit of hopefulness I hear?

No. Or…maybe. I'm torn. I want them to be at peace, but this isn't like friends moving across the country. I can't Facetime them, or set up a Zoom meeting. We can't plan a fun couples' reunion trip to Vegas.

It's a loss for all involved, sugar. Let yourself grieve it, but next time you see them, ask them to sit a spell and chat.

That's what you told me to do with Henry, when I first moved in. When I was trying to figure out if he was dangerous.

That all worked out pretty well, didn't it?

Tipsy had nodded, her throat constricting, but when Jane and Henry finally appeared and asked her to join them on the porch, she indeed agreed to sit a spell.

It was a Tuesday morning, almost two weeks after Henry had announced that he believed Jane about the pregnancy, and Tipsy had just returned from dropping off the kids at school. She had the whole day ahead of her, so if this sit-a-spell proved to be Jane and Henry's curtain call, she could squeeze in an hour for a good cry. She sat in one of the rocking chairs and propped her sneakered feet on the glass-topped coffee table. She nervously flexed her ankles. The chair rocked in little spasms that matched the jolts of adrenaline in her stomach.

Jane and Henry sat on the loveseat. She tucked her bare feet under her, and Henry crossed one leg over the other. He wrapped his big hands around his knees. "We come here today," he said, like a judge about to deliver his verdict, "to inform you that we have reached a conclusion about the *secret within a secret*. And all the other secrets that went along with it, before and after."

He paused, his jaw working. As the seconds stretched on, the fault line in Tipsy's stomach shifted. She had no idea what he would say, or what she *wanted* him to say. "*And?*"

"We've fully reconciled," he croaked out.

"Yes, we have," added Jane.

"Whew," said Tipsy. "I wasn't sure *where* you were going there—"

Henry wiped at his eyes, but one glittering tear snuck past his long auburn lashes. "I apologize. It's all very emotional, you see, and I've realized that I'm not as free with my emotions as I always thought. The most important ones, anyway."

Jane leaned toward him until her lavender dress blended into his white shirt, like frosting melting off the edges of a spring wedding cake. She wiped at his tear, but in an example of the fickleness of supernatural physics, her fingers passed over it. Still a sweet gesture, and he wrapped one arm around her shoulder and pulled her close. Why that worked and the tear swiping did not, Tipsy would never know.

"It is," said Jane. "I've wept enough sparkly tears to fill a hundred champagne bottles. We've discussed everything that…happened…back then. The good, the bad, and the uglier than homemade sin."

"Discussing it without anger or judgment—"

"But with compassion for each other," said Jane.

"And compassion for…him. Proctor."

"Wow, Henry," said Tipsy. "I can't believe you're saying that."

"I never thought I'd say it, even when I believed I'd found peace with it all." Henry ran his fingers up and down Jane's bare arm. "But Jane moved on so quickly, we never had a chance to..."

"To really *dissect* it?" offered Tipsy.

"That seems gruesome," said Jane. "Us being dead and all."

"But accurate," said Henry. "We understood the basic nature of our deaths, but there was no *detailed autopsy*. We never had got to explain our actions and understand where they came from. Without Jane here, we gained no true resolution. I perseverated on it more than I realized, and I eventually lost the clarity that I thought I'd regained."

Jane looked up at him. "As time went on—or what passes for time on the other side—I realized something was very wrong."

"It's supposed to be blissful in heaven. How can it be blissful, and very wrong?" Tipsy shook her head. "I wish you and Granna could explain it all to me. It might help me to help the boy across the street, Stephen. He's afraid that if I show him his death, he won't *move on* anywhere. He thinks he'll just be…*gone.*"

"I wish I could offer some clarity," said Jane, "but…it's beyond my ability to explain."

"But in a *good way*, right? At least I can tell Stephen that much."

Jane smiled. "Most definitely. I felt the presence of all my loved ones. My parents. Connie and her husband, Andrew, and little Louisa. Then later, our dear old Johnny and his lovely Ivy. We were all *together*, and everyone else seemed *wholly content*, but I once again felt the tug of the unresolved. When we were trapped in this house, something was drowning inside me. Trying to thrash its way to the surface. It quieted for a while when I moved on, but then it woke, more desperate than ever."

"The secret within the secret," said Tipsy. "The pregnancy you both wanted so badly, but never had a chance to tell Henry."

"That secret reached out through time and space and drew us back together," said Henry.

"That must have been what happened with those two men in Orangeburg. Y'all know what I mean. From my friend Helen's story. Those Quincy brothers."

"Now *what* about those Quincy brothers?"

Tipsy turned toward that singsong voice. "Helen! What's up?" Tipsy had texted with Helen about the latest developments with Jane and Henry, but she hadn't seen her supernatural mentor since their visit to Aunt Talia Parker. "You appeared like…well, a ghost."

"I'm alive and kickin' like a bee-stung mule. Just dropped off laundry for Mr. Q. Thought I'd stop by to share my latest ghost story with you, and then I hear the three of y'all…" She pointed between Tipsy, Jane, and Henry. "…talking about the Quincy Brothers."

Jane and Henry smiled at her recognition of them. "You must be Mrs. Helen Stokes," said Henry. "Esteemed deliverer of spirits and fountain of knowledge."

"That I am. You must be Mr. Henry Mott, sometime lunatic and kitchen destroyer."

"Unfortunately, yes. Although I feel much better of late. This is my wife, Jane."

"So nice to meet you, Mrs. Stokes," said Jane.

"And you, dear," said Helen. "I've heard a lot about you. You're as lovely as Tipsy said you are." She turned to Henry. "And you, Mr. Mott—"

"I leave much to be desired in the face, Mrs. Stokes, especially when compared to my beautiful wife and pretty Miss Tipsy."

"Don't sell yourself short. You're no Denzel, but there's something about your face."

"I have no idea who that is, but I sense a compliment."

Tipsy laughed. "The point is, your face sticks with people. It stayed with Stephen, and he only met you once when he was eight."

"Have you had any luck helping him move on?" asked Helen.

"Haven't had a chance to get over there and talk to him since he showed me that memory of his single meeting with Henry. His place has been crawling with construction workers."

"Perhaps you should try at night," said Jane.

"I'm afraid someone will call the cops. I've gotten pretty good at sneaking around private property to release ghosts in the past few years, but this is all a lot easier when you have easy access to the haunting space."

"True," said Helen. "That made it easier for me to talk to Pecan Ted and Grapevine Earl."

"Oh!" said Tipsy. "Did you go visit them?"

"I did," said Helen. "Auntie's story got stuck up in my craw, so I decided it was high time I visit the old family farm in Orangeburg."

"Is it still there?"

Helen nodded. "Some of the land has been sold, but the house is hanging on. I worried that the whole place would be built out and I'd be looking for the Quincy boys in a Family Dollar. House is run down, but someone seems to be living in it. Bunch of old cars in the front yard. A busted up trampoline. The pecan tree is still there, but the grapevines are gone. These days, it's Pecan Ted and Storage Shed Earl."

"Did you find them?"

"I did. Turns out their story was...*well.* Let's just say I don't know how it would have gone over with my mother and my Auntie, much less my Granny."

"What do you mean?"

"Remember how Aunt Talia said Granny didn't want pretty boy Ted coming around her girls? She had no need to worry, because Teddy had *no* kind of interest in *any* girls. At all."

"Ah," said Tipsy. "He was gay?"

"Gay as in having nothing to do with happiness?" asked Henry.

"Yes. When the brothers let me look into their memories, I saw..." As Helen paused to collect her thoughts, she gazed up at the haint blue porch ceiling. She looked remarkably like her Aunt Talia. "They *were* fighting over their mother's jewelry. That part was right, but it wasn't *all* right. Earl thought Teddy meant to give it to his sweetheart. That he had a girl somewhere. But the truth is, he wanted to sell it. To buy himself and his...gentleman friend...two one way tickets to New York city."

"Riiiight," said Tipsy. "Orangeburg, South Carolina, was probably not the place to be two gay black men in the 1940s—"

"It gets even worse. His gentleman friend was *white.* Some poor white trash young man whose father was a known member of the KKK. Earl found out and, then Earl lost his damn mind."

"I understand what you're saying," said Jane. "Or, *understand* isn't the right word, as I can't imagine how *any* of that could happen, but I *comprehend.*"

"As do I," said Henry. "So Earl attacked his brother?"

"He did. Threatened to kill him if he touched their mother's jewelry. Earl was convinced their dear departed mama was flip-flopping around in her grave like a beached bass over Ted's sinful ways. They tussled, and Teddy took off down the road. Earl went after him. Thirty minutes later, they were both dead in my Granny and Grandpa's front yard."

"That secret about Teddy's forbidden love life drew Teddy back to Earl and trapped them there until they sorted it out," said Tipsy.

Helen nodded. "Once they understood, they could both move on again, so off they went."

"Off they went," repeated Tipsy. She turned to Jane and Henry. "If resolution worked for the Quincy brothers…and y'all said everything is resolved between you…that means…" She took a deep breath and spit it out. "*So-y'all-can-move-on-now-right?*"

Jane smiled at her. "We can, honey."

"Yes, indeed. Both of us." Henry held out his hands, and wiggled his long fingers. "The feeling that I lost, and found, and lost again… it's back."

Tipsy forced herself to say what needed to be said. "Then y'all need to go. I love you both so much, but it's time."

"We will," said Jane, gently. "But there are a few things that must be done before we can leave you."

"Oh, Henry. Not THE GREAT STORY—"

"No," he said. "I let that go. If a GREAT STORY originates in me, I won't be the one to tell it."

"What do you mean?"

"Maybe it's the story of us. Me, and Jane. And you. And you're the one to tell it."

"I can't write—"

"Then paint our story."

"I appreciate your faith in my abilities, but there's too much nuance in this story for my artform."

"You have the rest of your life to put it on canvas. I'm not Mother Pearl Fischer, but I predict yours will be long and productive."

"What an amazing talent *that* woman had," said Jane. "Amazing, and terrifying."

"My own abilities vexed me during my life," said Henry, "but I'd rather see ghosts than see the future."

"I agree," said Helen. "I wouldn't know what to do with a glimpse of strange things past, or what may come."

"Right? So stressful," said Tipsy. "Mother Pearl had to decide, right then and there, what to tell Henry about his future, and she didn't know enough to save him from it."

"She did what she could," said Henry. "Without your young Stephen, we may have never figured out the secret within the secret. All thanks to the old maid in trousers, Pearl Fischer."

"So what is it that you still have to do here in this world, if not write the GREAT STORY?" asked Tipsy.

"We have to see you get married!" he said.

"But the wedding isn't for almost two weeks! Y'all can't risk waiting around—"

"We love you, Tipsy," said Jane. "We'll risk it, although, my *heart* is telling me there's no risk. Our path to eternity is smooth now."

"If y'all are sure. I admit your presence will make it even more special. Even if I'm the only person who can see you."

The four of them—two ghosts and two clairvoyants—lingered on the porch for a while, discussing everything from Tipsy's wedding to the confounding nature of the Motts' continued existence. "What am I, really?" asked Henry. "I've never spoken that question aloud, but I've certainly pondered it."

"As have I," said Jane. "It's enough to drive a person quite mad."

"We have no physical substance, yet we're defined by what we looked like at the time of our deaths. From my damnably messy hair to Jane's bare feet. Never aging in appearance, even as our experience of this world is relegated to the history books."

"It's permanent, yet so precarious. In the early days of my haunting," said Jane. "I wondered if I'd simply…fade away."

"Y'all sound like Stephen Ramsey. Poor kids thinks he'll end up like a bolt of lightning after it strikes the earth."

"Don't give up on him yet," said Helen. "You just started working on him."

"I've been surprised at how many ghosts are hesitant to accept my help. I'd love a nice simple exorcism one day. Like, one quick look into a willing spirit's head, and boom! Mystery solved and the ghost peaces out."

"You'll find some like that," said Helen, "but the hard cases will increase your skill."

"Think of stubborn ghosts like small children sitting for a portrait," said Henry. "The ones who won't stop moving. A challenge, but if you can understand the essence of those bright souls, the reward will be nothing short of a work of art."

Jane patted his arm. "Always the poet, darling."

Tipsy smiled at them. "I'll remember that, and I'll keep at it, but… Helen, this one might go faster if you come with me. You've done this so many times—"

Helen wagged a finger at her. "I told you. It's trial by fire, Tipsy. To borrow Henry's reference to artwork, I can give you pointers, but you'll only improve if you pick up the brush and practice with your own hand."

Tipsy sighed. "Yes, ma'am."

"You get a few more notches on your belt, and I'll happily work with you. Plenty of ghosts in this town need freeing, and I can't attend to them all. I've got to put in my hours at the laundry, and volunteer at my church, and spend time with my kids and grandbabies. Plus my walks…*and* my daughter wants me to take up CrossFit with her."

"You're taking after your Aunt Talia."

"We've both put in our time with spirits, although I'll never turn away from a ghost in need. Nice to know there will be someone to help me carry this load."

"I will. Absolutely." Tipsy thought about the ghosts she'd seen around town. "I ran into two ghosts on the beach at Sullivan's a few years ago. An enslaved man and a confederate soldier. Unsurprisingly, they didn't seem to like each other. I could start with them. And when I lived on Society Street, a woman in a hoop skirt wandered around on the sidewalk. Oh! The older man at the Whole Foods! He looked like a policeman, or something—"

"Get Stephen sorted out, then start on that list. You have any questions, shoot me a text. I'll keep an eye out for a big project we can do together. You know...someone famous."

"Anne Boleyn?" offered Henry.

"Why not? I've always wanted to visit London." Helen removed her keys from her pocketbook and pressed the button to unlock her Caddy. The car flashed its lights and *be-beeped*, like a mechanical wink and a wolf whistle. "Got to run. I promised my son I'd keep his kids tonight."

"Are you going home to prepare a lovely homemade supper for them?" asked Jane.

Helen laughed. "No, sugar. Nowadays, I only cook on Sundays. They'll have pizza and like it! Good luck with young Mr. Ramsey, Tipsy. You got this."

Helen got into her car and zipped down the driveway. As she disappeared, Tipsy turned to her friends. "Looks like I'm on my own with this one."

"I think Miss Helen is right," said Jane. "Some things one must learn for oneself."

"She's afraid you'll slow her down, Tipsy," said Henry. "She seems a very busy lady."

"When will you visit Stephen again?" asked Jane.

"Not now. It's a marathon painting day and I don't want to risk a headache." Tipsy rubbed her eyes, then dug her fingers into the sides of her skull. "Maybe I need a new approach, or I'm missing something with him."

"Don't worry about it too much, Tipsy," said Henry. "You're always worrying about something, related to the children, or Dr. Brandt, or your friends. Your artwork, or your house, or your sideways hustling as a buster of ghosts. I don't understand how one human brain can balance so many tasks. You drive yourself batty trying to sort things out, yet they always end up sorted."

Jane smiled at her husband again. "That's what *you men* never understand. Everything comes together *because* women drive themselves batty."

"That makes no sense," said Henry, like Little Ayers mulling over a difficult math problem.

"She means that it's the multi-tasking that gets things done," said Tipsy.

"It's a woman's way. A gift and a burden." Jane looked at Henry with a mischievous twinkle in her eye. "Some men in this age *ease* the burden. Look at Tipsy's Scott, cooking and cleaning like he was born in an apron."

Henry still looked confused. "You never wanted me in the kitchen, Janie. I would have unintentionally poisoned us both."

Jane laughed, and Henry launched into a story about the one time he tried to mop the floor and flooded the foyer, and Tipsy found her mind wandering pleasantly. She looked past her potted petunias on the porch steps. The yard was in full glorious springtime disarray. Fresh green grass, the old shrubs Scott had trimmed last weekend, and Jane's magnolia standing sentry in the corner, as it had for a century. Tipsy and Scott's long term renovation plan included new landscaping, but the magnolia would stay as long as the gods of nature held it up. She eyed some empty space along the fence line. The perfect spot for a new planting of wild indigo. False indigo, but as Jane had once said, if it was wild, it had to be indigo at its truest form.

A gift and a burden, she thought. That might be true about her clairvoyance, but that power had brought her the Motts, and they were one of life's greatest gifts.

Chapter 15

Tipsy stood in a patch of dried out grass, watching Ted and Earl Quincy sprint down a dirt road. Earl was yelling after Ted. Calling him *unnatural.* Saying their parents would die of shame if they weren't dead already. Reminding him that a man shouldn't be like this.

As Tipsy watched, Earl Quincy morphed into Pearl Fischer. Her blue pants flapped around her spindly legs as she pursued Ted. She was yelling, too. *"I'll teach you! It's not how a man should be!"*

Ted abruptly stopped, but when he turned around, he wasn't a handsome black man in his twenties. He was a white boy of about eight with a red splotch on his face. He clutched a bouquet of purple wild indigo flowers. He held out the flowers like a Mother's Day gift, but Pearl Fischer plowed into him. They tumbled onto the ground. "*It's for your own good!"* she hollered, as she pummeled him. *"You can't wear flowers! You can't wear flowers!"*

Tipsy woke, opened her eyes, and stared at her bedroom ceiling. She sat up with the dream still fresh in her mind.

Ted and Earl; Stephen and Mother Pearl.

She wanted to speak to Stephen right away, before it faded. Helen had suggested she seek him out at night. She got out of bed and looked at her phone. It was two in the morning. Can't get much more nighttime than that.

She peeked in on the kids, who were sleeping soundly. She traded her favorite old nightgown for her USC sweatshirt and taco print pajama pants, donned flip-flops, and walked downstairs to the foyer. "Jane? Henry?" she called out softly.

Jane appeared before her. Henry quickly followed. He stood behind his wife like a distorted yet protective reflection. "Goodness, it's late. Is everything alright?" asked Jane.

"Yes. I'm going to talk to Stephen."

"Right now?" asked Henry.

"Multi-tasking, remember? But the kids are sleeping and I can't leave them alone at this hour. Could y'all…"

"We'll watch over them," said Jane.

"I figured that would be okay, since Henry is…like…"

"No longer unintentionally demolishing kitchens?" he suggested.

"That *is* a correct assessment, right?"

"Oh, yes," said Henry. "All of my powers of telekinesis are firmly under my control." As if to prove his point, he raised one hand. He twirled his index finger, and Tipsy's keys left the key ring beside the door and floated toward her. She held out her hand, and they landed gently in her palm.

"Great, thanks. If anyone wakes up come get me, Henry. I'll be in Stephen's backyard."

"He will. We're *happy* to keep the children for you. You leave everything to us," said Jane, as if she were the kids' favorite babysitter. She turned to her husband. "Henry, I'll go back and forth between the girls' rooms. You watch over Little Ayers. They'll be as safe and snug as bunnies in a burrow."

They disappeared to assume their assigned positions. Tipsy crept out of her house, across the street, and around to the back of Pearl Fischer's old place. She held out her phone, flashlight on, and whispered, "Here, kitty, kitty, kitty."

Not sure anyone will hear you, sugar.

Practicing my lines, Granna. I have a great new cat alibi. If someone asks me what the hell I'm doing, I'll say I'm looking for a gray and black cat named Spring. It sounds too ridiculous to be made up.

She slunk along the neglected shrubs lining the foundation, tiptoed across the patio, and sat on the cool concrete. "Stephen!" she whisper-yelled. "Hey! Stephen. Can you come out?'

She waited a few minutes and then tried again. "Stephen! I want to talk to you about...about shirts...with flowers!"

He was suddenly sitting beside her. The blue luminescence wafting off him twinkled in the moonlight. He stretched his skinny legs out before him. So sad that he'd never had a chance to grow into those big feet. "That's an odd thing to say."

"Maybe, but it's equally odd that you're so interested in shirts with flowers." She waved a hand to correct herself. "These days it wouldn't be so odd. But in the context of a little boy in 1923, seems that it was."

He glowered at her. "You sound like Mother Pearl."

"In your memory, she advised you to back off that kind of thing—"

"Who was she to tell me to be a *real man*? She weren't a *real woman*. No husband. No children of her own. She wore men's clothes!"

"We're talking about you at the moment. When we first met, you told me she was awful concerned with you being a strong, tough boy. *I wonder*. Did she have a reason to be worried about your..." She didn't know if he'd understand the term masculinity in the way she defined it. "...manliness?"

"No! Or...well..." He looked into the moonlit sky, as if the correct answer was up there among the stars. "*Maybe*. She always yelled at the boys about being men and the girls about being ladies. But why would we listen to her, when she was some strange *in between* thing herself? She used to say she was trying to protect us. As if the girls' flowery dresses might fly on out of the laundry basket and smother me!"

Tipsy thought of Pearl Ramsey's statement in Stephen's last memory, about people who had certain...*opinions*...in the town. Even at eight, Stephen had thumbed his nose at them. "Will you think about Mother Pearl trying to protect you, and let me see into your memory?"

"Just because I let you see into my memory to help your friend, don't mean I'm ready for you to see into my head about...me."

"I promise you, there is a place where you will be at peace with the people you loved. My friend Jane was talking about it today. How all her family and friends were with her. Aren't there people you'd like to see?"

" *'Spose* so. A few."

"Like..." Tipsy kept pushing him. "....who? How about some names?"

"My real mother. Mother Pearl. My friends from this house. They must have all grown up, and lived, and died, by now."

"Like your friend Eldridge? You've mentioned him. The one who was gone when you woke up in your haunting."

"Yes. He was gone. So was his sister, Hannah. I never understood *why* they left."

"If you move on, you can see them. Find out what happened to them."

Somewhere in the oak trees above them, an owl hooted. Another bird responded with a repetitive chirping that seemed out of place in the still darkness. "Some-birdies are up early," said Tipsy.

"That's a nightjar. They sing at night."

"Ah. I wouldn't have known that. Would have assumed it was an insomniac chickadee. A sparrow, pulling an all-nighter."

"Mother Pearl said they blend in with the marsh grass, so I never actually seen one. But when I got older, we sat on the porch till late some nights. Me and her and Eldridge. Sometimes Hannah. Hannah was afraid of them birds. She said birds should only sing during the day. But Mother Pearl said it was clever for the nightjars to wait until dark, when no other birds would drown out their songs."

"Sounds like she taught y'all a lot."

"She did." He closed his eyes, as he had the last time. "Do it quickly, 'fore I change my mind."

Tipsy touched his pale knee. The nightjar's haunting song chimed in her ears as the darkness fell.

She wakes up to a chaotic scene that leaves little time to get her bearings. She's in an unfamiliar foyer looking into a sparsely furnished sitting room. Children are screaming and crying. Feet thud on the hardwood floor as they run up and down the hallway. Several people huddle over a crumpled form

sprawled in the entryway between foyer and parlor. She sees two bare feet and skinny, sandy legs.

Mother Pearl's voice rings out over the hullabaloo. "Everyone out!" she yells.

The children scatter, but Pearl barks more directions. "Hannah! Get me clean rags and water and…and alcohol!" A towheaded girl of ten or eleven in a red dress runs past Tipsy. Her white blonde braids bounce against her Peter Pan collar as she disappears down a narrow hallway.

"Eldridge! Come here!"

A boy about the age of the ghost of Stephen emerges from the adjacent room. He's very fair, with white blonde curly hair and pale brows. His blue eyes are bugging from his head and he's breathing hard. His feet are also bare, and he's wearing a dark brown jacket. There's bright red blood on his white hands and legs and some has streaked his nose.

Tipsy walks forward, and as she guessed, the mangled mess on the floor is Stephen Ramsey. He rolls onto his side and spits up blood. The back of his sweater is ripped, and she can see his pale shoulders and knobby spine. Mother Pearl pushes him onto his back and lifts the sweater. Thick blood pumps steadily from a two-inch wound on his abdomen.

Pearl's voice is steady, but her dark eyes are wide with fear. "What happened?"

"We were on the beach," says Eldridge. "Walking. Or…swimming. Uh…playing ball."

"Don't yank me around, boy! What were you doing?"

Stephen's voice floats up from the floor. "We were sitting. Talking. We were…"

"Hell's bells. Were you doing…unnatural things?"

"We were holding hands!" Stephen gasps. "He gave me a kiss. Just a little kiss on the cheek—"

"Stevie—" says Eldridge.

"It's the truth, El!"

"We said we wouldn't tell her! Or anyone! Not after last time—"

"Last time? How many times have there been?" asks Pearl.

"Only a few! We've been more careful since those boys…since they saw us—"

"God almighty! Who saw y'all? Who was it?"

"Three boys," says Stephen, in a rasping voice. "Laurence something. The boy with the big crooked nose. The Robbard brothers—"

"Pastor Robbard's children? The preacher from the Pentecostal *church?" She says it as if the Pentecostal church is a leper colony, or a maximum security prison.*

Hannah reappears with rags and a bottle of clear liquid that must be rubbing alcohol. Another older girl has a basin of water. Mother Pearl shoos them away once they deliver their supplies.

"What have I been trying to teach you boys all this time? You cannot!" She doesn't need to say what they cannot do. Everyone, including Tipsy, knows. "It's too dangerous! And now…Stephen…stabbed through—"

"Last time they only yelled at us, but this time, they came after us!" says Eldridge. "We weren't hurting them! We didn't do nothing to them at all!"

"You stupid boy! Your existence is a threat to them! Stephen! Stay with me!" She yells down into Stephen's face. His eyes are rolling. She presses on his wound, but the blood immediately soaks through the white rags. She barks up at Eldridge. "Then what happened?"

"Laurence had a knife. We tried to run from them, but he grabbed Stevie by his sweater and ripped it. Called us abominations. Devils. Evil perverts. Stevie pushed him a good one, and that's when Laurence stabbed him. They ran off, and I…I dragged him back here."

"Jesus wept," says Mother Pearl. "He's not going to make it. I think something inside him is hit. Maybe his stomach. Or his liver—"

"What do you mean? Is he dying?"

Stephen coughs. Blood shoots from his mouth and hits the scuffed, dingy white wall. It makes a pattern like a warped smiley face with a beaklike nose. Like Laurence is grinning at Stephen as he bleeds out. Hahaha, you pervert!

Eldridge kneels beside him. He takes both of Stephen's hands in his. "Stevie! Don't leave me. You can't!"

"El," says Stephen. "I'm cold…"

"Stevie! Pleasepleaseplease—"

Pearl tries to pry Eldridge's fingers from Stephen's, but Eldridge won't let go. He looks up at her with wild, teary eyes. "No! I won't. Just because you're a coward, don't mean we will be, too! We know what you are. You're the same as us! You're too scared to admit it!"

"I know how the world works!" says Pearl. "I've tried to teach you! If that makes me a coward, so be it."

"I don't want your lessons no more! Stevie's going to get better, and me and him and Hannah will leave here. We'll go to a big city, like Stevie always said. Where no one will know us and we can live how we please—"

"Don't you think if such a place existed, I would have gone there long ago?" Mother Pearl flops onto the floor on her skinny rear end and looks up at the ceiling. "Lord, I've done the best I could. You bring me these children, and I tried to protect them, and now you're taking this one away."

Stephen tries to push himself up on his elbows even as he grips Eldridge's hands. "El...El...Scared. I'm...scared..."

"Don't be scared! You're not *dying. You're not!"*

In the background, the other children are sobbing.

"He is *dying, Eldridge," says Mother Pearl, in a monotone voice. "He's leaving us. You and Hannah will have to leave, too."*

"What? What?"

"You can't stay here. Not after this. Everyone in town will know. You'll make it dangerous for the other children. You'll have to leave—"

"I don't understand—where will we go—"

Stephen's shudders. His head flops backward and his shoulders hit the floor. As his eyes cloud over, Eldridge screams again, and the light fades for Tipsy.

Stephen was silent as Tipsy explained what she'd seen in his memory. A ghost usually reacted with a combination of horror and relief upon hearing about his or her own demise. Horrified relief; relieved horror. Stephen asked no questions and requested no clarification. His face was like a blank page in a diary. No look of shock and comprehension.

She finished talking, and still nothing, so she leaned toward him. "Now that you've heard the story…does it sound familiar?"

"Yes. I remember it all now."

"Do you…have any questions?"

"No. I said I remember it," he said. "Mother Pearl made Eldridge and Hannah leave after I died."

"Sounds like it. She seemed afraid of what would happen once the story of your death got out."

"But did it ever get out? Did those boys pay for what they did?"

"I don't know. I can do some research—"

"Don't bother. I already know. They were nice boys from nice families. My mother was a barmaid and I lived on Mother Pearl's charity. And I was…how I was."

"You liked boys."

"I did. I'm already dead, so you can't kill me for it."

"Things are different now. There are still people who hold the same beliefs as those boys, but there are more people who don't care who you like. Men can get married to men. Women can get married to women. I spoke with Henry and Jane about it recently."

He looked at her like she'd just told him that the ocean was made of chocolate syrup. "That can't be."

"It's true. Nowadays, you and Eldridge could have gotten married. Mother Pearl might not have been a spinster." Tipsy shrugged. "If I'm correct in my assessment of her, she didn't stay unmarried because she never found the right man. She didn't want any man."

"She never said so, but that's what me and El thought. She was a… *hypo-krite*."

"Hypocrite," said Tipsy. "She wanted to protect y'all. She'd lived long enough to know that people like y'all were in extra danger. Given what happened, she was right."

"Now do you see why I don't believe in God? No *nice* God would have made me like this, and El, and even Mother Pearl, and made us be born when we were born. Why would God make everyone think our ways were a terrible sin? Let us get killed young for it, to boot, while people like Crooked Nose Laurence and Pastor Robbard's boys roamed the world, getting old and gray."

"You can't blame God for the messed up rules people have come up with over the last couple thousand years. I told you; I don't know what I believe in. But I don't think God has anything to do with what happened to you."

"He could have stopped it, if he's so powerful. Why wouldn't He?"

"Humanity has always asked that question. No one on this planet has been able to answer it. If you move on yourself, maybe you'll get answers."

"I wonder what happened to El, and Hannah and Mother Pearl."

"Only one way to find out for sure. Remember what I told you?"

"You said that once I understood my death, I'd be able to *feel* again."

"Do you?"

"Yes." He wiggled his fingers in front of his face. "Something deep inside is telling me I can move on now."

"Are you still afraid to go?"

"It could be God playing another trick on me. But if it's not, maybe I *can* find Eldridge. Him and me can be who we weren't allowed to be back then."

"That sounds wonderful," said Tipsy.

He stood and swiped his hands over his legs and his seat, even though no dirt and grass could stick to him. "No reason to hang around here forever, listening to all that noise from them carpenter men. The new owners…" He rolled his eyes. "They brought in pictures of how they plan to outfit the house. Every single thing in the whole place will be white. Walls. Ceilings. Furniture. Cabinets. Even the rugs."

"That's a popular aesthetic these days."

"It's terrible. I need color."

Tipsy smiled. "Then walk toward the end of the rainbow."

"I will." He took a few steps toward the house, and then turned around. "Thank you for helping me. I'm sorry if I was kind of…" He waved his hands.

"Bitchy?"

He laughed. "That sounds right. I just *didn't know*. Anything, really."

"Go find out."

Stephen blew her a kiss. As he ran toward the harbor, it seemed his blue flickering melded with the cascading white moonlight. Tipsy smiled as he disappeared, secure in the knowledge that he would go on, and on, and on. But now he wouldn't be alone.

She took out her phone as she walked back to her house. She opened a text box and sent Helen a message. I HOPE I'M NOT WAKING YOU, BUT I CAME TO STEPHEN AT NIGHT, LIKE YOU SUGGESTED, WITH A LITTLE INSPIRATION FROM MY OWN DREAMING BRAIN AND YOUR STORY ABOUT THE QUINCY BROTHERS. HE UNDERSTANDS HIS DEATH, AND HE'S MOVED ON. LIKEWISE, I CAN NOW MOVE ON TO THE REST OF MY LIST.

It was near three in the morning, but Tipsy did a few hop-skips on her way back to her house. Setting Stephen free came with a simple joy that she hadn't experienced with her other hauntings, when she had so much riding on the outcome.

If any neighbors peeked out their windows, they'd see a thirty-eight year old woman prancing across the street in a hoodie, taco jammies, and flip-flops. They'd surely think she was batshit nuts. Happily, that idea didn't bother her anymore. She had mastered her incredible supernatural powers and used them to help a soul in need, and if that made her nuts, so be it.

Chapter 16

"I can come with you," said Tipsy, as she and Henry stood at the St. Philip's cemetery gate.

"No, thank you," said Henry. "It's enough for me to know you're here."

"You feel okay? Like, the house isn't calling to you?"

"Not yet. Since Jane and I came to peace, my time constraints have returned to normal."

"Will thirty minutes be enough time for the two of you to make amends?"

"I suppose we'll see. If not, there's time before the wedding."

"Okay, well…good luck. I'm glad you're doing this, Henry. Even if you don't *need* to reconcile with Proctor before you move on, it seems like the right thing."

He nodded and his dark blue eyes swept the gravestones and obelisks, the trees and benches, and the uneven paths through the grass.

"I'll wait for you here," said Tipsy.

Henry walked into the cemetery. As he approached his own gravestone, Tipsy noted the pale form of Proctor under the closest tree. Henry stopped about ten feet from Proctor, and the two men spoke. Henry nervously wiped his hands over his hair.

Proctor disappeared, and for a moment, Tipsy felt panicked, but he reappeared on the closest bench.

Whew, Granna, said Tipsy. *For a second I thought Proctor was going to turn down Henry's overture of reconciliation. If he had, I would have gone in there and walloped Proctor upside the head with that olive branch.*

I hear you. It's mighty big of Henry to make peace with Proctor.

I think Henry and Jane don't want to move on and leave Proctor here, suffering.

Henry joined Proctor on the bench. He leaned forward and rested both elbows on his knees. Proctor watched solemnly as Henry talked at the grass below his feet. Eventually, Proctor leaned forward on his own knees, and started saying his own piece.

There's no excuse for what he done, said Granna, *but I can't help but feel a smidge kindlier toward him. He was a pawn in their jacked up game of romantic chess.*

He was. All three of them had a role to play, said Tipsy. *No one is always right. Kind of like how I know Kate is a pain in the ass given what Scott and Ayers have both said about her, but I also know Ayers is a piece of work. Not just a piece, a freakin' masterpiece. On the flipside, me and Scott have both acknowledged that we took the cowardly way out for most of our marriages by letting them both run amuck.*

There just plain ter-reeeble people in the world—look at Thomas Bonneau—but for the most part, we all have a role to play in the assholery.

Tipsy nodded and rested her butt against the stucco wall surrounding the cemetery. She pictured Proctor and Henry on the bench. A passerby—someone who could see them—might take them for a grandfather and grandson. The latter bestowing wisdom on the former. Tipsy knew the complicated truth. Her mental camera clicked, and she decided she'd paint them. She'd call the painting *Forgiveness.* Force the reader to wonder who was forgiving who, and for what.

Her phone dinged, and she looked at the screen. Helen had replied to Tipsy's late night message.

HELEN: CONGRATS, GIRL! YOU'RE ON YOUR WAY. CAN'T WAIT TO HEAR ALL ABOUT IT. EVEN IF I THINK YOU SHOULD KEEP PRACTICING ON YOUR OWN, I'M STILL HERE TO TRADE BATTLEFIELD STORIES AND FISH TALES, AS MY DADDY WOULD HAVE SAID. HE ALSO LOVED TO GIVE ADVICE, EVEN WHEN I DIDN'T WANT IT. SO, YOU BEST GET READY! ☺

TIPSY: I'LL TAKE ALL THE ADVICE YOU HAVE! IT'S SO GOOD TO KNOW YOU'RE A TEXT AWAY.

HELEN: YOU'RE NOT ALONE, REMEMBER?

TIPSY: YES MA'AM!

"Hey, Tipsy."

Tipsy looked up from the phone, and there was LeeLee Moretz in a short, pale green dress. Her dark hair spilled over her shoulders.

"LeeLee, hey! How random to run into you here."

"Not really, if you know what I mean."

"You got a supernatural DM about my visit to the graveyard near your office?"

"Pretty much. Thanks for having Trey over last weekend."

"No worries. He's a doll. Sorry I missed you when you picked him up, but I was running my girls around."

"How's the problem with your…dead friends?"

"The secret within a secret has been solved." Tipsy explained the recent events involving Henry and Jane, as well as young Stephen Ramsey and Mother Pearl Fischer. "I thought you might find that last part interesting. You and the late Mother Pearl have something in common."

"I do, especially since her premonition finally came home to roost. That's weirdly reassuring. I've had a couple readings in my life—"

"Readings?"

"That's how I think of them. Like…I'm reading stories in my head. But also listening to them. Kind of weird, I know, but there's no better way to explain it. Most of my readings about the future have eventually revealed a truth, but some are *so vague*. Nice to know the resolution might be waiting in another century."

"Without your vague premotions about the *secret within the secret*, my ghostly friends would have been stuck in my house forever."

"I'm glad I could help. I hate the thought of anyone being trapped in limbo for eternity. I've been in *emotional* limbo myself, and that's bad enough." She gestured toward the sky. "If they're not trapped anymore, does that mean they can go on to…wherever?"

"Pretty much. A comprehensive explanation will have to wait until we have more time, but they'll be moving on soon." Tipsy pointed into the graveyard. "Henry is in there now, working out one last issue before sashaying into eternal peace with the love of his life."

"Eternal peace. Must be nice."

"If anyone is ready for eternal peace, it's Henry Mott. Remember how we talked about people who are naturally turbulent? He's been a roiling whitewater since he splashed into this world in 1894. But now, he's so at peace, he's even giving up writing his magnum opus."

"Huh?"

"He's a writer, and he's always been obsessed with completing a novel. He even wanted to complete it after his death. He used to believe he had to finish it to find peace. Like, the novel *itself* would be his peace. Now he's found peace inside himself."

"I'm not *that* obsessed, but I understand the feeling of wanting to finish a story. I'm a novelist myself."

"Damn, sister. In all your spare time? Lawyer, mom, novelist?"

She laughed. "Yes. I can finally call myself that, because I finished my first novel. I'm finalizing the edits before seeing if I can get any bites from literary agents and publishers."

"A fellow creative *and* a psychic." This woman was more interesting by the minute. She seemed to be a storyteller in more ways than one, and Tipsy couldn't wait to hear *her* story. "You might be my new bestie."

LeeLee laughed. "I'm down. So when are we getting that drink?"

Before Tipsy went to bed that night, she got a text from Big Ayers. He'd been relatively quiet since their weird heart-to-heart on May Penny's driveway. Not totally ignoring her, or actively rude or abrasive. Just curt and to the point. Normally that was how she liked him, but given everything that had been going on lately, his aloofness raised her Spidey senses. She stared at his name on her phone. Would his message be good, bad, or confoundingly in between?

I almost wish he'd blow up at me so I knew where I stand, Granna.

The only way you'll know if it's a blow up, or a cry for help, or a joke about Little Ayers's dude-isms is to get swiping.

Tipsy nodded and did as Granna suggested.

AYERS: I'M MOVING BACK INTO MY HOUSE.

Tipsy exhaled her relief. THAT SOUNDS POSITIVE.

AYERS: THAT REMAINS TO BE SEEN, BUT KATE AND I ARE BOTH WILLING TO TRY. YOU CAN BRING THE KIDS TO MY HOUSE TOMORROW, NOT MOM AND DAD'S. I STILL HAVE THE TEAM BUILDING DINNER. I WON'T BE HOME TILL ABOUT TEN, BUT KATE WILL BE THERE.

Tipsy had promised to drop the kids off after Little A's lacrosse game so Ayers could attend that work dinner. Instead of May Penny getting the kids ready for bed, it would be Kate. The thought was momentarily unpleasant, but Tipsy immediately rationalized with herself. Such things came along with Ayers sticking it out with Kate.

Tipsy started typing. WILL DO. HAVE YOU TALKED TO THE KIDS ABOUT THIS YET? She resisted reminding him that this subject required a conversation with each child, not a group text.

AYERS: I'M CALLING THEM NOW. A FIRST, THEN THE GIRLS.

TIPSY: SOUNDS GOOD. I HOPE IT WORKS OUT.

AYERS: THX. His typing bubble lit up again. THX FOR YOUR INPUT THROUGH ALL THIS. Typing bubble again. AND YOUR SUPPORT.

She pictured him grimly typing out his gratitude as his pride rebelled against acknowledging that he'd ever needed her input or her support.

Not a bad sign, Granna. He's really trying to make changes.

The floor of rock bottom is even harder the second time around. If he can't change now, he's hopeless.

I never thought I'd say this about Ayers, said Tipsy, *but I do have hope.*

You've always been positive, sugar. A bit naïve at times, but positive.

I get it from you! The positivity, not the naivete. You were always wise.

Haha! Believe me, I had my own moments, said Granna. *But I held onto my faith in myself, and my fellow human beings, living and dead. If I passed that on to you, I did my job.*

You did all the jobs in my life. Thank you.

Tipsy let Scott know about the latest developments when he called to say goodnight, and they agreed it was a step in the right direction. Next came a discussion of logistics. Scott's informal move-in day (the day after the wedding), the estate sale for Miss Callie's old furniture (five days after the wedding), the closing dates on the sale of his I'On house and the purchase of Miss Callie's house (two weeks after the wedding), the anticipated date to move Scott's furniture out of storage and into Miss Callie's (one month after the wedding).

"If we have to sleep on blow up mattresses as the auctioneers are getting stuff out of here, so be it," said Scott. "It's going to be pretty chaotic, but we'll survive."

"Please don't worry. Henry and Jane will be moving on soon. In the meantime, Henry is perfectly sane again. Nothing is going to combust. No scary things going bump in the middle of the night."

"Baby, I'm not worried. Not like you seem to think I am. You told me the ghost stuff is sorted out, and I believe you. Even if it wasn't, we'd deal with it."

"Yes, but—"

"The rest of it is just…life. We know it's going to be a few stressful weeks. We've got a shit-ton of stuff going on, but Team Scipsy will triumph."

"I just worry about you."

"I worry about you, too. But I also know how strong you are, and I trust you."

"I feel the same way about you."

Do you now? asked Granna, and Tipsy felt a surge of guilty annoyance.

You know I do, but I've been trying to, like, ease his burden.

By making it all your burden. You should talk to him about how you've been feeling. How stressed you've been.

Not now. We can discuss it after the wedding.

Granna's sniffing laughter. *Now who doesn't want to discuss uncomfortable topics? If the prudish Motts can talk about their fertility problems, you can talk to your emotionally available fiancé about your savior complex.*

Good lord, Granna! That was all Tipsy could say. As usual, Granna was infernally correct. *Fine. I will! Let me find the right moment—*

"—kids bedroom furniture?" Scott's return to logistics cut off Tipsy and Granna's telepathic bickering.

"Umm. Yes. I told Jimmy we want to keep the stuff in my kids' rooms, and the front porch furniture. They're working it all into the closing costs."

"Great. We have my bedroom set, and my kids' stuff. The rest of my furniture. It will take a while to fill up that big place, but it will be a fun process."

"To get stuff we like."

"Our stuff."

"I love how that sounds," said Tipsy.

"I love you, Tiffany Lynn Denning."

"Ooooh, my country name."

"That's your real name."

"I know. I'm finally going to make the switch. I'll hyphenate my signature on my paintings with Collins, but I'm going to be Denning in my real life fairytale." They'd already discussed that Tipsy would not be taking Scott's last name. There seemed no point, and she'd had enough trouble shedding Collins.

"You know that's fine with me."

They chatted for a while longer and then said their goodnights. As Tipsy plugged in her phone and slid under the covers, she spoke up before Granna had a chance to prod her again. *When the time is right, I will speak to him about…whatever the hell is wrong with me.*

There's nothing wrong with you, sugar, said Granna. *If I came off that way, I surely didn't mean to. Remember that Scott's not the only one worrying about you. For years, I've watched you take everything on yourself. For your family, your friends, and even a bunch of dead people. You've always done what needed doing, and you rarely complain. If you have someone willing, then I'll push you to share your burden.*

I'm trying.

Think about how you'd feel about your own kids, and try a little harder.

The next day, Tipsy ran wedding errands (bakery, florist, seamstress), worked on a commission painting (two young black men selling palmetto roses on Market Street), and did some initial sketches for a new piece (Henry and Proctor on the graveyard bench). She checked the children's Dad-weekend bags for the necessities, loaded up the car, picked up the girls from volleyball practice and headed to Little A's lacrosse game. After the game, it was time to transport the kids to Ayers and Kate's house. As she pulled out of the school parking lot, she considered tactful ways to bring up the change in their father's circumstances, but Mary Pratt beat her to it.

"*Hi ho…hi ho…it's back to Dad's we go!*" She switched to her normal, somewhat shrill voice. "At least for this weekend!" She waved her hands like a conductor and started singing again. "*Hi-ho-hi-ho-hi-ho…hi ho—*"

"Bruh," said Little Ayers. "Stop tweaking."

"Not funny, M.P.," said O-Liv. "Seriously."

"Plus your singing is lowkey trash."

"Ayers Lee, that is *mean,*" said Tipsy. "It's not like you're…uh… Justin Bieber over there."

"Mom is right, Ayers. Your singing is as bad as mine," said Mary Pratt. "Come on, y'all. We gotta get hyped for Dad's house, and the hi-ho song is a *bop*. It slaps. It's lowkey—"

"M.P.," said Tipsy, "maybe we should talk about this instead of joking about it."

M.P. shrugged. "Sorry, y'all. Sometimes when things are messed up, I gotta joke about it."

"So you think it's messed up?" asked Tipsy.

"Yeah. I mean, sort of. I don't know." M.P. sunk into her seat. "We haven't been there in like a month. We haven't seen Tristan or Chloe or Kate."

"Now we walk in there like, *hey y'all, what's up?*" said Little Ayers. "It's so sus."

"You've talked to Tristan and Chloe, right?"

"Me and M.P. texted with Chloe on our group chat," said O-Liv.

"And I texted with T.," said Little Ayers. "None of us are babies. They knew something is up."

"How are they feeling about it?"

"They're weirded out because Kate told them Dad is a total jerk and this is all his fault, but he went back there a couple days ago and now she's acting like nothing happened."

"Dad's doing the same thing," said M.P. "I'm glad we're going back to the house with our own rooms in our neighborhood, but this is..." She shrugged.

"It's crazy town, not gonna lie," said O-Liv.

"Everyone handles conflict differently. Y'all are old enough to know that Dad has his own way of doing things—"

"That makes no sense half the time," said O-Liv. "But yeah, I get it, Mama."

"The best thing y'all can do is focus on the positives. You're going back to the house. Getting a break from Gigi. No big changes on the horizon with your dad and Kate."

"The horizon changes depending on the weather," said Little Ayers.

She looked at her sweet almost teenaged boy, who always impressed her with his wise observations.

"The horizon is always there, honey. The weather only changes how far we can see."

"Dad's weather is always stuck in hurricane season." Ayers looked her in the eye. "But you know how you're always telling us to, like, learn lessons all the time? Not school lessons. The other kind."

"Life lessons."

"Yeah, right. Dad has taught me some lessons. Like how *not* to be."

"Same," said M.P., who was more like her father than the other two kids, but at least she was already recognizing patterns she didn't want to repeat.

O-Liv, the tenderhearted one, said, "He's not all bad."

"Of course not! He loves y'all, that's for sure," said Tipsy. "And he's trying to make changes. He really wants to work things out with Kate.

So for now, all we can do is appreciate the peace and focus on the good things in each of your lives."

They looked out the window for a few silent moments.

"I'm excited to see Chloe," said O-Liv. "She's been waiting for us to watch the next season of *Glee*."

"That's nice of her," said Tipsy, who had acquired many cringy *Glee* cast versions of songs since her girls and Chloe starting binge-watching that old show.

"Hopefully Kate will make pancakes tomorrow," said M.P.

Kate's famous pancakes are always a winner, Granna.

Granna's sniffing laughter. *Even if her personality is not.*

Tipsy bit her lip to keep from laughing herself, then looked at Ayers. "You looking forward to pancakes, A.?"

"Sure, why not? I'm looking forward to beating Charleston Day at lacrosse Saturday morning even more. Then going to the skatepark with Tristan. Dad said he'll take us to see the new Marvel movie, too."

"Sounds like a great weekend," said Tipsy.

They pulled up to the house a few minutes later. The kids piled out, each with his or her Dad-weekend bag. The girls blew kisses and ran up the stairs, chattering away, but Little Ayers lingered to get his lacrosse bag and his stick.

"You got all that, Ayers?"

"Course I can, bruh—I mean, Mom."

"It's okay if you need help sometimes."

"This is one thing I don't need help with."

"Ayers, listen to me." He was almost thirteen, and he was wearing lacrosse cleats. Tipsy had only to tip her chin to meet his gaze. "Whatever comes up, I have faith that you can handle it, and I'm here to help you. So is your dad, in his…sometimes…odd…way."

"It's chill, Mom. I get frustrated with dad and school and like, life in general, but then I get reminded of stuff by you, and I feel better."

"Like what kind of stuff?"

"All that *life is pretty good* stuff."

She smiled. "Alright, dude. I'll see you at your game on Saturday."

"Sure, bruh," he said, and he darted away with his bag and his lax stuff bouncing on his back.

She tried to swat at his read end, but he was too fast, so she called after him. "I'm not your bruh! I'm your Ma!"

He laughed as he ran up the porch stairs. The front door opened. Little Ayers said hello to Kate, and then darted inside. Kate walked onto the porch with a watering can in one hand and a glass of white wine in the other. "Hey, Tipsy!" she called out. "How's it going?" She grinned and doused her overflowing flower boxes. From her bouncy blonde ponytail to her Lily Pulitzer sundress, she was the picture of domestic bliss.

"Hey, Kate," said Tipsy. According to Mimi's intel, Kate thought Big Ayers, Tipsy, and Scott had been conspiring against her. Little did she know, Tipsy had done everything in her power to keep them together.

Oh, well. Tipsy let her think what she wanted to think. "Everything's great," said Tipsy. "Thanks for watching the kids while Ayers is out."

"No problem!" chirped Kate.

Before she said anything else, Tipsy got in her truck and left. Her kids were settled in for the night, and for the foreseeable future, in their own beds. They had gleaned some positive perspectives, and maybe a life lesson or two. Tipsy had gotten pretty good at recognizing life lessons over the past few years.

Tipsy's party planning skills did not measure up to those of Shelby and Lindsey. Shelby was a social animal of the most evolved kingdom, genus, and species. Lindsey, an interior designer, made a living creating welcoming environments. As the wedding countdown kept on countin' down, Tipsy asked them to meet her at the GQB to review her checklist. Lindsey would know where she should set up the catering tables while Shelby reviewed her wedding playlist to ensure it was romantic but not cheesy.

To Tipsy's surprise, Lindsey swept into the GQB *without* little Paul Junior in tow. "*What's up*, girlies?" she said, with a smile reminiscent of the perky Lindsey of old. Shelby elbowed Tipsy while Lindsey checked her phone, swiped pink sparkles on her lips, and stashed her purse behind the sales desk.

"She's toddler-free," Shelby whispered. "Where's Lil' P.D.?"

"Don't bring it up," Tipsy whispered back. Little Paul was most likely with Lindsey's mom, and the mention of his absence would only remind Lindsey of his father's dereliction of duty.

"List! List!" said Lindsey. "Give me the list!"

"Me first," said Shelby.

"Tipsy asked *me* to figure out the best place for the catering table." Lindsey grabbed Tipsy's list and scowled down at it. "The forecast is literally perfect for the next week." She swiped Tipsy's pen and struck through *TENT*.

"There's no way they'll give her a refund," said Shelby. "It's too late. Besides, the tent will cozy things up."

"Can you get your money back on the tent?" asked Lindsey.

"As long as I cancel within forty-eight hours—"

"Call now! Right now!" Shelby was suddenly Team Tentless.

Tipsy grabbed her phone and called the tent rental company while Shelby and Lindsey happily squabbled over the perfect place for the ceremony (beside Jane's magnolia tree) and where Tipsy should make her grand entrance (Little Ayers would escort her down the porch stairs while Scott waited with Tristan and the three girls in purple junior bridesmaid's dresses). Shelby's attorney father would conduct the service, and Shelby promised she'd keep him on topic. "Big Billy Patterson loves to be the center of attention, but I'll remind him he's not giving a closing argument."

"What about your dress?" asked Lindsey.

"I finally got it back from the seamstress," said Tipsy. She'd borrowed an off-white beaded gown from Pamella. "I'm tall, but Pammy is *tall.* I had to get it hemmed a couple inches. Don't want to trip down the front stairs of my new house at my own wedding."

"Shoes?" Lindsey pointed at her own feet, encased in ridiculously tall springtime wedges.

"I'm wearing flat sandals."

"Tipsy Collins! Flats, at your wedding? *Come on.* It's your big day. Your footwear should be fabulous."

"She's going to be standing in uneven grass all day, Linds," said Shelby, the flip-flop aficionado, as the gallery phone rang behind them. "What do you want from her? Glass slippers?"

"Maybe," said Lindsey, as Shelby went to the desk to answer the phone. "Do you think glass shoes could ever be comfortable?"

"If they're magic, sure," said Tipsy.

"Maybe that's the happy ending all women should aspire to. Find super comfy shoes that still look amazing." Lindsey doodled a heart on Tipsy's list. "You found the proverbial glass slippers with Scott."

Tipsy laughed. "He's aesthetically pleasing, but more than that, no shoe has ever fit me better. I could run a marathon in that relationship, hike a mountain, walk a red carpet, or curl up beside the fire and read. He's everything from hiking boot to bunny slipper."

"Must be nice. I used to think that about P.D., too."

"I wasn't sure you'd want to talk about him, but how's it going? You've been kind of quiet about it all."

"We had the blow up of all blow ups about a week after our argument at Islander 71. I dropped the D word."

"Oh, shit. How'd he react?"

"He cried." Lindsey's own eyes watered. "He said nothing is more important to him than me and the kids. Emma and Paul, and this new baby. I believe him. I know he means well. Being a dad has been a huge adjustment for him. He's never dealt with babies. Emma was eight when we met. He imagined our children would emerge from the womb as third graders."

"A lot of men are like that. Ayers wanted to take Little A deep sea fishing when he was about fifteen months old. Just so he could pose that baby with a fish. He wanted me to go along to do the actual caretaking."

"Did you go?"

"Hell, no. I get seasick, and I was not going to force my squirmy toddler into a life jacket for ten hours."

"P.D. definitely misses his freedom."

"Moms aren't *allowed* to miss our freedom. People say, *cherish every moment.* I mean, I did cherish most of them when the kids were little. But I would have cherished a solo trip to the grocery store or a happy hour buzz, too."

"So true. Plus P.D. doesn't know *how* to help, which frustrates me. I get annoyed, and that makes him try even less. It's a mommy-daddy vicious cycle. But I'm trying to let him experiment more. Not hover so much.

"That's all positive."

"It is. We're going to therapy. We've been to three sessions. I feel more hopeful than I have in months."

"You seemed more like yourself when you got here, but now that we're talking about it, you still seem pretty down."

"I'm not down. Not *really*. Things are getting better. He's working from home today, and he offered to keep Paul for a few hours while I met up with y'all and ran errands. But still…" She looked up from her doodling. "When P.D. and I got married, I thought I'd found happily-ever-after."

"That's how you described it at your birthday happy hour at Muddy's."

"I know. I guess I never imagined it would be so complicated. That I'd still feel so hurt and frustrated, even with this man I adore."

Tipsy thought of Jane and Henry. How much they loved each other, and how blissfully happy they were on the day Henry proposed to Jane. They surely thought their fairytale would hold.

"The story doesn't end with the marriage," said Tipsy. "That's only the beginning. Even if Scott and I don't have the kind of problems you're facing right now, stuff will come up. We have five kids who are all heading into their teenage years. We're dealing with Kate and Ayers. It's going to cause strain between us at some point." Her own words reminded her of Granna's insistence that she address her need to shelter Scott from the recent supernatural drama. As those problems faded into the rearview, she saw her own issues more clearly. She could call it what it was—lowkey obsessive. She really did need to discuss it with him, so he could help her recognize it the next time they faced a challenge, supernatural or otherwise. "I've always believed that we're a team, and we can get through anything, but that doesn't mean I'm expecting the rest of my life to be a perfect fairytale."

"I remember I was giving you advice a couple years ago. Now you're the wise one."

"We've all gained wisdom over the past few years."

"We've had some good cries, and a ton of even better laughs." Lindsey reached out and squeezed Tipsy's hand. "Now it feels like we're all sort of...*settled.* I mean that in a good way. I'm happy where I am in my life, it's just...reality hasn't *quite* measured up to my daydreams. I'm adjusting to that."

"A couple years ago, I told this young woman I met—Sophie Yates, Jillian Yates's daughter—that I thought happily-ever-after was a state of overall contentment interspersed with highs and lows. The *contentment* part is the *real* goal. That's the best kind of love. Y'all get through this, and you'll be more in love than ever."

"We both want that, and I do love P.D.'s goofy ass."

"We're both lucky that we've found someone we want to ride out the hard times with. So is Shelby."

"So is Shelby what?" Shelby asked, as she hung up the phone. "What smack were y'all talking about me?"

"No smack," said Lindsey. "Just talking about how lucky we all are."

Shelby draped one arm over Tipsy, and one over Lindsey. She pulled them toward her until their heads about clonked together. "That we are, ladies. That. We. *Are.*"

Chapter 17

The week of the wedding, Scott took off work on Thursday and Friday so he and Tipsy could prepare their house. She dropped off the kids at school, and she planned to come right home and do some decluttering, but Scott sent her a text urging her to go to the gym.

SCOTT: YOU'LL FEEL BETTER AFTER A WORKOUT, AND I'M THE DECLUTTERING MASTER.

TIPSY: OKAY, YOU CONVINCED ME! I'LL HIT SOME WEIGHTS AND THEN I'LL BE HOME.

SCOTT: NO RUSH. I'M HEADING OVER THERE NOW TO GET STARTED.

TIPSY: KK. SEE YOU SOON.

The first thing Tipsy noticed when she walked into the house: a large painting on the floor in the foyer. The ornate old-fashioned frame leaned against the staircase, so she tipped it back for a look at its artsy side. It was an oil painting of a shrimp boat; a relic left behind by Miss Callie. Tipsy estimated that it had been hanging on the dining room wall for decades. She had always disliked it—dark and gloomy, with a wonky perspective—but it was still an original work from the 1920s, and probably worth a decent amount of money. She'd had no replacement piece, so she'd left it up when she attempted to personalize the house a few years ago. Now it huddled in the foyer like an old man who had tumbled down the staircase.

"Baby?" she called out. "What's up with this painting in the—"

"Heeeey!" Scott appeared behind her, from the direction of the dining room. He spun her around, so she faced the parlor. "You're home already."

"I said I'd be quick." She kissed him, then pointed down at the painting. "What are you doing with the S.S. Shrimp Breath? Going crazy with the magic eraser on the dining room walls?"

"I love me some magic erasers, but not this time. Lucky I'm fast with the hammer, or I'd be sending you out of the house again. As it is, you're just in time."

"What do you mean?"

He stepped behind her, then reached up and covered her eyes with his hand. She laughed. "Scott! What are you—"

"Hush up and walk." He maneuvered her in a circle, then gently pushed her forward, in the direction of the dining room.

"I can't see!"

"You don't need to see. I can see."

"Okay, okay." She allowed him to guide her. She basically knew where she was going, but it was still unnerving. She shuffled her feet and held out her hands. He kept one hand on her eyes, and the other firmly on her waist.

"I got you," he said.

They only walked about ten feet, but in those few seconds, Tipsy relaxed. *He really does have me,* she thought. *He's always had me.*

"Voila!" Scott removed his hand. For a second, Tipsy thought she had stepped into one of her own memories, because she was staring at *The Hand Study*. She looked around, but she was in her dining room, not the GQB.

"Wait, what?" She turned to Scott. "That's my painting."

He laughed. "Yeah, it is. In your house. On your dining room wall."

"But I took it to the GQB to sell it."

"And it sold."

"I don't get it. Who—" Tipsy suddenly understood. "Pamella."

"Yup. And Jillian Yates. It's a joint wedding gift, from both of them."

"Oh, jeez. This is too much. Shelby had it listed for…thousands. I can't remember exactly—"

"You know anything in the thousands is small potatoes for the combined fortunes of Pammy and Jillian. Pammy said she'd never seen you look at one of your own paintings with so much…longing. She knows how much Jane and Henry mean to you, and that they're leaving. She wanted you to have it."

Tipsy wiped her eyes and approached the painting. "I do love it. I *adore* it."

"Now we're keeping it." He rested his hands on her shoulders and whispered in her ear. "And in the future, if you adore one of your own damn paintings, we're keeping that, too."

"But I love all my paintings. They're all special to me, but they're also the source of my income. If I don't sell them, I don't make money."

"I understand. You're a fine art painter. Other artists keep something of their originals. Writers have books. Musicians can sing their songs over and over. Actors have their performances recorded. You create something, give it away, and then it's gone. But it doesn't always have to be that way. Not anymore."

She turned and wrapped her arms around his neck. "We have a big family, and a big house, and a lot of expenses. I want to pull my weight."

He squeezed her. "You do. Your income these days is no chump change. But you're not doing this all alone, and things aren't so tight for us that we can't keep a few of your paintings. We have this big ass house to decorate, remember?"

She looked up at Jane and Henry's peaceful faces, and then slid her own cheek into the crook between Scott's neck and his shoulder. "You're right. Thank you."

No time like the present, Granna.

She felt Granna's smiling encouragement, so she said, "I've been stressed out lately." As soon as the words were out of her mouth, her tears came in a flood.

"Hey, hey. It's okay."

"Like really stressed out—" She choked back a sob.

He pulled away from her and looked into her face. "Talk to me, Tipsy."

So she did.

Twenty minutes later, she'd cried herself dry and they were sitting on the staircase beside the S.S. Shrimp Breath. "I'm sorry I kept all this from you," she said. "I was just so worried."

"You didn't think I was going to like, bail, did you?"

"No. Not when I was being rational and going about our daily lives. Sometimes I feel like I don't deserve all this, when so many people have such hard lives."

"You've had your own hard times, baby."

"Not compared to other people."

"There's always someone who has it worse, and someone who has it better."

"Granna says that kind of thing all the time, but there's still this deep down part of me that's scared of…losing us. I don't even know what that would have looked like. I know we're committed to one another and our kids and we bought a damn house together and we have joint bank accounts and we're getting life insurance and—"

"But you were still scared."

"I don't want you to think I don't trust you. I really, truly do." She looked at him. "Do you believe me?"

"Yes. I really, truly do."

She sighed her relief. "Thank you. I've never had anyone I could count on like I count on you. And I've definitely never had anyone I could lean on about my supernatural stuff. I…I have this natural urge to protect people, and I *hate* seeing you stressed out. This time, with all the drama with Henry and Jane, that protectiveness went lowkey crazy."

"I have the same kinds of feelings about you. The idea that you've been dealing with all of this alone makes me feel awful."

"I'm sorry. I hate that you feel awful—"

He smiled. "You realize this is a circle. The opposite of a vicious one."

"That's good, right?"

"If we can channel it the right way. We've had this *argument* before. Where we *fight* about who is more worried about the other person. You want to do it again?"

"Sure."

"This time, you win."

"I won't try to out worry you again. Not about something important like this. As soon as I start feeling this way, I promise I'll tell you."

"Okay. If I sense you're in overprotective mode, I'll ask you about it."

"Deal," she said. "I love you."

"I love you, too. So…is this our first big conflict? Since you went crazy and broke up with me two years ago, I mean."

She snuggled closer to him. "It might be. I can't remember anything else."

"Not bad, if our one relationship issue in two years is you being obsessively concerned with my emotional health."

"And you being frustrated that I'm not letting you be as emotionally supportive as you want to be."

"Team Scipsy, for the win!"

"Rahrah-freakin' rah!"

"I think we got this whole marriage thing." He held out one hand, and she slapped him five.

"I think we do."

Tipsy and Scott got married in the backyard of Miss Callie's house—soon to be officially their house—on a beautiful late May afternoon. A simple ceremony, attended by the people dearest to them. Their kids. Scott's mother, stepfather, stepbrothers, and their wives and kids. Shelby and Lindsey and their families. Shelby's parents, Liz and Billy Patterson, owners of the GQB and Tipsy's surrogate parents since college, with Billy as the ceremonial MC. Under Shelby's direction, he kept mostly on topic. He told a single rambling story from a recent criminal trial, about a man who got a DUI on the way home from his own wedding.

Pamella and her husband Doug were in attendance, as were Jillian and Sophie Yates, the combined outfits of whom probably cost more than the entire wedding celebration. Mimi and Jimmy Lathrop held court with their boisterous kids. A few friends from childhood and college, some of Tipsy's former neighbors, a handful of Scott's colleagues. The invisible guests were equally important to Tipsy. In her own mind, her Granna watched over Tipsy, her new husband, and their family. She whispered *amens* and *hallelujahs*, like Tipsy remembered from their little mountain church in Martinville. On the porch, Jane and Henry were dignified, unseen ushers. Henry wrapped one arm around Jane, who cried sparkly tears and blew her nose into the handkerchief that he had in his pocket when he died.

Tipsy sniffled through their vows, and Scott teared up during their first dance, to *Stand by Me.* He spoke eloquently when he thanked their guests for joining them. Unlike her previous husband, he did not forget to mention his new wife in his speech. His tender salute to his bride reduced her to real tears. After that, it was a magical evening, complete with a Southern fried supper served on long picnic tables. The kids ran around barefoot and the adults carried on, laughing and shouting over one another and telling raucous stories. Tipsy didn't drink a sip of alcohol, but felt drunk on happiness.

She had a moment to speak with the Motts when she excused herself to use the bathroom while her guests chowed down on fried chicken and gourmet mac-n-cheese. They appeared in the foyer as she entered the house and shut the door behind her. Her pale, steady companions of the past four years.

"You're the *most beautiful* bride," said Jane.

"In the history of happy weddings," added Henry, "only my Janie outshone you."

"Oh, I know. I've seen y'all's wedding portrait." Tipsy's eyes watered. "Thank you so much for staying around. It means the world to me to have y'all here."

"We wouldn't miss it for all eternity," said Jane.

Henry smiled down at his wife. "She means that quite literally."

"And thank you for being my friends," said Tipsy. "I couldn't have managed the past four years without you."

"Henry was here for most of that time, not me," said Jane.

"That's true," said Tipsy. "Henry, you have been the best friend anyone could ask for. Your wisdom, your understanding—"

"My moody arrogance—"

"I'm serious!"

"You've taught me just as much, Tipsy."

She turned to Jane. "Even when you weren't here, you were with me, Janie. Through my memories of you, and Henry's memories. I would never have wished this crazy relapse on you, but I'm so glad I got to see you again."

"You've been *my* great friend, *and* you brought us back together. To say thank you, we came up with a little wedding gift for you." Jane turned to her husband. "Henry, could you—"

Henry waved his hand, and a smallish something levitated from the stairs behind them. It floated over Henry's shoulder and hung suspended in the air before Tipsy. She smiled. "The oyster shell dish!"

She held out her hand, and the shell dropped gently onto her palm.

"I couldn't run out to Berlin's for a real wedding gift," said Jane. "But this little piece is special to us."

"I hope you don't mind," said Henry, "but I took one of your skinny paintbrushes and autographed it. If you turn it over…"

Tipsy flipped the shell over, gold leaf side up. A little painted heart, and in Henry's spidery writing, the letters *H&J.*

"With love, from us," said Jane.

"You can keep in on your desk, as Jane did. Put your pretty rings in it when you're doing your lady things."

"Think of us, as I always thought of the night Henry proposed when I looked at it."

Tipsy gripped the shell. "I'll cherish it, y'all. No wedding gift could be more special."

"Now, get back to your guests!" said Jane. "Someone will see you talking into the thin air and think you've lost your senses."

"I'll take our gift upstairs to your room," said Henry. A gentle tug on the shell, and Tipsy released it. It floated toward Henry and hovered beside his ear.

"Will y'all, that is to say—"

"We won't leave today," said Jane. "This isn't *quite goodbye*."

Tipsy nodded, blew them a kiss, and returned to her party. She was glad it wasn't *quite goodbye*, because she didn't think her heart could take that much emotion in one day.

The next morning, Tipsy woke before anyone else in her house. She looked at her husband, sleeping peacefully on his back. They'd rolled toward each other in the night, and she woke in the crook of his arm.

She kissed him, and sat up. Jane and Henry's oyster shell sat beside her phone on the nightstand. She ran a finger over the purple splotch on its pearly surface.

"Where you going?" Scott asked, and opened one eye. "We've only been asleep for a few hours."

"I'm wide awake," she said. "Going to check on the state of the kitchen."

"The caterers cleaned it up."

"Then the state of the backyard…"

"You're going to say goodbye to Jane and Henry, aren't you?"

"They stuck around for me. It's not fair for them to linger."

"Do you want me to come with you? I know it will be hard."

"I think I need to say goodbye on my own."

"I'll be right here if you need to come back up and cry."

She got up and put on her COUGAR MOM t-shirt, her taco pants, and fuzzy socks. She ran a brush through her hair and wiped away the smudges of yesterday's mascara with a towelette. A quick brush of her teeth and she descended the stairs. She went to the front porch, where she'd spent so much time with Mr. and Mrs. Mott.

"Y'all?" she said softly, as she sat. "Hey, y'all?"

They materialized on their loveseat. Henry was grinding his teeth, and tears already glittered on Jane's cheeks.

"Good lord." Tipsy's lip trembled and her own eyes filled. "This is going to be freakin' hard."

"Hell, yes, it is," said Henry. "Now that it's time, we don't know what to say."

"We said it all yesterday," said Tipsy. "I just want y'all to go and be at peace."

"Like Proctor," said Henry. "He moved on, after we spoke. Finally, after all these years."

"Oh, wow," said Tipsy, and her tears overflowed their banks. "Can you…what happened…"

Henry waved his hand, and Jane took over for him. "They visited together several times, and spoke of many things. At first, they talked of forgiveness and redemption. All the good and terrible things that happened between the three of us. But then, it was only Henry and Proctor, discussing the mysteries of existence, as they did when Henry was young, and Proctor, not so old himself."

"He said speaking with me allowed him to forgive himself," said Henry. "Took away his fear. He was ready to face whatever waits for him."

"Do you think something *bad* is waiting for him?" asked Tipsy. "Like…Thomas Bonneau?" Despite everything, she hoped not.

"No. I watched him go. A serene exit, like Johnny and Ivy. I believe he's made peace with his God, and he's just fine."

"How do y'all feel about him?"

"It's a relief to both of us that he's moved on," said Jane. "The final piece in our story."

"Stories don't ever really end. That's a recurring theme for me lately," said Tipsy. "I hope y'all's doesn't."

Jane smiled. "Then let's think of it as the beginning of our *next* story."

"A sequel, shall we say," said Henry. "To THE GREAT STORY."

Tipsy thought of LeeLee Moretz. "You know, I met a writer recently. Maybe she can help me tell THE GREAT STORY. In words, not just paintings."

“There are many stories in the world, and many storytellers,” said Henry. “You’ll find a means.”

“Now…y’all *have* to go,” said Tipsy. “Please. Before I lose my nerve and beg you to stay.”

“Or we lose it, and decide to stay with you,” said Jane.

“This is the best path. We all know that.”

“We do,” said Henry. He stood. “Come, sweetheart.”

Jane also got to her feet. “We love you so much, Tipsy.”

“I love y’all.” Tipsy held back a sob. “I’m so happy for you both.”

“And we’re happy for you,” said Jane. “Remember, we’ll always be with you. We’re no more gone than your grandmother, or anyone else you’ve helped to *move on*. Just…somewhere else.”

Tipsy nodded.

“We can walk away from this house together now,” said Henry.

“Yes. Let’s,” said Jane. “Like we’re going for a stroll around the block. Like we used to do, when we were newlyweds.”

They walked down the stairs and across the yard. They paused at the gate, turned, and waved. Jane blew a kiss in Tipsy’s direction, and Tipsy’s mental camera clicked. She would paint her friends as she last saw them. Smiling and holding hands at the edge of the property that had once been theirs, and had trapped them all these long years. Framed by a white picket fence. Shaded by Jane’s magnolia tree. The late spring sun shining blindingly into their eyes. Hers light blue, his dark.

It was one painting Tipsy knew she would keep.

She waved back, and blew her own kiss, and forced herself to smile. Jane and Henry stepped across the threshold of the yard, and disappeared.

About a month later, Tipsy and Scott sat on the porch of their house—the former Miss Callie’s house—on a late June Saturday afternoon. They officially owned the place, although they were still in transition. Most of the old furniture and art from the estate sale had pulled an Elvis and left the building, including the S.S. Shrimp Breath. *The Hand Study* lorded over the empty dining room like a Renaissance masterpiece with its own chamber in the Louvre. They were waiting on the big furniture delivery after the sale of Scott's house in I'On, but they'd been transporting stuff in boxes and suitcases for days.

"I needed this beer," he said, as they sat on the loveseat with cans in hand. "The boxes are giving me anxiety."

"I know, silly," she said. "You're handling it well."

"Only because I have committed to being one hundred percent box free within two days of the furniture delivery."

"My whole body is sore," she said, as she set her beer on the glass-topped table. "I feel all thirty-eight of my years in my lower back."

"I feel all forty-one of mine in my knees." He clinked his beer against hers. "Here's to getting old and creaky together."

Little Ayers opened the porch door. "Mom, what's for dinner?"

"Uh...pizza? Sorry. I know we had Thai food last night. The kitchen is still a wreck."

"I'm not complaining. How about subs tomorrow night? Chick-fil-A the next night?"

Tristan's dark head appeared beside Little Ayers. He was a year older, but with Little A's growth spurt, they were the same height. "Yeah. Let's move every week so we can eat takeout food every night."

Scott laughed. "No dice, boys. I'm not going anywhere until y'all ship me off to the nursing home."

Tipsy swatted Scott. "No talk about nursing homes. We're not *that* old."

"Y'all *are* lowkey ancient," said Little A.

Tipsy laughed. "Y'all go find something to do, or I'm gonna make GiGi's famous meatloaf for dinner."

"Blech! Let's go, Tris," said Little A. "Believe me, you *do not* want to eat my Gigi's meatloaf."

"I've never had meatloaf," said Tristan, as they disappeared inside. "It sounds sus. Is it, like, really a loaf of meat?"

Tipsy heard chattering in the hallway and Mary Pratt, Olivia Grace, and Chloe graced them with their presence. “Can we walk to the Pitt Street Pharmacy and get ice cream?” asked M.P.

Tipsy and Scott looked at each other. “What do you think?” she asked.

“I’m good with it. As long as y’all promise to eat fruit salad with your pizza later. Gotta cling to something healthy during this transition.”

“We will,” said O-Liv. “Y’all want to walk, or ride bikes?”

“Let’s ride. It’s faster. I have money.” Chloe looked at her dad. “Over at Mom’s, I walked the neighbor’s dogs while they were out of town.”

“We’ll give y’all money,” said Tipsy. “No need for Chloe to spend all of hers.”

“It’s okay, Tipsy,” said Chloe. “Sisters always pay each other back eventually.”

Tipsy bit her lip as Scott instructed Chloe on where to find her bike amidst the stuff he’d stashed in the storage shed. Once the girls disappeared down the street, Tipsy wiped her eyes.

“It’s *so sweet*, seeing them all having so much fun. Chloe calling the twins her sisters…” She shrugged and pointed at her eyes again.

“Chloe always wanted a sister,” said Scott. “Given our unusual arrangement with Ayers and Kate, our kids are like real siblings.”

“I’m sure they’ll have their moments as they get older, but it’s nice to see them forming such a foundation. I always wanted to be part of a big family.” She leaned back into Scott’s arm. “I can imagine our elaborate Christmas celebrations when we’re grandparents.”

“What about our grandparent names? It’s a big decision.”

“I feel like Tipsy is already a grandma name. Maybe the grandchildren will butcher it.”

“Like…TeeTee?”

“Good lord, no. That’s what Granna used to say when she excused herself to use the bathroom during church.”

“I love that you think about that stuff, and I love that my kids are getting more comfortable with you all the time. I know Tristan can be a little standoffish.”

"He's a thirteen-year-old boy. We're lucky he talks to any of us, at all."

"You're right. But your kids are so…"

"Off the wall? Bonkers? Loud as hell?"

"I was going to stay exuberant. But if we can use those descriptors kindly, then yes. They bring mine out a little."

"Yours help mine chill out."

"I feel like you and me do the same for each other, depending on who is more worked up about something."

"You're right." They sat in comfortable silence for a while, until Scott broke it.

"What's next on the painting agenda?" he asked, as he set his beer beside hers on the table.

"That's a good question. I have to get organized. I have three commissions, including a lizard to match Richard and David's gator."

"Those guys love reptiles, huh?"

"Apparently. Then there's Henry and Proctor in the graveyard. The landscape of Aunt Talia's property on the Stono. Jane and Henry by the fence. And I'd like to paint Jane with her pony, Snowflake, as I saw them in her memory. I still want to paint Anne Boleyn—"

"You *do* owe it to posterity to capture that one."

"—and I finally have a good idea that will do her justice."

"Tell me, my lady."

"Well, in her day, portraiture was like an Instagram filter, or Facetune. If you were powerful enough to have your portrait done, you wanted something that made you look good. Arguably, better than real life. Look at the flack Holbein caught for his supposedly embellished portrait of Anne of Cleves. For people like Henry VIII, and Elizabeth when she was queen, that's how you showed off your beauty and strength and wealth."

"As the kids would say, go off king. Or queen."

"Right. Everything about those formal paintings screamed power. Anne Boleyn was damn powerful in her day. She fell from grace, and died in such a terrible way, and that's made her this tragic figure. But I bet a painting like that once existed. I could try to recreate it."

"That's a badass idea," said Scott.

"Thanks," she said. "So…to answer your original question, I have to work out a schedule for all the projects I just mentioned. I have a few more fantastical concepts, too." Tipsy's thoughts about Anne Boleyn and formal Renaissance portraiture had leached into those imaginary ideas. She planned to use paint to speak truth to power for Anne, and she had a notion to do the same thing for the fairytale princesses who inspired Lindsey and a zillion other women to keep doggedly pursuing mythical happy endings. Most women eventually figured out that happily-ever-after was complicated. What would those fairytale princesses be like once they learned the same lesson?

They'd be powerful, she thought. *Bad asses in their own right. Go off, queens.*

"More unicorns?" asked Scott.

"Hmm…what? Oh, yes. Probably. Nothing definitive yet, but ideas are percolating."

"You looked like you were off in fantasy land yourself for a second. Staring at stuff only you can see."

She smiled. "Painting ideas, or ghosts?"

"For the moment, the former." He rested a hand on her knee. "How you feeling about the Motts?"

"I miss them. That's the truth."

"They were your friends for a long time."

"They were, and Henry was with me at my lowest points. When I was crying myself to sleep over fights with Ayers or money. Or some terrible decision I made. Like when I broke up with you. I cannot believe I was ever that mentally unstable." She shivered. "I almost ruined my own life."

"You weren't mentally unstable. You were still recovering from your old life. We both were. But we walked through that fire together, and came out stronger."

"It didn't even take a century of being trapped in a house together to figure it out." She spun her wedding ring around her finger. "I always wanted Henry to move on, but maybe deep down I doubted he ever would, and that brought me comfort. I still had him, and through him, a link to Jane. I wish I could talk to them again. It's not like we can keep up on Instagram, with me viewing their latest pics from the afterlife."

Very true, said a familiar voice in Tipsy's head. *You can't send me texters, or call me on FacePhone.*

Tipsy sat up straight. "Holy shit. Henry?"

Scott looked around. "Huh?"

"Henry, is that you?"

I think it is. Well, I'll be damned.

"You're in my head? Like Granna?"

"What is going on?" asked Scott.

Tipsy held up one hand. This time, she spoke in her mind. *Am I really hearing you? Say something…Henry-like.*

You'll have to give me a moment to think of something appropriately melancholy yet arrogant.

It is you! Henry! Holy hell. I'm so happy to hear your voice!

I'm happy to hear yours too, my friend. Jane and I were thinking of you, and missing you. Poof! Here I am, right in your ol' noggin.

This is great! I should have thought of it, given my chats with Granna, but you and I aren't related.

Granna herself spoke up in Tipsy's mind. *We still don't know how all this works, Tipsy. You and Henry aren't kin, but y'all are both clairvoyants, and you're as close as brother and sister.*

Your grandmother is right, said Henry. *By the way, nice to meet you, Miss Stella. You did a lovely job raising your granddaughter.*

Thank you, Mr. Mott—

Call me Henry, please.

Henry, then, said Granna. *Thank you for being such a true friend to her—*

My pleasure, ma'am, always.

Whoa, y'all, said Tipsy. *It's going to be hard to follow two voices in my head. Can y'all…not talk at the same time?*

I'll retire and let y'all catch up. Love you, sugar.

Love you, too, Granna. She turned her conscience back to Henry. *I'm so glad to hear from you. Is everything…peaceful?*

Ah, such peace you cannot imagine.

And you and Jane are together?

Yes. With all our loved ones. I cannot thank you enough for helping us to get here, Tipsy. Now that I know we can speak, I'll be here for you whenever you need me. Jane, too, through me.

Thank you, Henry. I may need your help someday, if I'm going to become Helen's righthand ghost-buster. Like, what if we really go to London to see Queen Anne?

I'll come with you, naturally. Now, you best explain to Dr. Brandt what's happening. The poor man looks terribly confused.

I will. We'll talk soon?

Yes, my friend. Soon and often.

Tipsy opened her eyes and turned to Scott. "He's there, in my head. Just like Granna!"

"Wow. That's amazing. So you can talk to him?"

"I can hear him plain as day—you must think I'm crazy—"

"*Tipsy…*"

"I know you don't …but it is *freakin'* crazy."

"Yup. In the best way."

She leaned against him and propped her feet on the coffee table. Scott rubbed his bearded cheek against her forehead, and it was pleasantly scratchy. She thought of the adventures she'd had over the past few years as she watched bees and butterflies flittering over her new wild indigo bushes. She considered the people she'd met, living and dead, and the lessons she'd learned. She'd come to her own truth, as deep and rich as the tones of those purple flowers that Jane had loved so much. Her life was wonderful, and whether she deserved it or not was irrelevant. She'd keep seeing the beauty in that everyday truth, and everything would sort itself out. It always did, as Henry had said. Contentment ever after.

Tipsy would stay grateful, even if her gratitude didn't guarantee a perfect outcome. As she snuggled into the crook of her husband's arm, she felt especially grateful for the strange talent her grandmother's grandmother handed down to her. For the chance to do good, just for good's sake. Mysteries would surface and she'd solve them if she could.

Ghosts would appear and she'd help them disappear, forever. Some of them might be crazy, but that was life, especially in Charleston. Like Scott said, it was crazy in the best way. The only way she knew, and the only way she'd have it.

THE END

As I finish this fourth installment in the Tipsy Collins Series, I must first thank my readers, who have so enthusiastically embraced Tipsy, Henry, Jane, and their friends and families. Their constant positive feedback and demand for "more Tipsy" led me to spend more time with these characters than I ever imagined when I dreamed up Tipsy's world almost a decade ago. I'd also like to take this opportunity to explain my decision to wrap up the Tipsy Collins Series with *True Indigo*, which will lead to background on my work in general and news about upcoming projects.

My novels are character driven. The plot serves the character, rather than the character serving the plot, and I believe that plot-driven series are better suited to many volumes. At its heart, the Tipsy Collins Series is about Tipsy and her post-divorce emotional journey, and there comes a point where there must be a resolution to that journey. Without a resolution, readers will find her endlessly making the same mistakes (which can get annoying) or doing things that are totally out of character (also potentially annoying). I don't want Tipsy's story to go the way of a television show that should have ended after four seasons, but pushed its luck. It is possible I will revisit Tipsy in the years to come, but for now, I plan to leave her in a good place, with my best wishes.

I'm also ready to explore other characters and worlds, but there will always be common concepts that run through my fiction. Readers may notice that the Tipsy Collins Series makes multiple references to "happily-ever-after," a recurring theme in all my books, including my fairytale retelling, The Cracked Slipper series. My fantastical female protagonists are faced with different versions of the same universal conundrum. Women are raised on fairytale endings, but what happens when we wake up one day, look around, and realize that happily-ever-after is complicated? What do we do with this revelation? How do we make the best of whatever life hands us? Tipsy worked through these questions, as did Eleanor, the protagonist of The Cracked Slipper series.

On that note, I'm excited to announce the release of my next novel, *Mean Low Water*, in 2024. *Mean Low Water* features another woman who is struggling with challenges related to motherhood, her marriage, her emotional baggage, and her career. So who is this protagonist? Insightful readers may have noticed that a new character in *True Indigo* remained somewhat mysterious. Even Tipsy is anxious to learn more about her! Why, it's psychic divorce attorney LeeLee Moretz, of course! I can't wait to share LeeLee's story with my readers, as this tale of midlife strife, small town friendships, and the power of nostalgia is near and dear to my heart. It's a story about strong Southern women, set in the Lowcountry, full of magic, reflection, and humor, but I will warn y'all that Mean Low Water is more…*intense*…than the Tipsy novels. I think it's pretty obvious that I relish putting my characters in morally gray situations, and I have always promised myself that my novels will not succumb to formulaicness. Hopefully I have succeeded in both, and produced a new book that will appeal to Tipsy's fans and new readers alike.

I also hope that *True Indigo's* introduction to LeeLee and her supernatural abilities will prove a fun and compelling bridge between her story and Tipsy's. I grew up obsessed with the Stephen King multiverse, and I always delighted in finding connections between his many stories, whether through characters, settings, supernatural elements (the Beam, anyone?), or thematic elements. I hope my readers will enjoy exploring the connections between my characters, their worlds, and their happily-ever-after-ish stories, too! To that end, if you've enjoyed Tipsy's tales and you love magical stories, please check out The Cracked Slipper Series. There are multiple Cracked Slipper "Easter eggs" in *True Indigo*, and I challenge y'all to find them!

Finally, I must once again give thanks to those who have supported and inspire me as I toiled on this book: my three children (Eliza, Harper, and Cyrus), my mother (Dianne), my ride-or-die besties (Erica and Angela), and my siblings (Mary and Brice). My greatest gratitude is reserved for my husband, Jeffrey Cluver, who provides unfailing encouragement and support through this sometimes painful, often exhausting, but ultimately magical process of writing novels. Jeff, you are my happily-ever-after.

With love and gratitude,
Stephanie

www.ingramcontent.com/pod-product-compliance
Lightning Source LLC
Chambersburg PA
CBHW021954130726
47903CB00014B/1369